ZENITHS

by Josh D. Schroeder

DORRANCE
PUBLISHING CO
EST. 1920
PITTSBURGH, PENNSYLVANIA 15238

Dorrance Publishing Co
585 Alpha Drive
Suite 103
Pittsburgh, PA 15238

Visit our website at *www.dorrancebookstore.com*

ISBN: 979-8-88683-526-7
eISBN: 979-8-88683-614-1

ZENITHS

(NOTE: THIS BOOK HAS DESCRIPTIONS, DETAILS, AND SCENES THAT MIGHT BE INAPPROPRIATE OR OFFEND GROUPS OR CERTAIN GROUPS OF PEOPLE. IT IS FOR ENTERTAINMENT PURPOSE ONLY. IF YOU CHOOSE TO READ ON, DO SO AT YOUR OWN ACCORD. BUT KNOW THAT- YOU HAVE BEEN WARNED!)

PROLOGUE

With each choice we make comes with infinite possibilities for any future. Whether we choose to follow the sciences of logic and reason or the artistic or emotional, our choices define who we are as an individual. However, core beliefs contradict people, often making them choose to follow the same path rather than tread a new one. It is easier to do the same thing as another and be accepted rather than be persecuted for being different. It is true you're safer, but it is still false, for when you follow someone blindly to escape their hatred, you are just betraying yourself. For when you lie to the world about the true you, then you have given up on the being you were meant to be.

We may be born of the same organic material, but our personalities, culture, and decisions say we are different. That is what makes us unique, but through history we have seen the same patterns repeat. The thing that can make our history better is unity, the decision of the people coming together and doing what is right for everyone. However, there is another factor at play that can destroy our history and divide us - greed. All forms of greed come into play more often than what we were raised to believe. What is even worse is when another being is stuck with the price of that greed. For when you pass the price on to another, you darken yourself and the being along with you. Yet even if there is a steep price for someone's greed, someone will have to pay it, willingly or forcefully, and the price may be something so terrible, that even the gods turn away.

So, what would happen if the price were unforgivable or if you had no choice but to pay it?

CHAPTER 1

The darkest truth is absolute

During the warm winter December night, the half-moon begins to fall below the horizon as the colors of the dawn begin to illuminate the darkened skies. The stars fade away and the people of Wichita begin to awake and begin their day, but this day was the eve of the new year. The citizens rushed to get around and head off into the suns gleaming morning light. This day was a day of celebration for the end of another year and a chance of a better one. However, one man in Wichita was not going to be joyous as his alarm on his phone began to blare. The man woke up enraged by the sound and grabbed his phone. He shut off the alarm quickly and tried to lay back down for a little while longer, until it went off again, this time with a reminder.

"Work 6 a.m. – 4 p.m. 12/31/29. Also, happy 26th birthday."

The man heavily groaned. "Oh my god, why is it my company refuses to close for the day on the last day of the year, when they know business is going to be slow!" The young man rose from his bed in the basement of his home and began the day like he had done for the last eight years and prepared himself for work. The same old routine, waking up, making his bed, feeding his and his sister's cats, preparing his lunch, making sure the roads were clear, and dressing up appropriately.

"Same old, same old." He muttered to himself. As he went into the kitchen, he noticed the cat's bowls were already filled with food and they all seemed to be pleased and did not bother him with their loud moaning and crying. He stepped around the cats and opened the fridge where he had some leftovers from the other day stored away for his lunch, but when he looked inside all his leftovers were gone. He inhaled deeply as he turned his head towards the sink and not to his surprise, he found empty glass Tupperware with nothing left inside. The man gripped the door to the fridge as he began to shake with anger. He knew only two people would be stupid enough to steal from him and think they could walk away, his stepfather and his mother.

Davis rushed out of the kitchen, took off his pajamas, threw on his work clothes, grabbed his messenger bag along with his phone, and ran upstairs. With his anger guiding him, he remembered what he had given up on keeping his family from falling into financial ruin. The sacrifice he had to make to get them this far, the things he gave up for them, the things they did to him just to make themselves happy. He lived more than one-fourth of his life, he had been cheated by his family, and he had enough. As he opened the basement door to the main floor, he saw his stepfather and mother watching TV in the living room with some of his empty glass Tupperware on the table. The two were so deeply interested by the show that they did not even notice him, until he got in their way.

"Hey, is there something you need? We're trying to watch something here!" said his stepfather with a little anger in his one.

"Do not give me that attitude," said the man enraged. "We three need to have a quick chat before I head off to work."

"Okay, Davis, what?!" said his mother.

"The fact you two ate all my leftovers, including my lunch! This is the last straw you two have constantly and deliberately put not only your lives in jeopardy, but Alex's and mine as well," said Davis as he turned, he headed towards his stepfather with fury building in his chest. "Don, you have stolen from me, lied, and cheated into getting everything you want, regardless of the consequences and what's worse is that you dragged my mother into it by helping you cover up the lies!"

"I did what I needed to keep us in this house!" yelled Don back.

"So, when does stealing more than ten grand on a check from me and spending it on meth, woodwork tools that you don't use, alcohol, and a high-class prostitute have to do with keeping this house?" asked Davis with his raging burned eyes.

Don's anger vanished from his face and was replaced with fear, he didn't know that Davis knew what he had spent the stolen money on. "Don't be so surprised, Don, I found the pay stub in your pants pocket when I did your laundry, and after doing my own investigation I found out everything, so I have known for quite some time."

"Bubba I-" said Don before Davis cut him off "Shut your damn mouth. You didn't just rob me, you almost got me thrown in jail because of your choices."

"WHAT?!" screamed Davis's mother.

"Do you want to explain or should I." Davis said staring into Don's face.

Don said nothing as he stared back at Davis, his fear prevented him from talking knowing whatever he said was not going to help him escape this situation. He knew the answer, but he could not admit it to his wife, himself, or his stepson because he knew it was the end of his life with them. But Davis didn't care as he smirked and said, "You are such a coward. You have no problem screwing over others' lives, but God forbid it's the other way around. But now it's time to pay the devil his due, and I'm the devil in this scenario."

"You're such a liar!"

"Really Don, tell that to your friends who got caught and confessed to their aid in your crime."

Don's face turned red with anger, he stood up, and shouted "You got nothing on me you little "

"They already have enough evidence to link you to the crime, moron, they may not be able to pin it on you, but it's enough to hold you in a jail cell for the next 20 years with your friends." Davis said as he pushed him down into his chair as he turned to his mother. "And look at you, sitting in silence again because that is what is easiest for you, well guess what you both lost and this time it costs you so much more. As of this moment you are not getting any more help from me or my sister, you are both cut off. Now you two will make better decisions, get your lives together, and be able not to drag your family down with you."

Before either one could say another word, Davis went out the front door and slammed it so hard that the window on it cracked. As he got into his car and began to drive off into the warm morning, his anger dissipated, and he started to feel more alive and enthusiastic about the day and the new year. He felt the heavy load on his back, finally, fall off, and for the first time in a long time he felt free, just like so many people who had to deal with the burden of feeling like more of a lightning rod than a family member. He was proud in knowing that he chose a better life over a worse one, to make the right decision, and plotted a course to a new and brighter future for himself. Today even if they had forgotten his birthday, Davis would celebrate not the day he was born, but the day he was reborn as the person he had wanted to be. As he stared into the fading starry night, he could feel things were going to get better, eventually, but for now, he looked forward to the new year, a fresh start was right around the corner, and he had to figure out how to celebrate.

CHAPTER 2

The moments gone.

While driving down the highway, Davis was still re-living in his enjoyment after he had stood up for himself, but the moment did not last as he started to feel like a failure. He spent so much time feeling angry toward his family that he realized he was equally guilty for doing nothing about it. If he had just stood up for himself years ago, then maybe his life would have turned out differently. He thought to himself, "Who would I have been if I had not been someone else's punching bag?" In his high school years, he had an aptitude for chemistry, math, anthropology, and art. However due to his family's lack of support and constant disapproval of the things he wanted to do with his life, he never got to live his dreams. As he drove, he remembered when he was in third grade and he wanted to play the violin, but because of his mother's and stepfather's schedules, he never got to practice and when he did practice, they would get mad at him for it. Eventually his dream to play an instrument for fun had been shattered, one example of how his mother and stepfather took away his dreams. He had other dreams he wanted to fulfill, but he had to place them on hold just so he could "take care of them."

He wondered, what if he had just said "no" to them every time they came crawling for help, then maybe they would have learned that they needed to become organized, to not constantly make excuses for their ineptitude, and use their children to get away from responsibilities.

However, Davis in his heart knew that there was no excuse for him either, he could have resisted years ago, even if he got in trouble, it would have been far less bad than what he had to deal with. Maybe it was in Davis's head that he was just trying to cut them some slack, but he knew that they were his guardians, his protectors, the beings that were supposed to offer wisdom and insight through life. Being a parent is never easy, but the fact they could only put themselves in danger and not ensure their future showed Davis that he was better at making decisions than they were. The thought made him feel like a parent to them, how could they have failed so much, that he would look more like a parenteral role model than them? Davis hypothesized that their continuous strain of failures might have had him subconsciously learn from their mistakes, and him learning from his own made him a better person. It was honestly on the nose to him, but Davis did not understand how someone could make decisions based on the constant disregard for others. However, he reveled in knowing that those two would be forced into making tough decisions for the safety of their future without relying on him or his sister, but at the same time was disappointed in them.

Yet, despite his conflicting attitude towards the situation, Davis was now free from the weight of being a piggy bank and thought to himself all the things he could do more of his life. But when Davis began to think about his own future, he drew a blank. He spent too much time fixing other people's problems, that he did not even think about making a future for himself. His parents took so much away that he did not know where to begin. Davis started to have a panic attack realizing that he may not have a future to look forward towards at the rate he was going. As he pulled into his work parking lot, he reflected on his own words that he needs to get his life together. When Davis parked his car, he decided to make a list of all the things he want in his life and improve on himself to get them, he knew it was not going to be easy, but the last eight years of his life had not been either. Davis took a deep breath and was about to exit the car when he heard on the radio, "We have just received word that there is a shootout between gang members and police at the Shocker Baseball Stadium, everyone is advised to stay away until the situation is under control!" He turned off his car and sighed "Not the greatest way to start off the new year."

He exited his car to face the day at work, but with a fake smile on his face. He loved the fact that his coworkers cared about him but did not want them to worry to the point where they were neglecting their own duties. Davis walked on the cold pavement in the parking lot as he headed towards the shipping department at his facility, Ace Airs, a manufacturing plant for spaceship parts. It was ten till seven and as Davis was about to open the door to his facility, he felt the cold stair of someone watching him. Davis quickly turned around to see no one anywhere in sight but could not shake the feeling, he knew someone or something was watching him. Davis stepped away from the door and looked around on the ground and still saw nothing, but when he turned his head to the roof across the street, he noticed something odd. He could vaguely see something standing on one of the roofs across the street. The image looked obscured, like a ghost seen in a picture. He thought at first, he was imagining it, but after all the art classes he had taken in school, he could tell all the colors apart even if it looked identical. He got so good that even when the moon was eclipsed, he could still see the moon even when it was covered in shadow. But on the roof, he saw something in the shape of a being, yet he could not make out what it was. Suddenly the door behind him flew open and a woman called out to him "Davis, what are you doing out here? You're going to be late for work if you don't clock-in in the next five minutes." Davis turned to see his co-worker, Rosetta, looking at him with a worried expression. "Come on mi amigo we have to start work." said Rosetta.

Davis turned to the rooftop of the other building to see whatever was there, but it was now gone. "Davis is everything okay?" said Rosetta in her Spanish accent.

"Yes, I thought I saw something on the other roof, but I must be seeing things." said Davis as he entered the doorway. But as the door closed, he looked back out the window on the door before he headed to his workstation, he still felt like he was being watched, he knew he saw something, but he just did not know what.

Rosetta grabbed his hand and dragged him inside explaining the plan for the day, but Davis was barely listening, he was more concerned about what just happened than what he had to do. His tasks were like every other day, to make sure that the paperwork was complete and wrap parts up and place them in boxes with enough stuffing to keep them from getting damaged. Simple enough, but a little too simple for Davis's tastes. He once worked at the machines that made the parts but due to a work-related injury, they moved him to the shipping department for convenience. Though Davis did not like the idea, he took the job to give them peace of mind, but he did love watching the machines make the parts with each cut.

Davis sat down at his desk to clock into his shift, and decided to forget about what happened outside, he wanted to focus on his work rather than his family issues and whatever happened outside. As the day progressed, Davis started to find less and less to do, Davis had gotten so fast at doing his job that he really didn't have anything to do for a few hours, so to kill time he would help in other areas of his facility, but mostly just cleaned the floors and made sure he was busy. Unfortunately, when things were slow, so was the day, normally the shipping department sometimes had a steady pace of products moving to the department, but today things were too slow, especially for the end of the year. Normally it was their busiest time for shipping things out, but on the last day of the year, it was slow. This unfortunately made the higher ups upset, with twenty machines that made parts they thought they would have more, but since the machines were worn throughout the years they occasionally crashed, which slowed everything down. Davis was not in any mood to deal with this type of ordeal today, but he still did his best to make sure he did his job thoroughly. He made conversations with people from time to time, but still did his best to keep things professional. After a few hours of work and clean his area up the lunch bell rang. Everyone began to clock out and grab their lunches, except for Davis. He was fortunate that their break room area had vending machines with food he could stomach, however, the price of the food was absurd. He stood before the line machines and glared at the prices.

"I'm going to kill those two when I get back home!" he said as he grabbed a hamburger and a bag of chips. After heating up his hamburger in the company's microwave, he headed towards his desk, got out some paper, and while he ate made his list of things he wanted to do.

Pay off his debts and become financially stable in the next 5 years.

Revisit his social life by trying to find new friends to hang out with.

Try to find his missing half and start a retirement fund.

Have three kids each at least five years apart, so this way they could help each other if he were not around to do so and make his will.

Make sure his kids have a college fund set up, so they could have an actual future where he did not have to worry about them.

End the deliberate abuse of ADHD/ADD pills in his society if possible. Have a family reunion every two years so he could meet up with his children and grandbabies.

Finally, spend the rest of his life relaxing with his other half.

Even though he felt that his list may have not been very long, he still had another sixty to eighty years left to live and he was going to do his best to make it happened, even though he was fully aware that some of these things may not be possible, or he might die before he got them, he still wanted to try and get what he wanted.

"What's that, mi amigo?" asked Rosetta.

"It's a list of things I want to do before I croak." said Davis with a sincere smile.

"Oh, someone finally decided he deserved more and stood up for himself?" asked Rosetta in a playful tone.

Davis was shocked by her words and asked, "How did you—?" but stopped his sentence and rolled his eyes "Why am I even asking, you always know when something is up with me. But to answer your question yes, I did. I apologize for my French, but it felt so damn good."

"Well, I'm glad you finally did because your fake smile was starting to get on my nerves, I mean you're only 26 years old, you shouldn't be having to put yourself second, even for a family that doesn't seem to appreciate you." said Rosetta concerned.

"I know but after so many years of being put down and psychologically damaged to the point where you think that this is going to be your life, it's hard to make that change. Some people must hit rock bottom before they realize the one they think they love is really their worst enemy. I'm one of the lucky ones to escape that, few people aren't."

Rosetta grinned and tapped Davis's forehead with her finger. "Where has this wise guy been?"

Davis laughed and crumbled his hamburger into a ball. "Trying to keep my family from falling apart at the expense of my own life."

"Well, I'm glad that you're finally getting on with your life, but always remember there will be other people out there who will try to bring you down, including yourself. Things don't always work out the way you plan and when things get difficult people tend to complain rather than fix the problems, but I know for a fact that you're not one of them."

"How so?" asked Davis curiously.

"Well for starters, even though you would ignore your own problems, you never turned away from someone else's. Remember when you helped me with my kids."

As she asked him, Davis remembered the day when Rosetta's kids had lost hope in the future. With all the fighting, stealing, murdering, and cover ups from police and politicians they had heard about, they got scared of what the future would bring for them. "I remember that day, I came over to your house for dinner and when you were cooking with your husband I spoke to your kids."

"Do you remember what you told them?" asked Rosetta.

"The road ahead and the problems that came with it may have been caused by other people's greed, but it didn't mean they had to follow the same path. Their futures were their's to control. But if you give it willingly to another because you refuse to do the right thing and your life turns out horrible, that's your own fault. However, if you face the problems that come your way and you overcome them, then not only have you opened the door for yourself, but for everyone else, and the wisdom you gained from it, can be passed down to your kids so they won't have to suffer the same fate as others." said Davis repeating his words to Rosetta. "Exactly, you gave them the speech they need to face the unknown, something I couldn't do, and I'm their mother. So, take your own wisdom and use it for yourself, I can tell you that you have the determination to get everything on that list, and that your future will be-" Before Rosetta finished her sentence the facilities power began to turn on and off unexpectedly. The lights flickered, their computers turned on and off along with the machine. Everything kept turning on and off, until everything became quiet and darkness set in. The deepest parts of the facility were clocked in shadow with little light illuminating the polished concrete floors. Everyone was startled by the black out, normally the company gave a heads up when they were doing a power outage drill. Normally they did it to prepare for a thunderstorm, yet there was no warning, and the fact it happened right before lunch was over was strange to them.

"What the hell was that? A power outage?" asked Rosetta worried.

Davis got up from his desk and said, "No that wasn't a power outage, at least not like anything I have ever seen, and if it were, the backup generators would have started up by now. I suggest we find our lead and see what's going on."

The two walked away from their area and saw their lead at the front door with other leads talking about what just happened with other employees, but they too were at a loss. With the power out the leads gathered everyone into the break area to make sure all were accounted for, so no one could try to skip out on work and get paid for bailing. Which was understandable in Davis's mind, it would not have been the first time someone had done it. Everyone followed the lead to the break area and waited for further instructions. As everyone waited, Davis sat with his back against the wall and asked himself, "What the hell was going on here?" Then out of the corner of his right eye he saw the light on the floor flicker out on the ground. He turned his attention towards the light and waited. Nothing happened, and Davis thought he had just imagined it. Just as he was about to turn his head, a shadow appeared on the floor of the facility. Davis was startled by the shadow and quickly removed himself from the wall, he turned the corner of the break room and looked up at the window to find something looking into the facility.

"What the hell!?" screamed Davis as he looked at the window. Whatever it was it hung from the window like a monkey, it had four arms, and it was hairless. Everyone heard his scream and rushed over, but before they got a chance to look at the window the creature had climb onto the roof.

"What's wrong?" asked one the leads.

"Did no one see that just now?" asked Davis.

People shook their heads at him, he was about to explain what he saw, but the sound of metal bending stopped him. Everyone got up and looked around wondering where the sound was coming from. Davis looked at them and told them "I don't know what I saw out there, but it climbed on the roof."

Everyone turned their heads skyward and listened as they heard something walking around on the metal roof. Then it stopped, but only for a moment as the sound of metal bending intensified and a part of the roof was torn away. Everyone panicked thinking the roof was caving in on them, but as the sunshine down inside something stood in the path of the sun's rays with multiple six-winged creatures surrounding it. All became silent as Davis slowly backed up to Rosetta and said quietly "Stay next to me."

Rosetta grabbed Davis's hand quickly and said quietly "Si."

He could feel Rosetta shaking with fear from just her hand, as he tried to tell himself not to panic from this situation. No one said a word as they waited for the thing to do something. The seconds felt like hours and the strange being stepped into the hole, and fell three-stories, landing on its feet deeply cracked the cement floor. The creature rose slowly from the floor and revealed its full form in the light. The creature stood taller than any man or women anyone had seen. Its body was massive, accompanied by an elongated tail, and covered in greenish metallic armor with weapons on its back and sides.

Whatever this creature was it was clear to everyone, that it was not from their world.

The creature took out a small baseball sized orb and showed the crowd the metallic sphere. Then without hesitation the creature dropped the orb on to the ground, as it made impact the ding of metal echoed out. The orb opened small holes all over itself and began to spray black clouds out into the facility. Everyone went into a frenzy, trying to scatter in every direction to escape the dark clouds. Davis held onto Rosetta's hand tightly as he pushed through the crowd making his way for the furthest exit door. "Davis are you loco, why are you running to that door? There are three other doors behind us!?" said Rosetta shocked.

"Those doors are about to be swarmed with other people and they're closest to those black cloud, personally I don't want to stick around and see what it does. Which means we need distance between us and that stuff, and that door is closer to the faculty parking lot!" answered Davis while he was running through the crowds.

The clouds continued to expand into the facility and people began to push each other out of the way. Some fell to the floor and were trample while others tried to help them up, it was absolute chaos as Davis and Rosetta made their way to the other side. The clouds engulfed people left and right and was approaching Davis and Rosetta, who found themselves surrounded by it. Out of fear Davis quickly headed over to the wall with Rosetta behind. The two held onto the wall and became consumed by the clouds. Davis thought that this was the end as the clouds surrounded them, but found instead to be still breathing, but blind. Whatever this stuff was did not kill but made its so dark that not even the sun could light the way. The two kept their backs against the wall and listened as people still panic trying to get out.

Davis leaned into Rosetta and said, "Quietly sidestep to the door."

"Si, mi amigo." Said Rosetta scared.

The two slowly made their way to the door, as Davis kept track of how many steps they were taking to make sure they were not going to miss it, but he had miscalculated before, he just hoped he didn't this time. The cold wall guided them slowly through the darkness and when they reached what Davis assumed was the halfway mark, loud bellowing came from above followed by quick whooshing sounds. Davis grabbed Rosetta's shoulder with his hand and pulled her down the wall to the floor. He placed her hand on the wall and said, "Whatever you do don't let go of this wall or stand up. Crawl." They quickly began to scurry across the floor as whatever had escorted the creature decided to act, making its way inside, and doing God only knows what. All Davis could do was move forward with Rosetta as the screams of other people began to intensify. After all the terrifying minutes Davis felt the doors rim on the side of the wall. He stood up from the floor, and desperately looked for the latch. He rubbed his hands against the door to scan the area to find it as Rosetta grabbed his ankle. In his mind he kept saying "Where is it, where is it?" Panicking, he began to move his hand more until his left hand smashed into the latch.

He grabbed it and Rosetta, pushing the latch, and the door flung open; the two emerged from the black cloud outside the facility back into the sunlight.

Davis quickly shut the door behind them and took a deep breath and said, "Okay well that's new!"

"What is that thing!?" said Rosetta with fear in her voice.

"I do not want to stick around and find out we need to get to our cars."

"Davis?" She said as she raised her hand and pointed into the parking lot.

Davis turned his head and realized she was not just talking about the creatures inside, something was in the parking lot, and it was sniffing the ground around the cars. An exceptionally large creature, with horns, sharp fangs, and with two sets of eyes was sniffing out the area. It almost looked like a saber tooth cat in appearance, but with white fur with red designs on it. Davis quickly took Rosetta behind the trash bin in fear it was about to look their direction.

The two waited a moment and against their better judgement looked around the corner. The beast did not see them and the two sighed with relief, but Davis noticed it looked like it was standing guard. Unfortunately, Davis also noticed the beast was too close to his car, but it was further away from Rosetta's. He looked around on the ground to find anything that might help create a distraction or at least hurt it. The only thing he managed to find an old piece of aluminum that was scrapped, then he noticed the oil drums to his right, they were about fifty feet away, and one quickly movement he threw the scrap of aluminum at them. When the two metals clanged together it echoed out, alerting the beast to its presence. The beast looked towards them and began to charge with great speed, roaring loudly like a lion for an intent to kill.

As the beast past the trash bin, Davis quickly told Rosetta, "Run to your car and get home to your family, get them out of Wichita before things get worse!"

"What about you, Davis?"

"I'll head out when you leave, I need to stay behind so whatever that thing is doesn't pounce on your car when you start it. I can lead it into the old factory, then when I lose it, I will double back."

Davis knew there was no way they would be able to elude that thing without the other getting attacked, only one would be able to escape, and he knew this was her only chance to get out of there alive. She hesitated, but Davis saw in her eyes that she had to take it for her family. Before she left, Rosetta kissed Davis on his check, said, "Gracias!" and ran to her car. After two minutes Davis went out into the open and whistled at the beast, getting its attention. The beast turned towards Davis as he began running to the old factory, it began to pursuit him and as he and it ran past Rosetta's car, she quickly started it and sped off. Davis could hear the car take off as he entered the factory with the beast hot on his tail, and though he was glad his friend was safe, deep inside he was terrified, he had never feared death before, but now that it was about to happen it made him fear it.

Trying to get his baring's he looked around the factory, everything that was once there had been removed years ago, and the only people that ever came in here were the homeless and people addicted to illegal substances. The only place to hide down on the ground floor was nowhere. But thinking back on it, Davis remembered the old office area on the second floor and began to sprint towards the stairs that connected them to the factory floor, as the beast came through the wall. Once it got on its feet it and shook off the pain it began to charge after him. Davis could hear the deep panting of the beast closing in on him, every step he took, the beast took three more. Davis felt the air turn cold around him as the beast came closer, thinking back on his life, all the things he did with his family during the good times, but nothing came to his mind and made him feel ashamed.

He was so close the stairs, he was only twenty-five feet away, but then he tripped over his own feet, slid onto the floor, and scraped his right arm so badly it looked like someone had tried to skin him. Davis was stunned for a second and tried to get off the floor, but was quickly pinned down by the beast, he could feel the hot breath on the back of his neck as it panted from chasing him. Davis thought this was the end, thinking he was going to be mauled to death by a giant feline, but for some reason the beast did not attack. Davis was surprised that the creature didn't kill him right away like the carnivores of their planet would do. It just held him in place like it was waiting for something to happen. This creature seemed to be patient like a dog waiting for something to show up. In the back of his head, he thought this beast did not want its prey to get away until whatever it was waiting for showed up, and it was intent on keeping it that way. But he knew it was only a theory and he didn't want to stick around to find out if it was true. When Davis made the attempt to break free and run, the beast put the rest of its body on top of him. Davis became frustrated and tried to squirm his way out of the beast's underside. As the beast laid on top of him it became irritated and gently put its jaws around Davis's right shoulder. Davis stopped moving and waited for the creature to make its killing blow, but it didn't. He realized that it was a warning to stop, knowing that one bite would easily crush him. Davis was befuddled by this creatures' action; he realized this beast was highly intelligent and knew very well how to kill but had the will to resist.

Although he was astounded and terrified by this creature, his mind came to a halt as a red-light dot appeared in front of the two of them, Davis looked up at the office area and saw someone pointing a laser pointer at them. He thought what they were doing was idiotic, that they were going to give themselves away and get caught. But instead, the beast seemed interested in the red dot like a cat, mesmerized by its red luminescence. Then when the dot darted to the left the beast leapt off Davis and began to chase after it.

"Are you freaking kidding me right now?!" said Davis surprised as he saw the creature running around after the dot.

"What are you doing you, nitwit?" said a familiar voice.

Davis looked at the staircase to find another one of his co-workers standing on the first step. One who had trained him, befriended him on his first day on the job, and gave his tips about being coordinated, organized, and would make sure that no one tried to use him as a scapegoat.

"Mathew?!"

"No, shit now come on, before fang there gets wise!"

Davis quickly got up and made it to the stairs as Mathew lent him a hand. The two rushed up the stairs and into the office, barricading the door behind them. The two waited and listened to see if the creature was going to do anything, but all it did was roar out, and then went silent. The two quietly sat down on a desk and tried to regain their breath. Davis was overjoyed to see Mathew but wondered how he got away from the facility. His gaze started to wonder around the office, he saw stockpiles of supplies and the office looked like it had been turned into an apartment. He saw a man made the kitchen with equipment, a hammock, clothes, and a built-in shower.

"Wait a minute do you live here!?"

"I do live here, but its only temporary" said Mathew as he grabbed a medical kit.

"I noticed you disappearing now and again during your lunch, but I never would have guessed that this was the place you would disappear to."

"I have been doing this for a while now. I've always kind of an odd ball when it came to being prepared, especially for the end of the world." He said as he began to clean Davis's wound.

Davis hissed at the pain from the cleaning but didn't stop it. Through the pain Davis said, "This clearly isn't temporary, Mathew. I mean you managed to hook up power to your equipment and have a manmade shower with running water!"

"I like to be prepared for the worst Davis. I mean many people don't even care about the uncertainty of tomorrow, but I do," said Mathew as he finished cleaning Davis's wound.

"I understand more than you know, but you can't be afraid of it, otherwise you stop living," said Davis as Mathew dressed his wound up.

"Look, I'm fine here, okay, I know that I might be scared of the unknown, but a least I'm prepared for it."

"But for how long? Whatever attacked our work was far more advanced in technology than what we have. They might find you, and God knows what these creatures are doing to our coworkers."

"I appreciate the concern, Davis, but I feel safer here than out there, I'd rather take my chances here where I know it's safe rather than go out there and risk getting killed."

Mathew moved away from Davis and looked out the office window in silence. As the minutes passed Davis could feel that he was not going to be able to persuade him into leaving, but he still needed his help to get out of the factory. So, against his better judgment Davis had to leave him behind and get out of there. "If you wish to stay here, then I will not force you to leave, but please help me get past the beast so I can get home and find my family," said Davis.

Mathew looked to Davis and said, "You know you have a better chance if you stay here with me, there are no guarantees that your family is okay."

"I know, but I still have to try, if I don't then I might regret it for the rest of my life, not knowing is more painful than a bullet wound to the heart."

"That was cheesy, Davis, but regardless if you need to move quickly, you may only have a few minutes before it realizes that your outside again."

Davis said his goodbyes and thankyous to Mathew before they unbarricaded the door and headed out of the office and down the steps. The beast was looking around in the darkness trying to find its missing prey. It sniffed the air while making a few whimpering noises like a hurt dog, then would roar loudly trying to scare out anything hiding. He made his way down the old steps as he waited for Mathew to lure the beast away. Mathew made sure Davis was in position and used the laser like he did before, but it seemed the beast was not interested in it. Every time it did show interest it wouldn't last long and turned its head toward the stairs every time Davis would try to step onto the ground floor. After some time, the laser gained the beasts attention like before and began to chase it. Davis slipped out onto the ground floor and headed the way he came taking his time trying not to be spotted. Occasionally Davis would freeze as the beast leaped onto the floor trying to catch the laser fearing it might see him. When he saw he was good he would keep moving.

As he got to the entrance, he gave a gentle wave goodbye to Mathew, and quickly ran to his car. Without the creature in pursuit of him he managed to get to his car easily. He jumped in and drove out of the parking lot as the beast leapt out of the factory and roared as it saw him speeding away. Davis looked in his rear-view mirror one last time hoping that Mathew would be able to hold out until this was over, but he could not help feeling sorry for him. Choosing a life of loneliness over one filled with people made Davis feel distraught, unfortunately he did not have the heart to force Mathew to change his mind, all he could do was pray that Mathew stayed safe.

A mile up the road Davis made his way on to the highway, dodging the beast that lurked around they empty cars, and headed home. He could only imagine what has going on there, both his stepfather and mother were possibly freaking out and trying to get out of town, or trying to call him, or his brother and sisters. Davis grabbed his right pocket where he had put his phone hoping there was a message, but it wasn't there, he realized he had left his cell phone in his bag at work, so going home was the only option he had now. Whatever they were up to, Davis had to get home, and check on them, even if he was still angry with them, they did not deserve to be killed or left behind because of what they had done.

However, Davis's thoughts trailed off when he saw the once lively city of Wichita now in chaos. The city was being swarmed by what he believed was the serpents, there numbers were great, but it seemed their majority was only circling above the city, with only a few dozen or so dive bombing down into the streets below. Even from the highway he couldn't tell how much was going on down there but from what just happened with him at his work, he already knew it wasn't good. Davis stared at the sky watching them fly around in circles, it almost seemed hypnotic. He spent so much time looking at Wichita that he did not notice one of the winged serpents smacking into his car, sending him off the highway onto the hill that connected to it.

The hill flashed by, grass, dirt, and stone came through the busted front window. Davis screamed as his car tumbled down the hill, his head slammed into the steering wheel and faded in and out. He remembered little after that, except for a pair of narrow-pupil eyes gazing directly into his own for a few seconds before a small chirping sound was made, it quickly turned its head to its left, hissed in fear, and shot straight up into the sky. Then out of the corner of Davis's eye he saw four thin tentacles hovering a few feet from the ground heading straight towards him. Before Davis could get a good look at the creature, his sight faded to black, only hearing a soft cooing sound, and feeling something nuzzling his chin as he fell into the darkness.

CHAPTER 3

The city of Dis.

Awaking slowly, Davis's eyes flickered open in the light, blinding him for a few moments as he tried to get his baring's. His vision was coming into focus and when things became clear, he found himself under a bare willow tree. Collecting himself, he sat up from the ground, looking around to see where he was, wondering what happened. It slowly came back as he remembered the serpent that attacked his car and the strange chirping sound as he lost consciousness. Davis looked around a little more to find there were no creatures nearby but did see a light trail of blood on the grass and the car far off into the distance. He had no idea how he got there or what that thing was that scared the serpent away, but he believed that the creature that interfered must have had its own plans for him and he didn't want to stay any longer than he had to. Davis quickly stood up, but realized something abnormal, his body was not in any pain, not even his right arm which had been damaged not too long ago. As he grabbed his arm, he found it covered in some sort of mucus around his bandage. Davis tried to shake the stuff off his hand, but as he did, he noticed that there was a small cut on his thumb covered in it, and it began to heal it accelerated rate. Whatever this stuff was, it was healing his body and looked like it was cleaning the wounds at the same time.

Davis was surprised to see something like this anywhere on his planet, and his scientific curiosity was beginning to show. He wanted to figure out what this stuff was really made of and wanted to start a record of its abilities, but he knew he didn't have any time to check it. Davis had to fight his urge for curiosity and left it alone hoping that he could uncover its mystic healing properties later, if a there was enough to sample. He looked towards the sky at the sun, and saw it descending fast, he had to get moving if he wanted to get home before dark. With his car totaled Davis knew that he couldn't take the highway without protection and speed. He looked at the city and knew the only way home now would be to cut through the outskirts of Wichita. He pulled himself together and headed to the underside of the overpass, using it to hide in shadow and to keep protected from the serpents in the sky.

As he walked in the shadows, he kept himself alert for anything unexpected, just in case of the beast showing up or survivors looking for help. But in the back of his mind, he began to hear his subconscious bombarding him with questions. What were these things? Where did they come from? Why were they attacking? Where was the government or the armies? What were they doing to people? He did his best not to think about the questions, but they just kept popping into his head, for one like Davis, a scientific mind filled with wonder of the universe, would never stop asking questions until it had answers.

Davis said to himself, "You can do this, there is no room for questions or doubt right now, you need to get home to your family, granted your parents are moronic fools who seem to get in trouble a lot, but they are still family, and family comes first even if they don't put you first."

He shook off his doubts and pressed onward home while he repressed his fears of unknown and silenced the world around him. But as he walked, he found himself to a familiar sight, the south entrance to the city. This place almost looked like a gate into the city, welcoming all who journeyed inside. It was made of brick walls that looked almost curved by its appearance, with two large fans on top that looked like wings, and little lights below to show off its beauty even at night, or at least it did. What stood before him now was a half monument. Both the fans were torn from the top of the walls and lied on the street, one crushed and the other ripped apart. Though he was never truly attached to the monument, to now see it in ruins, Davis couldn't help but feel sorrow. Against his instincts, he approached the ruins to retrieve a small piece to remind himself of this place. As he drew closer, he could hear people screaming, beasts roaring, and the sounds of destruction coming from beyond the wall. Once he was out of the shadows, he noticed that the serpents were flying in the city looked thin, but the ones that came out looked chubbier. He cautiously snuck around the rubble of the entrance as the sounds of the world came back as he poked his head around the corner, he found Wichita in a war zone. Hundreds of people scattering in all directions avoiding the serpents and beasts, some were shoved on the ground and trampled, others were pushed into the creatures for others to escape, and some remained in the shadows hiding from the chaos only to be chased out by the beasts on the ground. Davis watched closely as some serpents dove into the crowds of people, tucking their wings in as they coiled around people and began to slowly eat them alive. Davis looked on in horror, thinking that was the worst way to die as he heard the muffled screams of the people being devoured. The beasts would pounce on the people, holding them down until a serpent notice them, when they did the serpent would squeeze under the beast, coil itself around the person, and do the same process.

Davis couldn't believe his eyes he saw these creatures were working in tandem. Even on earth he knew it was possible for this to happen in the animal kingdom, but he never would have suspected it from an entirely different species, which wasn't from earth. Though he wanted to look away from the horror in front of him, he could not, knowing that back in the factory that the beast was holding him down just so something else could eat him, it made his stomach turn. He was about to throw up, until he saw a woman with her child running towards the entrance with a serpent behind them. The two had almost made it, but the child had let go of her mother's hand. As the child fell to the ground the serpent quickly caught her, the mother turned to see what had happened to her child, but all she could see was the serpent coiling around her daughter. The mother screamed with fear in her eye knowing that she was going to lose her child, and in that moment her fear turned to rage, and she charged towards it. The mother tried to punch the serpent in its eye, but the serpent was too quick as it opened its jaws, swallowed her arm, and bit down. The woman cried out in pain as the serpent raised her off the ground and threw her into a car. The child called out for her mother to save her, but the woman was unresponsive. The serpent turned its attention back to the child and looked at her for a few moments before its slowly moved towards her head.

The child tried her best to break free from the coils, but all she did was make the serpent squeeze her tighter. Davis continued to watch the horror unfurl, but then something inside of his soul made him enraged. He could feel the flames of desire to protect reignite deep in his being, he reached down, and let it out. Davis quickly removed his belt from his pants and charged towards the serpent. Just as the serpent was about to swallow the little girls head, it noticed Davis approaching quickly. The serpent moved away from the girl's head and lunged at him, but Davis dodged out of the way. He hopped on its head and quickly wrapped the belt around its jaws, closing them shut, as the serpents grip on the girl became loose. Davis let go of the serpent and as he fell to the ground the creature managed to get the belt off. As it fell to the ground, Davis grabbed it midair and used his belt like a whip, hitting it in its eye. The serpent quickly let go of the little girl, shot straight up screeching in pain, and flew away. Davis quickly grabbed the girl and headed over to her mother, checking her pulse, he sighed with relief, then smacked her cheek forcing her to wake up.

"What the hell is wrong with… wait, Abigail?! Where's my..." she said panicking.

Davis quickly pointed to her child, as the woman saw her child, she quickly embraced her, but the relief didn't last long as Davis quickly grabbed the two by the arms and rushed them to the ruins entrance of the city. When they were hidden, Davis quickly explained that they needed to get to the countryside; the cities were a massive dinner bell for these creatures and lingering for too long would be unwise. The woman took her daughter's hand as she thanked Davis for saving her child, then quickly made her way south of Wichita, with some luck they could get home and stay safe for a while before they had to move on. Davis waived goodbye to them, thinking they were going to be okay, but as the two made their way under the highway, elongated javelins flew above the wall, towards the pillars that kept the overpass aloft. The javelins pierced deep into the pillar, and a massive explosion occurred seconds later, making the highway fall to the ground.

The force of the explosion threw Davis against the wall of the ruin and the air was knocked out of him. Gasping for air he saw out of the corner of his eye he saw some people trying to find a way over the collapsed highway only to get caught by the beast. As the air returned to his lungs, he speculated that the armored creatures were trying to cut off any exits that might make their prey escape, just like hounds cornering a fox. He saw the mother and child get to the other side before the highway fell. However, the beasts climbed over the rubble and managed to get on the other side. All Davis could do was stand there and listen as the beast roared and two serpents dive bombed on the other side of the rubble as the woman and her daughter started screaming. Then moments later, there was silence, two serpents flew up with full stomachs and headed to the west. Davis was devastated, but he had no time to grieve, he knew he needed to get out of there quickly, the way forward was blocked off and the only way to get home now was to cut across the river near Wichita, which he knew it meant he had to go to the bridge, upriver.

The bridge was through a portion of Wichita that was filled with open areas, like small fields and parking lots. These areas were great for viewing fireworks, carnivals, and other events, but not for an invasion of aliens. Unfortunately, the only other way Davis knew to get home would take three hours to get to the bridge down river. Davis did not have any other options but to move forward into Wichita. Weighting in on his options, he remembered something, Riverfest. It was a day of celebration for Wichita and its people. But, because of financial issues they had in the summer that year they moved it from a summer event to a new year celebration. Thinking back on it he remembered the parking lot they held the carnival in every year with a parking garage next door, and they both were next to the bridge that crossed the river.

"Okay," he said to himself, "You know what to do and where to go, so get moving." He tried to get his body to move, but his fear kept him grounded. Out of desperation he quickly slapped his own face, leaving a red mark, but simultaneously breaking him away from his fear. He jumped out around the corner and made his break to the parking garage before his fear could have a chance to take over again. Cutting through the crowds of people and avoiding the beasts and serpents in his path. Every once in a while Davis would whip a serpent that managed to coil itself around a person, he wasn't successful on all of them, but he did buy enough time for their prey to get away, however in one instance a serpent managed to grab his belt and tor it away from him as he drew close to the garage, quickly dodging out of the way of the serpent he managed to get in before it could find him, but then it turned its attention towards someone else. Davis looked outside to see the serpent coiled around another person and his fear became replaced with rage. His desire to protect overwhelmed him, so he let his rage get the better of him. He jumped out of his hiding spot and ran towards the serpent. Making an odd but still effective move, he took the tip of its tail and bit it off violently.

Violet colored liquid squirted Davis's mouth and cheeks as the serpent let go of the other person and flew off. The other being quickly ran for it as Davis ran back into the garage. When he made it inside, he waited to see if anything followed him, but nothing came. All Davis could hear outside the garage was the screaming, the roars, and screeching. Even though he wanted to help everyone, he couldn't, he tried to ignore the sounds and began to run through the garage. It seemed to him the focus of the creatures was on the streets, giving him the chance to escape. However, as he made his way to the other side of the garage, he once again felt like he was being watched by something. Davis noticed that the garage did not have anyone else in it, just cars, but that was not what made Davis feel uneasy. He had been watched by other people before and had gotten use to humans looking at him from the shadows, but this feeling was different, it felt like whatever was watching him was keeping a close eye on him, but for what reason he didn't know.

Davis scoffed it off as he made his way to the other side of the garage, and as he approached the exit, he saw the preparation for this New Year's Riverfest. Some of the rides were not up yet, and a few people were seen cutting through it with beasts and serpents following them, but the creatures were having a difficult time keeping up with them with everything close together. It seemed this year, Wichita wanted to go all out for new years and made the carnival bigger than usual, it started to spread onto the field near the river and there were signs that helped point out the directions of different rides, attractions, entertainment, and parking.

As he looked around one thing did catch his eye, one of the signs directed some parking beyond the river at the baseball stadium. Davis looked to the bridge that connected the west side of Wichita to the main city, it was still intact with its artistic architectures, but even from the distance he saw it was being guarded by many armored aliens. They covered both sides of the bridge and even climbed up the artistic architecture as high ground for better vantage points. For some reason they did not destroy this bridge and a few moments later Davis saw why. When people ran towards or ran in front of the bridge to get away from the beast and serpents, the aliens would shoot them with these elongated rifles, but it wasn't bullets that came out, instead it was a yellow beam of energy. The beasts seemed to be pushing people towards the bridge if they could not catch their prey as a last resort, relying on their masters to do the job they failed to do. With the bridge being so heavily guarded that it almost seemed impossible to get across. But despite the situation, Davis knew he had to get closer to figure out how he was going to get home.

Davis took a deep breath to calm his nerves and was about to start running until someone grabbed his arm and covered his mouth shut. Davis was dragged back into the garage, he squirmed to get free, and Davis decided to quickly drop his weight to the floor while doing a high kick, smacking whoever was attacking him in the face.

"OW, son of a bitch that hurt," said the assailant while hissing.

When Davis turned around, he saw an older man holding his nose as blood began to drip down. The man seemed to look like he worked at the carnival as one of the set-up crew, but it did not explain why he was in the garage, and why he attacked Davis.

"Well, serves you right for attacking me like that."

"I wasn't attacking you I was saving you!"

"Saving me?"

"Yes, whatever those things are out there, they wait for people to run into the carnival, then the big ones wear you down, and that's when the four-armed ones shoot you from the bridge." The worker was terrified and began to gasp for air as he continuously kept looking at the bridge and the beams of energy the streaked across the city. His fear was so great that he began to shake almost violently, and you could see in his eyes the regrets he had in his life.

"Really, because it seems the four-armed aliens are more concerned about the people heading towards the bridge than the carnival."

"Trust me it's a facade, those things out there are clever, there using our own environment against us, I mean they must have known we'd set up here, some of my coworkers were eaten by those flying snakes, and my boss just took off, and left me here when I was calling for help."

"Okay, just calm down."

"No way I'm going to calm down!"

"Keep quiet and listen carefully, we have to get out of here and find a place to hide, I'm sure that the military is scrambling to fix this, but till they actually come for us we need to survive on our own."

"Well, it's easier said than done!"

"Dude I just whipped twenty-three flying serpents with my belt and bit off ones tail like ten minutes ago to save fifteen strangers from being eaten, if I can do that then you can easily outrun a few aliens and if you think I'm calm, think again, I'm forcing myself to hold back my fear until I get somewhere safe, then I'll probably go insane for a while, after that I will get a plan together on what to do next."

The man just stood there blankly as Davis calmed down. Davis told the coworker that he was going to see if there was a way across the river and that the man could come with him if he wanted to, but if he chose to stay, then Davis would leave without him, though he believed that their best chance was together. In his heart he didn't want to leave this man alone, but he had to get back to his family. Davis headed back to the exit to the garage, looking carefully around to make sure he was not going to be seen. Then just before he left, the man grabbed Davis's shoulder and told him that he would go with him, but only till they reached the other side of the bridge, after that he was on his own. Davis nodded in agreement with the man then ran over to the flannel cake stand, using it as cover as one of the beasts ran by.

The man stayed put at in the garage, waiting for Davis to move again so he could follow from behind, as a look out for the aliens in the sky and on the bridge. Davis popped his head through the glass window to find another hiding spot and noticed one over by the twister ride and cotton candy tent. The space in between the two was covered in shadow making it difficult to see, it was also small so if something ran by it would miss them. Davis signaled to the man to follow, and they quickly made their moves. They repeated this process constantly, taking their time, and finding new spots to hide. As the two made it halfway, they became cut off when a few serpents chased someone running through the carnival trying to escape. Davis and the man saw the poor being get devoured, as some of the serpents started slithering around the area. The two quickly separated, taking different paths to avoid suspicion, but could see the serpents start to close in on them. Davis entered the mirror maze to hide in plain sight, hoping if the serpent did follow him in it would become distorted by the reflections. As he entered the maze dozens of himself appeared. Though Davis never really liked the mirror maze it was a perfect place to confuse his enemies. In his youth Davis often used the maze to escape some strangers, bullies, or his sisters when they tried to get him to play some rigged carnival games.

Fortunately, even after all the years he had gone to the maze, it never changed. The company that owned the carnival never really changed things, and the house of mirrors was one of them. He walked the path from his childhood and avoided the mirrors, but this time instead of avoiding his childhood issues, he had to hide from an unforeseen enemy. Though he made his way quickly into the center it didn't stop him from constantly trying to change his position in the mirrors to see if they were followed, to see if the serpent would enter. Looking carefully in the reflections he could see the elongated body of the creature slowly make its way inside, and as he expected, the creature became overwhelmed with its surroundings. It had no idea where it was or what was going on as constant images of Davis and itself surrounded it, making it feel disoriented. That is until it became aggressive, lunged toward a mirror, and shattering it into pieces. Davis rushed towards the exit as the serpent began smashing mirrors one by one hearing it bellow in pain from each mirror it shattered. When he reached the exit of the ride, he could see the serpent getting closer to him, smashing every mirror till it found its way out as he exited the maze.

Davis stepped down the small flight of steps and in a panic looked around for a place to hide but was too afraid to find a place. Then the man appeared out of nowhere, grabbing his arm, causing Davis to flinch. The man could hear the mirrors shattering inside the maze and without hesitation pulled him into the magician's tent. When they were inside the man looked out through the crack in the tarped door as Davis caught his breath. As the man looked out, he flinched as he saw the serpent shoot out of the maze and land hard on the ground. It was agitated and darted its head back and forth, searching for anyone to eat. Then a loud bellow called out into the skies around Wichita. The serpent seemed a little displeased, but quickly unfurled its wings and flew towards the direction of the bridge. It was a moment of relief of the two, but it ended quickly. Davis asked the man what was happening, but he said nothing as he walked away from the door. He could see the man was white as a ghost and against his own judgment looked out. As he peeked out the sun's rays stung his eyes for a moment before the world became clear and he saw why the worker was afraid. The aliens were commanding the beasts and serpents like trained attack animals, following behind them as they began to charge into the fray of terrified people.

Davis couldn't bear to look any more and said, "We have got to get out of here, before we end up like them."

The man didn't have to say anything to Davis, the fear that was in his eyes was good enough to say he wanted to leave. The two gathered their courage and made their way out of the tent, even though they were terrified with the thought of dying. They kept low and their eyes on the bridge while they got closer. They were 500 feet from the main road that connected to the bridge to the city and was the entrance to the carnival with the admissions both in plain sight.

But now that they were there, they had no idea how to get past the aliens or beasts that roamed nearby. Davis and the man hunkered down by the Ferris wheel trying to find a safe path. As they racked their brains to figure out anything that would help them out, they saw a couple of people who were hiding near the port-a-potties, but not doing a very good job of it.

One poked there head out too far as a beast looked in their direction, they managed to pull back in, but it already caught the attention of the beast, it began to slowly make its way towards the port-a-potties with a few other beasts in tow. The two began to panic as the beast moved closer and closer to the others and began to scramble to think of a way to save them fast. The two began to look around where they were hiding to find something that would distract the beast long enough to get them to safety, but there was nothing around them. The beast was now halfway down the port-a-potties as they began to sniff the air around them as the others tried to hide. Davis couldn't bear the thought of another person about to die in front of him, he looked around one last time for anything and noticed the man's work belt that had a flashlight. On the spur of the moment, he quickly told the man to stay put and pulled his flashlight out of his belt.

Davis quickly ran over to the other side of the Farris wheel just as the beast were only a few feet away from the other people. Davis turned on the flashlight and set it to S.O.S. mode, ran across to the admissions booth, and threw it against the aluminum wall with a bang. The sound echoed, the beast raised its head and turned, following the sound to the booth as Davis ran out the other side. He curved around the side of the booth just as the beast charged.

As they followed the sound Davis managed to slip around to the port-a-potties and said to them, “Follow me!” The group didn’t argue and followed him as he doubled back. Some of the others were stricken with fear like some many others caught up in this, but they still made the break, knowing if they didn’t, they were going to regret it. The others ran as quick as they could, past the beast, hoping with all their soul they wouldn’t be seen, as the worker ran around the Ferris wheel to under the bridge. With all the screams of the people, the roars of the beast, and aliens firing down upon everyone, their running was mute.

Davis managed to get there first and turned around to see the others running as quick as they could towards him. One by one each person made it under the bridge, leaning on the wall or sitting on the ground to catch their breath hoping they weren’t followed. Once they were all there, Davis gave them a minute to rest as he looked around to figure out the best course of action. After a while, Davis saw only one way across, and it was swimming. Davis was going to jump in, but then he turned his head towards the others, who were trying to sneak around the other side of the bridge.

“What are you doing?” said Davis terrified.

“We're heading onto the bridge." Said one of the other survivors.

“Are you insane!? We just hid from them as a way not to get killed!”

“We are going to use the rails on the bridge to shimmy across to the other side.”

“Again, are you insane? The best chance for all of you is to swim across the river!”

“Now that’s insane! You want us to swim in freezing cold water to get across!”

“It’s the fastest way across and we need to get some distance between us and those creatures!”

“You can do whatever you want to do but I am going to climb across,” said the survivor as she walked away.

"I'm telling you all that the best action to take here is swimming, but if you all want to die then be my guest, but don't expect someone to save you again." Davis said to the survivors as he turned away. He couldn't believe the people he just saved by risking his own life were willingly going to throw their chance to escaping away. Out of blind rage Davis punched his hand against the wall hard as the worker flinched. Davis checked his knuckles and saw them covered in open skin and blood, but he didn't care, he told the worker, "I won't stop you if you go with them, but I won't get killed because of a poor decision." He left the worker and walked up the riverbank as he stretched out his sore hand, though he felt bad leaving the others to free climb, he wasn't going to interfere with their plan, even though he knew it was going to end up a failure. As Davis made it up the river, he heard some footsteps behind him. He turned to see the worker and some of the other survivors following him.

"So, you changed your mind?"

"Thinking on it, you're right, we all would rather get across faster, rather than slower," answered one of the survivors.

"Glad to hear that, so if you're all done ignoring me here's the plan. We're going to use the rivers current to help get across. If we swim slightly against the current, it will push us into the shadow of the bridge as we swim across. If we swim calmly, we can get to the other side without drawing unwanted attention."

Everyone was still nervous about the plan and hoped it would work, but they were still nervous about messing up. Davis looked at them and said, "Look I know your scared, I'm scared too, we have never dealt with anything like this before, but regardless of what comes our way, if we face it together, we will see another day," before he plunged his foot into the water.

The first step in the Arkansas river was freezing cold. Davis could feel the cold move throughout his body the deeper he descended into the river. His body was already shivering fiercely even though only two minutes had passed. Regardless of the cold, he kept moving further away from the shore and began to swim across. The group, though still hesitant, began to slowly make their way into the water. The swim across felt like they were trying to swim from one side of the world to another, even though the river only was 700 feet from shore to shore. To them all it felt like they may never reach the other side before they died from the cold. As they swam, the shadow of the bridge blanketed them, and they hoped it was dark enough to get them the rest of the way without worrying about the serpents in the sky. The other shore was getting closer when Davis couldn't help but stop for a moment to catch his breath. As he floated, he managed to place his feet on the riverbed, not realizing it was close. He rose himself out of the water and found himself only waist deep in the rivers other side, so he decided to walk the rest of the way on foot. He rose out of the water as he made it to the shore, he turned around to see everyone's progress, but then he saw something else. The other group slowly making their way across the bridge, going one by one to avoid being seen, but just as Davis predicted, it didn't last long, and they were spotted. The group on the bridge was dragged off the railing and thrown on the ground. The creatures quickly shot them and in seconds the serpents came down and began to feast. Davis looked away knowing he couldn't help them, but as he was turned away, he heard a splash in the river. He looked up seeing a serpent that had dived onto one of the survivors, manage to drag them out of the water, it seemed that when the climber was discovered, so were they.

The survivor screamed at it to let him go as it flew onto the bridge, but it was too late for him. They others in the water succumbed to their fear when they saw what happened. They began to swim faster to the shore, kicking up the water in huge splashes, desperately trying to get away. But as they made it a shore they jumped out of the river and began to run in different directions. Davis tried to stop them, but the worker grabbed Davis's shoulder and hid around the corner of the bridge as the serpents came down after hearing the panicked group. It only took three seconds before Davis and the worker saw the survivors get dragged off into the sky like the others. However, one put up a fight and managed to free one of her hands and scratch the serpent's left eye with her fingernails, the serpent screech with agony, letting her go, and she began to fall.

Davis felt his blood go cold and the world slow down as he was going to watch another person die. He wanted to do anything to save the girl, and struggled to get free from the workers grasp, yet no matter how much he struggled all he could do was watch her scream as she fell to her death. The serpent dove down towards her trying to catch her, but even with it flapping its wings with all its might it was too late. The world went silent as she hit the ground on the hilltop near the bridge, her blood splattering into the air.

Davis couldn't look away from the hilltop, he couldn't believe that he failed again to save another person. He kept wondering why the other group didn't listen to him when they had the chance, if they had just swum across quietly, they all would have gotten out alive. Yet he knew there was nothing he could do that could have changed anything. The moment the other group was caught the so were they. The serpents were already on top of them the moment they started to panic, and if it hadn't been for the worker Davis would have been caught too. All he could do now was just wallow in his despair knowing he was again powerless to save another. As he felt defeat, the worker grabbed Davis and took him under the bridge as a few serpents flew down and began look at the lifeless body. Even in his depressed state his scientific curiosity got the better of him as Davis poked his head out to see what they were doing.

The serpents sniffed the body as one of the aliens approached. This alien was less bulky, it carried no weapon, and it wore no armor. It was adorned with simple cloths that were grey, its face was hidden by a cloaked hood with strange markings embordering it. The alien kneeled, and it look carefully at the body, but after a few minutes the alien stood up, bowing its head to the body, and pointed at Wichita. The serpents flew towards the city screeching as the alien looked downhill at the river. Davis quickly hid back in the shadows again trying to hold back the anguish, as the alien stared downhill. After waiting for some time, the alien walked towards the bridge, leaving the body behind.

Davis couldn't bring himself to look around the corner again even with the threat out of the way, the image of the girl's blood in the air was permanently burned into his mind, and just looking at her lifeless body would make him crack. The worker looked around the corner and said, "It's gone, let's go."

He grabbed Davis by the arm, but he wouldn't budge, the worker could see on his face that he didn't want to leave, that he had lost a bit of hope to live. He had to forcibly dragged Davis up the hill as he said, "You're not going to give up on me right now, we have to move." As they came near the top, Davis closed his eyes in shame so he couldn't see the result of his failure.

The worker guided him past the corpse as his sight remained in the darkness from his shut eye lids. It wasn't long before Davis heard the worker say, "It's okay, we are far enough away from the body, you can look."

Davis opened his eyes and didn't see the body anywhere in front of them, but he could still feel its presence behind them. The worker with a worried tone asked, "Do you know where we are?"

Davis slowly looked around in front of him to avoid looking back, in his sights he saw the baseball stadium. The stadium wasn't far from his home, he knew that this place was just north of it, by car it was only five minutes, but he wasn't sure by walking. He hoped they could rest and find transportation to get them to his house. As he stared at the stadium, he saw overhead serpents flying to the west and heard the roar of the beast. In a panic the two turned around to see the beast begin to cross the bridge with some of their masters. Davis feared that they got everyone in the city and now they were moving towards the outskirts.

"Run!" yelled Davis.

The worker and Davis ran towards the other side of the stadium, into the parking lot, where they found it covered in totaled cars and bodies were on the ground. Davis saw police cars parked with their doors open, but many of them were on the ground. This made both of their stomachs turn, but they couldn't stop to find another way across. The two quickly ran through the lot, desperately trying not to step or trip on any of the bodies. But as they made it halfway through, Davis loss his footing and fell to the ground. As he lied there, he felt the ground was wet. He lifted himself off it and saw he was drenched in blood. Then he remembered the morning news on the radio, "We have just received word that there a shot out between gang members and police at the Shocker baseball stadium, everyone is advised to stay way until the situation is under control." Davis's eyes became filled with sorrow and hatred, but this time he was done running and he felt himself change from deep inside his soul, too much blood had been spilt today and he had enough. He began to look on the ground for a gun that may have been left behind but found nothing. He stood up from the ground and something glinted into his eye from a beam of sunlight. He looked at where it came from and saw something caught in the wreckage of a car, it looked like some sort of alien tech. It had three-foot double-sided blades facing outside on each end, with a circular ring holding them together on a cylindrical pole five inches in diameter.

Davis was mesmerized by the beauty of this weapon even when he was angry, but then he saw the worker run past him yelling out, "What are you doing, run you idiot!"

Davis quickly turned to see the beast on the other side of the lot, beginning to charge through the cars, while crushing the bodies of the dead. The worker ran away from the stadium as Davis stood there, staring at the beast, refusing to move. Davis quickly grabbed the weapon and yanked it out of the car, he put both of his hands on it, and took his stance like he is holding a staff. He was infuriated by all the death and destruction by these things. All the people who could not get away from the city, the people who had died, all the people he couldn't save because of these aliens. Davis clenched his jaw down so tightly that he could break his own teeth just thinking about all of it. For him, he did not care what price he had to pay to try and make up for the loss of life that he had seen. But he refused to die here; he swore to himself he would live each day for them, hoping to tell the world how they survived and not let anyone else fall to those things. He promised himself he would keep trying to save as many people as he could even if it cost him his own.

With the beast only a few feet away from him, Davis channeled his rage into strength. He swung his body around with the weapon and as he did, he could feel the weapon heat up and turn black, the air became electrified, and right before the beast pounced on him, he swung it like a baseball bat. A massive wave of kinetic energy fired out the end of the weapon, making the beast take off like a baseball, along with some cars, ripping apart a portion of the stadium, and sent the debris flying into the bridge, crushing the beasts and aliens that still had remained on it. When Davis saw what he had just done, he felt strangely calm about it. Even though he had never fought like that before, it felt exhilarating to take down an enemy much stronger than he was. But in his mind, he believed that it was just a fluke and did not want to test it out, he took the weapon in his hands and made a run for it. Yet as he began to run the weapon disintegrated into dust and reconstructed itself into some sort of garb around his body. Davis was stunned for a second and he did not know what it meant, but he did not have time to figure it out. He quickly looked behind to see if the beast had gotten up, but found the clothed alien waving its hand, as if it were saying goodbye to him, which in turn made Davis run faster.

While running towards the other half of the highway, Davis found the worker hiding behind a car. He tried to get him to run, but the man refused to leave. He told Davis that he saw what he had done, seeing the alien wave to him, and that he would rather take his chances being alone than with him.

Davis felt hurt, but instead looked at the man in the eyes and tried to explain to him that he didn't know how he did that or why that alien waived to him, but he assured him he wasn't under their control, but the man refused to listen. Davis quickly grabbed his arm and told him that he was going with him and if he had a problem about it then he could take it up with the man-eating aliens. But the man then pulled from his backside a gun and pointed it at Davis. He told him he was being controlled by them now and that he was going to lead him to his death. Davis tried desperately to convince the man he was not going to hurt him, but the man told him to shut up and leave him alone. However, Davis was not going to leave another person to die, he could not leave another person to die by those things. The man ripped his arm away from Davis's grip and punched him to the ground.

The man pointed the gun at Davis as he started to tremble, he said in a broken voice, "I can't trust you. I don't know if you're just being used, but I won't go down like the others." Then the man took the gun and pointed it at his head and said, "If I'm going out, I'm doing it on my own terms," and squeeze the trigger. Davis tried to stop him, but it was too late, brain matter and skull shards flew out the side of the man's head and a moment later his body collapsed.

Davis stood there shaking with fear and thought to himself, "There was nothing I could do."

He grabbed the gun and looked to the sun in the west, then began to run south from his position in the parking lot, until a car with its hazard lights on caught his eye. He quickly looked in the car to find it abandoned with the key still in the ignition. He jumped in and sped off to his home as he saw the man's body lying still on the ground. He felt sadness for the man, but only for a moment as thoughts came into his mind, "Why did they only want the living? How could I have been able to use their tech? Why did it change?" Wherever the answers lie, Davis knew that he would probably find them in time, but for now all he had to do was survive, save others if he could, and find his family, until they revealed themselves, and hopefully end this nightmare.

Davis sped down the road while dodging other abandoned cars as he approached his street. A few beasts and serpents wondered around looking for easy prey in and around his area. However, he managed to slip by without drawing too much attention to himself by taking the back roads and managed to make it to his house. As he arrived, he saw his mother's car was gone and the front door was wide open. He quickly parked the car in the driveway, taking the keys out of the ignition he jumped out of the car, and he went to the garage or, as his stepfather put it, his "workshop." When he approached, he could hear something blaring almost like his alarm clock, the door to the garage was open and as he stepped inside, the blade of the electric saw was covered in blood, it still dripping, and on the ground below it was someone's left arm, covered in saw dust with its watch blaring.

CHAPTER 4

The wait is the worst part.

Davis was in a state of shock at the sight of his stepfather's workshop, the blood from the saw blade was slowly dripping from its teeth. The world became muted except the watches alarm. Continuously staring at the arm on the ground, Davis slowly approached it and kneeled on the dusty ground. His right hand slowly went towards it trembling, when he made contact, he could feel the warmth of the arm, as if it just happened a few moments ago, it seemed that the saw dust preserved its heat. He carefully pushed the saw dust off to find his stepfather's tattoo with his mother's ring in his palm. Davis took the ring and realized this was the ring he gave her for her birthday this year. The ring itself was $1,500, decorated with silver and a rose cut diamond in the center. Davis bought this for her to celebrate her fiftieth birthday, and to show her that she deserved better than a guy who constantly screwed up. In her life, not many people really gave her much besides her parents, but Davis believed that his mother deserved something major after all the years for being on earth, even if it was just a rock. But the one thing Davis did not know is why did Don have it? This was something to show that he loved his mother despite everything that had happened between them. Yet Don had something of great value, both in currency and emotion.

Davis snatched the ring for the severed arm and placed it in his pocket, but as he stood from the ground and was about to walk away, he spat on the severed arm. He made his way to the front of the house, making sure nothing saw him as he made his way inside. Once in the house he quickly locked all the doors and windows, closed the drapes to hide from the light, and then when things seemed clear he went down into the basement. His sister's and his cats started to gather around him crying for food as he made his way down the old wooden staircase. However, he wasn't concerned with that right now, he jumped on his computer, and looked at the security cameras to make sure they were still working. He was grateful the one thing Don did right was installing these cameras, even though he only did it after he stole from him to give him false security. But thanks to his idiocy, Davis was able to gain control of the cameras and watch him just in case he needed to report him to the police. Although he removed the front doors camera, he did not remove the one in the back yard, the ones on the side, the one on the back door, or the one looking at the garage.

Once he made sure everything was operational, he fed the cats to keep them quiet, and began to look at his food storage. He didn't know how long this invasion was going to last so he tried to prepare for the week, just to buy time for things to settle down and hopefully have the military act, but he only had a few days' worth of food that he could stretch out for a week. It didn't take him long to get things in order for survival and he knew he would have no choice but to go out and get some supplies later, yet in the back of his mind he had a strange curiosity. He went back to his computer and looked up the records of that day, to find out what happened to his mother and stepfather, though he knew there was danger lurking outside, he had to know.

He jumped back on his computer and found the video from that day, fast forwarding through the video he also was keeping an eye on the cameras outside. He would see a beast now and again looking in his neighborhood on his cameras, but they seemed to just only be there for a moment then run off. He didn't know why they were doing this, but regardless he kept his eye out just in case as he continued to look. Eventually he came across Don going into the garage at 12 o'clock, after only five minutes, he was confronted by a small group of men, and they looked shady. As Davis looked at the screen, he listened carefully at the audio hoping to hear their conversation. Even though the audio from the distance was low he could still hear them.

"Hello Don, it's been a while, how have you been?" asked the man, but before Don could answer he cut him off, "It doesn't matter what you say because it's about to become a living hell for you." The man looked at his other men and nodded his head towards Don, the men quickly swarmed him and grabbed his arms placing the left one on the saw table, as the saw blade was turned on. "I know that your stepson found out about are little arrangement with his check, but the one thing I don't know is how?"

"I don't know!" Don yelled!

The man took the saw blade and lowered it onto Dons arm. The flesh of his arm began to cut open as he screamed in agony, his crimson blood flying in the air and splattering the other men, he begged for them to stop, but the man didn't until he made it a quarter of the way down.

"I'll ask you three more times, if you keep lying to me, I will keep cutting your arm" the man explained.

"I am telling you the..." said Don before one of the other men took his pistol and shot his knee out.

"If you interrupt me or don't answer the question my boys will shoot another part of your body," said the man. "Now, I'm guessing your stepson found out about the check by something he came across, so how did he find out that it was stolen?"

Don looked shocked at what the men said, the man knew the check he gave them was stolen, but all Don did was say "I...I...don't-" The man took the blade down on his arm again, cutting deeper into the tissue. Dons screams echoed throughout the neighborhood, but no one came to see what was going on, no police sirens were heard, there was nothing. The man lifted the saw blade again and looked down at Don in disappointment.

"I thought you were a tough Russian scumbag, not a pitiful excuse of a human being," said the man with a little joy in his tone.

Davis continued to watch in horror as he could only imagine the pain Don was going through, he wanted to turn away, but he couldn't take his eyes away from it. Don shook violently in pain as his sweat and blood began to wet the floor. The other men kept Don from collapsing as the man was disappointed, their deal was simple, he provides money in exchange for items he can sell, he was basically a pawn guy or loan shark depending on the deal the man explained to Don. That it was a deal and sometimes Don got even more than what he bargained, the fact that he was trying to screw them over was unacceptable. Yet he was impressed that Don managed to get away with it for so long, and even more impressed that he was so cold hearted he was willing to sacrifice his stepson for himself, but the thing he did not like is where he set him up to take his place. However, he wanted to know how his stepson found out.

"Come on Donny, you are not this stupid to play this game, just tell me how he found out and this all will stop," said the man in a calming voice.

Don took with a fearful expression on his face didn't even take a second to think and spoke gasping "Okay, he found the pay stub to the check in my pocket last January."

"Anything else?"

"He knows it was premeditated and he knows how you got it cashed out."

The man looked at Don with a stern look and said, "I believe you." Then nodded to his men and they sawed the rest of Dons arm off.

The arm became detached from Don's body, falling limp to the floor, as the blood kept spilling onto the ground. The man took Don's handheld blow torch and told his men to hold him down on his side saying they were not done yet.

"You're not going to die so fast buddy. I still need your help in finding your stepson, only he can stop this madness, then maybe I will do him a solid and end you, but till then I need you alive, your life is my bargaining chip, and I'm not going to lose it," as he turned on the torch. The man pointed the blue flame towards the wound and began to cauterize it. Don tried his best to keep from screaming but caved in within a few seconds. After five minutes of burning the wound was shut and the blood was coagulated, but the men were far from done.

"Where is your stepson?" asked the man.

Before Don could answer he looked behind the man and then his eyes widen. The man turned around and saw something, but the video was facing the garage so the camera didn't see it, but a few seconds later a loud roar could be heard on the video as the men tried to scatter, but it was already too late, serpents entered the frame, attacked the men, and consumed their bodies. Don tried to get to the inside of the house, but a beast pounced on him keeping him down as a serpent approached. Davis paused the video now knowing his stepfather's fate, but he could not watch anymore, he feared if he did, he would find out his mother's fate was the same. He turned away from the video realizing this event showed him something significant. These beasts and serpents were already looking around in the neighborhoods before the attack on Wichita. They were all lying in wait for the perfect moment to strike.

Davis hoped this place would be a haven for him to hide out in, but now knowing that this place was already vaguely looked over, he knew it was only a matter of time before they came back. He didn't know what to do and became stressed out about this situation, so even though he knew the risk, he made his way into the upstairs bathroom and ran a bath to warm up from the cold Arkansas waters. He could not help himself, normally when he felt sad or scared, he would warm up his body with a bath to make him calm down and forget what happened, but today that was not going to happen. What Davis saw he could not just forget, so many people died in front of him, but for some reason he felt as if that many of them weren't really gone. Something in his heart told them they were okay, but in his mind, he knew they were gone, he saw them get eat alive and one fall to her death. Davis removed his cold wet clothes, and the ring from his pocket, but then he remembered the garb he was wearing as he took it off. With all the running and avoiding aliens, he forgot about it. When he took it off to examine it, it disintegrated again, and turned into a basketball sized sphere, hovering in the air motionless.

Davis was dumbfounded and waited to see what it was going to do, but after a while the bathtub became full, and the sphere had done nothing. Davis kept his eyes on it as he removed the rest of his cold clothes and bloody shoes, then entered the warm waters, and began to bathe himself. But eventually he began to feel uncomfortable, he did not like the idea of the sphere just hovering above him, it felt like he was being watched. He closed the curtain and continued to bathe himself while keeping an eye on the spheres shadow on the curtain. However, the dark shadow of the sphere kept him on edge. But regardless of it, during his time in the bath Davis tried to figure out what exactly the sphere was made of and trying to wash off the strange mucus on his arm, with no luck, it seemed that water wasn't going to wash it way easily. Though there were many things on his mind one thing interfering with it, "Why his stepfather had his mother 's ring?" It wasn't taken during the horrific remaining moments in Don's life, and it wasn't lost to the monsters outside, so he wondered how it got there.

Granted he knew there were important things that were going on, but he needed to know. After thirty minutes of relaxing, Davis moved the curtain and exited the bath while it drained. Wrapping a towel around his waist, he investigated the mirror then grabbed his mother's ring and examined it. He saw no blood, dust, or anything to show that Don had it on his person while he was outside, at least to what Davis could see. Then a thought came into his mind "What if mom left this behind to show she was alive?" A moment of joy came across Davis's face, but then vanished, even if she was alive, she was long gone and he couldn't go looking for her now, it was too dangerous to go outside. He gripped the ring in his hand and made a promise to himself, "I don't know how or when, but I will find you." Davis put the ring on his pinky finger and focused on his new tasks, figuring out how to beat the invaders, try to contact his brother and sisters, and save as many as he could.

As the water emptied from the tub Davis grabbed his clothes and shoes but wondered how he was going to get the sphere downstairs. He began to pull on it and push it from side to side to see if it would move, but with no luck. He became irritated by the sphere and decided to leave it there until he could make sense of it. But as he began to leave the bathroom, he noticed in the mirror the sphere began to follow him. Davis closed the door behind him quickly and waited for the sphere to react, but nothing happened, until Davis entered the living room. The sphere had turned into its dusty form, slipping under the door, and reformed itself into it sphere on the other side. He did not know why it was following him, but it seemed harmless, for now, so he let it continue to follow him until he could discover its secrets.

Once he was in his room again, he jumped onto his computer and was going to send a message to his younger brother, Martin, through an email in the hopes he was alright. As he looked through his email, he found five new messages from his brother sent that day. He quickly opened the conversation and began to read as quickly as he could.

"Hey bro I, just wanted to wish you a happy birthday and I hope to see you soon." Email received at 01:06 am Dec 31, 2029.

"Hey bro, I forgot to mention that I got you a present, but I forgot to send it, but the best things in life are worth waiting for, and I wanted to wish you a happy new year to, celebrate for me would you!" Email received at 01:15 am Dec 31, 2029.

"Bro, there has been a change in plans, the officers are telling us we are departing the shore at 09 hundred hours, which is weird, we weren't supposed to leave until after the first of January, but I guess it's a good thing, since that means I will be home sooner. I wanted to remind you, that once were at sea it's hard to get contact with any family, it's just standard protocol." Email received at 06:55 am Dec 31, 2029.

"Bro, I just got an email from mom saying she was leaving Don and that you were responsible for it, THANK GOD YOU GOT THROUGH TO HER." Email received at 08:45 am Dec 31, 2029.

"Bro, what's going on out there, the officers are telling us there has been an attack by an unknown enemy, they aren't telling us anything else, I tried to call you, but you weren't answering your phone, please pick up your damn phone and answer." Email received at 12:15 pm Dec 31, 2029.

Davis stared at his emails, wondering how his brother could have sent anything out at sea. In his mind he thought his brother might have broken protocol to see if anyone was okay. But Davis knew his brother would be in serious trouble if they found out what he did. He could not even begin to think about what they were going to do to his brother, especially if they found out during an invasion of their communications were being tracked. Davis shuttered to think about how his brother's ignorance could have gotten his crew and himself killed. His mind began to create images of his brother being attacked by the serpents, being devoured whole or the ship coming under attack by some sort of alien tech he has not seen yet that could destroy their ships or worse disintegrate them into nothing but particles. Then he feared that they might have captured him and were doing experimentations on him while he was still awake and watching what they were doing. Davis could not keep looking at the emails without thinking about the worst possibilities. He was about to close out of his email until a notification bell went off, it was a new email from his brother.

"Bro, I don 't know if you will ever see this, but if your alive please answer me. We have just been informed about what's happening on land, and there giving us a chance to send messages to our families. I have not been able to get into contact with anyone, not even Don, and he normally always keeps his phone on him. The officers tell us that they are going to start collaborating with all the other countries to stop this, but until they meet an agreement, we have orders to tell you help won't be coming for the next three months, so please hold out till we get there if we can." Messaged received at 4:55 pm Dec 31, 2029

Davis could feel his brother's anguish from his basement, unable to reach their loved ones was something far worse than death or any pain, but he gathered himself and quickly wrote him back, he needed to let his brother know he was okay and what happened.

"Bubba it is me, I'm okay, just frazzled. I was at work when we got attacked, but I was able to get away thanks to a friend of mine. To be honest I was up close and personal with those things. Don is dead, I do not know where mom is, and I left my phone at work in my bag I am currently downstairs with the cats, but Alex is not here. I'll try and contact our sisters and my father, but please let me know if you got this, quickly." Sent 05:00pm Dec 31, 2029

Davis quickly looked up his father's and sisters' emails and quickly messaged them and waited for a response, but nothing came. Davis turned away from his computer and looked at the sphere, wondering if his brother was cut off from the computer and unable to contact him back. All he could really do was wait until he got a response, however waiting was the worst part in these situations. Davis walked away from his computer and laid on his bed as some of his sister's cats jumped up and laid next to him. He stroked the cats fur coats as he waited, staring at the computer hoping to hear a ding, but the minutes turned into hours, and Davis had to eventually eat. He left his room and began sifting through his refrigerator to see what he had, but all there was were things he had to cook with a pan or throw in the microwave and neither one was something he wanted to do.

Davis knew he already risked his life with a bath but now he was going to have to do the same with food he had to cook. Granted he was still downstairs which made in more difficult to see him, but he didn't know how well the beasts or serpents smell was. In his hindsight, he realized he should have checked the upstairs pantry to see if there was some dry food he could eat till things settled down. In his anguish for food, he began to look around the basement to see if there were any places that might leak out the smell of cooked meat or veggies. When he believed he was okay, he carefully began to cook in the downstairs kitchen as quietly as he could and only chose things he could microwave for a few minutes. As he heated up some instant noodles, he remained silent watching the time carefully to make sure he could stop it from blaring its noise, but as he did, he became deep in thought. Wondering what he was going to do, for the next three months if he could not contact his brother or anyone else. He had plenty of company, but it was not the same, he wanted some actual contact with other people. Davis remembered how his sisters and himself would indulge themselves in conversation about anything, but now with them gone he felt like there was no need to talk. Once his noodles were ready, he finished it quickly then turned on his projector and watched some movies he had bought to pass the time with his sister's cats laying around him sleeping, keeping the volume down so only he could hear it. But eventually the clock struck ten and Davis decided to turn in, hoping he would awake to the sound of the notification bell and not some beasts roaring or aliens breaking in, but it never happened.

Time seemed to fly by as he waited for any message from anyone, the aliens seemed to have stopped their attack, and he was beginning to stress out on why they were there on earth, but with no real clues to anything involving them invading, he was stuck. He would check the cameras now and again to see if anything or anyone was nearby, other than a few serpents flying around, there was really nothing, even the animals seemed to be quiet. After three days of waiting, Davis found himself having a hard time sleeping and began to stress eat. However, things changed that night when the aliens made their move. As Davis was getting ready for another sleep deprived night, he heard someone scream from outside his basement window. Davis jumped on his computer to see what was going and that's when he saw them. The aliens were making their way through his neighborhood and were breaking into homes, catching whoever was inside, and letting the beasts feed. Every few minutes he could hear the screams of the neighbors echo through the night. Davis was too tired to put up a decent fight, he could not save anyone in his current state. He felt like a hypocrite for promising something he could not uphold, but they eventually approached his home.

He figured this would happen eventually, he jumped off his computer, and hid in the crawl space in the basement, hoping the aliens would not be able to find him. As he waited in the darkness, he could hear the aliens enter his home and began looking around upstairs and down in the basement simultaneously.

Flipping over furniture, ripping down doors, and even firing their weapons in the house to get a response. He desperately kept his mouth shut to the point where he had to put his dirty hand over his mouth just to keep himself from yipping. They spent hours looking through his house and when he heard less activity he felt as if they were nearly finished. Davis felt a great deal of relief, but it was quickly shattered when he saw a light enter the crawl spaces opening. Though he was out of the light's range, it illuminated the space enough where he could be spotted. Then a strange device poked into the crawl space and began to scan the area. Davis's blood began to run cold as he was close to being discovered.

Then out of the darkness his sister's cat, who Davis didn't know was in the crawl space, jumped out and startled the alien. The light and scanner were pulled away from the crawl space and Davis waited in silence for them to come back, but the light never shined in the hole again. He heard the aliens leave the house one by one as they closed the doors behind them, as if they were trying to leave no trace of them ever being there. Though Davis had heard the doors close, and their footsteps ceased, he refused to leave the crawl spaces darkness. Even for a full-grown man he felt like a child hiding from his dad. He didn't hear anything the rest of the night, but he didn't leave the darkness, and eventually passed out in the crawl space. When he awoke, he found himself okay, but in shock. He slowly gathered himself, crawled to the opening, and waited to see if something was there. But the only thing was his sister's cats meowing for attention. Davis with fear looked out the opening and saw it was clear, but noticed the door was still slightly open, he figured that they might have been there again when he was asleep. As he exited the crawl space, he noticed the sphere still following him around. That's when Davis realized that they were never able to find him, even with the sphere hovering around him. He thought that their tech would give off a signal, like a beacon to indicate it was nearby, but it seemed they did not even know they were missing something, which made him suspicious as the sun of a new day began to rise, and he was once again waiting.

After another three days Davis managed to clean his house up and watched the cameras on his computer for any sign of the invaders, but it seemed things were quiet, a little too quiet. All he could hear from the cameras was the wind and the occasional squirrel climbing. Once he was able to hear the kids playing in the street in the morning, but now it was so quiet, that made him feel isolated. Eventually he went upstairs and looked out the windows, seeing if there was anything nearby that his cameras couldn't see, but once again there was nothing. Davis retreated downstairs once he was done looking outside, he lay down, and as he lay there, he said to himself, "Okay, no more waiting for help, tomorrow it's time to get in gear and figure this out, I can't wait for help to come to me, and I can't wait for it. When or if I wake up, I need to strategize for the long haul."

The next morning, Davis woke up to no alarm and began strategizing for any run ins with the aliens, he even started to keep an audio journal about the things that had happened for research and as an account for others. Eventually he investigated his food rations and saw he was low. He decided that he had to make a run to the gas station for some food, though the superstore had better food choices, the gas station was closer and more convenient. Davis geared up and grabbed the gun he took from the dead carnival worker and walked out the front door, hoping it was going to be a smooth run. It only took him five minutes to walk to the gas station and when he arrived, he saw the place still stood, but was in shambles, cars totaled by collisions, the glass windows were broken, the doors were ripped off the hinges. What was unusual though was the blood on the shards of glass and cars with strange symbols on the doors. This was something that almost resembled a cult activity and it made him feel sick. He quickly entered the station, stepping over the glass, and grabbed a few bags of food, a couple of carbonated flavored waters, but something was off about this place, yet he could not put his finger on it. When he exited the station with his bags of food, he realized with the amount of blood there was, people would have died, yet there were no bodies. Though his curiosity was peeked, he did not want to see what made off with the bodies, so he ran back home.

As he entered his room, Davis began hating the idea for eating junk food as meals, but there was no other way around, he did not want to run down to the store even with the car, he believed the chances of getting caught were still too high. So, he stopped complaining to himself and dug into his chips, popcorn, and two flavored waters. Once he was finished, he laid down and stared at the ceiling as the sphere still hovered by his side, he wondered why it was still following him? He remembered what it looked like before as a spear or halberd but still wondered why it changed? He closed his eyes and pictured it in his mind, wondering how something like that could become so useless after one use.

Then suddenly a huge metallic clang made Davis jump out of his bed and land on the floor. He quickly looked around to find nothing was in the room with him, but the sphere was gone. Quickly making his way around the bed, he found the spear laying on the ground. That is when he realized the sphere materialized as a weapon the moment, he thought of it, and wondered if it reacted to memory or his imagination. He began thinking of a fictional claymore as he stared at the spear, but nothing came of it. Then when he thought of an old sword he once had, it changed. Whatever this material was, it would only respond to the user's thoughts and memories, however the sphere was not used up. It seemed that the sphere would only use a certain amount of itself to construct the item the user was thinking of, so whatever was left remained in its sphere form. From that observation, Davis realized depending how big the item was, meant how much of the sphere had to be used. He remembered when he was running away from the stadium, it changed into a cloth around his body, but when he had no use for it, it changed again. But thinking back on it he didn't wear something like that garb before and he didn't think of it, all he knew was that he was cold. That's when he wondered if it reacted to the beings needs as well as their thoughts and memories. There was so much to uncover about this sphere, but Davis decided that he needed to do more research before using this thing for anything, especially since he had no real idea of how this thing responded. Davis had no use for the sword, and it turned into dust, hovering back to the sphere and rejoining it. Things were once again quiet, as he lied back down for a few hours. Then Davis heard the notification bell from his computer, he quickly jumped on and saw a new email from his brother.

"BRO, I am so sorry I didn't respond last week, its chaos out here as well, the governments all over the world are going crazy, please message me if you are still there!"

"Bubba, I'm still here."

"Oh, thank God, are you okay? "

"I'm fine I have had a few close calls, but I'm still safe"

"Good, listen I have orders from my main officer that if we make contact with anyone on the mainland, we needed to get her, so I will be right back."

"Wait, what do you mean 'anyone on the mainland'?"

(Waiting for response)

"This is captain Marry Luvuntar, your brother's email is now considered one of the few communications we have in America, to whom am I addressing? "

"Davis Ring, Martin Ring's older brother."

"Can you prove your identity? "

"I duct taped my brother to the ceiling when I was eight."

(Waiting for response)

"Okay your brother says it's you... also how did you pull that off!

"We do not have the time to discuss that!"

"Good point so let me cut to the chase, we need information, we can't reach our people back in Blue Moon Bay, and the people we did contact would not help us. So, is there anything you can tell us that we need to know about these things?"

Davis messaged the captain through his brother's email everything he had seen, the two different aliens, their attack patterns, their tech and usage of their pets, passing over the dead and animals, and their strange armor. The only things he did not tell her was the strange sphere he had and the alien that waved to him, he did not want them to think he was being controlled by the invaders or scare his brother.

"Okay, this info is good, but we need more, is there anything else you might have seen?"

Davis thought for a moment and realized the only other thing he saw was the station and began typing. "I'm not sure if this is connected or not, but when I ran to the gas station for food today, there was blood all over the place and strange symbols on the doors, but there were no bodies, I haven't seen anything eating the corpses, but somethings telling me we need to be prepared for the worst."

"Thank you for the info, but now I need you to get photos and videos of everything you see and then send them to me, we will try to raise the military or air force base in your state, if we can, but till then Davis you're our eyes and ears on the ground."

"I'm sorry, WHAT!"

"Look I know this is messed up, but you're the only one we have contacted on the mainland that has helped us so far, we can't even get the President or many of our generals on the line, we need all the help we can get, and we need everything you can get your hands on. I know I can't demand you to put your life on the line, but I'm begging you for help. The world is experiencing the same thing, everyone is struggling to survive, it has already been a week and according to what we have heard, over sixty two percent of earth is already dead, we need help, our world needs help, otherwise we are done for!"

Davis knew what she was asking, but in his heart, it was worth the risk if it meant saving lives, so he typed her, "I will run to the super store after dark to get some drones, cameras, and SIM cards. This will be the ideal time to see if these things are nocturnal or have night vision."

"Thank you, contact me the moment you get back through your brother's email, stay safe and may god keep you from harm."

Emails sent and received from 03:56pm-06:00pm 01/07/2029.

Davis got off his computer and thought of the road he had just begun to travel down, he knew that his life would always be in unspeakable parrel, but it seemed he didn't have a choice, if no one else would do it then he was going to have to force himself to face the enemy. However, he had never really been in battle before, he had just started to regain his confidence, and this was not a situation where he could just reveal his true feelings about someone, this was a life-or death mission he had just accepted. In his life he had felt like the deck was stacked against him, yet now he was certain it was. If he refused, he would be a traitor, if he accepted, he would be gambling his life, but in the end his heart told him what he needed to do and spoke the truth. He could not allow others to die any further because of his cowardness. His heart told him that the road was filled with danger and at the end of it he would no longer be the same man, whether he was good or evil was up to him alone, but he could not forsake others because he was afraid.

Despite his better judgment, Davis decided to use the sphere, thinking of his jacket he had left at work, the spheres dusts surrounded his body and rematerialized. The warmth of this jacket mirrored his own to the last detail, and even though he was petrified. This was something he had never done before. This world changed so rapidly in a single week, humanity was on its knees, and no help was coming for a long time. Their leaders had vanished, and their military was scattered too thin. He couldn't begin to fathom how bad things were going to get as time went on. Yet despite his fears he knew he had to press on, not just for himself, but for the thousands of people still fighting, and counting on each other to find answers to stop this madness.

The waiting was beginning to bore him, but as he looked at his jacket, he realized he had time to try and figure out what this was or at least began to control it. "What the fuck am I doing?! I've been wasting so much time waiting for a message I didn't even try to figure out this thing yet, what's wrong with me!" he said aloud.

Davis took the jacket off and began experimenting with the sphere as he took notes on his audio recorder. The first test he did was a simple shape test to discover its modeling capabilities. He thought of a cube, then a pyramid, and then a decahedral dice. What he noticed is that though it made the shapes, it wasn't a solid form. It seemed to only make the shape of the object he wanted but didn't allow him to use more than what was necessary. Davis realized that this thing did have its own set of rules and if he could uncover them, then he would be able to control it better and hopefully use it against the invaders, or that's at least what he hoped. He changed it over and over, into different shapes and sizes, but the one thing he couldn't figure out was the kinetic wave of energy he unleashed. He tried to recreate the scenario and the feelings in his mind, but nothing came from it. He just couldn't create the wave of energy like before and wondered, what caused the waves reaction.

Once he was finished experimenting with the sphere he sat down at his desk and looked at the time. He did not even realize how much time had gone as the clock rolled over to 7:55 pm, the time had come to leave. As he walked out of his room, he imaged his coat and the sphere morphed around him as he headed up the stairs. He walked to the front door knowing once this mission started there was no turning back, he stopped for a moment, and he took a deep breath in and exhaled slowly out. He looked out the window to see the coast was clear and with his hand shaking he grabbed the doorknob, turned it, opened the door, and stepped outside into the night.

CHAPTER 5

The gamble.

The crescent moon hovered above the abandoned city of Wichita; the wind blew in Davis's hair as he walked away from his home. He could feel the winter winds begin to bite at him, almost like a sign that he needed to stay home tonight. Nevertheless, he began to make his way to the super store in the dark cold winter night. Davis was grateful that the weather was tolerable, but he did not like the idea of it icing over when he was out on the town, especially tonight. Though the walk was going to be a while, it was still a good opportunity to look around for supplies, weapons, and with luck maybe no aliens.

The winds howled in the night like a wolf at the moon as he walked down the road, it was the only thing he heard other than his own steps. He never really noticed how dreary the world was when there was no one around. Before the envision, all the people he saw driving by and walking around almost peaceful. But now he was always on alert for anything suspicious on the way to the super store. As he walked, he felt it again, the feeling he was being watched by something in the shadows. At this point it became apparent that he was being followed and it had waited for him, but by what, he did not know. He kept his pace as he continued down the street as whatever was following kept up. Although he knew he was being followed he did not hear any footsteps, it made him wonder how it was so quiet. Davis quickly investigated the reflection of a car to see something in the night sky slightly lit up by the crescent moon. Though the lighting was terrible Davis could make out large wings on its sides and an extremally small body with eight tails flowing in the wind, with three solid green eyes staring at him.

He stopped dead in his tracks and turned quickly to see what it was, but when he did the creature was gone. He waited for a few moments to see if the creature would make a move, but nothing came of it. When Davis turned around and investigated the reflection again it reappeared behind him. Whatever this creature was it had the ability to camouflage into its environment, like a chameleon, and yet it seemed to be cautious about who it was stalking. Whatever it was, it looked like it was keeping an eye on him, like it was waiting for the perfect opportunity to strike. This creature made Davis feel unsafe, for if this creature could easily find him and follow him, then any creature could. He felt like he needed to turn back to his home, but he could not, he knew what he had signed up for, and he had to see it through. So even though he was being followed he continued forward to the super store as the creature continued to follow him from behind.

As he walked through the night, Davis found himself at the southern bridge, still intact, and crossed over the Arkansas river, it felt nice to avoid the water, but then Davis realized something was amiss. The aliens and their pets were nowhere around, and this bridge was not being guarded or destroyed. The aliens had been in his neighborhood only three days ago and by the rate they were going he should have run into them by now or at least their pets. There was nothing, it was like being in a ghost town, but all the lights were still on. Davis got scared and quickly crossed the bridge, but his speed walking turned into running as he didn't want to be outside any longer. The rest of the way to the store was him running through the abandoned neighborhoods with no one around, just the lights on the street, and the darkness that surrounded him.

He stopped running when he neared the police station across the street from the super store, leaned on one of the police cars, and caught his breath, relaxing for a few moments before he continued. Suddenly from across the street, in the super store parking lot he heard gunfire followed by beast's roaring in pain. Davis ducked behind the police car in fear as he believed he was going to get hit, but eventually he raised his head above the car and looked across the street. The store was under siege by dozens of beasts trying to get inside, with people firing from the rooftop. The beasts were desperately trying to find a way in, but they couldn't. The people inside seemed to be making a last stand against the creatures and it looked like they were winning but their look was deceiving. After a while, the gun fire seemed to come less frequently, then everything went quiet. It had been apparent to Davis that the people inside the superstore had run out of ammo. Some of the people on the roof retreated into the store as others began to throw Molotov's onto the beast. As they broke on the ground the beast's fur did not catch flame, but it did force them to retreat, scattering in multiple directions.

Davis ran behind the police station as some of the beasts fled in his direction. As he hid in the shadow of the building, he could see the beast run past with fear in their eyes as blood fell from their bodies and their horns damaged. The beasts ran across the bridge and once they were out of sight, Davis looked around the corner to see the people on the roof cheering with delight, knowing that they had managed to push them back. When the coast was clear from the beasts, Davis quickly made his way over to the parking lot and headed to the store and began to see the damage up close. The parking lot was littered with bodies of serpents and beasts freshly killed and some that were already rotting away. Cars were pushed aside, flipped over, and trampled, a familiar sight he remembered from the first day at the baseball stadium when the beast chased him. When he stood in the middle of the parking lot, Davis never realized that this was happening so close to his home or that these people were struggling against the alien forces. The smell of gunpowder was strong in the air as he drew closer to the store, while avoiding the flames of the Molotov's burning liquid.

As he drew closer to the entrance of the super store, he could see it was blocked off with carts and other materials to prevent anything from entering from the front. He tried to peep inside the windows, till someone from the rooftop saw him and called down to him, "Hey, who are you?"

Davis was shocked by them screaming, wondering why in the world would they do that, especially since the beast could still be lurking nearby. But it seemed, even with the persons loud voice, that they were long gone at that point, the damage they received was too intense for them. Even though he didn't like the idea of yelling while he was in the open, he introduced himself to them. "Hello, my name is Davis and I'm looking for some help." Davis yelled back up.

"What person isn't," said the man.

"Fair point, but I'm not looking for a place to stay, I need some stuff from this place."

''What type of stuff and why?"

"I'm looking for tech, cameras, flash drives, recorders, and some drones if this place still has any."

The man on the roof became annoyed and asked him in a stern tone "Why?"

"Do you want me to explain everything, then let me inside before we get killed by those things, unless you prefer to chat inside a serpent's stomach!"

The man on the roof was first stand offish, but he pulled out a radio from his side and began to talk into it. Davis couldn't hear him from the ground, but it looked as if he was getting permission from someone. The man on the roof put down his radio and pointed to the corner. Davis looked where he pointed to see other people come around with guns and waited for Davis to do something.

"What are you doing?! If I was a threat to you, why would you come down here!" said Davis in anger.

The people lowered their weapons and escorted Davis inside, though he didn't like the aggregation display he could understand why they were doing it. They made their way to the back side of the store that was used for unloading stock items, but now it was the only entrance and exit to this massive place. Once they were all inside, they began to search for any weapons that Davis might have had on him, but the only thing they found was his gun. Even after they were done searching him, he was surprised by the fact they did not ask about the floating sphere behind him, they seemed to be calm about it.

"Hey question of curiosity, why haven't you questioned about the metal floating sphere that is following me around?"

"You're not the only one who has one, about two days ago a young woman about your age came to the rescue after a huge number of beasts and serpents attacked. She managed to take them down by herself and we didn't even have to fire a single shot. Afterword's she stayed with us for a few hours to rest up, we asked her to stay with us, but she refused, she said she had some family she needed to find." said another guard.

Davis became suspicious, he wondered "Why there were two of these weapons in human hands?" He knew it was one thing to lose one, but two, not likely. "These were very powerful and useful tools, so why would another race be so careless with them, and who had the other one?" He stopped thinking about those questions as he asked, "Are you all really okay with this sphere floating around your "base"?"

Some of the guards at the entrance said that they were cool with it, but Davis could see past their calm demeanor. "Look I can see that you're lying to me, so let's make this easy and let me explain why I'm here so I can leave before someone says or does something they regret, okay!" said Davis a little annoyed.

The guards were still skeptical about him and why he was there, but they gave him the chance to explain himself. He did not waste any time, he told them everything about his contact with the navy, why he needed the tech, and the chance of ending this war. Some of the guards looked at Davis with newfound hope, knowing their military was still trying to help everyone. But others seemed to be doubtful and didn't buy his story, thinking he was probably a bandit as they believed that there was no way he was the only one they contacted. The guards were divided, but they all agreed for him to speak with their boss and let him decide. They asked Davis to wait as they contacted their boss to see what he thought about the matter since they couldn't give him a straightforward answer.

However, before they could even call the boss on the radio someone yelled out "Don't give him anything!"

The group knew whose voice it was and turned to find a skin head approaching them at a fast pace. The group groaned with irritation, showing Davis this guy was going to be a pain in the ass. Davis could tell just from looking at this guy that he wasn't the leader, but his body language told him he was a very big problem. One of the guards blocked his path and demanded the skinhead to head back inside, that they had this covered, and they didn't need things to escalate out of control.

But this man didn't listen to the guards as he scoffed it off, saying, "I don't care what that little shit wants. This is my store and I'm not parting with anything to an outsider."

Davis instinctively knew what he was dealing with, an "entitled" man, and he became angry that he had to deal with someone like this during a war, but he kept his cool and said, "First off, are you seriously acting like this during the end of our world, second this isn't your store, and third I was asked to come here by the remaining Navy to gather supplies for research purposes. The research I'm going to be conducting is to hopefully help fight off the aliens and save our world."

Even after explaining himself to the skinhead, he still didn't care and said, "I don't give a damn if the order came from God, I am not going to part with anything of mine."

"That is not your decision!" yelled out another person. Everyone saw behind the skinhead a middle-aged African American woman standing behind him as she continued to yell at him "This place and its products do not belong to just you, there is plenty to go around and if this young man is telling the truth, then I say let him have what he needs."

Davis was happy that someone in this place had a voice of reasoning, but someone like the skinhead wasn't one of them. He became infuriated by her words and punched her in the face and broke her nose to silence her. She fell to the floor as she clasped her face, and the skin head began to kick her in the stomach. Everyone just watched in horror as he began to shout disrespectful and unacceptable words and slurs at her as he beat her to death.

"What the hell are you guards doing?! Stop him!" said Davis.

But the guards just stood there, some looked away, that's when he realized that these people were just that, people, and just like people some were taught to look away from things like this. Davis became enraged and materialized a baseball bat with his sphere and moved towards. Davis gripped the bat and took his stance as he said "Hey, batterer, batterer!" The skin head stopped kicking the women, turned his head around, and in that moment, Davis yelled out "SWING!" He swung the bat and struck the skin heads skull so hard that a piece of his flesh was torn off. The skin head fell to the floor and Davis stepped over his body as his bat dripped with blood. He helped the woman up and tried to comfort her as the guards just watched. Davis turned to the guards and said sarcastically "Thanks for the help!"

Davis looked over the woman as the skin head staggered up. As the skin head got his balance Davis turned to him and said, "Stay the hell away from us, you disgusting waste of life."

The man while holding his head and trying to see straight said, "What are you doing boy, this is a N-"

"If you value whatever your life is worth then you won't finish that word!" said Davis cutting him off.

"Why do you care what happens to her she's black and it's about time I put her in her pla-"

"SHUT THE FUCK UP!"

"Why the hell do you care about this N-"

"Because she's a human being, you jackass. Her color isn't something to be ashamed of, but your actions are. We're in the middle of a goddamn war and you still can't cut this shit out? You are an embarrassment to these people and humanity. Hell, you are not even worthy of being called human, let alone being in the presences of one or mine."

"I'm not worthy of being in your presence?" said the skin head in disbelief.

"Yes, because you think that your existence is so important that everyone else's is worthless. You constantly make excuses for your cruelty towards others just to make yourselves feel better about how pathetic you really are."

"I don't give a damn if your right or not, no black man or woman speaks to me that way," yelled the skinhead back.

"And no one should be brutally attacked for telling off an entitled, racist, failure!"

The skin head wobbled towards Davis as he turned his bat into a sword and raised it at him. The guards suddenly got between the two of them and told them both to cool their jets, they didn't want any more blood spilt on the ground. But despite their pleas, the skin head didn't listen and grabbed a pistol from one of the guard's holders. He points the weapon at his own group as he demanded them get out of the way. The group stood back and tried to reason with him, but they just couldn't reach him, he was too long gone. Davis was fed up and pushed through the guards, approached the skin head, and said, "You want to kill me then why don't I make it easy for you."

He took his gun and placed the barrel on his for head and told him "Pull it."

Everyone froze, they had never seen anyone in their life's do something like this before, other than in a movie. But the skin head was petrified to the core as he saw the rage in Davis's eyes. Everyone stood silently as they waited for someone to make a move, hoping that the worst situation would not come to pass.

"You think I won't kill you?" said the skin head nervously.

"I know you can't."

"Why's that?"

"Because the gun your holding doesn't have any ammo left to use."

"Let's find out then," said the skin head as he pulled the trigger.

The guards hit the deck as they feared the bullet would hit them, but nothing came out of the gun. The gun went click, click, click, but no bang came from it. Davis snatched the skin heads gun away from his hand and smirked. The skin head was shocked that Davis was right, but he wondered how he knew there was no ammo left to use. He looked at Davis's eyes and asked, "How did you know?!"

Davis smirked and said, "Its elementary idiot, your guards, who have been desperately trying to protect everyone here including your selfish ass, used up the rest of the ammo during the skirmish with the beasts outside."

The skin head just stood there and said scared, "But you couldn't have known if they actually used all the ammo! You still were going to test it just to save a stranger?!"

"Yes, because unlike you I care about people," Davis turned away from him for a second and then said, "Oh before I forget here's your prize scaring the shit out of everyone."

Davis took his sword and turned it into a gauntlet and punch the skin-head's stomach as everyone gasped in a bit of shock. The skin head kneeled to the floor as he refused to hold his stomach, trying to signify he was strong enough to withstand the pain of getting hit. But Davis could tell that he did some damage to his body, even if he was desperately trying not to show it. A moment later Davis asked the group if they had a place where they could put him until he was done. The group with newfound fear for Davis immediately swarmed around the skin head and took him to the storage room to keep him from getting in anymore trouble. Davis looked at the woman and asked the guards who remained behind if there was anyone who was a nurse or doctor in the store that could look at her.

Fortunately, there were a few doctors and staff members of the store that worked in the pharmaceutical department still there. The guards assured that she would be checked to see if she was okay, if she was, they would then send her back to her family.

One of the guards came up to him and asked, "How did you know he had no ammo?"

"I didn't."

Though that conversation was over Davis knew it was only the beginning. He knew violence wasn't always the best answer, but when it came down to it, he was afraid that he wouldn't have a choice but to use it. But what was done was done, and Davis had to focus on the task at hand, however, out of curiosity he asked one of the guards if the skin head had done stuff like this before. The guard explained that he arrived when the women with the sphere arrived, they first had believed they were a team, but after a while it was obvious, they were not, and the way the two interacted with each other was just like it was with him just now, it didn't take much to see how different they both were, and just like Davis, the women despised people like the skin head to almost a fault.

"So, if he was like this already why did you let him stay knowing that he was going to cause problems?" asked Davis.

"We thought that he would change his ways when he saw us all working together, but clearly that was a mistake," said one of the guards.

"You wanted to see the best in people and that's fine, but people like him never want to change. The thing that I hate most about humanity is people like him or rather what he represents, fear, division, and selfish behavior. Don't get me wrong I have done my fair share of idiotic things, but I know where at least the line is. But people like him don't see a line, those people are so ethnocentric that even when earth is in a situation like this, they still don't change."

"You can't change something they have been doing for years, not easily anyways."

"Really? So how many other people in this place are racist or have judgments against other people for just existing?"

The guard said nothing as he looked at Davis, he had no answer for him, but Davis could see it in his eye. "I'm guessing several, but I'm also guessing is that they are keeping their mouths shut, because they know this is not the time for turning on each other. So yes, they can change when its necessary, but there are some who refuse because they don't want their lighting rod taken away. However, there is no excuse to be complacent about that behavior, ever."

"Look I understand your stance on this but-" said the guard before Davis cut him off.

"You know what's worse is the fact that that you allowed people to act like this, it's unacceptable. Your people need a haven, a place with hope and guidance, if you don't get it together, then you might as well put up a sign that says, 'Human buffet here!' on the wall outside."

"It is not that easy, we aren't soldiers, we're not hardcore survivalists, or doomsday preppers. We weren't expecting an invasion of aliens storming our world and we have no real leadership."

"But you have each other, and the more you tear each other apart, the easier it will be for the aliens to finish us off. Now obviously there will be struggles, but if you show the people that you're willing to fight for them, they will follow. However, if you turn away, they won't trust you and that's something none of us need right now."

The guards were surprised by Davis's words but knew deep down inside their souls he was right. They had been taught to work together ever since they were kids, but back then it was easier because they didn't know how the world really acted when it came to working together.

Before any of the guards said anything, Davis said, "So first let me speak to whoever is in charge, then we will see how we can help each other before someone tries to kill another person."

The guards could see that Davis just wanted to drop the subject and took his hint. They escorted Davis into the store as his gauntlet merged with the sphere. As they entered from the back doors of the store, Davis became overwhelmed and now knew why the beasts and serpents had been attacking this place. There were crowds of people in this store and without an actual tally of how many people were in there it was anyone's guess. But even though there were many people, this place was far from thriving, it was the same thing Davis was enduring, only on a massive scale. People were either trying to get comfortable on the hard-tiled floor, complaining it was too cold, that there wasn't enough room for everyone, and that there wasn't enough food or water to share. This place looked like a fallout shelter, and justly so for an invasion. As he walked with the guards, he could see the desperation on people's faces, the fear of what transpired haunts them, and the meaning to live on seemed bleak.

When they arrived in the food department, Davis could see many people in line getting food and water, some were complaining on how much someone else had gotten, even though it was the exact same size. Some were even trying to steal food off other plates, even if the food had already been bitten into. It was terrible to see everyone fighting over what food they had, especially since the store was filled with years' worth of dry, canned, and box foods at their convenience. It seemed the leader of this store was trying to preserve as much food as he possibly could, but he might have been going overboard. It had only been a week since this all began and there was no actual shortage of food, water, or electricity. So, Davis thought, "Why was the boss hoarding food?" Then like a flash of lighting it became clear, he was trying to either control the people by making them starve or he was trying to make sure there was enough for outsiders.

The group passed the line of people and showed Davis to the back offices of the store where they held their meetings, strategized, and placed their guns for safety. This place was surrounded in stone, cement, and metal. It almost felt like this place was designed as a bomb shelter by the company that made the store as a last resort for a shelter. Though it was not that uncommon in Kansas, since the state also happened to be in "tornado alley," it made sense that companies would build stores with this type of architectural structure as a shelter. He knew it wasn't strong enough to hold up against a nuke, but at least it was structural enough to hold off aliens, hopefully. They entered the office area and two of the guards stopped Davis, they asked him to wait there why they spoke with him about his intent and the incident with the skin head. Davis willingly obliged, but asked them to be quick, for every moment they must wait is another moment that is needed.

The two went inside the store managers office, their leader's place of operation, and shut the door. Davis leaned against the wall on the other side and listened loosely through the door. He could hear them explain what happened at the door, Davis's mission, and the sphere that floated around him. After they were done explaining their boss spoke, "I'm not surprised that moron got his ass kicked, and honestly, he had it coming, he was here for only two days and the amount of crap he managed to get away with was unacceptable. Put him in the powered down storage freezer, until we figure out what to do with him as for the guy with the sphere send him in."

The two guards agreed with his decision and left the room. As the door opened Davis felt uneasy and for one reason, he had heard that man's voice before, on the video he saw with his stepfather being butchered. The guards turned to Davis and before they said a word Davis said, "I heard what he said, you go ahead, I'll speak with him."

The two guards left Davis and rejoined their group, as they walked away, they explained to the others what they needed to do. Davis slowly walked into the office and closed the door behind him, "I didn't think you of all people would run this operation." He said with the office chair facing away from him with the desk light turned on, and the man in the shadows.

"This is such a cliché that it makes me feel old," said Davis in a serious tone as he turned on the overhead light. The man did not turn around as the lights came on and refused to look at Davis. He simply sat in his chair benignly, as he waited for the words to come into his mind. Then after a few minutes he turned around and revealed himself. Davis wasn't stunned to see who it was after hearing his voice but wondered how he got away from the serpents and beasts.

"My name is John Markson and I'm the boss of this place," he stated in a serious tone.

"Really? I thought you were just a prop," said Davis sarcastically.

John sighed and said, "Look I know who you are, you're Don's ex-stepson."

"Don't say it like that putting an 'ex' in front of it sounds disturbing." said Davis in irritancies.

"Fine, I know you were his stepson, better?" said John.

"Yes, but I really don't care about that right now, I'm more concerned of what you do." said Davis in a strong tone. "I saw what you did to Don on the security cameras, and the deal you tried to make with him."

"I'm not surprised that you found out about it since you found out about the check," Said John benignly. "But you also saw that he set me up to, we're both victims here."

"You can play innocent, but the reality is you're just as guilty as him. I don't know how the hell you got away from the beasts and serpents, but whatever plans you have for me died that day," said Davis as he snapped at John.

"You're right and I'm grateful for that." Said John in a depressing voice

"What?!" Davis said surprised.

"Look I'm not a saint, throughout my life I have hurt and killed people to get what I want. I thought I was a god among the meek, but then all this happened, and I lost everything just like everyone else did. When I had to survive on my own, I realized I couldn't because I had fed off others. Then I found this place with people with no idea how to survive either, but they were trying. Many of these people knew who I was, but despite what I had did to them, they showed me mercy that I never did."

"So, what? you changed that quickly, I highly doubt that."

"You're right I haven't change that much. I still struggle to try and keep my impulse in check, but it's difficult. But the night we were attacked by the serpents and beast, I thought we were all going to die. Then out of nowhere that young woman came with two katanas and started hacking them to pieces. We were so grateful to her assistance, and she took nothing form us, but left us alone. After she left, everyone became depressed, the one person who was strong enough to push them back didn't want to help us. In that moment I saw what these people needed, someone to guide them, so in the first time in my life I took control, but not for myself. It was to do the one thing I never had done, give hope. Once I gained control, I began modifying this place."

Davis was unsure of John's story, but he did see that this man was not the same one in the video he had saw. He believed that nearly dying forced him to see the error of his ways and seeing the little hope people had made him see, may have found a way to help redeem himself. Davis heard the expression, "Your life flashes before your eyes and that you re-live every moment with more clarity," but for this man it was more of a punishment than a blessing. John was forced to see the man that he became and the pain he had inflicted on others in his pursuit of power, and it was terrifying to him, to see himself as a true monster.

"But I didn't call you here to talk about what happened, I wanted to thank you for putting that skinhead in his place," said John sincerely.

"I don't need your thanks, I just need your help," said Davis in a harsh tone.

"Okay, what do you need?" asked John.

"Technology, things that can record on video and audio, cameras, drone, anything that can help me get information about these aliens." As Davis continued to explain what he needed he could tell John was not paying that much attention to him, John's mind was someplace else. Davis snapped his figures to regain his attention and even though he hated to ask him he still asked, "What the hell is wrong?"

John rose from his seat and came around to Davis and sat down on his desk, "Look I am sorry, I haven't been listening, we're having a hard time trying to ration the food for everyone in the facility and tempers are flaring up so badly that people started to fight over the tiniest thing. Normally I had my guys do the 'fixing of my problems' but that's not an option and I don't know what to do."

"Wow, you have been a leader for just two days and you're struggling, what a shocker!" said Davis making fun of John. "It's simple, you prioritize, plan, and execute. It's not hard."

Though John understood what Davis was saying he just didn't know how to do it. He had always used fear and force to get what he wanted, but now he wanted to do things the right way, the ways he didn't know how to do. Though it was common knowledge in Davis's mind, it was unprofound wisdom to John. Davis became stressed out, this was supposed to be a straightforward mission and now it just got more complicated. He started to rub his neck to try to relax himself as he racked his brain to figure out what to do. Until he remembered one person that had a knack for preparing and executing plans.

"Look, I might know someone who can help you with all of this."

"Really!"

"Yes, but I'm not sure if he still around, but if he is then I will try persuade him into coming here, but I can't make any promises."

"What is so special about this person?"

"He is a doomsday prepper, he can rig running water and electricity, he knows how to organize, and is well versed in these types of situations"

John took a moment to think about it and told Davis, "If you can get him to come here and help us then we will help you in exchange."

"Then it's a deal, but know this, if you dare try to stab me in the back, I will make what you did to Don look like child's play," said Davis in a terrifying tone.

John became a little fearful when Davis said that but understood his lack of faith in him. John gathered his own courage and asked, "If he agrees, then when should we expect to see him?"

"Tomorrow at the latest, hopefully."

"Okay, let's hope he's okay and he does help." said John as Davis began to leave the room.

Davis could sense that John was being brutally honest with himself, that he knew that he did not deserve forgiveness until he could prove he could earn it. In this case, Davis wanted to believe that this man was trying to earn his forgiveness but was unsure. John was not trying to sway Davis's pity or ask for forgiveness, but the fact that he did not even try to apologize made Davis question his motive. "I don't care what you did in the past, it's irrelevant to what needs to be done now. So, for now, we are allies, but I'm telling you right now if you try anything I don't like, the next near-death experience for you, I promise, will be actual death!"

His thoughts became more doubtful about John's true intentions as he was heading out to the floor of the store. With his own eyes he never saw people change so easily before, in his experience it took years of fighting core instincts to change, but he could see in Johns eyes the battle for his humanity and soul. Not knowing someone else's intentions made Davis feel petrified, and with all the survivors in this store, and the aliens outside the wall of this place, made him stressed out. With his own thoughts, he tried to come up with a way to convince Mathew to join this group, but with his nature of being isolated he couldn't see how. But then his thought came to a halt as he heard someone yell "GET OUT OF MY SPOT!" He turned his head to see some people having an argument about a particular spot under a ventilation duct. One man was alone and the other had kids behind him, shielding them from the other man if things went violent.

"THIS SPOT IS MINE!"

"WE WERE HERE FIRST AND I HAVE KIDS WHO NEED TO STAY WARM!"

"SO, WHAT I'M COLD! NOW GET OUT OF THE WAY!" yelled the other man as he tried to shove the first man way from the spot.

"YOU LAY A HAND ON MY KIDS AND I WILL END YOU!" yelled the father grabbing the man's wrists.

Davis rubbed his eyes and sighed heavily "I could not just leave here without another confrontation, could I?" He approached the men as he said, "Will you two shut the fuck up?" The two became silent as Davis continued to talk, "Look I know this isn't ideal for anyone, but there is no point in fighting over something so trivial, if you're both cold then just put some more clothes or grab a blanket to keep warm, hell there's a fabric department with patterns to make quilts, clothes, and machines to sow with!"

Though Davis was being rational the single man refused listen as he drew out a knife and pointed it at the father. "This is my spot and I deserve it."

Then the father enraged said, "This isn't your spot, me and my kids were here first, and you had the nerve to point a knife at my kids!"

"WILL YOU TWO STOPS ACTING LIKE MANIACS?!" yelled Davis.

Unfortunately, the two didn't stop arguing and it had escalated to the point where the single man tried to stab the other man. In a panic Davis grabbed the kids and moved them away from the area. As his back was turned, he could hear one of the men scream with tremendous pain. The kids were crying and screaming for them to stop fighting.

"Stop, don't hurt our daddy!" said one of the children.

The situation was out of control and Davis had no choice but to do something drastic. Davis asked some other people to look after the kids as he reapproached the two men,he took out his gun, messed with it for a few moments as he saw the man with the knife and was about to slit the father's throat. Davis pointed his gun at the ceiling and squeezed the trigger firing one shot. The loud bang threw off the man with the knife as he turned to face Davis.

As he pointed the gun at the man he said, "Surrender or I will shoot you."

The man looked at Davis was fiery eyes and yelled out "Don't you dare point that thing at me, do you know who I am?!"

"No, and personally I don't care I just met someone like you at the front door and I'm not in the mood to deal with another selfish, entitled jackass!" Davis told the man. "This is your last chance either drop it or die."

But the man did not listen, he then decided to take the father hostage, even though he had a gun on him. He moved them both into a position that faced Davis and said, "This is how it's going to go down you're going to give me the gun so I can protect my space so next time if someone comes near, I'll give them a good scare or I'm going to spill this man's blood all over the white tile floor."

Davis didn't know if this guy was bluffing or not, but he couldn't risk the life of the father and leave two children without a parent in the world. At that moment he wished he had learned how to aim with a gun but seeing as he had no choice, he sat the gun on the floor and slid it over to him. The man let go of the father as the gun came to him had then jumped off the floor and point it at them saying "See, now this is my turf, and if I catch any of you near it you're all going to die." Even though the man gave his warning Davis immediately approached the man once the father was clear from him.

The man pointed the gun at Davis and yelled out "What the hell did I just say?" But Davis didn't care what he said he got closer and closer. Then when he was six feet from him the man yelled out, "I warned you," and with a cold stare into Davis's eyes, and squeezed the trigger. But the only noise to come out of it was only a click, not a bang. The man squeezed the trigger three more times hoping to hear a bang, but all anyone could hear was a click, click, click.

The man looked at the gun and said "What the hell is wrong with-"

Davis whistled to the man whose face became filled with a shock of horror. Davis wagged the clip of ammo in his left hand and cracked his knuckles in his right as some of the sphere turned into a gauntlet, telling him, "Bullets are bargained separately."

Davis then tossed the clip behind him to the floor as he rushed at the man, taking his right fist, and clobbering the man's face with a right hook. The man collapsed on to the floor with a single punch and fell unconscious. Davis began to breathe heavily as he picked up his gun from the floor knowing he put too much energy into that punch, but to him it was totally worth it, although he found it strange that the same scenario happened twice. As he gains a little strength back, he asked for help from some of the guards on duty. Though everyone was safe, Davis could not believe that the guards did nothing even when he fired a shot into the ceiling. Davis vowed that if he managed to make it back, he would help set up the rules and make sure the guards and leaders of this store were going to keep the peace and how to handle these types of situations to prevent any more heartbreak.

As the man was dragged way, Davis caught a peek in the corner of his eye of the father with his kids. Their father hugged them and soothed them as they cried into his body. The father turned his head to Davis and nodded a 'thank you' to him as he took his kids away to get checked up. Davis was glad they were safe, but something came over him as he punched the other man. Even in his enraged state he realized that he enjoyed hurting him. The adrenaline that coursed through him when his fist made impact, almost felt like an opium he had just taken. He could feel his soul almost revel in the pain he inflicted, and it made him sick. Davis looked at his hand and said to himself, "Don't let yourself enjoy this."

Davis put his hand down and quickly left the store, passing everyone who saw what happened, seeing them whispering amongst themselves. He passed the entrance and guards as they watched him suspiciously as he left the store, he had only been there for fifteen minutes and he already had a reputation, but he figured he could use it to his advantage as he walked home. Along the way he took the time to collect his thoughts about what he needed to do about the aliens and survivors. It had only been a week, and everyone was already at each other's throats and with the aliens attacking at random, there was no safe guarantee that the store would be a haven for long. He knew they were going to have to find a better place and soon, at least to hold out until the military came, he just didn't know where. As he continued to walk in the dark night, he stopped for a moment and listened to the quiet world. There was still no one around, but there were no cars driving, sirens blaring, gunshots heard from afar, and no sign of the aliens. When he realized there was still nothing around it made him believe that maybe the aliens weren't nocturnal or they were called back to wherever they came from, otherwise, he would have been in something's belly by now, or maybe they were just watching him from a distance. He was cautious before, but now he was starting to become paranoid, he wasn't sure where the aliens were or if this was some sort of trick into lowering his defenses, or anything really. In this world of danger, time passed slowly to Davis, unaware of any real danger, but he eventually saw that he made it to his street and out of fear he ran the rest of the way just so he could get inside. He flung opened the front door and closed it behind him then waited for anything to happen. He waited for a half hour before he realized he was fine, nothing had come to the door or followed him.

As he began to relax, he headed downstairs, jumped onto his computer, and opened his emails. He typed up his first report to Marry Luvuntar through his brothers email about his nighttime run. "Mrs. Luvuntar, the night run was disappointing, I had been out there for almost three hours and only ran into beasts when they were attacking the super store, which was apparently filled with dozens of people. Unfortunately, due to the severity of the survivor's situation, I must put a pin on gathering information until tomorrow. I will be seeking out someone who can help them and in return they will give me what I need and even contribute to this mission. Hopefully if everything goes as planned then I will be able to not only give you information, but you'll have an entire team on the mainland doing research."

Message sent 11:15 pm 01/07/2029

When he was done, he laid on his bed with the cats, tired, and worn from the emotional and physical day, waiting again for the little ding that would come from his computer. But just like before it didn't come so quickly and eventually, he gave up waiting. He closed his eyes and allowed the darkness and silence of the night take him back into the sleeping world, where he could dream of a world more hopeful than this one, where he didn't have to gamble other's lives.

CHAPTER 6

Memories of the flame.

The sun rose over the ruined city once again, another day of survival for all who lived in this world of war. In the basement of his home, Davis heard his notification on his computer ding with a new email. He rose out of bed and approached his computer feeling groggy as he desperately tried to keep his eyes open. When he looked at his screen, he saw an email from his brother, he sat down in his chair, and began to read the message.

> *"Davis we are glad to hear from you again, and happy that you have managed to contact others, but the order I gave was for you to be our eyes in the field not dozens of people."*
>
> *Davis shook off his grogginess as he retreaded the email, he became concerned the about the message, not truly understanding their intent. He typed back "Wait! Let me get this straight, you want me to do this.... ALONE?"*
>
> *"I know it is risky, but we don't need so many people giving us the exact same information and overload our systems."*
>
> *"That isn't the plan Sherlock, they provide me with the info, then I will go through it to make sure we can acquire every drop of data, then I will send you our hypothesis on the invaders with the dumb down version for you all.".*

"Okay, that actually makes more sense, but we still don't like the idea of too many people getting on this mission."

"I'm going to use anyone I can get, we both need help. So, do not be fussy, unless you want to come ashore and do it yourself."

"Okay fine, but please keep it to a minimum, we don't what the enemy finding out we are trying to figure out any of their weaknesses, and we don't want to have people trying out anything until we have proof it works."

"I can work with that, but next time maybe use clarification before you jump the gun."

"Very well, and as a personal favor from your brother, he asks if it was any possibility that you have found anyone else yet?"

"No, I haven't, but a lot of people are in the super store, I might have just missed them when I was there."

"I will let your brother know."

"Okay, and one thing tell him, you're my sweety pie, the apple of my eye."

"Why?"

"Hey, just because it's an invasion doesn't mean I can't embarrass my little brother a little. Get ready to laugh!"

Emails sent at 7:02 am-7:15am 01/08/2029

Davis smiled to himself as he exited his email, imagining his brother's reaction in his mind. Even when he was at home just hearing someone sing that little lyric made him angry, but it was the type of anger that made everyone in his house laugh. Once he cooled down, he would see a smile on his brother's face because he knew it meant they still cared. Davis's smile faded away as he got dressed to face the day, though he was grateful he had a moment to smile in this crazy life he was now in. Dressing in his warmest clothes he could find, he stepped out of his room and fed the cats once again, just like any other day, and headed out to the car. For just a single moment it felt like a regular workday as he was about to leave, and it once again made him smile because he felt the world was normal. Yet as he stepped outside into the quiet world it reminded him it had changed, and he had a new job to do, and messing up wasn't an option.

The car was still intact, just as he left it, but Davis was uneasy about going back into Wichita, even if the beasts and serpents were no longer inside the city. He was only on the outskirts a week ago and it was a nightmare, that day made Davis's soul shake in fear. The mere thought of being near the city again scared Davis to the point where he almost went back inside, but the memory of the girl who fell to her death came to him. He promised himself that he would do anything to save another person, if he backed out even before he started, he was no savior, but a deserter. "Okay, calm yourself, even if you can't use the highway that was the fastest route to work, you can still cut around the city. It has been a week so the city should be empty by now, hopefully, so with luck you might not run into anything," he said nervously to himself.

Though he was nervous about the chance of running into aliens it was Mathew himself that concerned him. Mathew was a person that could help organize the people inside the super store and possibly help gather intel about the aliens. But Mathew was a man who like to be in control of his environment. Mathew hated when things were disorganized or out of place, he became difficult to deal with when it happened and sometimes it would be unbearable, but regardless Davis knew he needed his help. If Mathew had problems with others, then they were just that, his problems. Although the situation demanded everyone stayed on their toes, Davis also knew he had to approach Mathew delicately, otherwise he might end up empty handed. He just hoped it would be in and out in the next few hours as he entered his car and sped off to his old work.

The drive on the outskirts of Wichita was calm and quiet with only the roar of the engine echoing throughout the area. Davis could see the ruins of Wichita as he was about to drive past the stadium, then within a fraction of a second Davis slammed on the brakes. He looked around the parking lot where he had blasted the stadium. The cars were still on their sides, but as he stared into the parking lot, saw something in the distance, something burning, and without hesitation, he parked the car and got out. Whatever he saw was on the hill next to the river, the same place the girl died. Though as he stared off into the distance he could feel something almost draw him to it, like it was calling him. Davis walked through the parking lot but still felt something else was off, yet he couldn't figure out what the problem was. Then as he passed the car, the same car where he had found the sphere, he remembered the body he had tripped on. Davis looked around the parking lot, this place once looked like a war zone between police and a gang, dozens of bodies had littered the parking lot, but now it was like they were never even there. The only thing the bodies left behind was the blood that stained the ground.

Though he wasn't surprised they were gone he knew it should have been the first thing he had noticed. He turned his attention back to the hill side as he felt whatever was there was still pulling on him, as he got closer, he was stunned to see the exact spot where the girl had died, but it wasn't the blood that stunned him, it was what was in it or rather, around it. It looked like a ritualistic alter, with three crimson poles that formed a perfect triangle, adorned with warm colored cloths that flowed in the wind, white gems, and a lime green fire floating in the center.

Davis approached cautiously, still mesmerized by the flame, he reached out for it, but felt no heat coming off it. He placed his hand in the fire and in his own mind he could see images appear. He could see someone fighting the serpent and as they looked down, they saw Davis looking up in horror, a gun fight between police officers and gang members, and news crews watching the travesty unfurl. Davis pulled his hand away from the fire and realized that this was a "burning memory," but he had only heard about these things from fiction. It was said that when someone died tragically their memory of their death would live on, with a piece of their soul alongside it, constantly replaying itself, repeatedly, until it drove the soul into madness, turning them twisted and grotesque. But he had never heard of one having multiple memories, it normally was only to one person at a time, or at least that's what he heard.

However, the fact that this was real made Davis's skin crawl, and it made it even worse that the last thing she saw before she had died was Davis looking at her in horror. He wanted to turn around, to get back in the car, and leave this place, but something told him to stay, to continue to watch the memories. Against his own judgement Davis put his hand in the flame again and saw all the fighting and death from the gun fight, but then he saw the girl fighting, seeing him, and eventually slip out of the serpent's grasp. But as she fell, she saw her life flash before her eyes, all her happiest moments in her life, birthdays, vacations, her schools, her brothers getting into mud fights, her joining the messy fun along with her parents. When she saw her life Davis could feel her smile knowing that she had a great life, it may have had its down sides from time to time, but it was her life, and she was glad she got to live it. When she was only a few feet from the ground she looked over at Davis one last time and smiled, thinking to herself, "Thank you for trying, I hope you know I don't blame you, and if I was going to die then I was glad that I died with someone who still tried." A second later her body hit the ground as she saw her blood rise out of her, she kept smiling, and then her vision faded away.

The flame vanished when her memory was over, and Davis stood there with his eyes beginning to fill with tears. He got to see the greatest moments of her life, and it made him feel a little envious of her. Granted, he was glad she did not die angry and even more so knowing she did not blame him for her death. Yet seeing her memories and feeling the joy and love she felt throughout her life, being able to remember the good and forget the bad, made him distraught. He couldn't remember much of the good that happened in his childhood and seeing someone relive the best moments of their lives made his envy and sorrow turn against each other. He felt terrible that this young woman was not able to live the rest of her life, never able to experience the joys of finding someone to spend her life with, if she ever wanted it, or making her mark on the world with her career. There was so much of her life left and she was robbed of it. But his envy made him feel bitter towards her, she got to have a decent childhood and had wonderful parents that raised her well. Her memories of bliss filled her mind, as the pain of the fall faded into nothing. She was able to feel the love of the world she knew one last time, even in death.

As he wiped his tears away and calmed himself, he couldn't stand there anymore, it was too painful for him, and his emotions ran wild. He turned away from the altar and headed back to his car, trying to get distance between him and it. But as he passed all the dried blood on the ground, he could see the memories of the people in his head who had died in the fire fight and felt their pain. He thought that when the flame went out the memoires would have stopped, but now he had a memory of everyone's memory from that day in parking lot. The pain and emotions of others filled his head as he began to stumble towards the car, it was like a classroom filled with kids, all screaming and yelling, but worse. He stopped and leaned on a car to clear his head, he wanted the memories to stop, but it was like an echo constantly bouncing off the walls and only got louder.

He stood up and took a breath and repressed his memory of the others just to quiet them. Normally he repressed anything that made him feal scared, afraid, or angry, which he knew wasn't healthy, but that's what he was taught to do by his teachers when it came to bullies and his family because it was the easiest way to handle a problem. The memory faded away into his subconscious and when his head was cleared, he just wanted to get away from there as fast as he could and get to Mathew, he had enough weirdness for one day. As he got off the destroyed car and made his way to his car, something gently stroked his right shoulder. He stopped dead in his tracks and looked around wondering what had touched him, but nothing was there. Davis thought he might be starting to go crazy, but then he felt it again, but this time on both shoulders, and this time with something talking to him.

"Don't be afraid, young one, there is much you need to know, but very little time for you to understand. So, know I will watch over you until the time comes, but till then keep yourself in darkness, and above all don't let any being find your pure self."

Even with whatever spoke to him, its gentle words made him freeze in place as he waited for an opportunity to strike. But then, he began to calm down, as it stroked his shoulders. It felt like the only thing it was trying to do was calm him down, like it was trying to show empathy. However, Davis was not in the mood for comfort, he just wanted to leave, so he turned and materialized a sword and swung it towards the unidentified creature. Before the sword could even get close the creature, a gust of wind forced Davis to stop, the gust was so powerful it almost lost his balance.

After the wind stopped, Davis looked around to find nothing, but he had a good idea what it was trying to comfort him. He looked to the blue sky, knowing whatever was there was still watching him. Though he didn't know that whatever was watching him was not a threat, it seemed strange on how much it followed him. It didn't seem like a threat, but he knew if it was, then it was a smart move to keep it close by. He didn't know why it cared for him so much but since it wasn't going to hurt him, he decided to let things play out, for now. He once again turned back towards the car, but as he took his first step, he ran into something. He did not even have to look up to see what it was, its greenish armor gave it away.

Davis jumped back quickly and pointed his sword against the alien ready to fight yelling out, "I'm in no mood for this crap so step aside before I make you!"

But even after his threat for one reason or another, the alien just stood there and did not even try to reach for its weapons. Instead, it just walked around him and headed towards the altar and disassembled it. The alien looked back at Davis and tossed something to him. As it came into his view, it looked like a baseball size clear orb with a black flame in the center surrounded by a ring of violet, orange, and blue colors. It looked reminiscent of the burning memory, but unlike the girls, this one gave off powerful emotions, it felt angry and filled with resentment. Davis picked it up, but no memories came, and looked towards the alien as it left, wondering what it was trying to tell him.

The alien headed across the bridge it yelled in at Davis in its native tongue. Davis was startled by the alien's language, but it did not seem threatening, it almost sounded like it was trying to give him some advice. Possibly about the sphere he had been given. However due to the language barrier, there was no chance that he would be able to figure out what the alien was trying to tell him, and he did not have the time to find someone that could. Davis put the orb in his pocket and headed back to the car. Once he was safely inside, he drove off as the alien headed its own way into Wichita.

Davis spent the rest of his drive in deep thought once again, asking himself so many questions about what he had just seen and done. From a scientific standpoint it made sense for him to try and uncover more of these creatures' ways, but it seemed the more he deeper he dug the more things did not make any sense. If they were such a huge threat to humanity, then why did they show much respect for their dead if they were just going to kill them anyways? Why did that alien just let him walk off without a scratch and give him the orb? Lastly, what was it trying to tell him, did it trust him with this orb or was it a weapon? In his mind he knew that he could not tell anyone about this encounter, not even the captain, for he feared that it could lead to them doubting his abilities and bloodshed.

"Just a massive pile of questions I will need to find answers for eventually," Davis said to himself. "I just wish they didn't come every single minute of the day!"

Davis found himself nearing his facility; his thoughts came to a halt as he noticed multiple cars blocking the road like a barricade. He stopped the car and looked at it, recognizing some of them from the facility parking lot. He figured that Mathew was able to hot wire the cars and place them in rows to try and keep people or the beasts out. However, Davis knew these roads as well as Mathew and he figured that he might have missed the back way in. This way was normally used as a detour to get around trains blocking the road and as a trucker's entry way for the loading bays to the other factories nearby. He turned the car around and headed to the back road, hoping Mathew had missed it.

But as he came upon the road, he noticed something was off about it. Out of his own instinct he immediately turned off his car and stepped out on the main road that connected to the back road. He took careful steps on the path and remembered from his drives to work that this road once had gravel on it, but it looked like someone, or something had cleaned them off. Davis was suspicious about this road, he turned his head to either side of the ditch, to find both sides were filled with the left-over aluminum scraps from his work. Anything that stepped or fell into these ditches was going to feel agonizing pain before they bled to death. Davis hissed just thinking about the pain it would inflect on someone. He turned away from the ditches and faced the bare road again, studying it, seeing what was different. Just from looking at it, the road seemed flat from his eye view, but then he thought of something. He remembered how some hardcore hunters would set illusions with camouflage to lure animals inside. But sometimes they had to make a funnel to keep them going in the same direction.

"This is so a trap," Davis said to himself.

He laid on the ground and saw these little hills in the road, almost like ant hills, but nothing was going in or out. Davis got off the ground and went back to his car and from the distance he used his sphere, turning it into a hundred of small marbles, and let them roll down the road. Then when the first one neared the hill Davis took cover behind the car, not knowing what was going to happen. The marble it the hill, but nothing happened, Davis rose his head from behind the car, and thought it was safe to cross, but he was wrong. An explosion followed a second later, the shock wave was so strong that it knocked Davis into the air and onto the ground. Though he was winded his adrenaline kicked in and he took cover behind his car. In another instance another explosion came and Davis quickly covering his ears, trying to block out the noise. Dozens of explosions went off one after the other and even with the loud roar of the sound, he tried to keep ears covered as dirt fell from the sky on top of him.

Then as soon as it started, it stopped Davis sat there petrified and waited to see if another round was going to go off, but nothing came of it. He rose slowly from the back side of the car and found that the road was now a long crater. He was angry that someone went to this length, but at the same time he became concerned, hoping Mathew wasn't responsible for this. He thought that if it was him, then Mathew was going overboard with the security, knowing that if any unfortunate soul went down this road that they only white light they would see would come from the blast. Davis carefully traveled down into the crater and began to make his way towards the end of the street, taking his time to make sure there was no other trap ahead as the spheres dust returned to his side, until a red laser shined through the dust cloud that loomed overhead. Then he felt something scathe his left arm and kick up some dirt behind him, he immediately knew that someone just took a shot at him. Davis panicked and quickly made a hemisphere from the spheres dust in front of him, blocking other bullets that might have been coming his direction, but only the one was shot.

The dust was blown away and things became clear, he opened a small peep hole to look down the road and saw a small band of people holding hunting rifles on their sides as they walked towards him. Realizing they might have tried to kill him because of the orb, mistaking him for an alien, he kept it up to keep himself safe just until they got close enough to see him. There were only six men and women that approached him as one of them radioed in what had they had found. Only a few feet from Davis as one of them called "Show yourself!"

Davis took a moment and figured this was the perfect opportunity to test the sphere once more. He thought of glass and its clear properties, being able to see thought the walls of buildings or the farthest stars. The hemisphere turned clear, and Davis appeared in front of the survivors, startling them a little as they flinched from him appearing.

"Are you an alien or a human?"

"No, I'm a being made of pure diamond, of course I'm human you moron! I just happened to find a bit of alien tech I can use to some extent." said Davis.

"What the hell do you want?"

"I have come looking for someone who might still be around here, I have a personal matter to speak with him about."

The person that looked like who led the group asked, "What is your name."

"My name is Davis," he answered, but when he did the leader looked like they were pissed.

The group leader raised her rifle at Davis and said, "There is only one other person nearby and if you're friends with then you're enemies with us."

Davis rolled his eyes at them and asked, "Why would he or I for that matter be your enemy? I'm pretty sure the aliens killing people are more predominantly our enemies than each other."

"After things began to quiet down, we went looking for a new place to hide, we found shelter in an old factory, but they did not know that it was inhabited by a psycho. We had lost three good people along with four kids, including mine. All because we tried to get into the upstairs office to get out of the cold. I will not let anyone deny my child's justice and if your friends with this monster then I will take personal joy in killing right now."

"Do you even try to make yourselves known before you entered the offices or better yet didn't you search the area?"

"Why does it matter if we did or not?"

"Well for starters were in the middle of a war between an unknown enemy and in a survivalist situation, people will shoot first and ask questions later. So, when you didn't look around for signs of life from another human being and tried to enter his home by force he panicked and possibly thought it was the aliens trying to break down the door. So, this is something that was started from a misunderstanding."

"Misunderstanding?! After we had buried our dead, we tried to confront him about what had happened, but when we had gotten to the factory a day later, we saw a massive number of defenses put up. When we tried to enter the doorway, he took a shot at us." Said the leader infuriated as she told her side of the story, but Davis got the feeling that she was not telling him everything about the incident.

"He is taking extra precautions after you tried to break into his home and is possibly now terrified of anything going into the facility. You can't blame him for something like this, especially when you're blinded by rage."

"WHAT?"

"I understand that you are all angry about this situation, but you can't deny that it happened because you didn't think to check the place out before you rushed up to the office. All it takes is someone not caring to do something, even when it's necessary to survive, to cause problems."

Davis could see her rage return in her eyes, as she put her finger on the trigger she was out for blood, and that made her blind to reason. Davis began to rub his templets and said to her irritated, "I am going to see him and try to get him to come out before someone else get hurt or someone does something regrettable."

"I will not give him any mercy or negotiate with a murderer. He will pay for what he has done. He killed intentionally and I will have justice for my child."

Davis could see that some of her group agreed with her as others remained silent, but he didn't care and spoke with a bit of anger. "Yes, he did intentionally kill, but only in self-defense and fear of getting killed. So know this, if you kill him, you can't not change your minds after, and the blood of an innocent man would stain on all your hands. Do you really want to live that type of guilt for the rest of your life?" Everyone became deathly quiet as his response shook them to the core, even their leader began to tremble with fear.

The leader looked at Davis with resentful eyes and then quickly turned away while saying "Do what you want, but don't come haunting me when he kills you."

"Just stay out of my way while I try to fix this, and let me make this apparent, you will not follow me to the factory or facility when I go and confront him. If he is trigger happy as you say he is, then you will just bring more trouble and secondly you will let go of this blood lust before you turn yourself into a modern-day Moby Dick," he said with an angered tone but with some concern.

Though some were skeptical about Davis's motives, most of the group was surprised by how levelheaded Davis was especially in this war. It was clear to Davis these people had seen others were either dangerous to both sides or too afraid to fight. He pushed his was through the group, he was silent, showing them that he was undaunted by their guns or their goal. The sphere returned to its original self as he made his way towards the factory and when he was about seven feet away, he could hear some of the group begin to start making bets with some cigarettes on whether he was going to come out of it alive.

As he continued to walk down the road as he yelled out without looking back. "Hey just because I'm walking way doesn't mean I'm out of ear shot and as far as I'm concerned you're all a bunch of jackasses.

He turned the corner on the road and vanished behind the building, out of sight of the group, and his old work facility was ahead of him. Even though it had been only a week, it had felt like a lifetime to Davis, and the haunting memories of that first day came back. The screams, bellowing, roars, and black clouds burned into his mind, a memory that would haunt him in this lifetime. He remembered that he saw something camouflaged on top of the other building right before his shift had started with Rosetta warning him that he was going to be late. He had hoped that Rosetta had gotten out of Wichita before everything went to hell and wished he knew if she was okay or not. But then another thought came to mind, his cell phone, he remembered he had stashed it into his messenger bag before the attack. Though he knew he had more important matters to attend to he figured he would stop at his old workstation quick and get his phone back before he headed to Mathew's, just to see if anyone else in his family had tried to contact him.

He rushed across the street and stepped into to the empty factory, but this place now made him feel nervous. This place once filled with dozens of people working hard laughing and yelling at each other, and now it was lifeless. There was a looming atmosphere, even in broad daylight, and with the machines turned off the echoes of his footsteps intimidated him. He looked around to see if anyone else was still in the building or if they had been spared by the alien's pets, but all he really saw was a flipped over desks, chairs, parts for airplanes scattered all over the floor, and a few splatters of blood. It looked like someone had tried to put up a fight to escape, but Davis knew that without someone else to aid them their chances were little to no chance. Davis tried to look away from the destruction as he headed to his desk, that was on its side, the computer monitor crashed, and found on the floor next to it was his messenger bag.

He picked it up and found everything he had left in it the day their place was attacked. There were a few pens, hair ties, soft peppermints, gum, his wallet, and his phone. Davis took a moment and thought to himself, "No wonder the women kept calling me a girl, it's for having this, it's just like a purse…. Oh well, I am still one of the sexiest bitches here."

Davis then chuckled to himself and wished that he had someone to share his joke with, but for him he felt like he was in a graveyard. His smile dissipated as he looked around, realizing how many people he had left behind in the literal dark, knowing that they could not get away, and being taken before their time. Davis quickly shoved those feelings aside and made his way to the back door near the parking lot. He passed under the hole the alien had made in the ceiling and it stopped him. When the light cascaded down on his body warming him, out of the corner of his mind, the night when the aliens invaded him at home came out of the blue. He remembered he had locked all the doors and windows, yet they managed to get in with ease. Davis was so terrified that he never gave it any thought of how they managed to get in. He kept thinking of ways that could be explained scientifically, but every scenario he produced just did not make sense. But then Davis remembered an important feature of the sphere, when it wasn't in use it would return to its original form. This made him make a theory of another use of being controlled. It did not just react to memory, it could possibly react to the user's needs. If this were true then with this information, he could be able to acquire new supplies, food, water, and medicine from anywhere. As he began to walk out of the ray of light he heard click from behind, and he felt something touch the back of his head. Davis raised his hands up and was about to explain what he was doing, but then a man's laugh stopped him from talking.

"You're a real pain in the ass, you know that!" said the man.

Davis immediately knew this voice and said, "Well if you used lube, you'd be fine, Mathew."

Mathew burst into laughter as he lowered his side arm, saying, "EW, you are such a prick. You know what, I'm not going to give you the satisfaction of getting another comeback."

Davis turned and smirked at Mathew as he realized what he just said and stated, "I would like to have that pulled from the record your honor."

Davis rolled his eyes and hugged Mathew while asking "How have you been?"

"I've been better, it's been hard the last couple of days, I got attacked by aliens, managed to kill some of them, and I had to move my home here. Did you know their blood is red, too?"

Davis hissed and said with an upsetting voice "About that Mathew, I need to tell you something, those weren't aliens, those were a group of survivors."

Mathew was stunned by what Davis had told him and thought he might have been messing with him, but the more he thought about it, the more things started to make sense. He could see in Mathew's eyes him thinking over the events that happened to him and saw the realization he was right. "No," he said repeatedly.

"Now it all makes sense, I have been trying to gather data about these aliens that kept attacking my home and why their blood was red. But the answer was in front of me the whole time, those were people looking for help!"

"Mathew clam down its okay, it was an accident."

"Why the hell didn't they just reveal themselves. If they had then maybe things could have been different," said Mathew as he tried to shift the blame.

"First of all, drop the victim card for a second! I know it was just an accident Mathew, but you still need to explain yourself to those people. You need to show them and tell them you're not an actual threat to them and try to make things right. I know it will be hard, but you need to give them peace."

Mathew hated the idea of confronting these people, especially now that he found out why they had been attacking, but he also when Davis was right, this was a misunderstanding that led to the deaths of innocent people, and both sides were at fault for what happened. Mathew gathered his courage and asked, "Take me to them." However, before he had the chance to talk to the group a bullet passed through his right shoulder, splattering blood on Davis's clothes, and forcing him to drop his gun. Davis grabbed Mathew's body as he nearly fell to the floor as the leader of the group shouted of her people to surround them, and to be ready to fire.

The leader approached the two as she said, "You two are going to pay, you for murdering our children, and you for aiding him."

"Are you all out of your fucking minds!?" Davis yelled.

"We are getting justice for our loved ones!"

"There is a thin line between justice and vengeance, and considering you all are here, then you know that from his reactions just now he was being genuine. But despite that information you're still going to kill him!"

"I WON'T BE DENIED!" said the leader pointing her gun at Davis.

"Wait!" screamed Mathew in pain "Don't kill Davis, look I'm sorry for what happened to your people, but I did not know you all were human, I thought you all were the enemy. But that's still no excuse, you can kill me for what I did, but please don't hurt Davis, he's a good guy, but he should not deserve to die just because he is my friend."

The leader yelled out "What about our people, did they deserve to die because they were our loved ones."

Mathew shook his head as Davis let him go and stood between them with his clothes soaked in blood, "Hasn't enough blood been shed already?"

"He has to pay!" she said as Davis could see her heart begin to break.

"Will that really make you feel better, because as far as I can see your trembling with regret!"

"WHAT?!"

"Look at yourself, you can't even pull the trigger, when he was right in front of you, and you could kill me in the street when you found out I was his friend. So, you know what that shows me, you don't want to kill anyone, you just want the pain to stop."

"You don't understand my pain!"

"I know I can't, I don't have kids of my own, and if I lost them like that, I would go crazy, too. But if you blind yourself by your pain then you could lose yourself entirely."

The leader but her gun down and said with tears in her eyes, "I don't know what to do? None of us do!"

"That's the point I am making, if you go through with this, you can't change your mind tomorrow, and wherever your child is now, do you think they could even look you in the eye anymore when you join them."

"But he has to-" she said before Davis cut her off. "Do you think you can say or do anything in this world that can make him feel worse than he already is? Be grateful she died in your arms and not in the belly of a serpent, not all of us got that luxury."

She began to shake as she could recall holding her daughter's lifeless body in her hands with her blood staining her cloths and body. "I just.... I never wanted her to die like that. She was only six years old, six years of loving, caring, nurturing, gone in one moment."

"Then you should be loving all those moments she was here, not hating the ones she not."

She turned to Mathew and gave him a look of disappointment, but it was not directed at him. She was regretting what she had done to him and saw a simulacrum of his lifeless body appear in her head. Knowing she was only moments away from taking his life just because of a misunderstanding made her feel terrible, and she broke down as she fell to the ground as others in her group began to tear up. The woman did not say anything, but everyone could tell she agreed with him. The group put their weapons away and headed into the generator room with Mathew, it seemed that he had moved his home into the facility for convenience since it was abandoned. As Mathew's arm was placed into an arm sling he swallowed some pain killers, and Davis told the group he needed to speak to him.

The leader stepped out along with her group and Davis immediately got into it even though he knew how rough his friend was. "Look I'm sorry but I need to talk to you right now and it can't wait."

Mathew hissed in pain and said, "It better be important, cause I'm in no mood!"

He explained what the Navy captain, Marry Luvuntar, wanted them to do and that he was going to need help doing it. He didn't sugar coat the situation about the store either, but if there was still a chance that they could reclaim their world then he was going to take it, but he was going to need a lot of help to achieve it. "So that's the situation, I need help to get things in order and to help our military with all or any information we can come across about these things. So, after hearing all of this, Mathew, would you consider heading to the super store and help them out to help me out."

"Sure, I can do that."

"What? Really?" Davis thought that Mathew would have relented, but he was surprised that Mathew agreed to help him.

"Well considering you stopped all of us from killing each other and saved all of us, it's the least I can do. But you do know when word get around, we will have to expand our operation to accommodate for more survivors."

"We can discuss that with the leader of the store when we get back."

"Actually I already have a plan for that, but when I get there I need to get my arm checked and see their stock list of items, considering how big the store is, we could convert it into a base for multiple survivors, and if they have working cars then we could make run to the other super store around to gather more supplies and other survivors, and even establish safe zones all over Wichita and the other outline cities."

"Damn Mathew, did you already have a plan in action or something!"

"Yeah for the east mall, I was going to use it because it has high and low ground with open space so we could see enemies coming from any direction and multiple local stores I could raid for more supplies and would have more room for people and their weapons."

"Dammit I wish I had thought of that, but you do know that it will take time to execute this plan, right?"

"Yes, I know, but I will still bring it up to the leader when things settle down at the store."

"Okay, then let's get you packed up and get out of here because we have to get going."

Mathew began to back up what he needed as the leader and her group began to talk in private outside the room. Even from the distance, Davis could make out their conversation. It didn't take long for them to pack and as they grabbed the bags they needed the leader of the group approached Davis nervously.

"Look I know things got heated and I pointed a gun at your face, but I ask you if-"

"Yes, you all can come and honestly, I will take any help that comes to offer it, just one thing.... Don't you ever pull a gun on me, that is the ninth time this week."

"How did you know I was going to ask?"

"Again, just because I'm far away doesn't mean in out of earshot." said Davis smiling.

Once everything was done at the facility, the group helped load Davis's car with Mathew's stuff. When they were helping load, Davis could still see some resentment in their eyes towards Mathew but wouldn't interfere any further unless it got to the point when someone was going to die, this was something he knew only they could work out. Afterword the group left Davis and Mathew by his car and left to get their things. Davis did tell them where they were stationed but also told them he couldn't wait, he needed Mathew to get checked out right away. As he drove off in his car, he wished them luck and to be quick, for he didn't know if they were being watched, or stalked. The ride seemed to be a lot shorter this time, with no delays or cars driving, it almost felt liberating to go faster than what he was supposed to, and Davis began to get better acquainted with this new adventurous life, but still had the fear deep inside of him treating him away little.

As he drove through the streets, he saw in the corner of his eye Mathew gazing at the city from his driver's side window. The fear Davis saw in his eyes said told him everything and even though Mathew was prepared for the worst, seeing everything in ruins, made him speechless. They passed neighborhoods, stores, the baseball stadium, everything between their old work and the superstore, Mathew finally got a good view of the destruction of the day. Both sat in silence the entire ride, they crossed the bridge that Davis took the other night and arrived at the super store. Shortly after the other group joined up with them with their supplies to add to the stores, they only had three trucks filled with themselves and supplies, but anything was better than nothing in the world they now lived in. The people on the roof were shocked to see Davis had come back with more people and in a panic radioed inside. He left his car and the supplies as he helped Mathew inside. He quickly asked if they had a doctor available for Mathew as he saw John come running down the aisle. John was thrilled to see Davis and the help he promised but was a little put off by the others.

Before he could even say one word Davis said bluntly, "This is Mathew, he's the friend you need, this group is going to help us, we need it, and I don't want to hear any arguments so live with it."

John immediately shut his mouth knowing he wasn't going to win this argument and he didn't want to heat things up. John asked two of the guards to help escort Matthew to the medical section to be seen by one of the doctors and given some strong painkillers as the woman and her team checked into the store. Davis followed behind Mathew and the guards but was forced to wait outside of the medical area as he went in. It took the doctor an hour and a half to just get the bleeding to stop and another four to get him patched up. In that time Davis and John were waiting constantly for any news about him. Eventually the women from the other group approached and sat down with them, and even explained why Mathew was hurt to John.

Though John showed he was a bit intimidated by her, he understood why she did it and confessed to what he used to be. The two seem to get along very well and eventually one of the doctors came out with some news.

"Mathew is going to be fine; it will take a few weeks of therapy to get his arm working properly again, but other than that he will be fine. Luckily however shot him was a lousy shooter." Said the doctor.

Everyone exhaled their breath with relief and though Davis did want Mathew to rest there was too much work to be done. They still needed to speak about organizing the superstore and the possibility of moving to the east mall. Davis told John to stand up and the two went to him and began to discuss things about the store and organization of supplies, but they did their best to keep it brief. During their discussion the east mall plan came up and John personally liked the idea of having a bigger place. He agreed with Mathew to let him handle the project once he was better and had a plan to get things in motion.

"You know the amount of responsibility we are going to be taking on, right." said John.

"Yeah, but how many people do you know who would willingly take a position of this type of responsibility?" asked Davis.

"We could just make a council this way no one can try to throw anyone under the bus." said Mathew a little groggy.

Davis looked at Mathew a little annoyed, "Damn it, even in his groggy state he can still come up with a good idea."

"It is a good idea, but we will have to set rules for everyone to follow to keep order, at least until we have a council to help aid us. Plus, when we move to the mall, we will all have our own areas to work at privately."

"That's a valid point too, but most of my work will be in the field. I need to get as close as I did on the first day when all this went down. Which means until the mall is ready to be moved into, I will stay out there."

"Are you crazy?" asked John concerned.

"Yes, but honestly what person in this world isn't."

"Fine," said John regretting, "But if you are going to be in the field then at least take a radio with you, this way if you need help then we can come to help."

"I can work with that, but for now I need to head home because this emotional day drained me quickly," said Davis as he left the medical area. "Get some well-needed rest Mathew, it might be the only decent rest you'll get for a long time."

They all said their goodbyes to each other, and Davis headed out. Before he went home, John made him take the radio and explained it could reach up to a hundred miles and made him promise the moment there was trouble he would give them a call. Davis got in his car and drove off in the midday sun. When he was home he headed downstairs again, but this time he wasn't greeted by the cats. He looked around, calling their names one by one to see if he could lure them out, but they never came. It wasn't time he checked the back room he knew why they didn't respond to him, the back door from the basement was open again. Davis closed it knowing the cats were long gone. He went into his room and checked his emails, but found no new messages, then remembered his phone and placed it on the charger to see if anyone had called him or left any messages, but it was going to be a while. He decided to lay down until he felt the sphere in his pocket press against his leg. Davis pulled it out and wondered what it was. He knew it was a burning memory, but it seemed different than the other one. Yet he wondered why he was given it, and what was the alien trying to warn him about.

Davis placed the small sphere on his nightstand, but he felt that he had forgotten something, then remembered he was still wearing the other sphere. He quickly removed it from his cloths, and it was once again hovering in the air.

He felt alone without his sister's cats swarming him and with the light of the computer it almost felt ominous. But then something came across his mind while he looked at the computer and remembered back at work, they had cut the power to the facility to kill dozens of people, but why did not they do it to the super store or the neighborhoods, and lastly why were they allowing communications to stay up? If they wanted to, they could have taken everything they needed away from them, they could have used it against them like they did with the environment, but they did not. Davis looked at the small orb again and wondered why they were not attacking anymore and where did they go?

Davis placed his hand on the small sphere and the moment he touched it he heard. "Seek the truth, for each one you find, I unlock."

CHAPTER 7

Rings come and shatter.

Back in the basement of Davis's house, he was startled by the voice in the sphere and more so surprised it was in English, but then after a moment of thinking he realized, after what he has seen already it was not that strange. Yet it did make him wonder what truth it spoke about, and it did not offer any clues of where to find it. Davis let go of the sphere and rose out of his bed and began to pace around, desperately trying to figure out what the truth was, and began to wonder if the alien he had run into was trying to tell him where to find the first one was.

"'Seek the truth, for each one you find, I unlock?' What type of cryptic bullshit is that and what truths are they talking about?" said Davis angrily at the sphere thinking it could talk.

Suddenly his thoughts trailed off when his phone began to ring, and it made him even more angry. This moment was a breakthrough to him, and he needed to concentrate on this sphere and its message, whoever was trying to contact him would have to wait. His phone rang over and over as he tried to calm himself down and focus, then moments later it stopped, and he could hear himself think again. He felt such relief as the quiet settled in, and he began to remember where he had left off, but then it began to ring again. Davis became enraged as that ring came back, it was infuriating. He grabbed the phone from its charger and in a fake clam voice answered it.

"Hello this is Davis Ring, if this was an emergency then take the law into your own hands like everyone else, after all this a war zone now between an unknown enemy and that apparently likes playing mind games with is, so please.... NEVER CALL THIS NUMBER AGAIN!" then he hung up.

As he began to once again recollect his thoughts his phone rang again. He took his phone and placed it on silent as he began to write down what had transpired from memory, though he only wrote the highlights or more critical information. But the more he looked at the information the more uncertain he was about it. To him things just did not add up with the aliens' tactics, if they were so advanced why use animals, and if the aliens were out for humans, then why did they stop their attacks a week later? Did they reach their goal? Or were they lying in wait?

The constant amount of stress was beginning to get to him as he could feel a severe headache coming on. He sat down in his chair and looked at the glowing screen, turned it off and gazed at his reflection, knowing this he asked himself, "why only just the first week?" He believed everyone thought the nightmare was over, but he knew whatever was coming next was going to be the far worse than any nightmare they could conger in their minds, or reality. Davis looked around his desk for some pain killers for his headache, he normally took some to deal with the stressful situations like this, but in the last year they took several bottles worth, and though he did not become addicted to them, it was still a problem.

Just like his mother and stepfather, he was trying to get away from the pain of stress or at the least escape it for a while. Though, unlike himself, his mother and stepfather would rather drink, smoke, or do illegal drugs to escape their problems. But after all the fighting and investigating over the money his stepfather had stolen from him, he couldn't keep up the benign audit forever. The months of having to clear his name and get his money back stressed him out too much. Normally he would talk to himself to walk him through the pain and come out the other side stronger, but that situation was just too much for him to handle. Yet even after all the fighting and arguing there was no conceivable way to get Don imprisoned for what he did. The stress was so intense that Davis had a heart attack and because he was using the pain medication for so long, he didn't even feel the pain in his shoulder, the pain that would have warned him about the impending danger on his life.

Davis managed to hide what happened to him from his family, if anyone knew what happened because of Dons actions, they would have been out for blood. But then he remembered the one day when Davis was visiting his doctor, Emily Montrosan, she confronted him about his problems.

"Davis, I might be a doctor of the physical body, but you also know I am of the mind as well," said Emily, concerned.

"I don't need phycological evaluation from you, just give me my prognosis on my heart so I can go." said Davis, annoyed.

"Okay, your heart is stabilized, and things are looking well physically, but emotionally you are in complete shambles."

"I said-"

"I know what you said, I was there three seconds ago, but as your doctor, it is my responsibility to make sure you are of sound mind and body. You're nearly twenty-six and you're in a situation no one should be in and the fact you still with them, honestly, makes you idiotic."

"What?"

"I know you what to help them, but the only ones who can help are themselves, this is basic stuff anyone knows."

"It's not that simple, how am I going to tell my mother her husband stole an insurance check from me, which the insurance company tried to charge me with fraud because of him, and nearly got sent to jail for five years?"

"It's not your problem, it's his, he was the one who made the decision to steal from you and screw over the insurance company, not you. If things fall apart, it's in his life and your mothers it's because of him, it's not your job to protect them."

Davis looked down at the floor to avoid Emile's gaze, he could not face her knowing she was right. "I mean do they even know what has happened to you, what is happening to you?"

"No," said Davis bluntly.

"Then either leave them or tell them, just do something before you die doing nothing, you need to save your life, not their's!"

As he remembered Emily's words from that day and looked up at the ceiling, knowing that wasn't an option. "What the hell am I doing?" Davis said upsettingly. There were hundreds if not thousands of people who were looking for someone to guide them, and without people like him to pick up the torch, their world would fall into sorrow, and the people would give up. Davis and the others at the super store had to be strong for everyone, so in turn others would become strong. But that didn't mean their emotions were not going to be ignored, they would still express their anger, their fears, and their sorrows, and with the help of the people, rise back up if they ever fell. Davis stopped looking for his pian killers and went to his phone to see who had been calling him, hoping they were still okay so he could tell them where to find help. The phone number was an unknown, but they had called over twenty-nine times, and left several voice mails. When Davis played the first one, he felt all the warmth leave his body, it was his little sister, Amelia, trying to contact him, and she sounded relieved but at the same time a little upset. Her emotions started to shift from sad to angry the more messages she left. Eventually Davis called her back and as expected she was not happy.

"Davis what the hell is wrong with you, I call you eight times and you basically ghost us?" said Amelia infuriated.

"Sorry, Kitten, I'm have been overwhelmed with my own crap to deal with."

"Do you have any idea what we have been through! Dear God it has been a nightmare for the three of us!"

"I'm sorry a lot of things have been moving too fast but look on the bright side we're alive, and we have managed to make contact again."

"I am glad you're alive, Bubba, but why do you take so long to answered me, do you know how many times I called?"

"Kitten, I was attacked at work, I didn't have time to grab my stuff, I just got my phone back today, so don't be pissed with me for desperately trying to survive and keep the peace between other people."

"Wait, keep the peace? What are you talking about?"

Davis then explained to Amelia what had happened in the last week and all the crazy stuff that came with it, but just like with the Navy, he kept the spheres secret for he didn't know how she would react. Afterword Amelia understood his predicament but still felt upset that Davis was unable to reach her for some time, and when she did, he ignored her. However even though she might have hated him for ignoring her calls.

"Look, Kitten I'm sorry for ignoring you, the call was unknown if I had known it was you, I would have picked up right away. But listen to me carefully, is still not safe out there, you all need to get to the super store as fast as you can."

"No, I'm not going to do that, I know you're doing things to help people, but you are not doing this without me! Where are you at we're coming to you and we can do this together and talk face to face!"

Davis truly wanted to see his little sister, he was about to tell her his location, but then he saw the floating sphere in front of him. He did not know how to explain this thing to her or the other sphere he had just got and if she saw it in person might freak her and her family out, just like the worker he saw commit suicide. So instead of telling her his location he told his sister that they would meet up later once things became calmer, and they could establish an order to maintain peace. However, Amelia refused and told him that if they were not allowed to even see him, then this would be their last time calling him, and that they would figure how to survive without their family. Davis knew that she was just hurting from everything that had happened, but he still couldn't let her know until he knew that her family was safe.

So, Davis raised his voice at her, "Amelia Ring, you will not speak to me that way, I do not care if you are nineteen and have a family of your own, I'm still your older brother, and right now I'm trying to get you to head some place safer, for your own safety, for your husband's and daughter's, and you dare threaten me like that! If you will not do as I ask because your angry that I had lost my phone for a week, then don't bother to call me back at all unless it's to apologize." After he was done, he hung up on her and but his phone back on silent as he laid back down and just stared at the ceiling. Hoping that after she had calmed down then maybe they could make up and find their way back to each other. However, he didn't hear from her the next day or the one after that.

The days turned to weeks since that call and Davis was worried for her, but he had to put his own feelings aside to help the people in the super store. Then first month came to its conclusion, one solid month since the invasion came with very little sign of the aliens or their pets, but the same could be said of the navy. Communications between them and Davis were only one way but despite that knowledge Davis tried to get back in contact with them. Yet during that same time Davis, John, and Matthew created teams and rules that both benefited the people and protected everyone from themselves, and during his escapades with his sphere Davis found out how to make it stay in place and call it when he needed it. At first it was a rocky start, especially with some beast's scourge for a few days, and entitled people finding ways to either complain about anything or try to take more than what they have got. Eventually things got it to a point where the majority was happy and a very rare few were unhappy, and even if they were it didn't last long. However, once and a while the few would become a problem, especially with the rules.

But regardless of the few people they still managed to press on. Davis, John, and Matthew established departments with them as the leaders to balance out the power and to organize what they had and in their spare time worked on the east mall for sustainable living. The groups were made up of ten or twenty people that were at the top of their field or at least studying in the field. Their goal in total there was going to be eight departments for the superstore, each one made specifically for their survival, in the beginning the only three: intelligence, security, and stock. Davis was head of the intelligence, John was head of security, and Matthew was head of stock each one trying to balance out the power carefully to make sure there wasn't a problem.

At the beginning of the second month, things became a bit fruitful for the super store. New departments came up along with familiar faces that began to arrive. The first to arrive with a few people in her care was Emily, who became head of the health, both mentally and physically, just like she had been trying to do her whole career. The second was the woman who had almost killed Matthew, she became head of the armory, though it was disturbing that no one had bothered to ask her name, everyone just called her "ma'am." Eventually they found out that her name was Jackie, but Davis felt so bad for not asking her for so long that he gave her his candy bars for a week as an apology. The third was a young teenager named Miller, who they found on a supply run, they caught him dissecting a coyote carouse in the middle of the store they raided. Everyone was grossed out by his study, but Davis saw opportunity, if they got lucky then maybe they could study one of the dead aliens or their pets to figure out how they work, potentially. On the same day they found a woman named Akio stopping some entailed people from causing problems and reestablished peace. She took it upon herself to become the leader of the peacekeepers, the fourth department, and personally no one minded, in fact they found it a blessing.

As they reached the halfway mark in the second month they ran into some trouble. Some vermin got inside and started eating anything they could get their hands on, by the time they were eradicated, they lost almost twenty-seven percent of their food. People began to panic, believing things were going to fall apart, and then they began to fight over what they had left for food. The leaders tried to calm them, assuring things were going to be okay, but they started to lose their faith in them. Then a man named Adalard came into the picture, helping Matthew take account for all the remaining food and some seeds that could be used to plant more later. Adalard showed his plan for distributing supplies out, the leads were impressed. He managed to turn their rations into a steady steam for their people, so the leads agreed that he was the new fifth lead.

With all the leads in the departments they thought things would go smoothly, but then people became fearful of going outside. Many didn't want to be in the supply run and eventually started to deny the request to do so. Even with every few beasts and serpents outside the walls of this place, they still didn't want to go. That was until an elderly man named Julian made his own department and started training people in secret to be gatherers. When he was discovered, the leads were overjoyed and added his department to the eight. When the groups were established, they formed a council with the heads, and took their operations and managed to move everyone to the east mall. However, every two weeks they would meet up to discuss issues, moral, and improvements, but the first four sessions were deplorable. Everyone spent the time arguing about what rules they needed, some wanted to keep the old ways of doing things, while others argued that they needed to change to survive. To Davis, this wasn't surprising, he knew in the beginning this was going to be a problem. Half were democratic and the others were republican, so making a compromise wasn't easy. Davis was the only one who wanted them to find the balance, but everyone didn't go with it, that was until the third month came.

The one thing they all agreed on was letting in people to help increase their numbers, but even though the order was given some of the security refused to let in certain people. When Davis and John found out they demanded to know why, and their answers shocked them. The guards told them there were people trying to force their way in, and that they were not having any of that. Even telling them of two teenagers who believed they were entitled to be safe and let in. Davis and John were both confused by the guard's response. The was no reason for the teens to attack, they welcomed anyone who would join. They thanked the guards for the information and let them be and as were they out of their range of hearing John said, "They are such bad liars, I've lied better than that!"

"And I can vouch for that truth, lets head to the security room and see what really happened."

When they got to the security room, they asked to check the videos from that week, it took them a while, but they found the video of the teens and what they saw infuriated them. The guards refused to let them in, then attacked them without probable cause, and when they were done, they pointed their guns at, the two kids fled, limping towards the direction of police station. Afterwards Davis told Akio to reprehend the guards that attacked them while John asked Julian to send out a search party for the kids, granted it wasn't their job, but they were more than happy to oblige when they found out what had happened. It took hours for the team to find the teens and longer still to get them to calm down.

One of the guards radioed back to John saying, "We found the kids, but they're in rough shape, I am requesting the medical department to be at the doors for immediate treatment."

"We hear you loud and clear, consider it done!"

After the radio went silent, Akio told Davis and John, "The guards are secure but there not answering any questions we have. Whatever the problem is they are trying to make sure we don't find out what it is."

"You think they're discriminating other survivors?" asked John.

"I would be that surprised if they weren't. But until the teens talk, we keep them locked up, then when and if we can talk to the kids, we will get are answers."

Akio and John agreed with Davis and waited with him near the front door. It wasn't long before Emily and her staff came out with arms stretched as the team came back with the teens. Davis could see from their faces they were terrified about entering the store, even with Emily and her people trying to calm them down. The teens were just two boys, covered in their own blood and bruises all over their bodies. Everyone at the door, the guards, the doctors and nurses, Davis, Emily, John, and Akio were disgusted by the damage the rogue guards caused. For them all this was a betrayal to the store and humanity. Seeing what those men did to these kids nearly made Davis puke. The teens were taken to the medical department by the stretchers that were brought as Davis, Emily, Akio, and John headed way from the front door.

"Emily, tell me the moment you clear them so we can speak with them. The faster we find out why they were attacked the faster we can get to the trail."

"I don't need to be reminded about our process Davis, I will get to what you need but give these kids a moment to breath and relax," said Emily.

Though he was being a little impatient he left Emily alone to do her work and went to his station, waiting for her response. His department was in the tech section of the store, filled with monitors, white boards of information and theories, and work desks with people talking to one another. Davis sat down at his desk and further tested his spheres morphing ability's and try to uncover its full potential as he waited. Its ability to morph into other things was nothing new or wonderous to Davis, but discovering it energetic power was what he truly desired. Even after months of research he still couldn't crack the secret of how he managed to fire the massive wave of kinetic energy that destroyed a bit of the baseball stadium. He even wrote down his emotions from that day to try to discern and recreate the reaction, but with no luck. It seemed whatever caused it may have only been a one-time thing as Davis saw it, or maybe there was something he was missing.

Davis looked through his notes again and again, trying to figure out how he did it, but he was frustrated to see anything new. Then his radio crackled with Emily's voice, "Davis, you there?"

"No, I'm on Mars, of course I'm here."

"No need for sarcasm, I just wanted to let you know the boys are okay and I got what I needed from them so meet everyone at the sanctum."

"Thanks, I'll be there shortly," said Davis as he got up and headed out.

The sanctum was basically a court room on the far side of the store with a few tables and chairs that formed and arch, so every could see and hear each other, as whoever was on "trial" would sit in the middle and be heard. But as the leads headed there, they started to see people whispering to each other and though no lead could understand them they already knew what was going on; after all, word gets around quickly when you have a small community.

As everyone made themselves comfortable, sitting down quietly in the chamber until Akio demanded, "What the hell where you idiots doing?" But the three guards still stuck to their story saying that they acted in self-defense.

However, Amelia gave her report to the council, saying "After a long examination I must report the injuries are severe, but not life-threatening. Unfortunately, I don't have the appropriate equipment to do a full scan of their bones or muscles, but for my observations I can see one boy has a fractured wrist, ankle, and collar bone. The bruises on his body show he was attacked viciously, and he was trying to defend himself at the same time. So, if you were attacked and it was self-defense, then why go that far and hide it?"

"Not to mention the group I sent out to find them reported they were terrified, and would not let anyone get near them, and even tried to shoot one, lucky they were lousy shots," said Julian taking the floor. The three guards tried to argue that they saw the gun and panicked, thinking that they were going to get shot at.

"I know what it's like when you panic when you think you're going to die or you lose someone, hell I nearly killed Matthew here because of a misunderstanding, but they were clearly out matched, and you three could have easily detained them, this wasn't an act of fear, and what Emily just told us, its sounds more of an act of anger." said Jackie. Then John pulled out the footage of them on the outside of the building and they had been caught attacking them, unprovoked, and even threatened to kill them if they didn't leave. The guards immediately tried to deny it was them, but the footage was as clear as a diamond, and their sign in sheets showed they were on duty when this incident occurred. Davis had enough of them beating around the bush and demanded, "Enough, we want the truth! Why did you attack two children who clearly were looking for help!"

The three guards just sat there in silence, until Davis said, "You think silence is bravery, we have someone here that came make you talk. Akio, do as you please until they talk."

As she stood up from her chair one of the guards yelled out, "We did it because they're fags." The other two looked at him infuriated, but it was clear that he was more afraid of what she was going to him than what they were. Davis remembered the rumors of Akio's "methods" when it came to the truth, but they were just that - rumors. So, he used it against them hoping one would crack and thankfully one did. The guard told them that they had been denying people who were homosexuals because they didn't what any abominations in the store or in the mall when they moved. That it was their right to beat down the nonbelievers and send the hell spawn of earth back to hell.

Davis looked at the three guards in anger and asked them, "Did you know that I happen to be a homosexual, or I guess in your case a fag?"

"What? No, you're not, and you don't have to lie to defend those people." said one of the guards.

"No, he is a homosexual, I knew him from before the invasions, we worked in the same place and my God if you had seen him back then, you would now not to argue with him about this subject. Hell, he even uses rainbows as his quote 'gay-dar'." said Matthew correcting them.

"Are you all serious?"

"What part of I am a homosexual and use rainbows for 'gay-dar' do you not understand!"

"And you all knew about this?"

"Yes," everyone on the council said. "When the council was formed, he told us to the very first day, now I grant you some of us weren't so happy about it at first, but he made us see that it wasn't our business and there were far more important things to worry about than prejudice behavior." said Julian.

"This is bull shit, how can you all stand with this embarrassment?"

"I'm sorry, but this embarrassment has been keeping your asses safe and fed for months, and if it wasn't for him this place wouldn't even exist!" said Jackie.

"Who he is, is wrong!"

"No, what you have done is wrong!" said Davis enraged. "You attacked two kids, unprovoked, denied them safety, and even tried to cover it up. If you believed what you did was right, then why go to the lengths of hiding it?" The guards didn't answer his question, so he answered for them, "I'll tell you why, because you knew what you did was wrong, despite what your religion says, your heart and mind betray it because you were taught to be empathetic towards others no matter what or how they are."

"Yes, we were taught to have empathy of people, our people, not everyone, just the people who think like us."

"And because of your lack of empathy towards others, you three attacked two kids without even knowing them and went behind our backs, making rules to only suit your needs, but not everyone's. You have learned nothing for humanity's mistakes and because of it you have made things worse."

"We did what we had-" said the guard before he was cut off by Davis, "Enough! This conversation is over. I am sure the council can agree with me that you three have been found beyond reasonable doubt guilty."

The council shook their heads in agreement and the guards were escorted out of the chamber for the council to decide their fate. They deliberated for some time but came to an agreement and called them back in. "We have made an agreement, the three of you along with the skin head we locked up a few months ago will be banished from this place, taken deep into the countryside, out there you can do whatever you want. But if ever dared to show your faces anywhere near Wichita again, I will personally become your grim reaper."

The council was dismissed, and the guards were sent way, along with the skin head, and after that day no one has seen or heard from them since. But things began to look up two days later, the teens were recovering nicely, and after all the struggles, they finally managed to get everything ready for the east mall. No one wasted a second of time and began to escort people from the store to the mall with all their supplies and families, being careful as not to arouse suspicion or get seen by the enemy. However, during that same week some gatherers had been running late, but when they returned, they found out why. All the leads including Davis were rushed outside to see what the commotion was about, when they saw what they had, Miller's eyes lit up like stars. They had found a fresh serpent body, a day old or so, lying on the road and they refused to leave it behind, they knew that this was a jackpot for humanity, so they used their truck and threw it in the back to bring home. This was the opportunity everyone one had been waiting for, to figure out how these creatures worked would give humanity a better advantage, and if they could learn their secrets.

That very same night everyone except Miller's department celebrated this triumph. What wasn't expected however was when Davis spotted Amelia and her family in the crowd, it looked like they had just arrived, and it looked like they were enjoying themselves. Davis wanted to speak with her, but he didn't have the heart to, not after the way he had left things. Later that evening while everyone was singing and dancing, Davis found his was up to the second level and stared down at the crowds. Most people would feel joy in this moment, knowing that things were finally going their way, and that maybe with the hope they just found, they had a chance to win this fight, but for Davis he felt nothing, this may have been a stroke of good luck, but he wondered how long it would last.

However, a female voice spoke caught his attention as she said, "Well you look like hell, Mr. Rain."

Davis recognized her voice, and with an overwhelming smile of joy he turned to see his sister Amelia standing on the last step, smiling at him as Davis said "Really, Mr. Rain? Kitten, I thought you would come up with something more creative?"

"Well Mr. Chocolate Lover was unavailable." said Amelia as Davis tried to take a gulp of his soda, but then choked on it.

Davis began coughing hard as he said, "I taught you to well."

"Maybe, but it does make me laugh to see your own humor turned against you," said Amelia while she chuckled.

After Davis had cleared out his throat the two stood in silent, waiting for the other to say something, but nothing came of it. The two were happy to see each other but the way things had been left off on their last phone call made them speechless. They simply watched the crowds of people below celebrating waiting for the other to say they were sorry about what they had said.

"FOR GOD SAKES WOULD YOU TWO JUST APOLOGIZE TO EACH OTHER?" Elliot screamed in a shriller voice over the crowd.

Everyone was startled for a second as they looked at Elliot wondering who he was talking to. Davis and Amelia above saw everyone's reaction to Elliot's shriller voice began to lose their minds laughing at the crowd's reaction. The echoes of the two siblings laughing began to become infectious as everyone began to giggle and laugh at what just happened. Elliot immediately felt embarrassed and filled with stage fright as he carried their daughter away through the crowds, walking back to their living quarters.

The two were glad that he had broken as Davis said, "You have got a crazy husband there."

"Yes, I do, and I love him for it."

"Look, Kitten I'm so-"

"No, I'm sorry Davis, I know you told me about all of this before, but I was just scared that I would lose you. Hell, I don't even know if our other family members are still alive and after everything Elliot, Diamond, and I went through, just the thought of losing you made me angry, and I didn't want to see it happen. I know I can't make you abandon this mission or these people, but-"

"I know, Sweetie, you don't have to explain everything that happened. But there was something I did leave out from that call." said Davis as he began to reveal to her about the spheres, the encounter with the alien, and the cryptic message.

As he revealed to her about the spheres and message her smile vanished from her face and was replaced with fear. She with a scared tone of voice asked, "Does anyone else know about this stuff?"

"Everyone knows about the morphing one, but the only ones that know about the small one is you and the council, but just like I told them, keep it on the DL until I figure out what they want." Amelia agreed to her brothers request but was skeptical about the council members, wondering if they could keep his secret and if they were worthy of his trust. In her own mind she believed she had to keep an eye on the council, just as a precaution.

As night came and left the warm spring winds began to stir in the air, and there were still no signs of the aliens and their pets. Whatever was going on out in the world made Davis feel suspicious as the communications between him and the Navy stopped. Though he knew they wouldn't answer throughout the third month Davis sent message after message to the Navy and his brother, wondering if they were on land or not, but with no reply and he eventually gave up and focused on his research and more importantly why the aliens had disappeared. However, one night Miller came crashing through Davis's department saying he needed to speak with him immediately. Davis began to follow him, but for some reason he could hear the call of the small sphere, saying "Seek the truth, for each one you find, I unlock." Davis's eyes widened as the sphere kept calling him, almost like it was wanting to go with him. He quickly grabbed the sphere from his safe and followed Miller to his department on the opposite side of the mall.

Miller took Davis to the back and showed Davis the opened serpent carcass and began explaining his reach to Davis. "Okay so you know I have been looking at this thing for weeks now, but this creature's anatomy is way more different than I thought, and it was a pain in the ass to figure out, but this was a huge success, and I began to write all my findings in my books and-".

"Miller! Please slow down you are giving me a headache here."

"Sorry, I had discovered that the membrane around this creature is more inapt to expanding their bodies and their bones which turn out to be low on marrow and light weight. I've also discovered that these creatures-"

"Miller, please give it me in English or were going to be all night."

"Let me show you two particular things about this creature." Miller looked excitedly at Davis as he showed him two beakers that contained the stomach acid from the serpent and placed a slice of ham in the left one, but nothing had happened, it had just floated on the top, it wasn't dissolving. Then Miller took a strawberry and dropped it into the right one and in mere moments it began to dissolve. Davis was confused and wasn't sure what Miller was trying to prove.

"Okay what are you trying to tell me?"

Miller couldn't hold it back anymore and yelled out, "There were herbivores, they only eat plants, fruits, and vegetables! It can only dissolve plants because their acid isn't strong enough to dissolve meat!"

"What?! Are you sure?!"

"Positive!"

"If that's true then why were they eating people?"

"They weren't!" said Miller as he quickly dragged Davis over to the table where the serpent lay.

Miller showed him the organs of the serpents but pointed out the strange sack he had taken out. He had found it in between its four lungs, and it connected to its esophagus and surprisingly attached to two of the lungs, but it wasn't another stomach. "Whatever this is it some sort of sack that expanded whenever something entered in it. Let me show you!" He took the small sack and demonstrated, managing to put his whole body inside it. Davis was surprised to see that small sack managed to stretch out so far, as he could see Miller's body and clothes in an almost perfectly outlined shape. Miller removed the sake as he continued to explain, "The sack is possibly used for caring their young, like a kangaroo with their infant, and the connection to the lungs indicates that whatever was inside it at the time would be given a steady supply of air. These animals used this sack as a means of transport, if their young were unable to fly, and that I don't think that these animals are cable of attacking anything unless there provoked or if they were trained to do so!"

Davis then realized what he was getting at and said, "So these creatures weren't eating people." He could feel the sphere become hot in his pocket as he gently pulled it out, his hand felt warm against the sphere as he looked at it and said, "They had kidnapped them." The sphere erupted with orange light, and he could feel the heat intensify for a split second as he dropped it. When the light dimmed, the orange ring shattered and collapsed into the black flame, and in the center of that flame a small speak of orange light could be seen. Davis could hear a voice in the sphere say, "It's a deal… Here is what we promised…We don't have a choice." Davis tried to investigate the flame, but no images or memories came of it, only the voices. As he went to pick it up, he could feel the temperature change from hot to cold and when he placed his finger on the sphere it felt as cold as ice.

"What just happened?

"You discovered a hidden truth, these aliens are not here to kill us, they're here to take us."

"But why…. why do they need humanity?"

"I don't know, but the truth might be in this sphere. At first, I thought they were just wasting our time, but now, its irrefutable something happened between humanity and them."

"Wait, so what did it do?"

"I think it gave me a piece of a memory or at least some audio bits, and the strange part is, the voice was a human."

"Every time it says, 'seek the truth, for each one you find, I unlock.' It sounds like an AI voice, but when I heard this voice, it sounded like a human man."

"If that's true then we need to tell the council, they need to know what we have just found out!"

Davis agreed with Miller but before either one of them got the chance, John rushed into the department, sweating. "Davis?! There you are. There are a few dozen trucks coming from the east and they are coming in hot!"

"Get everyone inside the mall and the guards on the roof, we might need to prepare for an attack or siege, let hope it's not either one! Also, next time just radio me its way faster than running to find me."

Before anyone could do anything, John's radio crackled with one of his guards speaking through it, "Sir you need to get up here and see this!"

"See how easy that was!" said Davis as him and John ran out Miller's department.

Rushing to the roof they saw dozens of peacekeepers and guards heading in the same direction. Whatever was going on outside was getting intent quickly as the crowds of people ran to the roof along with Akio by their side. Pushing and shoving one another many found themselves on the roof, looking to the east. Davis, John, and Akio pushed through them all and stood near the edge and saw in the distance the trucks, but also saw a black saw following close behind. Davis grabbed a pair of binoculars from one of the guards and looked out towards the trucks, what he saw made his skin crawl with fear. The trucks were being pursued by a horde of beast and serpents and they were closing in on them.

"Oh my god," said Davis with fear in his voice. "We are going to need a lot more ammunition up here!"

"Everyone, find your posts!" said Akio as the trucks turned off the highway.

All the guards and peacekeepers prepared themselves for what was to come as they saw the truck near the entrance of the mall. One of the drivers jumped out as the truck nearly come to a stop and started screaming, "LET US IN, WE HAVE KIDS AND WOUNDED, THOSE THINGS WILL BE HERE ANY SECOND!" From the distance all could hear the roars and bellowing of the serpents, some had managed to get further ahead of the hoard and charged straight at the people below. The people with guns got out of their trucks and began to fire upon them. The beasts didn't stand a chance as the bullets found a new home in their bodies, but the amount of ammunition they were using was too much. Their guns became empty as they took down the beasts, then the serpents began to dive towards the trucks, trying to snatch up any who strayed away.

As the hellish battle was going down below, the people on the roof felt their fear begging to rise in their souls. Davis saw his people's pale faces, them shaking their guns, and some looking away. Some guards began to slowly walk back inside, pretending not to hear the screaming people below or their gun fire. As one approached the door and began to open it Davis yelled out, "WHERE THE HELL DO YOU THINK YOU ALL ARE GOING!"

"Davis, I know you want to save them, but we can't, we would be putting all of our lives in jeopardy to save some strangers!" said one of the peace-keepers.

"Really, because last time I checked I was once a stranger to all of you, but despite that, you let me in, how is this any different? This is the exact situation we have always been in, nothing has changed, and just like before we will not abandon our people to die!"

Everyone looked shocked at Davis as his words rang out, they could feel his confidence, but then their faces turn to terror as a serpent flew at him from behind. Davis grabbed a guard's pistol and turned around with rage in his eyes and yelled out "IM TRING TO BE MOTIVATING HERE!" All it took was one flash of the gun firing and the serpent fell to the ground on the roof top with one bullet hole in its body. The serpent lay dead on the roof as Davis through the gun to guard he took it from saying, "We need everyone who can wield a gun up here, NOW!"

Davis went to the ventilation duct and called out to everyone in the mall knowing they would be able to hear him. "Everyone!" he said first as it echoed inside the mall. All could hear his voice and listened, "We need everyone who knows how to wield a gun to come to the roof with extra ammunition to help fight off a horde of alien pets and save some survivors outside, I won't lie it's going to be tough and some might not make it back, but we must fight, not just for us, for everyone who didn't make it. So, let's make this a day where humanity sticks back, and if we're going to die, let's see how many of these things we can take down with us!"

All in the mall sat inside silently and hesitant, the mall seemed almost life-less. Everyone was scared of what was going to come, they didn't want to fight, they didn't want to die. In the living quarters, Jackie came in and saw no one moving, she tried to find a way to inspire them, but she didn't know how. But then Elliot raised out from his seat saying, "Davis, my brother-in-law, no my brother, and the council has done everything to keep us safe from harm, given us a second chance at life, and now we're going to deny others the same thing? If you all can live with that then you're not human, I would rather die fighting to protect others in the light, rather than cower in the dark. As he walked towards Jackie, Amelia grabbed his arms with Diamond in her arms saying, "You better come back and with my brother, otherwise I will make you both pay in the next life."

Elliot smiled at Amelia and kissed her as he made her let go of his hand. As he turned away from her, he said, "Hey at least I get to spend some time with my brother-in-law if I die. Heh, I think the universe just screwed me, but it's so worth it."

As he could feel Amelia's sorrow flow out of her, Elliot charged out of the living quarters and towards the armory with Jackie. She handed him an AK-57, a few mags of ammunition, and showed him the way to the roof. As other people saw Elliot run out to battle, they saw his resilient courage show. Though they didn't know why themselves, many headed to the armory to gather weapons to fight. Many were scared but they all knew if they didn't, then the next morning would never shine as bright ever again.

Back on the roof, Miller called Davis on his radio and asked, "I know this is bad timing but what about the-"

"Just put it into my safe for now, I know you know my combo so put it there, and make sure everyone who is still down there stays clam!" said Davis and he headed towards the edge again.

"Alright everyone give the people below cover, we have the high ground, they have the low, so give them everything you have got, don't hold back!" said Akio with confidence.

The sounds of multiple guns firing filled the air and echoed through the land as everyone began to fire down at the beasts from the roof and the people on the ground began to fire at the serpents in the sky. Bodies of both beasts and serpents began to drop like flies to the ground along with the shell casings from the guns. The blood of the aliens began to pool on the ground and the roars and bellowing of agony came and gone. Some serpents made it past the trucks and began to head towards the roof top, getting past the defenses on the ground. As they drew closer, Davis snapped his finger and a few moments later, out of the vent, the dust from his sphere came to him. As he got his sphere, a serpent managed to get its coils around someone and the moment he saw it, Davis became enraged. He formed a halberd with his sphere and with one motion of his blade, slashed the serpent in half. Its blueish blood spilt to the ground and covered Davis's blade as its corpse fell on the ground. The person he saved was fine and immediately got off the ground and started firing at the beasts again, doing everything in their power to push them back.

Davis kept the ones that got too close at bay while the everyone kept their eyes on the ground and sky. More and more bodies dropped to the ground as the battle raged on, but then the beasts bellow began to move around to their side of the mall as the serpents began to circle high above. People left and right were being spread out to thin on the roof, desperately firing at the beast trying to get around them. Bullet after bullet, body after body, they stop them from getting around. The serpents kept diving onto the roof when they saw an opportunity to attack, but always met a swift end by Akio and Davis as they worked in tandem. It seemed to Davis they had a chance to win this fight, but then his radio crackled with Amelia's voice.

"Davis!"

"Not now, Kitten!" said Davis as he answered her while fighting with Akio by his side.

"DAVIS THEY'RE RIPPING THE WEST SIDE ENTRANCE DOWN!"

"WHAT?!" yelled Davis as he ran to the west side of the roof.

In his disbelief, he saw the beasts ripping apart the entrance and barricade they had made. Davis could hear them breaking down their stockade even with the loud noise of the guns. Davis realized that they were so busy fighting off the beasts on the south side of the mall they forgot to cover the north side. He let go of his halberd and it returned to its former self as he grabbed a gun and began to fire down towards the beasts, imagining the people inside begin to panic and scatter in the mall, trying to find a way out. Akio joined him by his side and as the two managed to push them back a serpent managed to swoop in from behind and grab Davis by the arm, dragging him over the edge.

"DAIVS!" Akio screamed in fear.

As the serpent tried to get Davis around its coils Akio put a bullet into the serpent's head and the two fell six stories down to the hard concert below. As they hit the ground hard the serpents body managed to soften Davis land as its blood splatter the ground and him. But even thought he was unharmed, and nothing was broken he unfortunately got the wind knocked out of him as he desperately tried to get up and gasp for air. From the roof, Davis could see

Akio was relieved he was fine as he gasped for air. He managed to get out of the body of the serpent still gasping as Akio yelled out, "LOOK OUT!"

Davis looked towards the west entrance seeing one of the beasts come charging towards him, he figured it must have seen him fall. Davis was still trying to recover, he needed more time, time that he didn't have. Akio tried to stall it, but every shot she took missed the beast, and eventually she ran out. The beast drew only a few yards away as Davis realized this was it for him and he said to himself "I'll see you in h-"

Then from behind him a mighty gust of heated wind passed his left side and struck the beast, turning half of its body into ash. Davis was shocked by what happened and turned to see a hooded woman approach him with a katana in her right hand that was pointed at the ground. She moved her blade way to her side and approached him. She lifted him off the ground and said, "Take a moment, okay, you took a rather nasty fall."

As she spoke, he instantly recognized her voice, he was thrilled to know that she was okay, but before he could even get a word in, she thrust her katana forward as a kinetic wave of energy came out, throwing the beast away from the door. Davis was amazed that she was able to do something like that so effortlessly, he spent months try to uncover that secret and she could do it effortlessly.

"How the hell did you do that, I have had my sphere for months and I can't even do that!"

"You think that's cool, I'm about to make things hot!" the woman said smiling as the beast got off the ground.

It roared at the two and begun to charge at them as she lifted her sword skyward, the blade turned orange, then red, then white. She shoved the blade into the ground and from the swords hilt, a diamond pattern appeared on the ground, and as the beast passed into the pattern the concert turned molten red. The beast began to roar in pain as their paws began to burn and eventually fall into the boiling rock, the beast howled in pain as their bodies started to become one with the molten rock. Some died from the pain as others tried to escape the molten lake. The woman removed her sword from the ground and her blade began to shoot out sparks of electricity. She swung her sword horizontally towards the tar, as lighting swung down into the tar and traveled towards the beasts, electrifying them, and eventually killing them. What was left of their bodies fell into the molten rock as their fur beings to burn away along with their skin. The serpents in the sky saw what she had done and immediately began to dive towards her. She looks into the sky, takes her blade, and points it towards them. In a second her blade turns to dust and forms small spikes, and fires like a buttle towards the enemy. The serpents begin to fall to the ground as the spikes penetrate the bodies, ripping them to shreds. It was only for a moment, but the serpents seemed to know they couldn't get near her. After she was done, the spikes returned to her and reformed her katana, she just stared at them with a look of fear. The remaining serpents and beasts began to panic at the sight of her and fled to the west. Everyone was startled by their swift retreat but was overjoyed that they managed to win and began to cheer.

Davis and the woman stood in the parking lot hearing the people on the roof and near the front entrance began to cheer as Davis said, "Thanks for the help."

The woman chuckled to herself and said, "I still have to look out for you even when you're an adult and the leader of a society, huh?"

"Well, you always have, after all it is you job.... Alex" said Davis smiling.

Alex laughed and said, "I demand a rise, I don't get paid enough to keep saving your ass."

Davis was overjoyed to see his sister and had so many questions about where she had been and what happened to her, but something came over him. He didn't know what he was feeling, but it almost felt something evil was nearby and coming in fast. He looked behind his sister and just like on the first day he saw that monkey like shadow again. He turned his head skyward and saw a four-armed alien, drawing out a small orange dagger. It landed right behind Alex and began to make its thrust movement, it was moments away from killing her. Without thinking, Davis shoved Alex out of the way as it thrusts its blade toward her. As she was moved way Davis opened his hand to reveal its palm and the blade sank into hand.

His own blood began to drip heavily from his wound as the blade piece all the way through and squirted blood onto his arm. Even though there was a blade in his hand he still stood his ground. The adrenaline helped ease the pain, but he knew it wasn't going to last long. What truly caught his eye as he stared at his hand was the blade, it's no longer orange, but looked like it original silverly look. Alex was on the ground when she saw she was about to die, but her fear turned into rage. She took her katana and it turned white, as she sliced it down at the four-armed alien she yelled, "GET THE HELL AWAY FROM HIM!!!"

It quickly removed the blade from Davis hand and jumped backwards over the molten rock as her blade came down, releasing another wave of heat. The wave hit a nearby store, it exploded with flames and turned into a bile of melted rock and metal. Davis fell to the ground clasping his left hand in pain as the adrenaline wore off, desperately trying to keep the blood from leaking onto the ground. Alex got in front of her brother to shield him as she asked in a worried voice, "Davis, are you alright?!"

"I have a hole in my hand, what do you think?"

Alex wanted to help her brother at that moment, but she was so enraged at what that creature did she became blind to it. She would not allow someone, or anything, hurt her brother and in the heat of the moment she created a gut of hot air and used it to make an updraft. The heated wind swirled around the tar like a twister, raised up from the ground like spiraled pillars and headed straight towards the alien. Davis was amazed as he saw what his sister could do with only three months of wielding her sphere. The alien itself didn't move as the molten rock flew at it, it seemed victory was at hand. But it was thwarted as it was just a few feet away it flung its left arm towards the side, in that moment the tar turned from its boiling state back into its black solid mass. The siblings were stunned by what it just did, it somehow managed to remove all the heat and energy that was inside the tar. Alex wanted to give chase to the alien and finish this battle before it got away. But she could hear her brother wincing in pain from his hand. In that moment her rage dissipated, as she turned around becoming more concerned about her brother. She saw the blood pour out of his wound as he started to lose his grip on it. She quickly grabbed Davis's arm and rushed him back to the front of the mall, as some people looked down from the roof tops wondering if they both were okay. Alex nearly made the corner when their spheres turned back and floated around them as she turned back to see that the alien was already gone, it looked like it had fled, at least for now. As they broached the front doors of the mall the beast and serpents that survived the slaughter had retreated and began to flee into the west as the sun began to fall.

Inside people from the trucks rushed in with Alex and Davis, getting away from the outside world, relaxing and knowing the day was won. Alex rushed Davis to the medical department as the caravan was being comforted by the guards and peacekeepers with a few medical staff on hand. It seemed that no one had been hurt or lost in the fight, but the emotions and terrifying memoires of this day would haunt everyone. Pushing and shoving through the crowds of people she found her way to the medical department. Emily happened to run into the two and saw Davis's hand, her face turned white.

"Davis what happened to your hand?!"

"An alien stabbed his hand as he pushed me aside to save my life." Alex explained.

As the two were talking Davis focused on his hand, squeezing his wrist to stop his blood from falling, yet he began to feel his hand become less painful it almost seemed like it was asleep. Emily grabbed Davis and plopped him down onto a chair and began to look at his wounded hand. As she carefully examined his hand, she saw something that had thrown her off. The wound started to shrink down in size as tissue, muscle, and bone started to reassemble themselves.

"What the hell?"

"What is it?" asked Davis.

"Your wound is healing at an accelerated rate!"

Davis was just as surprised as his sister and Emily about this and it didn't make any sense. These creatures were kidnapping humans not trying to heal them, it made Davis ask, "This doesn't make sense, why are they now doing this?"

"Intelligence is your department not mine, maybe you had some experience like this before?"

Davis thought for a moment and remembered the mucus from this first day, but it didn't seem like it was on the blade, he felt like there was another form of healing, something he didn't know about. Once his wound was closed, he clenched his fist, but no pain came from it, it seemed he was in the clear, but before he did anything Emily wanted to check his hand after it was clean to see if there were any scars or anything out of the ordinary. He had no reason to refuse her request, so he washed his hands to find that it was healing and there was a long scare on both sides of his hand, but for some reason it was indigo colored.

Alex and Emily were grateful for his hands' recovery but didn't know how to react to it or the scar's color. They both distanced themselves from Davis and talked privately about this situation. As Davis waited for them to stop talking something kept eating at him. He wondered why did it try to kill Alex? Was it after her weapon? If it was, it didn't make sense. If it were after the sphere then would it have attacked both to get them both, and if his sister were so powerful then why make the attempt to steal from her?

The only conclusion that made sense was that it was maybe after something else, something she had, something that not even she knew about, but even if it was why try and kill her? There were far too many questions and things were just getting stranger with these aliens. Davis wanted to tell her about his thought on the subject, but he couldn't bring himself to do it. There was a time and a place for everything but after today everyone just wanted to rest up and be at peace at least for a while. When they came back Alex said, "Okay, listen carefully, we don't know what that thing did to you so for now let's keep a glove on it as not to cause a panic."

"I have no argument with that."

"You don't get a choice!" said Emily scolding him.

A black leather glove was placed on his left hand as Alex laid down on the medical bed, resting her body from her long journey. Amelia, Elliott, and their daughter found their way to the medical department and saw him sitting in a chair, waiting for Emily to give him the "all clear." It only took Amelia a moment to scold him for being reckless and irresponsible. Amelia even asked him with tears in her eyes, "What would have happened if you died?"

Davis looked past her and said, "Then I guess you be stuck with her."

Amelia turned to find Alex laying on one of the beds, waving with a smile as she says, "I'm your nightmare, both in your sleep and in reality."

Amelia was stunned to see her older sister alive and began to feel lightheaded. Alex got up from her bed and helped Amelia onto it as Emily came in with some pain medication. Davis was thrilled at the fact that some of their family was reunited, but he couldn't tell Amelia what had happened to his hand, even though Davis knew she would be furious when she found out.

Later that night after everything had settled down again, the newcomers became comfortable with their new surroundings as Akio and Jackie explained the rundown of the place. Davis was back in his office, wanting to lay down, and rest after the hell he just went through. But as he was about to lay down, he noticed on his desk a note from Miller. He picked it up and read it. "I put the sphere back in your safe, but I need to let you know when I did your email notification went off. I don't know who's out there trying to contact you, but you might need to read it!"

After he read the message Davis immediately got on his computer, he checked his email and saw not one but two new messages, both from his brother Jacob. "Bro, I am sorry that I haven't been able to contact you, but the captain and some generals are saying that we are no longer allowed to communicate with people from the mainland, and they say the reason why is because of the picture I sent you. They think it's some sort of communication that might be able to intercept ours. Whatever it is, you better figure it out fast, it sounds like they might be preparing for the worst!" The next email showed a satellite image of a massive structure located in some of the largest deserts in the world, and America's was in the Great Basin Desert, west of their current position. Davis needed to know more about this structure, and what exactly they were doing there, though he had a fairly good idea of what it was. But two things were known certain to Davis. The first was now he knew why the enemy kept going west and the second was after what had just happened there was no way that anyone would just casually go towards the enemy.

He just couldn't believe it, he didn't even get a moment to rest before this information bombed on him. He racked his brain to figure out what to do, everyone one was exhausted from the fight and weren't fit to travel, furthermore with all the ammo they just lost they wouldn't be able to hold off an attack on the road, whatever was left had to be reserved for the people that was left behind. He also knew it would be lunacy to go into another battle against something that big and unknown. Davis looked at his sphere and saw his own reflection in it, he knew so little about his sphere and its abilities, but regardless it was the best weapon they had even if it wasn't fully understood. His head started pounding from the amount of stress he was enduring. All this time he wondered and questioned everything that was happening, being so patient and desperately trying to keep everyone's hope alive that things would go back to before. But at this point he was fed up. He was done with all the running around and waiting for help when it clearly wasn't coming. He was fed up with all the cryptic nonsense from the aliens and forcing away their pets.

"No more waiting!" Davis said to himself. "I think it's time I have a little talk with those creatures."

There was no way that Davis was going all the way to the Great Basin Desert, it was too far, and without knowing what it was out there, he wasn't going to risk it. He decided to look for the one that stopped him. He did pray that that thing was still around nearby. He gathered a few supplies and started to head out to the front door, but then as he turned the corner, he found his path blocked by his sister Alex with her katana at her side saying, "What are you doing?"

CHAPTER 8

The blood of the guilty.

Alex stood in his path wanting an answer for his sudden exit "Why are you leaving in the middle of the night after a huge battle?"

Davis looked at his sister with a scornful look, but in his heart, he knew she was worried about him, so he explained "I'm going to go look for the bastard or bitch that stabbed my hand!"

"You're not going out tonight, we don't even know what that thing did to your hand!"

"I have to Alex! I just got a new message from our little brother a few minutes ago about a massive structure in the Basin Desert and I'm sick to death of all the cryptic mind game bullshit! I need answers and going to get them one way or the other!"

Alex seemed shocked to hear Jacob was still alive and so she said calmly without screaming with joy, "I'm glad our brother is alive, but that's no excuse to leave like this, bedsides if you want answers, I can help with that."

"What do you mean by that?"

"Where do you think I have been for the last few months! You're not the only one with a scientific mind in our family you know."

"So, what have you learned?"

"That's a discussion we can have if you go to your office."

Davis was angry at his sister for stopping him, however it wouldn't be the first time she had done this, she always seemed to be the one to calm him down, to help him think rationally rather than rashly, and he did value her opinion above all others. Even when he was younger, she was able to help him be more logical but still have his strong emotions in perfect balance and in some cases complement one another. She herself flowed her own ideology for logic and emotion but she wasn't as good as her brother, Davis. He did as she asked and the two walked back to his office, quietly. When both got comfortable, Alex began to explain herself, where she had been, her misadventures with some of the aliens and humans, but most of all a structure out in the Great Basin Desert.

"So, you have seen the structure out there!"

"That's why I came back. Before I left, I heard you were leading in the intelligence department at the superstore, and when I noticed all the aliens were gone, I remembered they flew west, so I followed my instincts and tailed them for a few months. After weeks, I found myself near Salt Lake City and over the mountain I saw the sky lit up. It was almost like night never set in the desert, even at midnight. I climbed over the mountain and that's when I saw it, I didn't have a camera at the time but from what I saw through my binoculars, it's a massive strong hold, maybe a prison, and on its roof, I could see some laboratories."

"Laboratories?" Davis said, concerning.

"Yes, I couldn't see too well, even with the binoculars, but it looked like there were these hemispheres on the top of the roof made from glass, I think. I saw them looking over a human body, and they began to scan it. Then they sent the body away and brought in another, honestly, I think they were looking for something specific."

"Well, that's disturbing, but on the plus side, we now know that everyone is still alive, sort of, and I now know that the information I was given is accurate."

"What information?"

Davis answered her question thoroughly, telling her everything he had seen, heard, and done. He even showed her the small sphere that the alien had given him, but it seemed that she wasn't that surprised by it. Davis could only surmise that his sister's reaction was pitiful because of all the things she had seen before. At this point nothing really surprised her about the aliens anymore. But then again, he knew his sister wasn't the type to get surprised too easily, especially after all the hell she went through in her life.

Alex rose out of her chair and said, "I know you want answers and for all of this to end, but you can't go out there blinded by rage, you know what happens to you when you do, besides which you may be able to summon whatever you want with that sphere of yours, but you can't energize it yet. If you left now there would be no chance of you ending this and more so, brute force isn't going to solve this nor will allowing your emotions to get the better of you."

"I know," said Davis quietly.

As Alex left his department she said, "Don't worry, Bubba, well figure this out, but for now, let's get you stronger. Tomorrow I will start to teach you how to energize your sword, and more importantly how to release it on command."

The following days became calm for the survivors of Wichita, the beasts and serpents were once again nowhere to be seen. Davis told the council about the orb and the strange message, and Alex did as she said and began to train Davis not just with morphing his weapon more quickly, but even showing him how to energize his weapons. She explained to him her theory, she believed whatever the spheres were made from were microscopic, allowing them to manipulate the matter that surrounded them, allowing them to put anything in any state of matter. For her "heat wave" she causes the plasma and air that surrounding the blade to intensify, to the point where it could incinerate anything in its path; in short, she creates a low-powered solar wind from her sword. However, the weapons can only be charged by emotions. She didn't know how it did, so but she did admit afterword's, the anger or stress had vanished afterwards, like she never had it.

After she explained her theory, Davis remembered the stadium he destroyed on the first day, the anger he felt, and fear that coursed through his body, that day. But what he didn't understand was why it never worked afterwards, he had tried to recreate the situation over and over with no results. So, he asked Alex what he was doing wrong.

"Think it through Davis, if you need a memory to create a weapon, then you need an emotion to charge it, in short, the weapon can only charge if you give it your emotion! I still don't fully understand it, but I believe the material becomes an extension of our bodies and when our brains realize chemicals, it reacts to it."

"It can sense it!"

"I believe so. Since this all started, have you ever used its ability without knowing?"

"On every first day I got so angry and scared when I was about to be pounced on by some beasts that I blasted them and the baseball stadium by accident."

"You did that? Damn Davis, that a little over kill isn't it?"

"Said the woman who made a giant lake of molten rock and incinerated giant beasts."

"Okay… you got me there. But besides that, you have done it before, the only issue you had was to aim it in one direction. When you fired it, you didn't give it any real direction other than forward, so it resealed its energy in all directions in front of you. With these weapons, you must be precise with direction. When using my 'heat wave,' I use the command straight forward in an arch strike. The blade creates the wave I want, I execute the motion, and on the same command I tell it when to let go of the energy."

Davis finally started to understand his sphere's abilities and managed to get the waves of energy his sister made and force he had made on that first day. It wasn't as good as his sisters, but it was strong enough to lead aid when it was necessary. Things seemed to be fine but eventually someone began to stir up trouble. A week and a half later a Christian priest with a caravan began to have service in the morning before breakfast, nobody minds, and it was uplifting to hear someone try to bring confidence in the masses. Even Davis would attend occasionally, to hear what this priest had to say, but always stayed out of sight as to not intervene or have them panic, a council member near them might cause them to feel intimidated. However, looks can be deceiving, one day the priest began to preach people to repent for their sins and that hell awaits all who dare not believe, and it did not stop, it only got worse. He began scaring the masses and intimidating them for not repenting for what they had done in life.

It wasn't that shocking that the priest was doing this, many people had seen men and women like this before the invasion, but something about this priest began to make Davis warry of his action and what he said. The council began to keep a close eye on the priest and his followers, making sure that they didn't do anything that could disturb the peace, but their main priority was finding out about the sphere. One day the priest and his followers had a meeting with the council about making Christianity the main religion of their society and mandatory services, but the council refused to pass a rule like that.

"America was founded on the principles of freedom, though America has fallen, that doesn't mean the teachings are gone. We all thought the value of being free and had the right to choose who we are. You may be whatever you wish but we will not pass any rule that forces people to think your way." said Davis.

Once that was said the priest demanded that the council stand down for their heresy. But all he really did was make the council laugh. The priest and his followers were laughed out of the court room that day, and the real hell began to take hold. It was one thing to fight against the aliens, but now after all this time, the priest started a war with humanity. He started preaching every morning, noon, and night, trying desperately to gain more followers to worm his way into power. But this matter to the council was trivial at best and a waste of time. They knew the priest would not get enough followers to overthrow them and even if he did, Alex and Davis could immediately stop anything that threatened the whole mall. But what they didn't account for was his malice.

In the mid of April, on a warm morning everyone in the mall was begging to work, Davis rose from his bed and began to look at his notes about the sphere and any clue he might have missed, but then he smelt smoke and people screaming, as Akio crashed into his department.

"Akio, what's going on?"

"It's that fucking cult! They set fire to the peacekeepers department!"

"WHAT?!" said Davis as he leapt over his table rushing out of his department.

Even from where he was, he could see the smoke rising quickly from the ground level as he shoved his way through the crowds of people running away from the fire. Looking over the catwalk he saw the cult throwing Molotov's into the store as some peacekeepers tried to put out the fires with their fire extinguishers. The cult was screaming and yelling verses of their religion as they began to assault the peacekeepers.

Davis yelled out to the cult "HAVE YOU ALL LOST YOUR MINDS!"

But as his voice echoed out no one in the cult could hear him. Then in the far back of the crowd he saw the priest, smiling at the destruction. Davis ran down the stairs and approached him as he formed his sword yelling out "YOU THINK THIS IS FUNNY, YOU EVIL FUCK?"

"I'm smiling because I did what was right." he said calmly.

"WHATS, RIGHT?! THE COUNCIL AND I HAVE SPENT MONTHS FIGHTING EVERY SECOND TO STOP NOT JUST THE ALIENS BUT PEOPLE LIKE YOU. YOU DONT GIVE A DAMN ABOUT HUMANITY AS LONG AS YOU ARE IN CONRTOL." screamed Davis as he points his sword at the priest.

"I did what was best for God's children."

"CUT THE CRAP! WE BOTH KNOW YOU'RE JUST TAKING ADVANTAGE PEOPLE'S FEAR, GIVING THEM FALSE HOPE!"

"It matters not what you do to me, I have already done God's work and you can't change anything about it, the blood of the sinners will stain the floor."

"I couldn't agree more!" said Davis as he began to walk towards him.

Some of his cult saw Davis approaching him and began to surround him, trying to block his path. "You see god is protecting-" said the priest before Davis beat the life out of the people blocking his path.

"Some of you I spent months trying to protect, sheltering you, feeding you, giving you a reason to live on in this hell, and you all gave it up for a coward who can't even fight his own battles without having puppets to control."

The priest stood in fear seeing Davis beating up his cult members as he drew closer to him. The priest started to walk backwards towards the crowd, seeing Davis's rage in his eyes stare into his own. The priest then fell to the floor, clawing backwards towards his followers, as he saw the reflection of the fire in Davis's eyes. He started to call for his people to help him. But their own blindness made him invisible to them.

"Well look at that, you made them so angry that they can't even hear your cries for help, just like the people you burn alive!"

The priest tried to get his feet to move, he started punching his legs to try to make them move, but it was like his body was placed in cement, and Davis stood right in front of him with his blade pointed at him. The priest sat on the floor as Davis winked at him and said, "Tell Lou I said 'hi.'" Then with a quick motion he spun around and with a single stroke, decapitated the priest. His head fell to the floor along with his body and his blood began to pour out on the ground. The blood pooled around Davis's shoes as his sword dripped with his blood. Then from the crowd of cultists one started to scream in fear as everyone turned around to see what had happened. The blood began to pool around some of their feet to and started gauging, shaking, and some even fell to their knees.

"The council and I took you all in because we saw you needed hope, and how did you repay us? By betraying us and our families, just so you could get what you wanted, even if it meant the end of humans in the process. No one can look away at what you all have done, you are all going to be punished!"

The crowds of people tried to disburse, but the security department came rushing in with the medical department and surrounded them, taking them in one by one. Some of the people in the department knew the followers, and they couldn't even look them in the eye. Just knowing what they had done was too painful for them, the people they grew up with, their families had betrayed them and everyone. War can happen, but it never should be the first thing people run to when things aren't going great or trying to divide themselves because they feel like they were cheated. There is always another way to stop evil, but if it comes to it, then you must stay yourself for what you need to do to survive, but if you do it out of greed or lust, then you have betrayed not only humanity, but yourself, and that unfortunately is what these people did when they followed the priest's lust for power.

The cult was gathered up, the fire was put out, and the injured or dead were taken away to be treated for and incinerated to prevent the spread of illness. Emily stays in her department working around the clock with her people, taking care of the injured as the rest of the council gathered in their chamber trying to discuss what they needed to do with the traitors. However, their discussion was almost like a brawl.

"What the fuck are we going to do to these people?" screamed Jackie.

"There is no way they can stay here anymore, they're too dangerous to be around."

"Well, if the security department had done their job in the first place, none of this would have happened!" stated Akio.

"How the hell were we supposed to know that we had a maniac in our midst, and he was going to attack our base like that?" yelled John.

"How the hell did they even get Molotov's, Matthew?" asked Julian.

"Hey, I take and distribute materials, not make weapons, that's Jackie's department!"

"Don't look at me, all the ingredients to make Molotov's are under lock and key. Besides which Julian you head of the gathers department, some of those people in that cult worked in your section."

"Almost everyone in that cult worked in all of our sections except Davis's!" said Miller.

"They planned this out from the beginning, this way if they were told no then they could exact their revenge."

"Look it doesn't matter at this point how it happened, we need to focus on now." Davis said concerned as he tried to end their fight with each other. "What are we going to do?"

"We need to lay down striker rules and show are authority; we will not allow this type of behavior to go unpunished."

"That's not going to work." said Alex walking into the chamber.

"What are you doing here?" asked Julian.

"I am here to give you my input. I know what has happened is horrible but if you start to make striker rules and show off your authority then you will only be making more trouble. Only the guilty should be punished, not the innocent. If you all do this, then they will start to loss hope and if that happens, they won't turn to you for help."

"I'm sorry but you have only been here a few weeks and no nothing about the strife we have been through. We have been dealing with problems with people being unhappy for the last few months, you have been out there living however you want, so your voice isn't needed." said Julian.

"Excuses me!" yelled Alex.

Everyone in the chamber started yelling and screaming at each other trying to get a word in with one another until Davis yelled out, "EVERYONE SHUT THE HELL UP!" The council grew silent as they saw Davis staring at them with cold dead eyes as he continued, "Fighting with each other isn't going to solve this one. Look I am not going to lie, they made their choice, but don't forget it was the priest who started it. He found weaker personalities and exploited them, only when he faced me did he realizes how weak he was. But nevertheless, they still chose to take his side, but in this world, we can't be on any side other than humanity's. So, what are we going to do with these people?"

"Well, there's no doubt they need to be punished for what they have done, the question is what punishment would fit their crime?" asked Akio.

"I'm not sure, it was one thing getting rid of entitled jackasses, but murderers, I don't know." said Davis sighing heavily.

"Why don't we take some time to think and reflect on this, let's meet back up here in fifteen minutes with some ideas."

"Agreed but let's all agree one other thing whatever the punishment is, has to be a clear message to all of them but not an insult to impaired families." said Akio.

Everyone did agree with Akio and left for a short recess to relax from their screaming and yelling. Davis looked over the catwalk to where the peacekeeper department once stood and rubbed his forehead as he headed back to his department. Alex joined him and began to rub his back, trying to get him to relax as Akio walked in.

"So have you made up your mind yet?" said Akio almost emotionless.

"I just got back in my department, Akio; I need to think." said Davis.

"There is nothing to think about, they put us all in grave danger and hurt people, they can't walk away from this."

"Akio, I know you're upset because of what happened, but please this is not the time to seek revenge."

"Revenge? You think I want revenge? I want them to pay because they put all of us in danger, not because it was my department."

"Akio you can lie to yourself and everyone else, but not me. I have known you far too long, and I know you do not let something like this side. The last time someone pissed you off you nearly chopped their head hands off when you found out it was personal."

"That was a completely different situation, Davis."

"No, it's not, you once again feel threatened, and you want to make sure they can't do it again. We cannot spill anymore blood."

Akio faced away from Davis as Alex said, "Wait so did you come here to try and sway my brother into killing more people? Are you insane?"

"Easy for to say, it wasn't your people who were attacked!"

"So, this is about you! How selfish are you?"

Akio shuddered for a moment as she looked away from the two siblings as Davis said "Enough, both of you."

"No, Davis, she has no right to say this was an assault only aimed at her, when this was an assault on everyone in the council and everyone here." yelled Alex.

"I understand that, but put yourself in her position, it was her department that was attacked, it was her friends that are in critical condition, how do you think she was going to react? Now yes, this was an assault on all of us, but this is far more painful for her, I mean if it were my department, you know full well, I would be furious too." said Davis unrestingly.

Alex looked to Akio kind of feeling bad that she had yelled at her, but she said nothing as she looked to the siblings with tears in her eyes. In all the time Davis had known Akio, she had never shed tears in front of anyone, it truly showed him that she was devastated. The minutes that passed felt like time had slowed down, and the air felt like everyone had just inhaled cement as no one said anything else. After a ten long minutes, Amelia came rushing in with tears in her eyes. Akio immediately went to her and tried to get her to calm down and talk to her.

"Amelia, what's wrong?" asked Akio.

With tears in Amelia eyes and her stuttering voice she said "Elliot….and Diamond… they were…in your department…when the fire started."

Davis and Alex's blood ran cold as they over herd the news, Alex and Akio ran to see if they could find Elliot and Diamond as Davis compilated what they needed to do with the people, even though he was desperately trying to hold back his anger and tears.

"Well?" asked Amelia.

"Well, what?" asked Davis.

"Aren't you going to help them look?" yelled Amelia.

"No, I can't right now, Kitten, I still need to figure…" said Davis before Amelia shouted "You can't right now? How can you even say that? Your niece and brother-in-law could be dead, and you say you 'can't right now,' what type of jackass says that?"

Davis sat down at his desk, placing his hand on his forehead, and said, "I can't look right now because I am trying to find a way to keep everything together. We are dangerously close to having everything we worked hard for fall apart. This place and everyone in it.... may no longer be safe."

"Davis you can take a minute to look for your family, screw everyone else." yelled Amelia.

Davis rose from his seat quickly and kidded the chair aside. He staired deep into his sister's eyes and yelled "Don't you ever say those words again!", Amelia was startled by her brother's tone of voice and began to shake as he continued to yell. "We have twenty-three in custody, God knows how many dead people we have right now or who are dying on those beds, and now two missing. Do you really think I have time to solve everything in thirty seconds! I am doing the best I can and you harping at me isn't going to solve shit! So back off, I will help you find them later, but right now I can't!" Amelia became silent after he was done yelling at her, but she didn't seem upset in his eyes, he only saw fear. She lifted her hand up as she trembled trying to get the words from her mind to come out of her mouth, but all she could do was mumble. Then she pointed at his desk, Davis looked down, and saw his sword sitting on his desk, still covered in blood.

Amelia managed to get out one question from her mouth as she stood in front of him shaking "Did...did you kill someone?"

Davis wanted to explain what had happened to his sister, but he saw that she looked like she was on the verge of tears. He wanted to lie to her so she wouldn't run, but he stopped himself. He lied about his injured had and the small sphere to his sister because he was afraid, she wouldn't understand why he kept lying to her. However, he was caught red handed, literally, and so he said, "I decapitated the lunatic priest."

Davis dematerialized his sword and told Amelia that he was sorry for scaring her, but right now everyone needed help and he could not stop for one person, even though it was crushing his soul. Not knowing whether his own family was okay terrified him, but he couldn't stop to check when so many others were suffering too. Amelia looked disappointed at Davis, she knew he had a lot on his plate, but the fact that he was refusing to try and find his family made her hate him.

"I don't know who you are any more, Davis. The brother I grew up with would never turn his back on people or even kill them. You clearly have shown that your power is more important to you than us!"

Davis's anger dissipated as he became confused at what she had just she had just said "I'm not choosing..." but before he could complete his sentence Amelia spoke up, "From now on I no longer know you, from now, I disown you!"

Amelia turned and left his department as Adalard came in, seeing Amelia walk away, and Davis falling back into his seat. "Is everything okay?" asked Adalard.

Davis felt his heart crush into dust as she said that, but he calmed his heart and said, "It's nothing to worry about."

"Okay? Do you want to talk about that or-?"

"No, why are you here, Adalard?" snapped Davis.

"Whoa, no need to be hostile, we don't have to talk about that. I just want to tell you the guards and my department are cleaning up the mess those idiots made, and they did remove the priest's body so no one else would see it." said Adalard, but even with him talking Davis's mind was somewhere else. He was thinking about his little sister coming to him asking for help when it came to making friends or just playing around but those days seemed like a dream now. After a few moments he asked, "How are you holding up?"

"I'm fairly sure you already know how I am," said Davis in apathy.

Before Adalard could speak Davis asked, "Could you send some of the reaming peacekeepers into the lower stock rooms to see if my brother-in-law and my niece might have fled there when the fire started?"

Adalard looked puzzled and asked, "I thought my department had the only keys."

"You did, but I had found one of those key duplicating machines at the super store on one of my runs, so I made a copy and gave it to him for emergencies, if we were ever overrun by the aliens or other humans, they had a way out," said Davis as began to head out.

"You know the rules we made said that no one, not even a council member, has any right to interfere with any of the departments." said Adalard with a stern look.

"I know," said Davis as he passed him.

Adalard stood there for a moment and then he smiled and turned to walk with Davis back to the council's sanctum. As they were walking Adalard said, "No matter what your sister said, know that she still loves you, even though it doesn't seem like it."

"Thanks, Adalard, but this situation is something that can't be fixed so easy." said Davis as they arrived at the sanctum.

Davis said nothing as their time was up and headed back into the chamber. Once inside they found the other council members sitting in their chairs as Adalard asked one of the guards to look in the lower floors, while Davis made his way to his seat. Once they were seated, they picked up where they left off without Akio or Alex in attendance. Emily had finally managed to get to the chamber and explain the severity of the situation in the medical department.

She stood before all the council members and said, "I'm not going to lie to you all or sugar coat this. There were seventeen people in the peacekeepers department, two are deceased, the other fifteen are in critical condition, they are suffering from second-and third-degree burns. Even with all our resources we won't be able to save all of them. Some will die from the pain, others from infection, and the ones that do survive will spend years recovering and the rest of their lives unable to move without feeling pain."

After hearing all this the council came to an agreement and believed they all had a fitting punishment. The traitors would be sent off like the three guards, leave them in the middle of nowhere, let them survive on their own without their families, and not let them have the chance to say good-bye. Everyone in the council agreed and decided to do it in that night. Under the cover of the moonless night, they gathered guards and what was left of the peacekeepers and had them put groups of four at random into cars with their heads covered and sent them off.

They had over two hundred people in that mall and now they were down to one-hundred and eighty, all because a few couldn't be happy with what they had and allowed themselves to be easily manipulated by a man who lusted for more. After three hours one of the guards radioed Davis and told him that one of the women that was sent off was begging to be let back in, to be with her child, and that they would never step out of line again. However, no matter how much she begged Davis refused to let her come back. She didn't step out of line, she crossed it. When she joined that flock and allowed herself to be a killer, she put everyone in danger including her own child, and that made her too dangerous. Though Davis knew he had no idea how painful it was to lose a child, Davis couldn't allow the child to be near anyone like that. Davis told them to leave her in the darkness, and hopefully one day when this is all over, she can find her child again.

Hours had passed and the warm colors of the dawn began to light up the sky as the guards came back. They all exited from their cars and one by one entered the mall, looking defeated and tired. Davis could tell they were emotionally distraught over this decision but said nothing. When everyone was inside the one that radioed came up to Davis saying, "When we drove off, we could hear her screaming and yelling at us come back, it had echoed for miles."

Davis told him without hesitation or emotion, "They betrayed all of us they knew what they were giving up. I can understand her pain, but we can't allow such evil to enter these walls again. This time we were lucky, but next time it might not be." Davis felt the guard put his hand on his should and patted it as he stared off into the sunrise. Once everyone was inside Davis had everyone sit down in the mall sit down for an announcement even though a part of him didn't want to.

As the crowd of people gathered, Davis and the council headed up to the second floor and looked out to everyone. Everyone became silent on their own as they saw Davis looking down at them as he clears his throat. "I wish you all a good morning, but I'm afraid that's not possible right now. As some of you already know we had an…incident yesterday which resulted in the deaths of three people and fifteen injured. The people who are responsible for this have been banished from this place, indefinitely. Now I know many of you had a relationship with these people and you cared for them. I know that many of you are furious at us for sending them away instead of killing them but understand we didn't take any pleasure in doing this. It broke our hearts to send them away and destroy families. However, we will not allow this to happen again!

Anyone who wants to volunteer and help in the medical department or peacekeepers are more than welcome to train under Emily or Akio. We will maintain order but not with an iron fist, we will always have time to hear about ideas that can help this place and your concerns, but don't hold back on them."

After the announcement, they all had the people take time to reflect but things after that became difficult. Davis didn't need glasses to see the people were still far too intimidated or they just didn't want his of any of the council members help. It was easier to complain about what made them unhappy then rather than helping to fix the problems. This type of false philosophy was what made Davis's blood boil. They all offered a chance to make things better, but all they did was just wallow in regret and anger.

Yet a few days later Davis's rage turned into joy as Elite and Diamond were found in the lower levels unharmed. But then soon after he began to hear Amelia along with many others began to speak about the possibility of leaving and going somewhere else, some place better. Davis was devastated by this news, he couldn't believe what he was hearing, after everything they did for them, all the strife they put up with and the months of fighting each other to find the balance, and creating a home in a world at war, these people were just going to leave. In his mind he thought to himself, "Was this the extent of humanity's ability, to just run away. They stood up against a foe not of their world, pushed them back, and saved countless strangers, but now, they just wanted to run. They all fought together and survived together, now because of one incident they were going to just give?"

Davis could not accept that as he stormed to the living quarters and entered Amelia's living area. "What the hell is wrong with you?! I heard that you're planning to leave this place!" Davis yelled.

"This place isn't for us and after what that man did, after what you did, how can you expect anyone to stay!" said Amelia.

"I'm not asking you to stay for yourself, I'm asking you for Diamond!"

"Davis, it's our responsibility to look after her, and right now she needs to be away from this place and someone so dangerous!"

Davis was shocked to hear their words as he said, "I'm dangerous?! All I have ever done is try to keep this place and our people safe. If it wasn't for me or the council taking charge, then you all would be out there dying. We open this place to protect the innocent and keep humanity going. If you all begin to leave this place, this sanctuary, possibly the last place of humanity to make their stand then we all have failed!"

Amelia scoffed at his remark and told him that, "You should have thought of that before choosing power."

The moment she said that Davis snapped, he had enough. All he had ever tried to do was the right thing and save as many as he could. But the constant blaming and hurtful things that had been said were too much even for him. His eyes felt like they were lit with fire as he yelled back, "You know what, fine, you want to risk your lives, you want to gamble Diamond's life, then go. We offered you peace, hope, and a chance to live, and you're willingly turning it away, because you're not contempt with what we offered!"

"You clearly showed us that power was more important to you than us!" yelled Amelia back as she picked up Diamond as she began to cry.

"Really, because I was the one who saved Elliot and Diamond!"

"What are you...." said Amelia before Davis cut her off, "I gave Elliot a key to the lower levels for safety just in case if we ever got overrun with the alien's pets. So, all of you could escape unharmed and out of danger. I went against our own rules to make sure that you all were safe. But no matter how much I sacrifice, I am still always the villain, that's my role in your eyes. Hell, that's my role in everyone's!"

The two remained silent as Diamond continued to cry, Davis could see that they were frightened by him and his rage, but he didn't care, he was done with all the hate for doing what was right. Once he was done, he turned around in disgust at them and he left the room with his blood still boiling as Alex came around the corner, "Hey Davis, you..." But before she could finish her sentence Davis pushed her aside hard and continued to walk away.

Once in his room he lied face up trying to calm down and think of what he needed to do next as Jackie came into the room. Normally Jackie kept an eye on everyone when things got desperate, but this time it was depression. Jackie leaned on his desk and waited for Davis to notice her, but all he did was stare at the ceiling, concentrating on his breathing, trying to relax.

"You know it would have been better if you had just told those two to take your place for a day," said Jackie.

"You know you're right, I should have, but I couldn't put them under that type of stress, especially since they have a kid." replied Davis.

Jackie sighed and said, "I know how it feels to be under appreciated when it comes to family and the masses."

"Everyone feels it, Jackie, it's just people like me are willing to acknowledge it and do something about it."

"Davis, you know it's far more complicated than that, I am sure your sister and brother did not mean it." said Jackie in a stern voice.

"You don't understand Jackie, before all of this I was always the bubbly type of guy who always tried to find peace in battle, but now, it's like if I try to keep balance and order by making the hard choices, I'm labeled as a monster." said Davis while continuing to stare at the ceiling.

"Oh, I am well aware Davis, everyone on the council feels that way, no matter what we do it seems to never be enough, even though we are desperately trying to keep everyone together, no one cares about the hardships we have to take on day after day. But that doesn't mean what we do don't matter, it doesn't matter what they think because they are just going to make any excuse they can to get more." said Jackie.

"You know that's not entirely true, not everyone does it." said Davis.

"You're right all it takes is a few to start the fires then all hell breaks loose. Speaking of which Alex is coming?" said Jackie.

"Oh, great here we go!" said Davis, sitting up.

His sister slowly entered his room, but she instead of being angry she seemed understanding and calm. "I talked to Amelia and Elliot, there still upset but after a quick chat with them I managed to get them to stay, for now. But Bubba, you must help with a family issue like that; granted yes, it's hard but you have at least tried and make the effort."

"Alex, I love ya, but you know I can't plan or agree to something like that, no one on the council can. If they want to stay or go that's up to them, put they can't demand I sacrifice the lives of the many for a few." Davis said as he turned on his side, facing the wall.

Alex approached her brother, sat on the bed and said, "I know you can't, but put yourself in their shoes, they're hurting right now. Elliot had no idea if him and Diamond were going to get out of there alive or if they were last to survive the fire and Amelia had no idea if her husband and daughter were gone from this world or hurt badly. For the two of them this was a terrifying experience."

"Do you honestly think I don't know that? I can't even begin to fathom the fear they went through, and neither can you. You and I don't have children or a significant other so the pain we feel is nearly nothing. But it's not just their pain I must deal with, its everyone's. The people in this place, the families and friendships destroyed from one incident that might never be repaired, puts all of us in danger. I know family is important, but when trying to protect everyone I can't hold them higher than any other person." said Davis a little annoyed by Alex's statement.

Before Alex could say anything, Jackie jumped in, to stop the siblings from getting into an argument. "Alright you two quit while your head. You both make good arguments and you're both right about the situations of other people, too. But my advice for your family is to talk about it, get it all out in the open, and come to a new understanding with each other. We have all changed to survive in this world but that also means we need to find new common ground with each other."

Alex and Davis said nothing to each other, Davis knew Jackie was right, but he didn't know if his sister agreed with her. Alex rose from the bed and quietly left the room as Jackie followed behind. Left alone again, Davis kept staring at the wall, wondering, and praying Amelia would understand, but also know he still loved her and everything she had. The hum of the air conditioner was the only thing he heard in his department as he rose out of his bed. He never realized how quiet it really was until he was alone. He was so busy with trying to get everyone comfortable with each department he forgot to get help for his. In all the months of looking for the clues he needed, he never asked for help, and couldn't even remember the last time he wasn't fighting or taking a break from all the chaos.

Thinking back on it he remembered all the time when people came and asked if they could help with anything, only to be shown the door by him. He realized he was so caught up in trying to save humanity, he forgot to let them help him. Davis giggled to himself as he put his hand over his face, say, "I isolated myself for so long that I blocked out the world and the people who wanted to help."

"You do have a nasty habit of it, too." said John accompanied with Mathew and Adalard.

Davis removed his hand and asked, "What are you all doing here now?"

John raised a bottle and some shot glasses in his hands and said, "After all the hell we went through this week. Adalard figured you'd like a drink."

Davis smiled at their kind effort to cheer him up and said, "No thanks, besides I thought we all agreed to no drinking during the day?"

"It was, but after all the hell we decided to bend the rule a little, we're allowing one shot to ever adult in the morning a day for the rest of the week." said Mathew.

"We all know drinking your sorrows away won't solve the problems, but at least for a short time, we're allowing it, at least to help try and cope with what happened." said Adalard sitting down in a chair.

"Come on, Davis sit down with us have a drink." said John pouring the shoots for everyone as Mathew sat next to Adalard.

Davis got out of bed and was handed a shot glass as John continued to speak, "You won't become an alcoholic over one shot, Davis, just make sure if you do drink it's on your terms and not out of depression. Granted I'm kind of a hypocrite for giving advice to people to cope, but I'm not so sure about you, I think whether you drink it or not, you be fine."

Davis picked up the shot and moved it towards his mouth, but at the last second, he stopped and gave it to John. He turned away from him as he said, "You can have mine."

"Always the one who faces his problems head on, huh?" said Mathew nervously joking.

Davis quickly responded with a simple, "yes" while John asked, "Even if it slowly eats at you like a cancer?" All Davis said was, "yes" but with an upsetting tone.

"Okay enough of the gloom. Would you all like to talk about... well anything, we really haven't had the chance since this place was made." asked Adalard.

Davis was shocked by his words as he realized he was right, they hadn't just talked in a long time. But all Davis could do was just sit there in silence wondering what could he talk about? Most days he spent his time preparing meetings, researching, and explaining the ideology of how they did thing around there to newcomers. Yet in all the time he had been surrounded by people he never had a conversation that wasn't about work. But now, he didn't think it was relevant anymore with everyone in the world gone and them desperately trying to survive, it seemed pointless.

"What is there to talk about anymore, we have been so busy surviving, we haven't had a regular conversation." said Davis.

"Well, if you don't want to talk casually then maybe we can talk about that small sphere. Have you come up with any new ideas about where to find these cluses?" asked Mathew.

Davis winched at the question and said, "No, nothing, after months of searching for clues, we only found the one and there still two remaining." He got up from his desk and pulled it out of his safe and placed it onto the desk to show them.

"Davis?" said John concerned, "We all need to know, how bad is it right now?"

Davis looked at them with a blank expression and said, "We already know that they haven't been trying to kill people, they have been taking them, but honestly if we don't figure this out, humanity will fall."

The three, terrified at his response, took their shots. Everyone in that room began to believe that maybe the aliens were just toying with them, making them squirm before they came for them. But to Davis, it didn't make any sense, why give him a memory, and make him work to find the truth if it was so important.

Davis explained to them, "Look I don't know what these beings want, even with all my research I still don't have the answers I need to save our world. Maybe they are just toying with us or maybe this is a legitimate test to the see if we are capable to go the distance to find out the truth. No one on earth can tell you the what's in someone else's mind, whether they were from the same planet or the deepest parts of the known universe. All anyone can do is make an educated guess. Like I said if we don't figure this out soon, I'm afraid humanity will, and even if there are survivors after this, the road to recover would be nearly impossible to achieve.

Davis's remark made John and Mathew understand where Davis was coming from. The fate of their only planet might hang in the balance of figuring out the truth but just didn't know where to start looking.

Mathew asked, "Has the sphere even tried to give you a hit or something?" Davis shook his head in disappointment. All it had been doing in the last month was sitting in his safe gathering dust with no indication that another clue was nearby.

John laughed and said jokingly, "Well it's a test, so what if you already have a clue but you just don't know it?"

"Wait, what?" asked Davis surprisingly.

"Well, you, I mean what if you already have the clue in your mind but it's so simple you would overlook it." said John grabbing another shot of tequila.

But before he could pour a shot he stopped as everyone sat silent for only a minute, realizing what if it was true? What if Davis really did find another clue but missed it? It would explain why the sphere hadn't given anything new because he already had seen it.

"Something hidden in plain sight!" screamed Davis with joy as he jumped out of his chair and began tearing through one of his filing cabinets. "Okay I'm going to need a lot of help, you three pull out every file, check every video and witness reports, look for anything that might be a clue!"

The three dropped their drinks and the four immediately started going through all the information Davis had obtained on the aliens, if there was answer to save their world it had to be there, but everything he had was simply basic stuff. Two hours of looking through everything in the cabinets they found nothing. They began to look through the data journals about the operations and video sightings of the alien's pets, but still found nothing. After six hours of searching and the department littered with documents, they still had nothing. They had been searching for so long that Davis had lost track of time as Emily came to check on Davis only to find his office a mess with the four men looking through biological behavior patterns, alien tech, and cultural ideology.

Emily got concerned and asked, "Are you all okay? What are you trying to do?"

"Emily sorry I forgot about our appointment, but this is crucial for humanity."

"Making a massive mess is crucial for humanity?"

"What? No! The small sphere that the alien gave me unlocks when we find clues about the truth, remember? So, John figured that I might have a clue already, but I just missed it!"

"Emily, could you help us, please?!" said Mathew concerned and worn from looking.

"Okay, but after I check out Davis."

"This is kind of important right now!"

"So is your health, Davis! You can't save anyone until I'm sure you're okay!"

Davis growled with anger as he told John and Mathew, "Continue looking while I get checked up!" Before neither one of them could object this checkup, Davis had run past them and followed Emily to the back corner of his department. It had been a month since he had check up done on him and Emily was concerned about his hand. She told him to keep an eye on it every day just in case something changed, but for Davis it was a tedious task. Every time he tried to check on it someone would be looking for him, would want to talk to him about new updates about his research, or simply ask for some information about lost family members. Davis never had the chance to look at the scar that the alien had left in his hand but to him if he wasn't in any pain then there was no point to look.

Emily had Davis sit down and slowly took off Davis's glove. As it came off both of their hearts nearly stopped. The indigo scar had grown and now there were veins with a metallic silver color that had spread out from the scar and wrapped around Davis's fingers, palm, and a bit of his wrist.

"Oh my god! Davis why didn't you tell me this was happing?"

"I haven't even had the chance to look at it yet either with everything going on!"

"Davis, this is serious! We have no idea what that thing did to you and now it's spreading, I don't know if I can treat this."

"Calm down we will figure this out but right now we have more important matters to attend to." said Davis as he put his glove back on.

Davis saw in the corner of his eye John and Mathew coming and put his hand away while quietly saying to Emily, "We'll deal with it later, when we don't have a crowd."

Before she could say anything, John and Mathew came in and said, "Sorry to bother you two but Davis can remember anything that might be a clue from before any of this?"

Davis was shocked by the question and asked, "What, why?"

Mathew explained, "These aliens play differently from humans so I believe that maybe the clue we're looking for could exist outside the information you already have. Something that maybe you may have not written down because it was somewhere else or irrelevant." Davis could see what Mathew meant and began to relive what happened every first day when earth was attacked.

After constantly retelling the story repeatedly as the sun was nearly beginning to set as everyone became annoyed. John stood up and yelled out, "There must be more to your story. Are you sure you're not leaving anything out?"

"Well after telling it to you about thirty-six times, no." said Davis irritated.

"Okay, Davis one more time." Emily said disappointedly.

Davis sighed heavily and repeated his story again until he got to the emails about his brother. He paused for a moment and thought of something. He couldn't believe he didn't think of this sooner, the emails he sent had information about everything he sent to them, but he never considered the things they sent to him there could be something in there he missed. When he thought this the sphere lit up with a violet color for a second, and Davis took it as a sign that maybe he was right.

He rushed over to his computer and began looking through the emails from his brother at the beginning and looked carefully, but he couldn't see what he was missing. That is until Emily stood behind and asked him to go back to a specific email. Davis showed her it and she asked, "When did you see the strange creature on the roof?"

"Around 6:55 am, Why?" answered Davis then questioned her.

"Look at the time your brother sent this email," Emily said as she was pointing at the time.

"Bro, there has been a change in plans, the officers are telling us we are departing the shore at 09 hundred hours, which is wired, we weren't supposed to leave until after the first of January, but I guess it's a good thing, since that means I will be home sooner. I wanted to remind you that once we're at sea it's hard to get in contact with any family, it's just standard protocol." Email received 06:55 am, December 31.

Davis eyes widened as he realized what she meant and said under his breather "They…. knew, they knew they were here, and they left us to die." Suddenly a violet flash of light fills the room then dimes as the violet ring collapse into the black flame, and a small violet light floats in the center of the sphere along with the orange one. Davis looked at the sphere and picked it up, and as he stared into it he began to see a memory in his head.

CHAPTER 9

The deal of the Venvoss.

Memories of events that had long since passed spun around Davis's head. Until he began to see a clear image of some people in the middle of a desert. Davis could see some sort of operation take place with everyone around in a panic as scientists and military personnel were taking positions. It seemed Davis was seeing an event that brought some together, but for what? Even amongst the chaos, Davis could see through the waves of men, some ambassadors from different countries stationed in a few tents. After moving in more closely he could see that these ambassadors were from the United Nations, but for some reason only a few had attended this event.

In total there were only four ambassadors, ones from China, Russia, America, and Canada. They were sitting in around a dining table discussing what they intended to do with their translators explaining. The ambassador from Russia argued that it would be ludicrous to make any type of deal with the Venvoss, especially with the current state of the earth after the end of the second world war. The one from China disagreed, he believed that maybe the Venvoss were possibly here to help humanity. However, the American ambassador intervened and explained that it would make sense to attack us when the whole world was just starting to recover, when everyone was at their weakest.

The Canadian ambassador stopped everyone's conversation and explained that, "No one knows why these 'Venvoss' are coming besides the obvious. We all received the same transmission, they wanted to talk about making a deal with humanity, and they wanted us to hear them out. If they wanted to attack us, then why not do it from space they clearly have the technology to travel between stars I'm sure they have the technology to destroy a planet. Secondly, we don't know what the deal they want to make is, so no one needs to panic. We have military from all of our country's here to help with any problems that may accrue along with our scientists to help supervise this event and help try and translate their language. Finally, maybe they are here to help us. With the wisdom of these people, we might be able to avoid any more conflict between each other or it could backfire in the worst of ways. But until we speak with them, we need to show our soldiers and scientist that we are not going to be phased by what comes next. For whatever they throw at us we will face together."

Davis liked the Canadian Ambassador's way of thinking, it wasn't too far one way or the other, it was dead center, and his motivational speech to the others was nice. However, the other ambassadors disagreed, they told him his ideology could get them all killed or worse, embarrass them in front of their soldiers. They explained that leaders needed to lead with an iron fist, otherwise no one would ever take them seriously. However, the Canadian Ambassador stated there was nothing wrong with being flawed, everyone was, so why should anyone fear it? The other ambassadors looked at him with discontent from his words and told him that they needed to look fearsome and in control otherwise if they didn't, they might appear weak.

The Canadian ambassador rose from his chair and told the other three that they were on their own. If they were not going to listen to reason and allow their fear to control their actions, then there was no point in staying to see what their actions would bring. The Canadian ambassador left the tent and ordered his people to abandon this mission for the other ambassadors were too afraid. But before he and his people could leave the moon became eclipsed by a massive object as it began to descend towards the earth.

Once it had landed Davis could see that it was a giant ship. He speculated it was possibly as tall as a mountain, but it's appearance soon faded, it seemed to have some sort of clocking technology. Which gave Davis his answer about how they got on the planet unseen. But it was strange, the ship he saw in the picture was so much wider and longer. Davis believed that maybe this was a different model from the one he saw, but even if it was, these creatures clearly made some massive steps in their technology. Davis continued to watch as the military of four different nations gathered around the ship weapons ready at the first sign of trouble, as scientist prepare for first contact.

The ambassadors of China, Russia, and America approached cautiously towards the ship, but the Canadians refused to stand with them. He stayed with his soldiers and scientist, telling them to record everything they saw and to be prepare if the others screwed up. The other ambassadors made it to the front lines as a door opened on the ship. But instead of being greeted by aliens there was only darkness. The ambassadors ordered lights to be shined inside to see who was there but became appalled when they saw nothing. Not even the light from their labs could penetrate this darkness.

Everyone began to squint to see if there was anything inside, but the only thing that caught their eye was a shimmer in the darkness. It seemed there was some sort of glass between the door and the darkness, possibly used for a safety precaution so there wouldn't be any accidents. However, this event turned into a standoff between these aliens and humanity. Both sides were waiting for someone to make the first move. After a few minutes, the Canadian ambassador sighed angrily and bushed through the soldiers and other ambassadors making his way towards the glass while saying to everyone, "You all are talk but no bite huh!" As he approached the glass door parted down the middle and the darkness began to pour out on to the ground in a black clouded mist. The same mist that was used at Davis's work when the invasion first started.

As the mist began to flow on the ground, light began to pierce the darkness from both outside and inside. Standing a few feet from the door were three figures starting to walk towards the ambassador. It was the four-armed aliens, one in armor and two in cloths. However, Davis noticed something about the armored alien. This alien was decorated in different armor than the other ones he had seen, it had white and sliver armor with tints of blue, and an elongated loin cloth decoder with what Davis believed to be the alien's planetary symbols. The eye in the center with a star and eight golden spikes extended outward, with three rings, and two lopsided four-pointed stars. But its most striking feature was the three basketball sized orbs that followed it.

The Canadian ambassador didn't seem to concern with the small details as he started up at this massive creature trying not to show fear, but he was doing an extremely poor job at it. The alien kneeled to be at eye-level with the ambassador and spoke in its own language while giving him a small sphere, it almost looked identical to Davis's. However, this sphere didn't look like what he had, the one the ambassador had was filled with a gray material. Once it was in his hand, he could hear the alien in his foreign tongue as did Davis.

"Can you understand me, human?" asked the armored alien.

"Ye...yes, how did you..." asked the ambassador before one of the thinner aliens cut him off, "We don't have time to explain our technology to you."

"Shenral!" said the other thin alien. "Don't speak to him like that he has a right to wonder how."

"Yanton is right Shenral, and we need their help so don't get agitated over a simple question." said the armored alien as he turned his head towards the thin alien. Shenral became silent as the armored alien introduced himself to the ambassador. "I am Icin, the Zenitharus of the Venvoss, me and my kind have come a great distance for your assistance."

"Our assistance? What could humanity possibly offer assistance for an advance race like yourself?"

Icin stood up and explained that an unknown disease somehow made its way from Earth to Tenatros, the home world of the Venvoss. It started off slow in small villages around the coasts of their home world but now it has somehow hopped from planet to planet. In the Milky Way alone there were seven known planets with life, and each one had two different races on each, seven races have unknowingly fallen victim to this disease, and even with their supreme technology they couldn't figure out its origin. Until they got a transmission from this planet about its races and cultures. This makes them the fifteenth known planet and possibly the origin of the disease. They sent drones to their planet years ago and discovered trace amounts of the disease on the planet, but it wasn't exactly the same one they had deep in space.

"Millions of beings around the galaxy have been taken by this disease, and more are yet to journey across the stary sky and rejoin their loved ones in the next life, but there is still a chance to save the remainder of the seven races, and time to stop it from spreading any further." said Icin as he turned his sphere into a screen, showing images of what was happening on the other worlds. "This disease is far worse than anything anyone of the other races have seen and it's not just infecting our races anymore, it's also infected our animals and planets. We don't know how it got from your planet to ours, but you seem to have a resistance to it. That is why we have come, to ask for your help and knowledge."

The ambassador just stood looking at all the pictures of the disease, the decaying death that surrounded the galaxy world. The ambassador called out to the others, "You need to see this, right now and bring over some scientists!"

The ambassadors came over quickly with some of their best people and Icin showed them the images of his dying world. Many were intrigued by the device but were more horrified by the images they had seen. But as they discussed the pictures and possibilities with the ambassadors, something caught Davis's ear. China's ambassador sounded familiar, but he didn't know why. After viewing the pictures for an hour, chatting with one another, and concluded what they were dealing with, one of the scientists said aloud, "I think it's a more deadly version of the bubonic plague from the fourteenth century."

"WHAT?" said all the ambassadors in unison.

"What's wrong?" asked Icin as he jumped on his feet.

"The bubonic plague was one of the deadliest diseases in the world seven years ago. It killed one third of the European culture." said the Canadian ambassador.

"But how could have it gotten so far?" asked China's ambassador.

"Maybe we released it into space?" said the Russian ambassador.

"We don't have the ability to send it deep in space. Even if we did it would take centuries with our technology." Said the American ambassador.

"Regardless of how it got to Tenatros, is there anything you can do for us now!" said Icin, distort.

The ambassadors looked to their scientists and gave them a look, one that Davis could see meant, we need an answer fast! But even with their minds combined they had no answer to this problem. They didn't even know how it stop centuries ago in Europe and since they didn't live through it, they could only speculate on how it stopped. One scientist stood before Icin and said, "I'm sorry, but even we don't know how to help you. If our technology was more advanced then maybe we could help your kind, but...." Then Davis saw three of the ambassadors faces light up like they had some sort of realization.

They stopped the scientist's words and Chinas ambassador said, "What if we made a deal?"

When Davis heard the word "deal" he realized this was the moment from the first clue he found and the voice he heard was the ambassadors. This was the moment that made the Venvoss attack earth, the reason why they came back. Davis got closer and listened intently, he didn't want to waste this opportunity to learn more about what happened years ago.

"I can make any deal if is justifiable," said Icin a little concerned as he leaned towards the ambassadors.

Though they were uncomfortable by his stature the American ambassador said, "Well… you have the technology we need, and we have a good idea of how it works, so why don't we combine our technologies and knowledge about the plague. Together we can create a vaccine to save not just your worlds but also save ours and advance it."

"In other words, if you help us, we help you, and it saves us all. But if we do it alone and without your technology, then it could take years if not decades to figure it out." said Russia's ambassador.

Icin took a moment to think, from his body language he seemed worried about this deal and the consequences as he slumped down a bit and tapped his foot repeatedly. Davis could only guess what Icin was feeling that day, but he knew if the roles were reversed, he wouldn't know what to do either. Icin stood tall and said, "I can accept your terms, but you do know that we are in a hurry, so you must make sure the cure is perfected, otherwise I fear things could only get worse."

"Don't fear Icin, I'm sure we can get this all sorted and who knows, maybe one day you'll come back to greet all of humanity on good terms." said the American ambassador.

Davis shook his head in disbelief as he said, "If only all knew what mess you all left behind."

The memory changed and showed him the ambassadors, scientists, and Icin with some of his Venvoss, beginning to discuss the plan for the cure and the other aliens that were infected by the disease. By the Venvoss' account they have witnessed the first spread of the disease was thirty-six years ago by earths standard time and spread from planet to planet.

"But how could it have spread?" asked a scientist.

"Our systems are calibrated for now diseases and or viruses. It can't identify something new unless we have dealt with it and updated our systems to identify it. Many planets and races use the same technology to keep their societies safe."

"So, when you found out what you were dealing with it was too late." said the Canadian ambassador.

"Yes, and as I have said my race isn't the only ones that have suffered from the disease. There are Shosci from Molvoben, Zatran from Aqunaua, Casvat from Nortrovif, Falion from Derinjath, Polirians from Termperana, Wanyakai from Rolpemban, and the Knivos from Xenstranvolam. I will use my sphere to give you a better visual of what you're dealing with."

Icin began to form the figures on the table in front of them, but then something happened at that point. The memory that surrounded Davis went black, there was nothing but darkness for a few moments and the memory returned with the figures being dismantled. "What the hell just happened!" said Davis worried. It seemed that this particular part of the memory was kept from his eyes, but he didn't know why. Though he was appalled by how many different races there were in the milky way galaxy and there's still another eight that were unknown to humanity. He wished they had gone into detail about the others but sadly they were to remain a mystery to him. The memory speed up showing their progression and their failures for months, but after those long tedious months, they had finally perfected what they believed to be the cure they needed for the seven races. They did one final test to be positive it worked, and it showed a ninety-nine percent rate of success. Icin was grateful for humanity's aid in this endeavor to save the seven worlds and allowed humanity to keep their technology as promised. Once they had the serums recipe they took to the stars and returned to their home world.

When the Venvoss left everyone who was there that day took a vow of silence, to never speak about what they did that day in fear of their world retaliating against them. All the information they had was to be hidden from the world, but not destroyed. They believed one day humanity would be ready for the knowledge that beyond their world was one bigger than they could ever have imagined, but then things changed. People who were there that day began to disappear or mysteriously die and all their records from those mouths of helping the Venvoss had vanished. It seemed to Davis that someone was going to great lengths to hide the events of that day, but for what reason he was uncertain. The memory began to break down around him and once it was over some random picture of the hope diamond appeared in Davis mind until he found himself laying on his bed with Emily using some eye drops on his eyes.

Emily was shocked to see him blink and said, "Jesus, Davis don't do that."

"Davis, you have no idea what happened to you don't you?" asked Emily concerned.

Davis shook his head and asked, "No, I don't, could you tell me."

"After that violet light went off and looked in the orb, a beam of that color went into your eyes and you fell to the floor! We tried to get you to snap out of it, but you were in some sort of deep trance. We lifted you on the bed and I have been watching over for the past hour, you didn't even blink, and gripped the sphere so hard I thought you were going to crush it! I even tried to pry it was from your hand, but I was afraid of breaking your fingers." Emily said as she checks Davis out, making sure his physical reactions were responding.

"That's shocking." Davis said as she checked him.

"Well, it seems like you're okay now, and the violet color has dissipated from your eyes, so I would say you're good to go, but I have to ask what happened with this sphere this time, what did you see?"

Davis lifted the sphere as he looked at it, making Emily flinch as he said, "I saw a hell of a lot more than the first time!"

"What did you see?" said Emily concerned.

Davis got off his bed and said to Emily, "I need to find Alex and I need you to gather everyone into the chamber, they all need to hear this."

"Why?"

"Because this isn't the first time these aliens have been on earth!" he said to Emily with a stern tone of voice.

Emily was silent as he went running through the mall looking for his sister, calling her name hoping she could hear his voice and come running. But she didn't respond to him, he got worried, that is, until then he found himself near Jackie's department and could hear his sister's voice coming from inside. He was about to enter until he stopped, Jackie and Alex both were in deep conversation with one another, and he didn't want to interrupt, but out of his curiosity he did listen.

"Amelia is still pissed with Davis and he's too busy to try to make amends." said Alex, worried.

"Alex, I understand what Davis is going through I just wished that your sister could see it too." said Jackie trying to comfort her as she rubbed her back. "Look she doesn't have to support his choice, but she needs to understand why he had to make it. We as the council can't overlook these things and we must make tough calls. But he keeps his head high because he knows these people need it. To be honest Alex, I think it's torturing him."

"I know, but I'm the older sibling I shouldn't be allowing my little brother to make such a call and carry the hardships that came with it! I have always given him guidance when he ever left lost or scared when he was little. I helped him through the hard times when he started to have misgivings about the world and wanted to hurt people in the most inhumane ways. I never wanted him to go through something like that. He took the life of another person and when I saw what he did, I thought I saw him smile, I feel like I failed him." said Alex as she began to cry with sorrow.

"Alex you are a wonderful sister, and you did a great job being there for him. What he can do shows how far he has come because of you. I would have quit months ago if I had to put up the amount of crap Davis must do daily. The fact that he can carry the burden of a leader or a decision that nobody else wanted to carry, made him stronger than anyone here. In my opinion I don't think he is evil, but he did strike it down."

Alex looked to Jackie and told her, "It's not just what he just did. It's what he did for me when this place was attacked a month ago."

Jackie was about to speak, when Davis knocked on her door and popped in around the corner saying, "Jackie, Alex, I need you both in the council chambers right now, I have acquired new information about the aliens and you all need to hear it."

Jackie rose from her seat and asked, "Were you eavesdropping on us?"

Davis darted his eyes around the room and said, "Well...I'm not admitting to eavesdropping on you two."

Alex and Jackie were both about to yell at him, but around the corner Adalard and Julian came out and asked what Davis wanted in the middle of their shifts? Davis told them to head towards the chamber and he would explain everything about what the sphere had shown him. It took everyone to understand what he had meant, but when they realized that he was talking about the small sphere, they immediately rushed out to the hall, all except Alex. She sat in her chair and asked him, "You were listening to us Davis, don't think your loveable stupidity will get you out of this argument."

"Yes, I was, Alex, you shouldn't blame yourself for what happened, and Jackie is right. You don't have to be proud of what I did but be proud that I can make the hard choices, so you don't have to. I know you blame yourself for what happened to my hand, but I don't. You have always been there for me when barely anyone was. But now it's time for you to let me take care of you and don't give me that 'you're my younger brother it's my responsibility to take care of you no matter what' shit." said Davis trying to imitate Alex's voice. "I don't want to hear it from you, all I want from you is to be happy that I grew up the way you wanted me to."

Alex wiped away her tears and said seriously, "Davis.... I do not sound like that." Mocking Davis's ill willed attempt at mimicking his voice.

Davis rolled his eyes and told her, "See you're already making fun of me, that's a good first step in the wrong direction. But your wrong is always somehow in the right, so good work!"

Alex smiled at her brother, but Davis was not a fool. He could still see that his sister was tormented inside, even if he reassured her everything between them was okay. Davis helped his sister from the chair and took her he the chamber to discuss what happened decades ago. But along the way the two ran into Amelia and Elliot. As they passed them no one said, anything. The silence between them was definite, there was nothing to say about what happened, and that he wasn't going to stop them from leaving. But then the silence was broken when Elliot said, "Davis...thank you. Thank you for the key and for trusting me with that responsibility."

However, Davis said nothing and continued to walk towards chamber as he could hear Elliot whisper to his sister, "Amelia, come on we talked about this."

"I know, I was there.... but after what I said I don't think he would forgive me so easily. At least not now."

Davis stopped in his tracks and told Alex to keep going as he turned around to face his sister. The two stared at each other as Davis used the hand sign to follow him. Amelia was surprised by her brother's gesture but followed him to the chambers while Elliot stayed with their daughter. However, Amelia was underwhelmed that she was only now just being let into one of these meetings. In the last few months, she wanted to be on the council, but Davis as well as Alex refused, which made her irritated. Amelia wanted to join because she thought they were just trying to control the masses and she wanted to stop them. However, she was now going to get a crash course in what the council really does behind those doors.

When they arrived at the doors, Adalard was waiting for Davis and was happy to see him, but it quickly faded when he saw Amelia. "What is she...?" asked Adalard.

"Don't worry about it, okay?" said Davis.

Amelia said nothing as Davis followed Adalard into the chamber were all the council's members where sitting in their spots chatting quietly about why he might have called them there. Emily, John, and Mathew were already aware of the situation, but did not tell anyone else, they wanted Davis to tell them with his own words. Adalard sat down in his chair as Davis asked Amelia to sit in his. The rest of the council was just like Adalard, surprised to see his younger sister sitting in on this meeting. Alex was not surprised she knew it was only a matter of time till Davis was going to let her in on the secrets of why they truly gathered, she just wondered if Amelia was going to be able to handle the truth.

Julian asked innocently, "Davis are you sure you want your sister Amelia here, tonight? You know you can't take back anything you say once you start."

"Yes, I know." said Davis. "We all have had to make sacrifices to keep this place alive, some more than others. For months Amelia has asked to join the council, but Alex and I kept her away due to the fear of what she was going to hear. But after what happened with the priest, I have decided that we need to show not just her, but everyone the truth of what we all have been doing back here. Finally I want to discuss what Emily, John, Mathew, and myself discovered with the small sphere."

Everyone in the council didn't understand his intention with Amelia, as they believed it wasn't the time to tell everyone the truth just yet. However, Davis reassured them after he told them what he found out they would. The council remained on edge as Davis explained the events that happened a few hours ago before he was in a paralyzed state. Then he went into detail about the Venvoss, the other races in the Milky Way, and the deal that was made between some of humanity for the technology. At first the council seemed a little skeptical about Davis's account of what happened, but the more he told, the more they listened. At the end Davis did let them know that the memory stopped, but there was one truth remaining to finally figure out why they came back, and he believed it had to do with the Hope Diamond in Washington D.C.

From his view he could see the council was in absolute disarray, their faces were filled with fear and they couldn't believe what he had just told them. This whole time their government knew and they left them just to save themselves. What made matters worse is that they made them do their dirty work by demanding them to do their research for them to save their world and race when they abandoned them. The council members started fighting with one another and debating with each other. After yelling in a complete and utter rage everyone calmed down and asked why. Why did they leave us? Amelia looked at the council and told them, "It's because we are expendable to them."

Davis could see the tears being to swell up in her eye. She now understood the weight that these people had to carry, and all for nothing. All these months, struggling to make sure their people survive, the arguments they had, the research they had done, was for nothing. Their government betrayed everyone and left them to die, sending them on a wild goose chase, just to try and sway their own guilt.

"This is not over yet," said Davis trying to uplift their spirits. "Yes, our idiot traitorous leaders abandoned their countries and left us at the mercy of the Venvoss. But we are still here, and we haven't fallen yet. I know this road hasn't been easy but look what we managed to accomplish without them. We held back a horde of beasts and serpents, made a stronghold out of a mall, and discovered things that we didn't even know about the universe or the other races. We can make it without them, we only have one final ring to break, and the answer lies with the Hope Diamond. Right now, we have the advantage, they don't know that we know about their traitorous act or the spheres me and my sister have. They don't stand a chance against all of us and with my sister Alex and me by your sides, there is no way we are going out without a fight for our right to live. One more ring and we will finally know the truth, one more and we can stop this. Whatever they did to start this war, we will end it. They might have put all of Earth in danger, but all of us will never let it fall!"

"My brother is right," said Amelia, "If Davis is telling the truth, then we must stop this. It is our duty to protect each other."

Akio sighed and spoke up, "Look Davis even if this is true, were not just taking on our government, we are possibly taking on every government."

"Don't you think he hasn't already figured that out!" said Julian. "If this information is valid, then this could be the actions of a few trying to cover it up. Just like Davis said, 'to sway their own guilt.'"

Miller spoke up questioning, "If this is true then why is the Hope Diamond the next clue?

Personally, that doesn't make any sense to use a gem to hide information." Then he thought about it for a moment and said, "Then again, if you put it in a gem only every few can touch it, it would be the perfect hiding spot."

"Look, even if the Hope Diamond is the next clue, we can't send off our guards, peacekeepers and gatherers to go get it half a country away and if you're wrong we could be putting more of our people in danger." said as John rose from his chair as he slammed his hand on the table.

Adalard spoke up against everyone saying, "Davis has done nothing but be honest with us. Why would he make something like this up?"

"It's not that we don't trust him it's that we don't trust these Venvoss. I mean why only have him be able to see inside the sphere? Why not Alex too? Why not us?"

"Maybe it's because they don't trust humanity anymore." said Alex. "I believe they are testing the new generations to see if they are worthy of being part of the universe. What better way than to put us through a test and only have one person to I be able to find out the truth. This forces us to work together and actually get to the bottom of this nightmare."

Davis rose from his own seat and made his way towards the center of the chamber as he said "No one here has an answer for their actions, but the one I have given you all is what's at stake right now. I still question their motives, but regardless we have an answer, and we need to stop playing defense, because if we do, we will never see our home rebuilt in any generation."

John sat back down and calmly explained, "I trust you Davis, but I just-" Before he could finish his sentence Akio interrupted, "We all get it, it's a lot to process, but he can't stay here like this forever, always in fear of the enzymes of the world." Akio got up from her chair and joined Davis's side and said, "I would fight to live to see tomorrow than cower in the dark."

"Okay so if we agreed to this then how are we going to do it." asked Jackie concerned.

"It's simple." said Davis with confidence, "I will take a group of volunteers to Washington D.C. and find the diamond. One group will take to the skies and the other will be on the ground. The group that takes to the skies will be entrusted to wait for the ground team and set up a perimeter at the airline. The ground forces will be tasked with heading to the rendezvous point and finding survivors."

"Davis it will take the ground troop four days, driving nonstop to get to Washington." said Julian.

"I know it will be a long drive, but this might be the last chance for all of us." said Davis with a concerned voice.

The councils sat silently for a few moments, then Adalard stood up saying, "I volunteer to go." The council wasn't shocked that he was the first to volunteer but then when Akio did it caught them off guard. Davis knew Alex would go no matter what he said, but four wasn't enough. Davis told the council in the morning they would tell everyone the truth about what was going on. Granted he told them everyone was going to be pissed, but maybe they could get a few more people to join on this mission. The council agreed and told each other good night. But it seemed that they were nervous about how the people were going to react. Davis wasn't surprised by that fact, but they didn't have a choice.

Davis returned to his room and lied down on his bed trying to get to sleep. But he couldn't, he kept thinking about how far they had come and what the last truth was. Too many questions kept him awake and when he wasn't thinking about what the last truth was, he worried about the road ahead. Even if they did get some people to join their cause there was no guarantee that they might come pack. What made matters worse was the fact they had been abandoned, forgotten, and betrayed. He didn't know how well everyone was going to take it in the morning, but he could only imagine the heart break they were going to feel.

Eventually Davis passed out around two am. However, he woke up to something in his room falling on the floor. Davis's eyes shot open, and he materialized his broad sword in his hands, pointing it into the darkness of his department. As his eyes adjusted in the dark, he saw it was just Adalard moving trying to get to his bed. Davis shook his head in disbelief and asked him, "What are you doing in my department?"

"Sorry but I just needed to speak with you."

"You couldn't wait till morning?" said Davis as he groaned.

"No, it can't." said Adalard as he sat on the edge of the bed. "I'm worried about everything that's going to happen, honestly I'm worried about you."

"What do you mean?" asked Davis as he dematerialized his sword.

"The way you're constantly calm and confident scares me. It's like you don't understand the severity of this situation. You're not reacting the way someone normally would, I thought you would be pissed, but the way you spoke in the chamber, it's like you're not ever phased by everything that's happening." he said as he faced out into the darkness.

Davis could hear the fear come from his voice as he spoke his mind. He placed his hand on his back and said, "Do you honestly think I'm not scared or that I know how screwed up this is?" Adalard turned his head towards Davis as he began to grip the back of his shirt. "This a complete nightmare!" Davis continued with his head down. "In all of my life I have been afraid of many things, but in the twenty-seven years I have lived, I never imagined my life, or anyone's for that matter to turn out like this!" Davis lifted his other hand to Adalard's shoulder and began to squeeze down hard on it. "I have nightmares sometimes of people who I couldn't save or help, but then when I wake up for a split second, I think to myself it's over, but then it dawns on me it's not! I don't know what lies ahead more than anyone else, but the moment I stop having hope, I know it's over! That's why I don't stop for a second giving as much hope as I can, the moment hope dies, so does everything around it."

Adalard hissed in pain by Davis's hand digging into his shoulder, but he could understand now why Davis is so determined to fix this mess. Adalard removed Davis hand from his shoulder but held onto it as he said, "But you can't keep these emotions bottled up forever! I don't need to be an empath to tell me how much pain you're in! Your actions tell me everything, you're becoming more distant from everyone, and you never tell anyone how you feel! Sometimes you don't say anything to anyone for days and it's scaring me!"

Adalard then pulled Davis's arm forcing him into his chest as he grabbed his back and pulled him in for a hug. Davis could feel Adalard shake as he held him close saying, "I..." he stopped and reshaped his sentence. "We...are all scared that you going to crack under all this pressure, we're your friends, your family. But what point is there in saving the world if you're too broken to enjoy it."

Davis let go of Adalard's shirt and hugged him back gently. He could still feel his friend shake and could hear his heart beating loudly as his ear was to his chest. Davis never knew that Adalard was this concerned about him or the fact his feeling towards him were strong. He wondered about many things in his life, but he never imagined anyone other than his family to feel this concerned for him. Looking back on it Davis realized Adalard always was close to him in one way or another, whether it was helping with his documents or analyzing data, he was always there. He didn't know if Adalard's feelings for him were real or if it was his imagination, but regardless, he wanted Adalard to know he was okay, even if it meant lying to him.

"Adalard you're a good friend, but I can't stop, not now, especially since in a few hours we're about to tell everyone the truth." Davis said as he pulled away from Adalard's body. "I am angry, sad, disappointed, every negative emotion I can think of, I'm feeling right now, ever since the beginning. I will deal with it when this is over, but this is the burden of being a leader. Sometimes you must break a little bit just so others can be contempt with their lives. It the price of doing what's right."

Adalard took his hand, placed it under Davis chin, then raised it so their eyes met. "Doing what's right, doesn't mean you give up your own happiness or someone else's."

Davis couldn't help but smile and said, "That's something I would say."

"That just shows how wise you are, but you should take your own advice." said Adalard as he lowered his hand from Davis's chin. "Let me ask you something Davis, and I want the truth. Do you think we can really win this war?"

Davis stared into Adalard's eyes and said with confidence, "I don't think it, I know it."

Adalard smiled and put his hand on his shoulder but said nothing, he nodded, then got up from the bed and walked away. He turned around as he was about to leave Davis's department and waved to him, saying, "good night," as Davis waived back. When Adalard was out of sight Davis laid back down and closed his eyes trying to get some sleep before the announcement, but before he drifted off, he began to let out some of his pain and began to have a breakdown in his pillow. After his breakdown, he passed out in his bed, his pillow covered in his tears, his face red from his repressed sadness and anger that he piled up, but for the first time since the beginning he found peace as he went back to sleep.

CHAPTER 10

Six swords cross.

Davis could see in his mind a familiar sight: the bridge and alien that gave him the small sphere. It seemed he was reliving that memory of that day, but something was off about it. Davis was already holding the sphere, but it was clear like the one the ambassadors used. In the distance he heard the alien call out, "When you find the truth come find me and be careful some of your kind will stop at nothing to keep what they did a secret," in perfect English. How was this possible, Davis wondered. That was not how it happened, it didn't speak English it spoke in its native tongue. Yet in his dream he could hear him as clear as a bell.

Then his left arm began to feel inflamed as he held the sphere. He looked down to see the same diseases the Venvoss had been fighting begin to take hold of his arm. His skin became black as his blood began to burst through the cracks it had made. Yet after a short while his skin began to fall off showing his muscles and tissue. Eventually that too began to rot and fall off, it made Davis panic. He desperately tried to find something to remove the arm, but it had already spread to his legs and other arm. He could see all his skin begin to fall off along with his muscle, feeling like he was being torn apart while he was still alive. Davis fell to the ground and felt the pain stop. He waited on the ground for a few seconds before he lifted his head to see nothing but a waste land. There was no city, no river, no bridge, only an endless desert. It was like something had taken all the life away from the world.

Davis felt something grasp his shoulder and he froze. When he turned to face it, he woke up as his sister Alex was shaking him awake.

"Davis are you okay?" said Alex worried. "You were screaming in your sleep!"

"I…was?" said Davis as he got up. Davis could feel the cold sweat on his clothes as he sat up. When he turned, he could see that even his bed was drenched in sweat.

"I tried to wake you up, but you were such in a deep sleep I had to slap you, and that didn't even work!" said Alex exhaling deeply, "Whatever your dream was about was intense, wasn't it?"

"You have no idea!" said Davis as he got out of his bed, got a bottle of water, and guzzled it down.

Then through the doorway of his department Jackie and Adalard came rushing in looking like they were in shock. "What the hell's going on in here?" screamed Jackie with fear in her voice.

"Davis are you alright? I heard you from the other side of the mall!" asked Adalard, panicking.

Davis but down his drink and said calmly, "I'm okay, I'm okay, I just had a really messed up nightmare."

The two sighed with relief as Jackie got on the radio and spoke into it "Its okay everyone false alarm. Davis just had a nightmare."

On the radio Akio's voice crackled in saying, "The way we heard him screaming sounded like he was dying! Are you sure, he's okay?"

Davis nodded his head to Jackie, and she replied, "Davis is right in front of me, and he says he's fine."

"Alright, just no more nightmares, that was horrifying."

Jackie put her radio away as Davis got up from his bed and sat at his desk, he could still feel the sweat covering his body and clothes as he moved around. He went to a cabinet where he kept his clothes and grabbed a towel from inside. He began to gently wash off the sweat from his neck and arms as his friends and sister spoke in whispers to each other. As he washed off the sweat he felt a tingle in his left arm, it felt like his arm was asleep. So, he pushed it off and focused on getting cleaned up. Adalard came up from behind and asked, "Do you need anything?"

Davis faced him with the towel on his shoulder and said, "No, I'm good, I'm just glad it's over."

"Well, I'm glad you're okay, but remember our talk from before. You said you had nightmares all the time, but you never screamed before."

"Not like that one, it was different."

"What do you mean?" said Adalard as he grabbed Davis shoulders.

As he was about to explain, he felt his left arm begin to feel sore, like he had just done dozens of exercises. Davis made Adalard let go of his shoulders and said, "Let me get clean off first and then I will tell you." Davis excused himself as he grabbed some new clothes and headed into his private bathroom. He turned on his shower and got undressed, but as he removed his shirt and glove, he's face turned white and made his heart drop. The injury to his hand changed, what was once a scar from battle turned into something else. His indigo scar remained, but now his veins from his finger to his shoulder and his pectoral were silver in color. It made him feel sick just looking at his arm and in a panic from what he saw, he ran to the toilet and vomited.

Alex's knocked on the door and asked, "Davis are you alright, you sound sick? Do I need to come in?"

Davis raised his head up from the rim and said, "NO, don't come in, I'm not decent, I just drank the water too fast."

Davis could hear his sister's foots steeps recede from the door and as he thought he was okay; he investigated the toilet to find a more distributing view. What he had thrown up wasn't food, or water, or bile. It was blood, his blood, and it was red with signs of indigo mixing together. Davis was panicking in his mind, he couldn't figure out what was happing to him, he felt like was about to lose his mind. However, something had crossed his mind that had stopped him, everyone else.

Davis could not let anyone see him like this. They were so close to ending this nightmare and bringing peace back to world, that he wasn't going to let a little discolored blood stop him. Davis stood up from the toilet, flushed, then entered the shower, allowing the warm waters to clean his body from all the sweat and blood. It was only for a few minutes, then he dried himself off quickly and threw on his new clean clothes. But as he began to put on his shirt, he heard another knock at the door. "Is it alright if I come in now?" asked his sister, Alex.

Davis finished putting on his shirt and placed his glove back on as he said, "I am already done."

Davis stepped out of the bathroom as Adalard asked "So are you going to tell us about-"

"Yes." said Davis cutting off Adalard's sentence.

As he promised them, he explained what his dream was about in detail and the pain he felt from it. When he was done, he could see them all with concerned looks on their faces, especially Adalard's. He had always seen his sister's face filled with worry, but Adalard's felt to Davis somehow more important.

Alex looked like she was about to say something, but Adalard stopped her and said, "Would you mind if I sleep the rest of the night in your department, just to keep an eye on you?"

Davis was going to argue back, but after what he just went through, he had no case to argue back. He sighed and said, "I won't mind, but we're not sleeping in the same bed, okay!"

Adalard understood and grabbed a few pillows, a blanket, and was about to lay on the floor as Davis said, "You're not sleeping on a tiled floor!" From under his bed, he pulled out a queen size mattress and said, "You will sleep on this." Adalard got up and threw his stuff on the bed as Jackie and Alex left the room saying their goodnights. When they were gone Davis began to change the sheets from his own bed, then Adalard began to help him remake it with the new fresh sheets and blankets. "So do you want to.... talk about it?" asked Adalard.

"I would rather not, just be thinking about it makes me..." said Davis as he began to quiver.

"Was it really that terrible?" asked Adalard, concerned. Davis only nodded his head slightly as he tried not to think about it. Adalard saw that whatever Davis had dreamed about was intense and it seemed to have damaged his psyche. "I know you know this already, but it was only a dream, it wasn't real."

Davis could see that Adalard was trying to comfort him, but he knew that if he had ever found out about his arm and what he had vomited up in the bathroom, it would terrify him, and possibly make it impossible to go on the mission in a few days. No matter the cost Davis had to pay to get to the last clue was worth it if it meant his family and friends were safe from harm. So, Davis put on his best smile and turned to Adalard to say, "I just hope some dreams don't come true."

Davis's façade was good, but he believed Adalard could see past it, that somehow, he knew something was up with him, thankfully he didn't ask too many questions. Yet all Adalard could do now was give him some space and let him tell him in his own time. The two laid in their separate beds waiting for the first one to fall asleep. It felt like it was a game to see if one or the other was trying to get in the same bed once one fell asleep. However, Davis did not want to play anything right now. The images in his head were burned into his mind and it made him unformattable. He wondered what it meant, what happened on Tenatros? Why did the disease just stop when it almost killed him? Why was earth nothing more than a desert? These questions kept Davis awake for the rest of the night as he heard Adalard snore on occasion.

Davis could feel the time of the world move faster the more he waited for the sun to rise. It was like even the universe itself was wanting to help Davis get the meeting over with and honestly Davis agreed. This meeting was not going to be easy. After decades of their government hiding the truth from them, now they were forced into telling their's. But in his experience, he only saw pain when it came to revealing the truth. Granted this was going to be painful, it would be better if everyone knew what they were about to get into, their people deserved that. His mind kept wandering before he could not take it anymore, and deicide to go for a walk around the mall.

Davis was still feeling the effects of being worn out and groggy as he roamed the catwalks and descended to the lower floors. He would occasionally run into a guard now and again telling stories of how they got lucky with a chick or guy, or how they fought off a dozen beasts. He sometimes would be decent enough to just tell their stories to hear their tales, but other times he would screw with them and add or subtract specific information, by the end of their stories in made so little sense people would just laugh of how impossible it was. Davis loved to see people getting along, even if it was just for a short time. But in a few hours the way they looked at him with joyful and accepting eyes, could change into being vindictive. Soon he found himself in front of the burnt down ruins of the peacekeepers department in the food court. The blackened store was a painful reminder of what happened when rage takes over the mind. He hoped that maybe they would understand, but inside he knew that they had the right to be angry for withholding the truth. Davis turned away from the store and sat down at the nearest table and began to think about what he was going to say during the announcement and what would happen when things hit the fan. But then a voice called to him saying, "Howdy Davis, would you like a cup of coffee?"

Davis was startled by the voice as he jumped up from his chair and saw a young teenager who was startled by his movement. "Whoa, calm down cowboy, I just wanted to know if you wanted some coffee?"

"Sorry, sorry, I didn't mean to scare you, but yes would like some Ms…"

"Molly, my name is Molly."

"Molly? Wait didn't you arrive in on the caravan?"

Molly looked shocked as she said, "You remember that! Honestly, I didn't even think you would even know me!"

"Personally, no but knowing you as a survivor, yes."

"Okay, well at least it's something, but other than that, what do you take with your coffee?" said Molly as she got out a pen and note pad. Davis told her what he liked and in a few minutes his coffee was brought to him. Molly sat it down right in front of him and he began to sip from his mug. As he took a few sips he noticed Molly staring at him, it was begging to make him uncomfortable.

"Is something wrong Molly?" Davis asked worried.

Molly stopped staring at him and sat herself down in front of him, "Nothing is wrong with me, but I can see you have a problem."

Davis said nothing as he tried to enjoy his coffee, but then Molly gave this look that was reminiscent of his sister Alex's, it said, "Either tell me the truth or I will rip it out of your soul."

Davis put his coffee down, then slouched into his chair saying, "Okay first, please stop looking at me like that, it is making me nervous. Second, there is going to be a meeting after breakfast about every disturbing information and we as the council fear what might happen afterwards. I'm trying to figure out a strategy, but I'm coming up with nothing."

Looking into her eyes he could see Molly thinking about something, then she said, "Well my mama always used to say, 'Breaking bad news is better than hiding it and making it worse along the way. Eventually things get better with time if you give it a chance.'"

"That's the thing Molly, there might not be much time left, and we found out something that never should have been found and now it could tear us all apart."

Davis looked to his coffee while grabbing it and said "What I must, no matter how steep the price is. Even if it costs me my life, I must end this war".

Molly walked away but instead of being upset she smiled and said, "I think you have done enough for us, don't you?"

Davis smiled as he took a sip of his coffee and as the warm vanilla and caramel mixture warmed his soul, he heard something tapping on some glass. Davis looked around and eventually found his sister Amelia pounding on one of the old cell phone kiosks on the second floor looking down at him. Eventually Amelia came down and sat next to Davis as Molly came with a coffee already in hand for her. When Molly walked away the two sat quietly while occasionally sipping their drinks and waited for the countdown to end. The main clock in the food court clicked on and on, Davis could see that she was struggling to talk. Whatever she wanted to say clearly made her feel uncomfortable. Davis stood up from his table and was about to head off when he could hear Amelia say quietly, "Please don't leave just yet." Davis turned to face her and stared her down as she looked at her cup.

She still refused to talk, but Davis saw her shaking, like she was afraid, but clenching her fist so hard she would shatter her mug, trying to hold back her anger. From just looking at her, he could tell the information was too much for her to handle. She understood why they hid this from everyone, but it only made things worse for the two of them. He could see that she wanted to ask so many things, but she couldn't bring herself to say anything without either blowing up with anger or crying.

All this time she thought her brother was seeking more than what he already had. But he was holding back the truth because he didn't know how she or anyone else would have handled it. Eventually the chime on the clock struck 7 am, the time they made everyone get up and face the new day and get breakfast into their systems. Amelia finally came up with the courage and finally asked, "How can you do it, knowing that people will hate you for keeping secrets?"

"I must, I'm afraid the only chance we have now to fix this is to tell them everything. People will be infuriated at us for keeping this from them when they had every right to know, but if there is even a chance that some will help us end this, then we need to let them know what they could be dragged into." answered Davis, upsettingly.

Amelia looked like she was about to say something about everything that had happened, but then she stopped herself. She only asked one question for her brother, "Are you ready?"

Davis turned away from her and looked at the crowds of people coming into the food court as he said, "Are any of us?"

Amelia could see her brother almost on the verge of tears as he answered her. The pain that he was going through she couldn't even imagine. The pain of taking a life or causing someone else pain to save the lives of many. To her it was a simple choice, you do what's right for others, but what no one ever told her or anyone else is the price you will have to pay for it, and today the council was going to pay the price in full. Amelia stood up from her seat and looked at Davis one more time before heading off to her room to get Elliot and Diamond for breakfast. She could tell from Davis's expression he was nervous as well as frightened.

As soon as Amelia was out of sight Davis headed up to the catwalk and stared down at the crowds of people getting breakfast. They seemed to be in a better mood today than in the last few, but it was only going to be shorted-lived. Davis could see some families comforting the children whose parents had been involved with the priest along with some teachers talking about the plans for today, and the gauds signing in and out at the end and beginning of their shift. It almost left like a regular day to Davis but seeing what little joy they had made him feel ashamed to be the one to take it away. Little by little, the clock began to tick down to the moment the meeting was going to take place and he could see the council along with Alex were just as nervous as he was.

When it was time, the council joined up with Davis on the catwalk and then he whistled to get everyone's attention. Everyone looked skyward towards him and began to whisper among themselves as Davis spoke, "Good morning, everyone, it's a very beautiful morning this day and I would like to give a round of applause to the volunteers for their service to the medical department and peacekeepers. You have all done an amazing job in the last few weeks, so everyone please let them know how much you apricate their service."

"On that same note the people who were harmed in the fire from the cult are making a remarkable recovery and with the medicine and medical techniques these men and women will make a full recovery." said Emily butting, in on Davis's speech.

"More good news to hear in these troubled times. Whatever good deeds still await us will hopefully come to pass soon." said Davis smiling. But then he came to the part of his speech he didn't want to say, but he spoke the words anyways. "Now for some grim news, there are things we as the council have been keeping from you, but not because of our position, because we feared how you would take the news." All eyes were now set on Davis as the people began to whisper to their neighbors what he meant, and his blood ran cold. "The truth is that there are things from our worldly past that have come back to haunt this new generation, and you have the right to know it all. No matter how terrible it might be." said Davis, trying to convey his courage through his voice. Then he finally began to explain everything to the crowds of people everything they had learned from the past six months and as he did, he could seem nearly all of them look at him in shock.

Eventually they began to fit the pieces together, and it didn't take long for people to understand that they were lied to for the last few months. The people began to stand from their chairs and began to scream and shout at the council. The people had felt betrayed by the council they had trusted, the men and women who swore to protect them and now they were expected to help them. People began to toss and turn over chairs and tables and began throwing food at them from below to only have it miss them. Plates and cups fell to the floor breaking and spilling everything on the floor while children began to cry in fear of the coward's rage.

They began screaming, "Everyone on the council is insane and needs to die!"

Men and women began to storm up to the second floor with anger covering their faces and with the determination to kill.

But before anyone got even close to them Amelia managed to push through them and came up next to Davis and told everyone "SHUT THE HELL UP!" her voice echoed through the mall..

Amelia stood by her brother and sister grabbing their hands as she said, "I know this is crazy and yes, I'm pissed too, the council and my brother should have never underestimated us with this information and should have told us sooner. But they didn't do this out of spite or for control, they did it because they didn't know how bad everything was till yesterday and they didn't want to drag anyone into this hell they had to go through! They wanted us to live our lives in peace and safety, so that way whatever time we all had left wasn't terrible. But I'm not angry that they kept this from us. I'm angry because they had no right to face this problem alone. We're all in this together whether we like it or not. I know that what they have done is terrible, but the best thing for all of us is to stand together now more than ever for not just ourselves, but for all the people out there who still need us to be strong."

Many people in the crowds agreed with Amelia and did understand what she was saying, but the sting they felt from their betrayal was too much for them and they didn't know how to feel now. Davis let go of his sister's hand and said to the crowd. "Look we know we have no right to lead you now unless you want us to. But we still needed volunteers to help us get to Washington D.C. So please if anyone would like to volunteer for this, come speak to me or my sister, Alex, in the intelligence department." But no one said anything they just stared him down and then eventually began to disburse to do their daily routine. Some spent time turning over chairs and tables as the council began to have second thoughts about what they had just said and done.

Three days had passed since the meeting and no one had signed up for the journey to Washington besides Adalard, Alex, Davis, Akio, Jackie, and John. They only waited for so long because they wanted the masses to calm down a bit to make a rational decision, but it was becoming apparent that no one was going to help them, it seemed that six were all that was going on the trip in the next four days. So, the six gather in the intelligence department and discussed what the plan was. The original plan was thrown out the window because they didn't have the required number of people and the ones who knew how to fly were possibly not going to sign up. The new plan was to drive all day and night till they got to Washington D.C. It was about an eighteen-hour trip so everyone would switch out every six hours driving. They agreed to have two cars and two week's worth of food if they got delayed or lost.

When their meeting was almost done, Molly and four others came in and asked if they still had room on the sign in sheet. This caught everyone off guard, they never expected to see people actually show up and help after what they lied about. Molly assured them that they had calmed down after the meeting and agreed that if the roles were reversed, they would have done the same thing. But they made it clear they were never going to let them live this down. The six knew she was just giving them a hard time, but they honestly knew they deserved it.

However, though the six appreciated them wanting to help, they couldn't let them. The six didn't have to say anything to each other, all they had to do was look into each other's eyes and knew their answer for them. They were still kids and had a chance at a life when this was over, they couldn't risk their lives for them.

"Molly, we really do appreciate your all wanting to help, but the best thing for all of you is to stay here, where its safe." said Davis as he looked at her and her friends.

"Oh, like you all have a massive amount of people just waiting to line up for this?" Molly said irritated. "You guys need the help of dozens of people, there's no way in hell you all are going to do this alone."

"Kids, I don't think you understand the severity of this situation." said Adalard, concerned. "It's going to be dangerous, we have never traveled outside Kansas before, we don't know what we're going to run into or who we might run into. Its better if you kids stay here."

"We don't care! I understand that you all don't want us to go, and I get that. But what's the point of having a future that you feel useless in. I don't want to personally look back on my life and say to my kids, 'Ya at the final battle of our home I was sitting around pouring coffee into mugs of other survivors.' This is our home too and we have every right to fight for it!"

"Molly, we will fight for our home so you don't have to, we're not going to gamble your life!" yelled Alex. "Besides kids there is no guarantee you would make it back alive and even if you did there is a chance of serious and life threating injuries, ones that we would be unequipped for." said Alex, worried.

Molly was about to say something till Davis said sternly as he slapped the table, "Kids this isn't up for discussion, you're not going!"

The teens were about to argue with them some more before someone from the guards came around the corner and told John out loud, "Hey there, Venvoss in a dark-colored armor approaching the entrance of the mall!"

Davis became annoyed by the guard coming into his department yelling for help when he had a radio at his disposal and said, "I know this isn't relevant to this situation but, people we have radios, you don't have to run around looking for people every time there is a problem. Just give a shout out through it."

Davis saw the guards face turn slightly red as she realized the reality of the situation and said, "Sorry, in hindsight I should have just done that, it would have saved me some time."

Davis groaned in anger and stood up, "Sis you're with me, John, get your people prepared for any surprised attacks, kids you all stay here!"

Davis and Alex both quickly got away from the table and bolted out of the intelligence department. John rushed out soon after them and ran the other way, yelling on his radio to get his men and women ready for anything that came their way.

The two siblings ran up to the roof to see men and women running around getting ready for a fight. They loaded their guns and aimed them below to the ground of the parking lot, waiting for the signal to fire. When the siblings approached the ledge, they saw the armored Venvoss approaching slowly towards the doors. Alex materialized her sword and waited for the first sign of an attack just like the guard, but Davis didn't draw his weapon. He wanted to know why the Venvoss came to them now and furthermore, what it wanted. As they waited for the Venvoss to get closer something caught Davis attention as he began to twist and turn his head all around looking.

"Sis, last time we faced a Venvoss it had a horde of beasts and serpents, right?"

"Yes, you were there, remember? Wait, why do you ask?"

"Where the hell is the horde?"

Alex began to look around as well and realized he was right, there was nothing. "Davis, I don't like this, why would it come alone?"

Davis paused for a moment and said with a little fear in his voice, "Either to surrender or fight us to the death."

As they stopped talking the Venvoss looked at the top of the roof and could see everyone pointing their guns at it and saw a few people shaking with fear. It didn't say anything, but it did point to Alex and Davis. Everyone looked to the siblings seeing if they would react to the Venvoss' pointing, but all Alex did was flip it off as a response. Davis grabbed her hand and told her to knock it off as he forcibly lowered her hand. He looked at the Venvoss and spoke aloud to it, saying he knew they could understand them, and he wanted to know why they had come to them. The Venvoss stopped pointing at them and lowered its hand to its side and spoke in its own language for a few moments before Alex screamed out "SPEAK ENGLISH, PLEASE!"

The Venvoss stopped talking and took a second, then spoke up, "I am here for my vengeance." Everyone looked stunned to hear an alien speak English so perfectly but was terrified that it was there to harm them. Suddenly it materialized its own sword and stuck it down in an arch, a flash of light bolted past the two of them and left a trail of molten rock on the once concrete ledge. Alex and Davis could feel the power of that lighting as it shot past them and Alex became pissed that it tried to attack them like that. She took her katana and pointed it and while making her terrifying expression that she gives to anyone when they cross her path with hate. The wind starts to pick up and the two siblings hair starts to flow in the wind as the alien demands, "Accept your fate humans and let my people have their retribution."

Davis looked at Alex and said a little afraid, "This got intense fast."

"Ya, it did, and I don't like his attitude towards our people either!"

said Alex as she jumped off the building while simultaneously creating an elongated pole from the ground to the roof with what she had left of her sphere.

As she descended to the ground on the pole Davis yelled out to her, "What are you doing, you psycho?" He began to run off the roof to follow behind her as he said to the guards, "Keep an eye out on it but not to interfere, we will handle this for now, but if things get too intense, then get everyone underground without us." As he ran inside, he could hear the sound of swords clashing with one another. Panicking not only for his sister but also everyone he used his radio and called Akio. "Akio! Things got intense fast, Alex is fighting outside. Get everyone underground, something tells me it's going to be a clash of titian in a few minutes!"

"Roger that, Davis!" said Akio back.

In just moments an alarm sounded throughout the mall, it was the siren for a tornado, but they used it because it was a familiar sign to get underground quickly. As his feet touched the ground floor Akio and her people split into teams, escorting the injured and impaired to safety first as the other survivors followed behind. He rushed down the hallway and turned so fast that he slipped and fell on the floor. He got up, shook off his pain and continued to rush to the front door. Drawing in closer to the door he could hear metal ring out more and more, clashing frequently, to the point where it started to hum like a song. He got his own sword out and pushed open the door to see his sister trying to keep her ground and block all attacks. But because of its four arms and blades, she could barely keep up with it.

Davis rushed into the fray of battle as the Venvoss swung all its blades down on Alex at once. She managed to block it, but she fell to her knee due to the strength of all four swords. It pushed down with its blades harder, and Alex begun to bend backwards. She began to tremble at the pain from the position she was in.

The Venvoss with its swords atop of hers said, "Humans are so weak."

Davis quickly used some of his sphere and turned it into a gauntlet and jumped towards it with his swords and his side and his fist raised ready to strike. "Get away from my sister!"

The Venvoss looked at Davis for a second and that was when his fist connected with its helmet. In one punch he managed to hit the Venvoss away so hard that he flew into one of the old stores that was raided months ago. Davis panted for a few seconds before his sister got up and said, "Damn Davis, where did that come from!"

"Don't know, don't care, look alive." said Davis as he pointed his sword at the building.

The Venvoss come out of the darkness of the building and picked up one of its swords. It rolled its neck for a second and then rushed towards the siblings with great speed.

"Davis, you take the swords on the right, I've got the left!"

"No complaints here!"

The Venvoss was right on top of them, but the siblings dodged out of the way, and were now on opposite sides of the being. The two rushed towards it and they began to clash with it. Swords clanged out and sparks flew as the siblings and the Venvoss of his swords crashed into each other. They were at a stalemate for a second before the Venvoss turned its swords in its right hands down, it quickly spun its swords along with Davis's in a circle, then flung his sword way from its own. Then it did a three-sixty around to Alex's back side and kicked her into Davis. As she was flung towards her brother Davis used his sphere to make some boots to get his stance back together, he quickly grabbed her arm and did his own three-sixty, flung her back at the Venvoss. She quickly understood what her brother was doing and got her sword aloft. The Venvoss tried to ready its fall for her sword, but when she was in range she tucked her body in, flipped over, then extended her legs. The Venvoss noticed that she too was wearing the boots that were made from the sphere and as she made the connection its body arched backwards as it stumbled. It dropped two swords as Alex landed on the ground safely, then Davis hopped over her with his sword and smacked one of its remaining swords out from its hands.

The Venvoss took its remaining sword and swung it down at Davis only for Alex to block it. Then the Venvoss looked to its swords and the three flew directly to his hands. It swung its swords horizontally at the siblings, but they quickly ducked and in unison, both extended their shoes length to their thighs and swept its feet. As it fell to the ground, the siblings rose and with their shoes smashed the heels of their feet into its chest. The force of the combined power from the siblings made it crash into the ground so hard it cracked the cement around it. The Venvoss let go of its swords and grabbed the siblings' legs and shoved them off, making them fly back a few feet. It staggered off the ground and yelled "HOW? HOW AM I LOSING TO YOU?"

"Unlike you, the two of us spent years learning how to fight and preparing for something like this!" said Alex as Davis and here were back-to-back.

"How humiliating that you can't even take down two humans by yourself and you even have four arms to do it with." said Davis as he pointed his sword along with Alex's at the Venvoss.

Saying that made the Venvoss angry and it blindly charged towards them with only two swords. The siblings charged at it together and once again the swords clanged. As their swords constantly contacted one another it took one of its arms, grabbed Alex by her shirt and flung her to the side. Davis turned his sword around and flipped over the shoulder of the Venvoss, dragging its arm along with him. With it distracted, Alex used her sword and summoned a wave of heat and unleashed it on the Venvoss knowing Davis was protected around his body. As the wave raced towards the Venvoss it too summoned a wave of heat and fired it at Alex's, canceling both out. Then it took its left arm and punched Davis in his stomach, hard. Davis lost his grip and when he did the Venvoss flung Davis back over its shoulder and punched him again in the same place, sending him flying across the pavement. Davis rolled on the pavement for a few seconds as Alex ran at the Venvoss making another katana to use with her sphere. Davis staggers up and coughs up a bit of blood, then he takes his sword and follows his sister's lead and makes another sword and rushes into battle again. As their swords constantly contacted one another as the six blades began to become heated almost like they were charging themselves, the energy around their blades began to affect the air as they saw it began to crackle with electricity.

The energy between the three was getting intense and out of fear for everyone, Davis ordered, "Everyone on the roof get inside, take shelter inside, NOW!"

Everyone hesitated for a moment because they didn't want to leave them out there without cover. But when Alex's sword crossed the Venvoss's, and a bolt of lightning came out from the collision, firing over the roof, missing everyone, but it got them moving. The guards were gone now and when it was just the three off them left, the battle went into sudden death. The force of energy that they used when flinging their swords intensified and when they collided with the Venvoss's, a powerful wave of sound rages out cracking the pavement on the ground and some nearby windows. The two could feel their skin begin to burn like it was on an open fire and saw their hair and clothes were beginning to singe with scorch marks. They could smell the flesh on their hands begin to cook as blood began to find its way through the cracks and tears of the skin, as the blades turned hot white. They both started to feel dizzy, and their vision was becoming blurry, as the Venvoss waited to see what they were going to do next. The two were tired, and on opposite sides of the Venvoss again, but as a final attempt to stop this creature, Alex used the last of her strength to swing down her sword in an arch to release a heated wave of energy. The wave made its way towards the creature; the heat was so intense that bolts of lightning followed its path as she fell to the ground on the verge of passing out.

The Venvoss turned and blocked the wave of energy and lighting bolts with all four of its swords, its back facing Davis. Though his vision was blurred he saw a chance to end this but didn't know what to do. But then realized something, even in his state, the armor it was wearing was made from the same material as their spheres which meant it could reradiate heat or at the very least absorb it. Davis stood tall and in desperation took a shot in the dark and formed thousands of marble sized orbs around him from his white-hot sword and the remaining sphere. He imagined the energy being transferred from one to another and had each one hover in midair. As the small orbs glowed white like stars Davis used his mind to throw them with the same technique Alex used on the flying serpents.

Cutting through the air, hundreds of small spheres flew towards the Venvoss as trials of lightning bolts began to follow behind. The creature saw what was coming towards in the corner of its gaze, but it was too late to act. The orbs contacted the amour and quickly bounced off with a pinging sound and no longer glowing white, but its simple silver color. For a moment, the creature didn't understand what he was trying to accomplish, but then a moment later, its armor began to turn red and began to burn its body from the inside. Davis was right to think the material could not pierce the same material; it could transfer energy and heat that it absorbed. All the energy and heat he had gathered was now being forced it into the Venvoss's armor, quickly cooking it alive.

The Venvoss began screaming in pain as the armor started to turn white, it seemed victory was at hand, until another Venvoss jumped in the way and created a shield, blocking the rest of the orbs. Once he was out Davis called his orbs back to him and rematerialized his sword, as the other Venvoss disintegrated its shield to face Davis. It stood in front of him as it turned its head around to see the wounded Venvoss remove its armor quickly, getting away from the pain and discomfort. When its armor was off Davis could see this creature looked reptilian even with its scales burned and damaged. Though he was curious about the Venvoss's appearance, he put it off and faced the one in front of him as Alex rejoined him quickly.

The two were careful, though they were still tired and feeling dizzy. This was a perfect opportunity to attack, but then Venvoss didn't. Instead, it approached them casually and gave them both a vial of clear liquid, but by earths standards it was more of a bottle than vial. It looked down at them for a moment to see the damage that had been caused by the fight. Both were exhausted and in pain but still breathing well to an extent.

When it saw that they were okay, it kneeled in front of them and said in English, "Use that when you're inside, you might like the results and please forgive Vomanin, he just grew impatient, he has lost so much, and he couldn't bear to lose anything else."

Davis stood there wide-eyed, he recognized the voice, and in a surge of adrenalin he shouted out "ICIN?!"

Icin was surprised to hear his name, he figured that they would have found out, but not so soon. "I'm impressed young human, you managed to figure out who I am." Said Icin as he stood up.

"You said Icin?" said Alex confused.

"Yes, this is the Zenitharus of the Venvoss if I remember correctly."

"This is wonderful, I knew I could trust the common humans to help my people rather than your leaders and it seems you have learned a lot."

"I'm glad you approve, but why aren't you going to tell us what happened between the Venvoss and humanity?" asked Alex.

Icin's tone of voice changed from being joyous to stern as he said, "I understand this situation isn't ideal for anyone of our species, but we had already tried to inform your leaders of the situation between us and the other worlds, and they have refused to aid us in our crisis. I know it's frustrating not being told why, but the reason I'm having you all search is to prove your worth to the stars. The moment I stepped on your world I saw opportunity not only to help, but also to evolve beyond anything any of your kind would ever dream of. This is a chance for not only your people to seek the truth because it shows how far you will go to do the right thing, but also show you all don't think the same. This will show the other races that you all might not be one, but it will also show them you can't be judged by a few humans' mistakes."

"But whatever is happening to your people you're just letting it continue. You're making them suffer even more, is it worth it?" Asked Alex.

"Of course, it's not. But I still believe humanity is cable of being part of an endless universe and grow with it. Besides what's happened to my race along with the others isn't something that can kill us like before. Granted it is still an issue that can lead to the end of multiple races, but not for a few more years."

"Wait, what?" said Davis, shocked and confused.

"Then what was the purpose for attacking our world, why attack any of us!" yelled Alex with rage.

"We were promised that we would have a cure for our race and the other seven, and it did work but not without a side effect, now instead of immediate death, we now face a slow one. Your leaders have tried so hard to hide the truth and because of it we had to act. That is why we have taken so many of your kind, to force their hands into doing the right thing. But the fact that they let their own be taken and held captive shows what they are willing to do to stop the truth from being known. That was why when I saw this young human being, I took a chance, and my faith in him has proven fruitful."

Icin turned away from the siblings and help Vomanin up to his feet as he said, "But know, this little human, to fix the mistake of your world's past, the price that will have to be paid might be a steep one."

Before Alex could yell at Icin some more he grabbed Vomanin and used his sphere to create a pair of wings and took off into the skies with a few winged serpents following behind them.

She was pissed that they just left them with every vague answer, "GET BACK HERE, YOU FUCK, POOR EXCUSE FOR A REPTILE, DON'T YOU DARE LEAVE US WITH ANOTHER ENIGMA, DAMN IT!" While Alex was cussing at them as they flew away Davis could understand Icin and his people's intent, this wasn't just a test it was a second chance. Besides, it wasn't like they didn't know what to do now. But what made him uncomfortable other than his burns and cuts was what Icin said, "The price that will have to be paid MAY be a steep one." Davis wanted to know what happened even more than ever and he believed that Icin knew what he was doing, or at least he hoped.

Davis grabbed his sister's shoulder and told her, "Sis, it's okay, let them go, this will be over soon anyways, so there's no point of arguing."

"I'm sorry, Davis, but I'm so sick of this crap!"

"How the hell do you think I feel?" said Davis snapping at her, "I'm pissed too, but regardless, we have to keep going."

"Fine, but next time I see him, I'm going to smack the scales off of him!" said Alex, moving away from her brother and heading inside.

Davis followed behind but then heard a familiar chirping sound, he didn't stop on his way to the door but knew what it was. It was that strange creature again, the one that had been following him. He nearly had forgotten about that creature, but the fact it was still watching him made him feel like he was being stalked as he entered the mall. As he entered the main hall with his sister, Akio and John rushed over. As Davis was about to wave at them, he remembered his left-hand glove. He faced the palm towards his face, and it was in ruins, revealing his scar from the stab wound and the silver veins. He quickly put his hand to the side as others came up hoping they wouldn't notice its singed.

"Are you two alright?" asked John.

"We're fine, John." said Davis.

"Are you sure, we should get you both to the medical department to get checked out."

"That won't be necessary, we have this," said Davis as he showed them the bottle of ointment.

"What's that?"

"Icin told me and Davis to use it when we got inside."

"You're not going to, are you?" said Akio.

Davis then investigated the bottle from the side and tried to swirl it. When he looked at the context it looked more like a mucus than an ointment as he saw it. When he used the word "mucus," he remembered the first day of the attack, right after the crash. There was something on his arm that healed his wound and was mucus-like as well. "Wait, I think this was used on me once before."

"What, when?" asked Alex.

"The first day this all happened I got into a crash, but before that I got hurt, my arm was scraped badly, but after the crash I found this strange mucus like substance on my arm, and it was healing it."

"You think this is the same thing?" asked John.

"Only one way to know!" said Davis as he opened the lid of the bottle and had his sister pour some on his right hand.

Davis quickly rubbed his right hand with his left, making sure none of them saw his palm. After a few minutes his right hand began to heal quickly, the burns were gone, and the scars it would have left, never came to be. When the three saw what was happening to his hand, Alex began to use the ointment as well. Within moments their bodies stopped aching and searing with pain.

"Wow, that stuff is amazing," said John.

"And better still, there is enough for the rest of the injured and impaired." said Alex with joy in her voice.

Davis noticed Akio staring intently at the bottle and then their hands. Then she looked at Davis in the eyes, coldly, like she was studying and trying to figure something out. Davis thought for a second that she had noticed his burnt glove and saw the sliver veins. But she didn't say anything to him, she just stared at him.

"Akio?" said he said, nervously. "Why are you staring at me like that, you're scaring me!"

Akio closed her eyes and said, "Sorry, I am just concerned. It seems you have more experience than anyone dealing with these things, and you only know as much as we do. Yet somehow you have found yourself in the middle of this, intentionally."

"What do you mean by that?" asked Alex, concerned.

"It just seems, that this has been staged since the beginning, that's all I'm saying." said Akio after she opened her eyes and stared at the floor.

The others didn't know what she was talking about, especially Davis. To him it almost sounded like she didn't trust him, that he was hiding something from her. Davis knew she wasn't wrong, but the only thing he hid was the scar and the strange effect it was having on his body, other than that he wasn't sure what she was insinuating. Akio turned around and walked away, quietly as the others stood there appalled.

"What was that about?" asked Alex.

"I don't know, she's been a little weird lately, but I wouldn't worry too much about it. Akio is just being Akio." said John trying to drop the matter. "I know that stuff was good for you guys, but why don't we get Emily to check you both out when we get everyone up from the basement."

The siblings felt fine, but the way Akio acted and John's insistence they thought it wouldn't hurt to give them peace of mind. The three began to walk down the hall as the sirens turned off and John ordered everyone on the radio to come up from the basement. Just like before, the injured and impaired were escorted first and everyone followed. People were scared at first to come up, but when some stepped back onto the ground level of the mall and saw Davis and Alex they seemed released. It wasn't long before everyone was out, and the people returned to their living areas. The siblings pushed back some of the crowds and entered the medical department where it seemed Emily was already in wait. She did her standard checkup, except Davis had deliberately hidden his left hand from her. After all she hadn't seen it since the day he got it. It seemed however luck was on his side as she seemed to overlook his hand entirely. He assumed she just thought with his glove on, his hand was fine.

After they were done Emily said, "You two are good to go."

As they were about to leave, Alex gave her the bottle and explained what it did to them, how it was able to heal them. Emily seemed doubtful at first, but after all she had seen so far she went against her own code and used something that wasn't modern medicine by human standards on her other patients. The siblings let her be with her patients and as they left many people waited for them outside and began to cheer. The crowds of people were overjoyed it was over and that the two siblings came out of it alive.

But Davis wasn't a fool, he knew many of them were still angry about the secrets they kept from them; however, they might have been grateful. Eventually everyone went back to their routine and just as the battle started and ended, so did the day.

Things that night started to quiet down, and people were beginning to eat dinner as Davis sat at the furthest table and began to chow down on some spaghetti and meatballs. But as he ate, Molly came out of nowhere and said, "I'm glad you're still alive and all, but what about the mission to D.C.?"

Davis cleans his mouth of and said, "Molly, we have already discussed this, you and your friends can't go."

"WHY NOT?" screamed Molly as her voice echoed out. "You don't get to deiced what's best for me, I want to go and fight." People tried to ignore her shouting, but some could not help but just stare at her.

Davis sat in his chair and yelled back "You are too young and after what my sister and I had to put up with today, its painfully obvious things have gotten worse! The leader of the Venvoss is starting to lose control of his own people and it took me and my sister everything we had just to bring one down. Not only are you not going, but after that battle I think it would be safer if me and Alex went alone, at least we stand a chance." Before he could continue with his explanation one of the people stood from their chairs and yelled out, "WILL YOU STOP PLAYING THE SELF-RIGHTEOUS HERO FOR GOD SAKES?"

Davis stopped talking and looked behind Molly, towards a woman standing up as she continued, "You can't keep underestimating us, that's what got you in trouble to begin with. We may not have your spheres or fighting abilities, but we are not useless, damn it. Now yes, many of us are still angry that you lied, but you are not going out there on your own to risk your lives to save the world while we here pondering whether or not if we should do the same."

Many people began to agree with her knowing that she was right, they would rather go out there and help than be constantly thought of as weak and helpless. The women walked towards Davis and demanded to give her the sign-up sheet for the mission and let her and Molly sign up because weather he liked it or not, he was getting their help, and if he had a problem with it, he could stick it. Davis was surprised at first but then smiled faintly, he got up from his chair and went to his department, grabbed the sign-up sheet and headed back. When he came back with the sign-up sheet there was a line of about fifty people waiting to sign the paper with Molly in the front. In that moment Davis was afraid of them dying but was proud that they were not going to listen to him and felt like a hypocrite for underestimating them like others had done to him. He handed the sheet to Molly, who snatched it out from his hand and pulled out her pen and signed her name on the first line and told Davis to stick it. One by one, people began to sign and tell Davis to stick it, but he didn't care at this moment he was so grateful that they were going to help he didn't give a damn.

After everyone had signed up, the total number of people they had went to fifty-six people. To Davis, this meant the world to him, not because of how many stood with him, but by how many were brave enough to fight; they still and hope and found a new fire to ignite for themselves. Davis got out his chair and stood on his table and said to everyone who sighed up, "Thank you all so much for helping us, but now comes the hard part, pulling it off, this is just like a heist people, we only get one shot at it. So tonight, get a good night's sleep and at seven o'clock sharp, come to the intelligence department to discuss the plan." No one argued with the time and went off to their living quarters to slumber away before the big day.

Davis went back to his department and looked at the list again with joy. But as he held the piece of paper, he saw his destroyed glove. He went over to his desk, placed the list down and grabbed a new one to replace his ruined one. He slipped it on and then looked at the list again, then laid down in his bed and sighed saying, "Here we go! Let's just hope everything goes smoothly." It took him some time but eventually he managed to get a PowerPoint presentation to work with everything they needed, their schedule, what route to take, and above all watching out for their safety. Once everything was in place, Davis laid down in his bed and tried to force himself to sleep till the sun rose again.

Soon it was the next morning and when Davis was cleaned and more presentable, he began to welcome people inside and had them sit down as Adalard, Alex, Akio, Jackie, and John approached the department.

"We have everyone one?" asked Akio.

"Seems like it."

"You ready to do this?" asked Alex as she saw her brother's nervous demeanor.

"No, but I'm going to do it anyway." said Davis as he entered the department.

"Good morning, everyone, I hope everyone slept good last night because we have got a lot of shit do before we take off so please pay attention."

With his introduction over he and began explaining the plan to them. Two teams, one in the air and one on the ground, when they meet up, they will take a small team of twelve to get the Hope Diamond and figure out what they needed to do next. The remaining people would stay behind and keep their temporary base operational till the mission was over and would gather supplies and find survivors, they would also rotate teams on guard post and supply runs for efficiency. But if things went sideways, they needed to meet up with everyone at the edge of D.C. If everything went according to plan, then they could get in and out quickly with no problems.

"So, with that said we have the route already planned out and somewhat of and idea of what to expect so anyone have any Q's for me before we adjourn?"

"Yes actually, you want to fly there but how do we know we won't be intercepted by those winged freaks?" asked on of the pilots.

"I'm head of the intelligence department for a reason. Over the last few months, I have seen these creatures attack humans because they have been capturing them. However, I noticed something, they don't seem to attack anything larger than them. Once I saw them at the Sedrick County Zoo when we were looking for food and it was facing off against a grizzly bear. It didn't win and fled in fear at it because I believe it was too small for the challenge. So, if you get a large enough plane, it might confuse it for a predator, besides these things are herbivores not carnivores so the chances of being attacked are minuscule even with a massive pack. Plus remember their job is to capture us not kill us." "Oh, that makes sense, I think? So, what type of plane do you want us to use?"

"The biggest and fastest you can get your hands on! Any other Q's?" asked Davis, but when no one responded he said, "Then for the next three days well will be looking for vehicles and taking out supplies from the basement for the road. When we get the teams made up, we find a plane, get it fueled, and in the ready position for takeoff. Air team give yourselves a two hour's head start before the ground team takes off so we have boots on the ground when we get there and you all have time to set up. Everyone clear on what to do?"

Everyone in the department gave an uninspired 'yes,' which Davis wasn't having any of "I SAID IS THAT CLEAR PEOPLE?"

The people got the hit of what Davis was doing and said with confidence, "YES, SIR!"

"Then meetings adjourn, let's get to work I want this stuff done like we did it a month ago!"

For the next three days people gathered supplies from the basement and vehicles they needed to get to D.C. The tensions were high, for in just a few days the journey towards the future was about to begin. Everyone, though they were anxious to get underway, they kept themselves calm as they prepare. With a lot of hard work and determination,they managed to salvage ten large semi-trucks for their supplies and their people, along with some small trucks and cars for extra room while they found a 747-8 model plane sitting in persistent condition at Eisenhower National Airport in one of their hangars. Then they began to assign people to ground and air teams. Alex was going to lead the air team with Jackie and John, and they would have a two-hour head start to get the plane in the air. While Davis would lead the ground with Adalard and Akio. When the air team arrived in D.C., they would have sixteen hours to wait for the ground team, which would give them time to get everything ready, once they meet up it was game on. When everything was nearly done Davis asked to see his sister Amelia in private.

As men and women alike were running around with supplies and maps, Davis found his way to the living quarters and saw his sister Amelia playing with Diamond. "Hey, Kitten, can I talk to you for a moment?"

Amelia could hear the seriousness of his words through his tone and asked Elliot to watch over Diamond as she talked with her brother. "What's wrong, did something happen?"

"No, no, no Kitten, it's just with half of the council gone things might get a little hectic around here without us. So, I was wondering if you could look after things when we leave?"

"But, why me? Why not Elliot or that wired boy with the mad scientist lab?"

"Because I trust you to do what's right, plus I get to piss off your husband for not choosing him and all the other haters who can't stand a woman in charge."

Amelia giggled at his joke and said, "If you want me to I will, and I promise I will do my best."

"I know, sweet heart." Davis said while hugging her.

Davis said goodbye to his sister, brother-in-law, and his little niece Diamond as their sister Alex entered in to say her own goodbyes. Davis left the living quarters and did one last inspection with Mathew before they went to get some dinner. Everything was in order as Mathew told Davis, "Thank you, by the way. Thank you for opening me up to this craziness, it might not be what I was expecting, but I'm glad that it did."

Davis said nothing as he gave him a nudge with his first on his cheek as they began to head into the food court for their one last dinner together for a while. The night was filled with laughter and joy as people seemed to forget that tomorrow was their departure. Everyone cheered and cried as they said their goodbyes to their own families, wishing them luck on the road ahead, and to come back safely. But the fun was short lived as time flew by too quickly for anyone's comfort. Davis could see that everyone had lost their sense of joy as they all realized that the clock struck ten. As everyone began to depart from the food court, Davis said his good nights to everyone and that he would see them in the morning as Adalard accompanied him to his room.

"Well, that was fun, too bad it's over."

"For now, imagine the overwhelming joy the world will feel when this is over, and everyone is reunited with their families and friends."

"I'm glad to see you out of the slump."

"I am, too. Depression doesn't look good on me, does it?"

"It doesn't for anyone, you little shit!"

Davis began to laugh hard with joy as they came up to his department. The two said their good nights, but tonight, they had another guest, Emily who had fallen asleep on this air mattress. "It seems she can't handle her alcohol." said Adalard.

"You can just sleep in my bed tonight." said Davis. Adalard had no objections and so, the two decided to share one bed, at least for that night, soon Davis could hear his friend snore occasionally as he began to fall asleep. When his eyes shut, he was surrounded by the darkness that aided him his whole life, for rejuvenation, but then just as he lost his senses his alarm blared off and he jumped out of bed with the determination to face the day alone with everyone one else. He got Adalard up and both made their way to the food court where men and women alike were crying and saying another goodbyes to the air team as they began to load up the trucks. When they were ready many of the air team members began to hug their children tightly showing them how much they loved them. The children saw their mothers and fathers leave them behind to fight for their future and their freedom to grow up without living in fear, but even Davis could see like anyone else there that they didn't want them to go.

Once the air team was on the road and then out of sight, the ground team began to pull around their trucks and began to pack as well, waiting for the air team to get airborne. As soon as the ground team was ready to go the air teams plane flew over. The ground team saw it as their signal and as the plane shrunk in the distance, they got in six trucks and six cars, waved one last time to the loved ones, and began the on journey to D.C. As they did the people from the mall managed to get onto the roof and waved to them hoping they would see them, knowing they were there to see them off.

"Alright everyone let's hit it, we got a lot of ground to cover, and remember, we are coming back!" said Davis encouraging his people.

"Wait, Davis! Where's Emily? I thought she was going to see us off?" asked Akio.

"She came to my office, but she seemed to be a little out of it so I told her to lay down until she felt better, I'm sure she will be just fine, and when we get back, we can see how she's doing." Davis replied as he got into his car.

Akio shrugged it off and got in the car with Davis along with Adalard and Molly.

Every vesical fired up their engines and as they roared, they begun to move, and soon the trucks and cars took off towards the highway, in their rearview mirrors they saw people on the roof begin to shoot off fireworks and cheer as the left to the toll route. The trucks blared their horns and called in on the radio asking, "Did you know they planned that?"

Davis picked up the radio and said, "No, but let them have it, after everything I think they deserve it!" As Davis saw them celebrating in the review mirror, he began to feel a severe pian in his left arm. To him it felt like it did when he was on fire in the dream and the pain started to spread to his chest like something was trying to smother him. Davis knew that whatever was happing to him was now beginning stir up and was only going to get worse. But in his heart, he couldn't tell anyone out of fear they would call this mission off, or he would be left behind. He kept quiet as they made their way down the road. When they made it on the toll road, they burst through the pole and continued onward.

"In hindsight we should have taken that down when we had the chance." said Molly.

"Don't worry if anyone asks the aliens did it." Said Akio, smiling.

Everyone in the car giggled and laughed at Akio's joke, all except Davis that is, all he did was look out the window of the car, he saw Wichita off in the distance grow smaller and smaller until they turned a corner and it was gone. Davis feared that that image of his home was possibly going to be the last one he ever saw and under his breath said, "Good-bye."

CHAPTER 11

19 hours of hiding.

As the ground team advanced down the toll road was nearly completely bare, like someone or something had cleaned off the roads just for them. But for their own safety they kept an eye out for anything suspicious or out of the ordinary as they headed towards D.C. Looking out into the countryside that remained vast with no damage in the fields or forests since the war started. SSmall towns they passed on the road were empty and without people, wild animals were the only things the team could see, and it looked like they seemed to reclaim their lost land. All the stores for construction, gardening, and landscaping outside of Wichita, were empty, even though the team believed that there were many supplies still left inside. In the front of this massive caravan of people, Davis's car led the way, guiding them to their destination. Adalard sat in the back seat with Davis while Molly and Akio at the wheel sat in the front. All were quiet and deep in thought but as for Davis he looked at his maps of the toll road to plot out every possible detour to account for any obstacles that might get in their way while the others talked to each other. Davis did like hearing their conversations but kept to himself as much as possible to keep anyone from noticing he was in pain. Then a voice broke the silence.

"Davis do you really think we might be the last humans free right now?" asked Molly as she stared out at all the window into the empty world.

"I don't know, the Venvoss took many people, but I don't believe they caught everyone. There might be people hiding out somewhere like in the towns that we passed."

"How can we be so sure?" asked Akio.

"I don't know. Currently most people keep to themselves, not many people can handle having to protect hundreds of people let alone face an alien force from beyond the stars."

As Davis plotted out alternate routes his radio crackled with a female's voice "Davis you there? You, okay?"

Davis picked up his radio and answered back "Yes we're fine up here everything okay back at your end?"

"Ya, it's just.... Please tell me you've noticed it, too."

"You mean the fact that there are cars thrown into the ditches and the road is mostly cleared, yes."

"It's not just on this side, I looked over to the road heading west and its cleared, too. What do you think moved all the cars?"

"I don't know for sure, but I'm betting it was the beasts, on day one when they chased me the crushed and moved cars out of the way with their bodies, there like living bulldozers." "Wait?! what then why would we drive there then if they're that strong!"

"They are strong yes, fast, no, I clocked them to be about 34 miles an hour, we're going nearly eighty, so odds were going to flatten them like a pancake before they even get a chance to attack."

Davis could hear on his radio a sigh of relief from everyone driving on the channel as he looked out the window to all the abandoned cars. Wondering how did the people get caught? As he began to take deep breaths to try and nullify the pain in his arm. Then Davis went back to his maps and counited to look for detours. Hours passed since they made it on the highway and things out there on the road seemed quieter than normal, even with basically a caravan rolling around. Each moment passed seemed to be forgotten as quickly as it came, and the hum of the car made everyone tired. Davis had experienced this before on the road and planes, but this felt distraught. Unlike the other times he was able to complain about the pain in his back or his behind. But the only pain he had known now was his arm and chest. He remembered back to the days before their journey when Emily wanted to check on Davis's hands and his body after the fight they had with Vomanin. However, Davis refused to let her check his body and became aggravated when she would ever try to inspect him. He knew she was only trying to help, but he couldn't let her see him like this, especially now that they had the help. Eventually Davis began to keep his distance from Emily and made sure she would try to sneak a peek at his arm or torso when he was sleeping. Even putting a camera inside his department and room to make sure she couldn't sneak up on him. Yet on the day before they left, he couldn't escape her, so he did something to her to give him time to get away. But he remembered why he did it, to give humanity their chance.

That night...

"Davis I'm here to speak with you!" asked Emily as she walked into the intelligence department.

"Not now Emily, I'm trying to make sure everything is in accordance with the plan and making sure we have alternate routes, and when to switch drivers." said Davis rummaging through his papers.

"Davis!" she yelled as he ignored her. "I haven't seen your arm in weeks, you keep putting it off or ignoring my request to check it. You are about to go halfway across the country with an unusual infection that we know nothing about!"

Davis got up from his desk and started to move around Emily as he said, "We can't worry about that right now."

As he passed her again Emily had enough of this waiting game. "I must check on that arm of yours before you go!" She said as she grabbed his left arm after she stormed in. Even though she had only just grabbed him gently, it felt like someone had just punched him.

Davis wrenched with pain, hissed, and flicked back for a moment, but that was all that she needed to see. "Davis did that hurt? I barely grabbed your arm and yet your response wasn't what I was expecting. Please show me your life could be in danger."

Davis managed to get her to let go and said, "Look I will show you later tonight I have other things to do that are too important, but when I'm finished then you can do what you need to."

Emily sighed and told him, "I can't believe I'm agreeing to this, but, fine. I will be back here at seven thirty sharp, and you better be here, otherwise I will bring your sisters in on this!"

Davis became angered that she threatened him with his sisters but kept a calm look on his face and agreed and both went their separate ways. Throughout the day he could see that Emily was keeping an eye on him from afar as he was finishing up a few final touches on trucks and cars that needed done before they loaded up the supplies they were going to take. Once everything was accounted for Davis asked one of the medical workers to pack some sleeping pills for the road to get everyone who wasn't driving to rest properly so they could switch out after a few hours. It didn't take the worker long before she gave Davis the pills to put into the supplies, but as he did Davis managed to slip a few sleeping pills from the supplies away.

"I hope I don't have to do this, but I will if I must." Davis thought to himself.

He didn't want to do what he was about to, but it was just as a last resort if things went south. He headed back into his department and immediately began to make some tea for them both. Davis took the pills from his pocket and crushed them into a powder and mixed it in with the sugar, as he waited for Emily. He felt terrible that he was going to do this, but there was too much at stake to be stopped now.

Right on cue Emily walked in at 7:30 and wasted no time when it came to her patients. She approached Davis and saw him drinking some tea and asked bluntly, "Alight, no more games show me your arm."

Davis was hesitant at first, but knew he needed to wait and see what she said before he had to drug her, though in his heart he truly wished he weren't going to. He placed his cup down and removed his glove to show her his hand. The metallic veins moved up his fingers and made his fingernails turn red and the once indigo colored wound had mixtures of black and orange surrounding it. The area only had been in his left hand, but now it had spread further, all the way around his hand. Emily asked, "Davis this hasn't spread, has it? Please remove your shirt." Davis did as she asked, and her face turned white with horror. She could see this thing move up his arm and across his chest. In her eyes Davis could see she couldn't believe it, and in her mind, she screamed to herself, "Why did you for any reason would Davis keep this secret?" She knew in the beginning how bad it was, but she never thought it would get this bad!

As she examined his arm from a distance, she saw there was a bruise from the place she had grabbed a few hours ago when she tried to confront him. She didn't even grab him that hard and yet there was a massive bruise right above his wrist. Emily sat down shaking and asked, "Davis are you in any pain or sort of discomfort?"

"To be honest when you grabbed me it felt like someone who lifted heavy weights had just punched me."

Emily immediately started to scream at Davis, "Are you out of your damn mind? Why the hell did you keep this from all of us, from me? For God sakes you could have exposed whatever that is to someone else without even knowing because you didn't want to say anything!"

"It's not simple and you know that!"

"Davis as your friend and GP I'm ordering you to stay here under close observation until this war is over. I mean we don't even know what this is yet you pull this bullshit off!"

"Emily, you know that's not an option, I'm the only one that can see into Icin's sphere and no one else can!"

"We don't know!"

"Emily you were there when the second clue was discovered remember, you, John, and Mathew didn't see shit! That's proof that I'm the only one who can!"

"Then let them go get it and bring it back Davis, if you go on that mission, you're not just putting your life endangered, but others as well, you would be a liability!"

"I know the risks, but you said it yourself we don't know what's happening to me or what this stuff is. I could be dying for all I know, but if we wait for them to get back it could be too late to get the information. This is a race against time, time that I might only have a little of. The only logical answer is to go and get it, even if I die you all still get the information you need to end this! If I must die so others can live, then so be it!"

"I'm a doctor, Davis! I took an oath to save lives not let them run after death!"

"So, are you willing going to let billions die to save one?"

Davis could see Emily's frustration as she began to rub her eyes, desperately trying to figure out what to do. Davis sat her back down and said, "Look why don't I pour you a glass of tea and we can try to work something out."

Emily said nothing as he went to the tea kettle and poured her a cup. In the pits of his soul, he could feel himself being torn apart by what he was doing.

He never wanted this to be the outcome, but he needed to get there, even if he had betrayed his most loyal friend, and so he began to mix in the sugar mixed with the sleeping pills into her tea.

Davis handed her the cup and said, "Lavender tea always calms your nerves and I made it just the way you like it."

"Thank you, Davis." she said as Emily took the cup and quickly began to chug it down. When she was done, she said, "Davis, I'm just scared for your. safety, I need you to stay here so I can keep an eye on you and try to stop, whatever this is. Alex and the others can handle this mission without you, and I know it's not in your nature to be selfish, but please stay-" Then without warning she stopped talking and tried to shake herself awake. She stood up and started to lose her balance as she said, "That's strange why do I-" she looked at Davis and she saw on his face his guilty look as he grabbed the cup and put them back where he got them. "What did you-"

Davis faced her and said, "I'm sorry Emily, but you can't stop me from doing this, and I can't have you standing in my way."

It didn't take her long to realize that she had been drugged, but it was too late to do anything, it was already in her system.

"You drugged me!" she yelled as she fell to the ground.

"Just enough to make sure you stay asleep until after we are long gone. But I'm sorry, maybe one day I can regain your trust and your forgiveness, but I can't risk everyone else's lives for mine, I can't risk yours either. Please understand I'm doing this because there might not be another way, I will not let anyone else fall. Not even for me."

Soon after that, Emily had passed out as Davis prepared his air mattress for her and later, he and Adalard came back to find her as they too fell asleep till the sun rose in the sky, the mission was finally underway, and everyone began to head out including Davis. Emily was sound asleep when he left his room and hoped it would stay that way for a few more hours, just to make sure they were out of range with the walkie-talkies. But after almost four hours of driving, they didn't hear anything, it seemed that Davis had gotten away with it. But Emily's words rang in his mind. She was right, eventually his condition would slow them down and everyone would find out the truth. He knew he would have to deal with it eventually, but for now he needed to focus on the task at hand.

Adalard could see that Davis was in deep thought again and asked, "What are you doing writing a book in your head or something?"

Davis turned his head to face Adalard, "I'm just worried about what we're going to find in D.C."

Akio was driving spoke up and said, "Everything is going to be fine, we have Alex ahead of us, and she is strong, plus with her own sphere weapon she would be hard to take down in a fight."

Davis appreciated her sentiment as she praised his sister, but he was a little concerned about someone else: Emily. He hated the way he left things like that but in that moment, he didn't see any other choice. But then as soon as this thought came it left when Molly asked, "Hey not to jump off topic, but I have a question for Davis?"

"What's up is something wrong?"

"No, it's just did you or are you and that guard Michael an item?"

"What does that have to do with our mission?"

"I'm asking because it's a long drive and I would like to get to know everyone better and I'm asking because he said you two were and I told him I didn't believe it and now here we are."

Molly's questions caught everyone off guard as Davis asked, "Michael Brook?"

"Ya, he said that you two used to date before all of this, back in high school anyways." replied Molly.

"Well, we were, but it was a secret romance scene he played football and was going for a scholarship we had to keep it on the supper D.L."

Molly turned to face the front window as she said, "That is just complete bullshit. You shouldn't have had to hide yourself because your secret love was a football player."

"Molly, he didn't ask me to, I was the one who told him we needed to keep it on the D.L." said Davis.

The news surprised her, and she refaced Davis saying, "WHAT? WHY?"

"Molly you must understand even in both of our generations it is still considered taboo to be gay or even curious about it. Eventually that fear turns into anger, even hate. Honestly, I feel sorry for them, they live in so much fear of the unknown that they're not living their lives, that the only way they can live is now, is to make enemies of people who don't believe the same as they do."

"He said you do it because you were ashamed? That you never wanted to move forward with your relationship?" said Molly questioningly.

"I was never ashamed, I was scared that if he chose me, he would have lost a chance of getting a good life and education. That scholarship of his was his ticket to a great future and I didn't want him to give it up, not even for me."

"But he didn't want to lose you, he was willing to give up everything for you, and you turned him down because you didn't want him to?" said Molly a little upset.

"I know, but when you love someone, Molly, you will do anything to make sure they're happy, even if it means you aren't in the picture with them. That's what love can be, giving and sacrificing for the person you care for above all less in this world."

Molly turned back towards the front window and said, "Honestly it sounds like you made a decision without him, and in doing so you hurt him…." Then she took a moment to process and realized why he did it. "So that way he didn't have a reason to look back, so he could move forward without you!"

"Precisely, Molly, I knew that the price was steep, but I paid it willingly so he wouldn't have to." said Davis in an upsetting tone. "Do you ever think you find another?" asked Adalard.

"I don't think he could even if he wanted to." answered Akio. "Davis cares about people so much that he would never let them get hurt or ruin a chance to be happy. His ideology is that everyone comes first, and he comes last. So, to him his happiness isn't worth much, but the joy he gives others is worth everything."

Molly turned to face Akio as she wondered how anyone could think like that. Everyone was entitled to their happiness, yet his only came from the joy he gave to others. She couldn't understand how someone like that could think in this type of world. But then she thought to herself maybe that was exactly what the world needed. People to help each other bring joy through and little things that make life so wonderful. Rather than worrying about how different each person was. Molly looked back at Davis and wondered after everything he had done so far just to make the many happy, she wondered what she could do to help return the favor. Even though his latest escapades have only been to keep everyone in the dark.

As she turned back in her seat one more time, she noticed that Davis seemed a little uncomfortable as he was holding his left arm but said nothing.

She figured something was wrong with his arm and decided to hide it from everyone. So, when she turned around, she asked, "Is your arm okay?"

"Yeah I just pulled it when we fought that Venvoss, Vomanin, I talked to Emily about it before we felt, she said it would get better in a day or two I just have to take it easy for a bit, then I'm all set to fight again," said Davis innocently.

A few hours later everyone in the cars and trucks switched places as Davis called out to the others to take a quick bathroom break, they needed to hurry up as Akio and Adalard switched places. Molly stayed in the car as the two switched as Davis reentered after everyone was done with their business. It didn't take long for them to do their business and when they were positive everyone was there, they began to roll out on the road. The four in the car remained quiet for three hours as they had nothing to say. Davis eventually decided to take a nap to pass the time and as fast as he fell asleep.

Three hours later the car came to a stop and Davis was awoken from his sleep by Adalard. It was his turn to drive and the last few hours before they made it into D.C. and the sun had just gone down. Davis got out and told everyone to take their breaks, switch, and fill up on gas, that they were in the final home stretch of their goal, in six more hours they would be in D.C. and meet up with the air team. People began to switch and go do their business as Davis filled up the tank with their gas can, but then he could feel that they were being watched. Once he was done, Davis closed his door to shut off the car lights and could see that strange creature flying overhead again.

This time it seemed more at ease being around humans especially this many. Thinking back on it this thing might have been watching him the whole time he was inside the mall and going on runs. After all this time this creature didn't leave him alone, it just stayed in the shadows watching his every movement. Davis was impressed that this flyer could keep up with them going seventy-five miles an hour for a twelve-hour period, but eventually it would have to rest at some point. Davis heard the honk of the truck as the driver yelled out, "We are going or what?" The driver startled him, and his eyes turned away for a second to face him, but when he turned back, he saw the creature gone again.

"Everything okay?" asked the driver.

"Ya, just a little tired, let's move out," said Davis as he put the gas can in the trunk and got in the drives seat. He readjusted his seat and mirrors as he looked into the dark skies, wondering where it disappeared to. He started the car and began to drive off into the night with the others following behind now accompanied by that creature.

Davis kept his eyes out for the flyer just in case it tried anything as the others slept throughout the drive. Eventually Davis let his guard down about the creature, thinking that there was no way that little thing could possibly keep up right now. It was late and even though they were beginning to run on fumes, not matter what it was, it needed to rest at some point. As they drew closer to their destination Davis could swear that he was hearing something on the road ahead. Davis called the other cars and trucks and asked everyone to stop their vehicles for a few minutes. When everyone came to a stop, they asked Davis what was going on. He had no response for them and got out of his car listening to the sounds around him. He could hear something on the wind, almost like someone or something was humming.

Davis called the others on the radio and asked, "Does anyone hear that humming or is it just me?"

"It's not just you Davis we all hear it," said one of the other drivers.

"Someone check to see where we are please!"

After a few minutes another driver called on the radio, "I think we're near Mount Hope in West Virginia."

Davis liked to hear they were closer than he first thought to D.C. but didn't like the idea of going anywhere near Mount Hope. It felt like something was lingering in the air, something ominous. Davis didn't like the idea of getting any closer until he made sure it was safe, so he radioed everyone "Listen something isn't right here, why don't you all to stay where you are, I'll drive up the road and see if anything a wrong." Everyone didn't have any arguments and agreed to stay put.

With everyone still sound asleep, Davis carefully rolled his car up the road and began to see a very thick fog begin to roll over the road. "Oh well that's not even remotely ominous." said Davis sarcastically to himself.

As he went deeper into the fog, he could hear the humming sound get louder, it almost sounded like a few men and women from mass about to sing a hymn. But then it became soft, then softer, until it was silent. Davis stopped the car and waited, wondering why the humming stopped. Everything was far too quiet for Davis's comfort and as he peered out the front window trying to see through the dense fog. Then he heard a small pitter-patter of something hitting the car. Like something had just scurried across the side. Davis looked out the side window but saw nothing. Then he heard a different noise, something scrapping something against the other side of the car. He turned his head in the other direction but saw nothing again. "What the hell is-" he said before a loud pounding sound comes from behind him. He turned and saw a human's bloody hand on the windshield, it startled Davis, it was dragged off to the side. Davis thought at first someone was hurt, and they needed help, but before he could exit the car, another hit came from behind on the back window. Then Davis hit the brakes, stopping the car dead in its tracks as more bloody hands began to make it into the car and windows. The blood was beginning to cover the entirety of the windows as the faces of people began to take shape in it. Davis tried to turn on the windshield wipers, but even they were not working, and when he tried to open the door, it became jammed.

"WHAT IS THIS?!" yelled Davis as he began to hyperventilate. He heard his heart bound in his chest to the point where he felt it was going to burst out.

The hands continued to smack the windows and metal of the car as Davis closed his eyes and placed his head on the stirring wheel saying, "This isn't real!" repeatedly. He lifted his head from the wheel and looked over at his friends, wondering if they could see what he was seeing. He turned his head towards Akio, but he saw something that made him shiver with fear. Akio was lying still in her seat as blood dripped from her body, her skin ripped away from her stomach, and her organs hanging out on the side. Davis was frozen for a moment and then regretfully looked behind at Molly and Adalard. They two were in the same condition as Akio, lifeless.

Davis looked away and said again, "This isn't real," repeatedly.

Feeling the overwhelming fear Davis started to lose control of his breathing and became dizzy from the shortness of breath. He almost began to cry when a new sound entered his ear, it almost sounded like a fly, or dozens of them. He didn't want to look again, but against his own instinct to look away, he peeked into the corner of his eye. Akio's body now was rotted and covered with maggots and flies swarming in and out of her mouth. Davis froze again and was on the verge of passing out, but then a scream came out from behind him. Davis couldn't look behind him, but he guessed it was Molly's voice.

The corpse of Molly jilted forward and pointed out the front window, still screaming as Davis tried to ignore her, putting his hands on his ears, desperately trying to block out everything. Then the corpse grabbed Davis by his shoulder and started to shake him violently.

Davis grabbed her arm and said, "Don't touch me!" as he looked away.

As he was busy dealing with Molly, he placed his hand on the cars horn and accidently pressed it, releasing its loud booming sounded, which echoed into the night. It was for a few moments, but as it roared out, everything that was happening before had vanished. The hands disappeared, the blood was gone, and everyone in the car was fine. Molly stopped screaming and looked down at Davis and said, "Did you see that!"

"I don't know what you saw, but I saw was horrifyingly scaring!" said Davis trying to catch his breath.

Molly sat back down and asked, "Davis what's going on?"

"I don't know! Tell me what you saw out the front window!"

"It was like a skinless human snake with eyes on its chest and a mouth on its stomach and it was screaming in pain."

"Okay, I didn't see that, I saw hundreds of bloody hands all over the windows, and the three of you were corpses."

"What?"

As Davis breathed deeply, he took a moment and thought to himself. Then it all became clear to him as the fear dissipated from his mind, he was right it wasn't real. "We need to get out of this fog!"

"Why?" said Molly looking around.

Davis put the car in reverse, turned to face the review window, and sped out quickly as Molly braced herself, "I don't know why but there is something in this fog that's messing with us!"

"What do you mean something is messing with us?"

"Nothing happened this entire trip until we got inside this fog, we need to see if whatever is in here can follow us out!"

Davis kept his foot on the gas as he drove backwards, waiting to see the clearing, and the lights of the other cars. Yet as he drove backwards, him and Molly started to hear a loud thud, in front of the car. Davis refused to look forward as the thuds became more frequent and louder, he knew he had to focus on the road behind him. Molly was panicking and she started to mumble something to herself. Davis wasn't sure what it was, but he wasn't too concerned with it at the moment. As the thuds grew louder the fog began to thin out, the fields and road were beginning to come back into view. Then just before they got out of the fog a massive roar was heard in front of them. Davis couldn't control himself and he looked back as Molly covered her eyes and ears screaming. The shadow of a very large creature was coming into view, but no real details of the strange beast came from beyond the fog. It lunged towards them as the car sped out of the fog, trying to take a bite out of them, only to disappear as they left the fog.

Davis drove further back, made the car come to a stop, and began to look into the fog as Molly tried to catch his breath and reopened her eyes. "You alright Molly?"

"Davis, WHAT THE FUCK WAS THAT?" Molly screamed with terror.

"Don't know, but whatever it was, didn't follow us outside the fog, in fact it vanished." Davis said trying to calm her nerves and his own."

"This isn't some sort of cartoon mystery on T.V., that was real, it couldn't have just vanished!"

"Molly, you need to calm down! Whatever it was, it scared me too, and I don't know what's going on but I'm going to check it out." said Davis as he got out of the car. It was strange how the door was unlocked unlike before, but he thought to himself maybe he wasn't actual grabbing the door handle, maybe he just thought he did.

"Are you insane?" Molly said as she grabbed Davis's shoulder. "That thing is huge even you'll die from it!"

Davis was adamant and told her, "Let me go, Molly! I have got this!"

He forced his arm away from Molly and stood in front of the car in its head beam lights. He stared into the fog and whistled of his sphere which came out from the trunk of the car. As the dust approached him the silhouette of the creature was back, but this time he could see more detail. He saw this thing had hundreds of human arms holding severed heads all looking to him. Their eyes lit up yellow like a cat in the dark and kept a fix on him as he stood still. He could hear from behind him Molly screaming, "Davis please get back in the car!" as the thing began to make little lunges at him. But he didn't move from his spot, he made his halberd, and pointed it at the creature. It began to inhale deeply, and it looked like it was going to spit something out at him, but he still didn't move.

"WHAT ARE YOU DOING, RUN!" screamed Molly.

But he still didn't listen to her, instead he was trying to listen to the world around him.

Things became silent and still, but then he heard something from in front of him on the ground. He quickly turned his halberd into a staff and swung it down under the creature. As it lunged itself forward releasing a massive cloud of yellowish gas.

Molly was confused as she yelled out, "WHAT THE HELL ARE YOU DOING?"

As he completed his swing the creature, its attack, and the fog faded away into the winds of the warm summer night.

Molly found herself dumbstruck, she had no idea what just happened, she quickly stepped out of the car, and heard something whimpering in front of the car. Davis bent over and pick it up as Molly asked out of fear "What is it?"

"I don't know?" said Davis as he dematerialized his weapon and showed her the creature in his hands. He held a small grey creature in his hands, it had six legs, two in the front and four in the back, it was roughly the size of a soccer ball, with four eyes in a diamond formation, and it had a mouth on its head.

"I've never seen something like this before!"

"Neither one of us would have, this creature clearly isn't from Earth, but I don't think this thing is used for war purposes. If it was, we would have seen it months ago."

"Wait, how did you know it was there, and where's the other creature!"

"There is no other creature, this little guy was the one of the many that caused all the trouble, and the only reason why I knew it was there was because I heard its foot steeps."

"How is that even possible for a tiny little thing lit this to do that much!"

"Molly, I said one of the many, I don't know how these creatures do it but there is no way one of these little guys could do all that alone. I guess that its kin fled after I swung my staff, how they did it I don't know, but I think they might have some sort of aqua-kinetic abilities and might be telepathic, allowing us to see and hear things that aren't there."

"Maybe we should keep it." she said as she took it from Davis arms and held it close to her body.

"Molly for God sakes it's not a pet! It's a wild animal from another world! If anything, once this is over, we need to inform Icin about this, I have a suspension that these little guys are an invasive species. They need to be sent back to their original home world."

Molly looked disappointed as she stared down at the little alien, as it held onto her with its legs like a child grabbing onto their mother. Though Davis couldn't read minds he could read body language and Molly showed hers to be upsetting. A few moments later Molly put the creature on the ground and scooted it away with her hands trying to make it leave. The creature looked confused at the two and darted its eyes in all directions possibly thinking there was going to be a sneak attack, but when nothing came it bolted into the trees and bushes around the toll road. Davis told Molly that she did the right thing as he went into the car to fetch the radio. Molly followed slowly behind and entered the car slumping in her chair. Once Davis found the radio, he called to the others behind them and told them they were good to go. The other drivers called back answering Davis's response and said that they would be there in a few minutes.

Davis was glad that this was resolved and saw that Molly was still upset about the alien creature. He shook his head in disbelief and wondered how someone could fall in love with something that fast, he hadn't met anyone who could, and it made him feel a little ashamed. As he turned his head to check on the others, he could see that they were still asleep. Then he quickly realized they were still asleep after all of that?! Davis quickly opened Akio's door and shook her until she was awake. Davis just needed to know if the two of them were okay and why were they asleep for the entire ordeal. As Davis continued to shake Akio she slowly began to wake up and, in her irritation, punched Davis in his chest. Davis could feel the wind get knocked out of her as he staggered up trying to get his air back.

Akio awoke to see that they were stopped and wondered why, until she saw Davis holding his chest in pain. She realized what she had done in her sleep and got out to see if he was okay while taking out some earplugs. Davis got his answer about how they were asleep but was pissed that they did that, if this had been a life-or-death situation then death surely would have won. Akio told Davis to get in the back seat to check up on him as Adalard woke up on his own accord. Akio apologized so many times about hitting him that hard, but honestly though Davis was in pain and angry he was genuinely impressed by her strength in her sleep. Akio told Davis to get all the way in the back seat and she would drive the rest of the way for hurting him, but Davis didn't want her to do that. He knew it was an accident, but he did tell her that they could not wear earplugs any further and explained why.

When Akio heard of what transpired when she was asleep, she felt great shame. They all could have been killed because of her and Adalard's mistake. Davis could see in her eyes that she was furious at herself and tried to get her calm down and that things were okay now, they just needed to be more careful in the future. However, Akio was adamant and told him that she was taking the wheel and she didn't want to hear another word about it. Before Davis could even say anything, Akio slammed the door shut on him and got into the driver's seat as the other trucks and cars started to roll up. Akio put the car into drive and began to speed down the road as the others began to speed up.

Adalard finally was fully awake, and he removed his earplugs and asked, "What did I miss?"

Davis and Molly, both gave him a cold dare stair and told him in unison, "A lot, sleeping beauty!"

Two hours later they were finally nearing the end of their long trip and they could see from the toll road over passes the ruins of neighborhoods of the outer lands of D.C. Everyone in the caravan wondered how any leader could leave their people to fight their war while they ran off to save themselves. But soon their thoughts faded from their minds as they saw a few strike eagles fly overhead. In the distance they could see helicopters hovering over Wichita of D.C. and smoke rising from certain parts of it. Whatever was going on it was apparent that it was a military operation, but the question on everyone's mind was, why now? After months of hiding why just suddenly come out?

The caravan made it off the toll road and headed to the airport on the highway and tried to be quick so they wouldn't arouse suspicion. But as they made their way there, the highway suddenly just cut off. The overpass that went to the airport was destroyed and the only other way was to cut through the surface streets. Nobody liked the idea of this because it made them think it was a trap, that they were being funneled in. Unfortunately, they didn't have much of a choice, they had to get to the airport and rendezvous with the others. Davis pulled out his radio and turned it to channel seven to see if he could raise his sister. He kept calling and calling her as they made their way there, but something wasn't right, normally she was always so punctual. Yet now her being quiet wasn't a good sign in his book.

They were about another thirty minutes from the airport when his radio started to crackle with his sister's voice coming in and out. Davis tried to radio back to her, but something was jamming the signal. Davis started to shake the radio, trying to regain the signal, but with no luck. Then Akio slowed down the car and said, "We have got company, people."

Davis, Molly, and Adalard looked outside the windows and saw movement in the bushes and building on the street. "You think they're friendly?" asked Molly.

Akio stopped the car and said, "Why don't you ask them?" Akio parked the car and pointed out the front window with her hand on the wheel. Everyone looked out the front and saw a military squad with their guns pointed at them. Davis gave the radio to Molly and told everyone to stay in the car as he exited with the sphere turning into a powder and followed him out. Davis approached the squad slowly, as the dust followed behind, he wanted to see what they wanted and if they were friendly, but just in case he wanted the element of surprise.

One of the soldiers yelled out for Davis, "Hold it!" and he did as the soldier asked, "Identify yourself!"

"My name is Davis Ring, I'm from Wichita, Kansas."

The guards looked in shock for a moment and asked, "Can you prove that?" Davis slowly reached into his back pocket and pulled out his wallet and tossed it to them.

"Is this your wallet? Why do you still have this?"

"Just in case if my body is brutally mutilated or lost then that can help identify me and help find my husk's way back home."

The supposed captain looked at his I.D. and gave the order to stand down and asked, "Okay you're clear, but I need you to come with us."

Davis nodded his head in agreement and began to head back towards the car when the captain said, "No, just you alone."

This caught him off gaud as he turned around and asked, "Why?"

"It's classified and were ordered to take you by force if we have to!"

This made Davis weary, but he could risk the lives of his group or men and women who were just following orders. "Fine, but let my people pass unharmed and get to their destination."

The captain hesitated for a minute and told her guards, "Alright, people, you heard him, get off the road."

Davis radioed behind him to the others saying, "Get going and keep going, I don't want a firefight, will meet up later."

Many of the drivers protested him leaving, but he made it clear through the radio, "Priority right now is to the airport so we can find and get the Hope Diamond as quickly as we can. I will deal with them, otherwise I fear we're going to lose this chance."

After his words were delt nobody argued and continued down the road without Davis as he to steeped out of the way. Seeing everyone drive away made him feel more relaxed and when they were out of eyesight. Davis headed towards the square and demanded, "Alright they're gone so where are we going?"

The captain looked at Davis seriously and told him, "The same place as your friends are going, the Ronald Reagan airport."

Fearing he just sent his team to die he quickly materialized his broad sword and pointed it at the captain's throat and was going to force him to talk. He asked, "Then tell me, what makes you think I won't just kill you for basically sending my people to a slaughter."

"Because they won't be killed, but they will be lied to!" One of the other soldiers said aloud.

"Oh, let me guess, whoever is running the airport doesn't want the truth getting out, so they trying to lie their way out of it because all the deaths in the world are currently on their hands and they're trying to clean it off so they can have a clearer conscious about their betrayal not only to humanity, but the aliens too, right?"

"How the hell did you guess all of that?" asked the captain.

"Because I saw it, all of it. But the truth isn't all there just yet, there is one more piece that is missing and we're going to find it here in D.C." said Davis as he continued to point his sword towards the captain.

"That's what we want, too." said the captain. "Things in the last few months have gotten worse in the circles of politicians, their arguments are strange. It almost sounds like they knew why they attacked and they're just beating around the bush until it just goes away. That's why some of us have stopped taking orders from our generals and politicians, they know what's going on and they're keeping it from us."

Davis dematerialized his sword and asked, "So you want to know why they came? Then answer me this why do they want me?"

The captain took a moment and said in a calming voice, "Because they think you have something that can lead to their undoing and personally, I think they're afraid of you and your sister."

"Why be afraid of us, they don't even know what we are capable of?"

"Actually, they do, they have been watching you from a satellite and someone in your mall is a mole for them. They have video of you and your sister practicing with your spheres and the fight you had with the alien along with the conversation you had with…Icin."

"So that's why they stopped contacting me, they knew I would discover the truth for myself, which would in turn make me turn against them."

"The politics have joined up with your sister at the airport along with some military, but it's all of publicity. She knows that they can't be trusted. We are on her and your side, your sister asked us to be the moles inside of the opposing military operations and let you all know where and when things are going to happen. This way you have no surprises and get what you need for the last clue and stop this war." Said one of the other soldiers.

"If you are telling the truth, then prove it!"

One of the silent soldiers gave his radio to Davis and told him to just press the button. Davis pushed it and spoke into it asking if anyone was there. It only took a moment for Alex to pick up and she sounded relieved to hear her brother's voice. Davis asked if this squad was trustworthy as he had doubts, but Alex reassured him that they were good. Davis told her that he would be there in fifteen minutes and that they were going to speak with the politicians when he got there. She agreed to his idea but also told him there was a surprise waiting for him when he got there.

Davis rolled his eyes and gave the soldier back his radio and told them to get out of there before they were spotted. The squad wasted no time as they took off pretending not to notice him and Davis had done the same as he took back his wallet and headed towards the airport. It wasn't a long trek through Wichita especially since there was no cars or traffic, and Davis found himself near the airport in a matter of fifteen minutes. When he approached it seemed that there was a lot of upgrades to the walls and fences around it, he couldn't see what was going on inside, but he approached cautiously. When he approached the front door, it opened on its own, and what he found inside surprised him.

CHAPTER 12

A politician's complication.

Staring inside the airport it almost looked like a familiar sight. He stepped in and the doors close behind him as he found himself surrounded by dozens of people running about. This place almost seemed like the mall back in Kansas, bustling with life and activities. But upon further inspection Davis saw that unlike the mall this space seemed more chaotic. People seemed to be rushing around in a panic, instead of pacing themselves. Davis thought to himself, "What is going on?" as he began to stroll into the crowd. He was amazed at this set up these people had made, but something told him that things were about to get more complicated. He didn't know why he thought this, but he listened to his instincts.

Walking through the crowd he began to take notice that men and women were beginning to stare at him and whisper to each other. He didn't understand why at first, but then remembered the sphere floating around him. In his own perspective, his sphere would make anyone start to question the being that carried it. He started to feel uncomfortable coming into his place and then he began to fear the worst. Eventually someone yelled out from the crowd, "Hey you there, the one with the sphere!"

Davis looked around trying to figure out where the voice came from. But then from behind, someone grabbed his left shoulder. The moment they grabbed his shoulder they grabbed it, hard. Davis knew they weren't trying to hurt him, but whatever was happing to him, made his shoulder feel like it was hit by a baseball bat. Davis restrained himself from screaming in the middle of the crowd but couldn't stop the tears from his eyes from flowing. He was spun around to face the person as they asked, "Who are…Hey, are you okay?"

The person standing in front of him was a soldier from the military and she had her hand on her gun. "You look like you're in pain." She said worried.

Davis knew he couldn't hold in his tears, but if she or anyone around him saw his hand it would be over for him, so out of desperation he made up a lie. "I got into a fight with an alien and my left arm took some damage, it is still really sore and you grabbing it isn't helping!"

The soldier let her hand off his shoulder and said, "Sorry, but I need to ask you are you Davis Ring by chance?"

"Yes, I am, and thank you for the pain." said Davis irritated as he whipped his tears away from his cheeks.

"My apologies sir, I'm Major Dehart, your sister and the politicians asked me to look for you. Your ground team told me you were kidnapped, and I was about to head out looking but then I saw you enter the doors, it looks like you handled yourself well."

"Thank you, I guess, but I want to know where my sister is and who is in charge."

"That is why I'm here sir. I was instructed to find you and take you to the conference room the moment you stepped inside." Major Dehart said as she walked past him. "If you please follow me."

"Hold it, I need to make sure my team knows I'm okay, also what do your leaders want with me." Davis asked curiosity.

Major Dehart sighed and said, "I only have heard rumors, but if they're true, if things have gotten even worse, then we might have to do something drastic."

"What does that mean, Major?" said Davis concerned.

"I don't know what they're planning, but I was asked to take you to them, even if I have to use force." Major Dehart said as she faces him with a cold stare and her hand still on her gun.

Davis didn't want any conflict especially with so many people around him, so reluctantly he agreed to go without hesitation and Major Dehart led him away from the terminal. The walk made them go through their armoires, warehouses, and even their storage areas. Davis was amazed by it all, but as he walks through those places, he started to notice that many of the routines are his malls routines. He didn't think much of it but something in his mind told him it wasn't a coincidence that they thought of the same things. He wanted to ask Dehart some questions but before he could the two found themselves in front of a door with two military soldiers standing guard.

As they approached the guards asked a question with their guns raised and pointed at them, "What's the code?"

"I'm not going to even tell you to shut up. You, Satan reject!" said Dehart without hesitation.

The guards lowered their guns and stood in attention just like before as Dehart opened the metal door. As it opened, multiple voices carried out into the hallways. Men and women alike arguing over something that Davis couldn't understand because they kept interrupting with one another. Dehart enter the room and Davis followed behind her but tried to keep a distance. As he entered the room the door behind closed as Dehart tried to get the people to stop yelling at each other. The men and women kept arguing over each other and ignored each other as Davis stood silently waiting for them to stop. As they argued no one noticed Davis standing near the door and yelled out, "Everyone, shut up!"

They all looked to her and all she did was point to Davis as he stood before them, "You all said you wanted to speak with me?"

One of the men spoke up, "Are you Davis Ring?"

"Yes, I am and you all have a lot to explain!"

The men and women looked at each other as each sat down and calmed themselves. The same man spoke again as one whispered something to Dehart and she left the room. "We heard you were kidnapped."

"It's not kidnapping if you go of your own free will." said Davis as he sat down. "But that's beside the main issue we have here."

One of the others spoke and said calmly, "We were worried about your safety."

"Okay let's cut the bullshit, if you all were worried about me or any of the people that you all left behind, then you would have sent out your armies months ago. So, what the hell have you all been up to for the last six months?

Why didn't you come look for us? What happened with the Venvoss that your so scared of that you refuse to say?"

"Davis, we know you're angry and scared, we will answer your questions, but this is all still new to us too, and we might have a bigger problem than just the Venvoss." said another leader.

"What problem is bigger than a galactic war!" said Davis enraged.

Before anyone could answer him, the door opened back up and coming thought was his sister Alex and someone, he didn't think he would run into, someone that made Davis almost cry.

"Jacob?" yelled Davis in surprise.

"What up, you noob, or do you prefer mister rainbow?" said Jacob grinning happily.

Davis jumped out of his chair and hugged his little brother with delight even though the pain in his arm began to stir again. But he was so happy that he didn't care about the pain, he was just happy to see his brother alive and well. "Jacob! I'm so relieved you're okay, but why haven't you answered any of my messages for months?"

Alex pulled Davis away from Jacob and told him, "Davis I know you're happy that we're reunited, but we can celebrate later. We might have a bigger problem than just the Venvoss."

"That's what they said too, what's going on?" Davis asked worried as he let go of his brother.

"Let's sit down and discuss this. Plus, you can shed more light on how bad everything is on our end." said Alex pulling Davis back to his seat.

Davis became worried by her words as one politician stood up and said, "Welcome Davis to the Seekers, my name is Mrs. Tenor, and we're here for the same reason as you all are, to end this war. As you are already aware decades ago the people of Russia, Canada, and China made a deal with the Venvoss for advanced technology in exchange for a cure for the bubonic plague. However, we don't know why they came back. According to their records the cure was made to perfection and worked flawlessly. We have heard that you were on the verge of ending this, so we want to help. But we have another problem the A.K.R. - alien killer renegades - want to kill the invaders and we have had no success with taking them down. Therefore, we need your help now more than ever, your sister said that you had something that only you can use to uncover the mystery and end this. We need to stop this before more people die or worse."

Davis wasn't surprised that these fools couldn't understand the severity of the Venvoss situation, especially since they had no clue about why they had come back, but he knew one thing, they were lying to him. The American ambassador had also made that deal with them, Canada refused at first, but only joined in after to help with the research. Furthermore, there were no records left in the world, so how did they find this information? In his mind he thought of three possibilities. Either they thought they could try to pin it on other societies, they had something to do with the Venvosses failed cure and documents destroyed and hidden, or they were lied to as well and didn't know what to think. Yet to him it didn't matter, for now, he would keep an eye on them, but the most important thing was to end this war.

"There's one other thing Davis the A.K.R. is looking for the presidential football."

"You mean the controls to the American nuclear missiles, why?"

"We believe the other side is going to use it on the structure out at the Great Basin desert."

"Wait hold on, if I have heard correctly, the football can only be activated by the current president's thumb print and unlocked by three keys held by separate men and women around the country?"

"That's true.... except there is an emergency release on the football if you enter in a special code, and it was hidden on the framework of the Abraham Lincoln portrait in the white house, which was taken by the A.R.K. two days ago."

"What?" Davis said angerly. Before anyone could say anything, Davis rose out of his chair and said, "Everyone shut the hell up for a damn second! Are you telling me, that without provocation you all put a back door on the most dangerous weapon in northern America!"

"It was a failsafe, besides what's the big deal they have killed billions of humans, why should we care if they use it?" said another politician.

At that moment Davis with so much rage pushed his chair out of the way and approached the politician turned him around and got into his face. His face was filled with fear as Davis said, "Maybe on the general notion that structure out there happens to be the place where the billions of our races that weren't kill are right now. So, if you or anyone uses it on it, which we have no idea if that structure is made from the same material as our spheres or if it has a protective coating, you would be committing genocide of not just of the Venvoss, but of our own and if that doesn't work then you're going to piss them off further which will make the war last longer and will decimate an enter area of our planet for eons! I am making sense now!"

Everyone in the office was dead quiet after hearing and seeing Davis's rage and the news about the structure. As he looked around the room, he could see from their shocked faces that they had absolutely no idea that the structure was a facility. Davis got away from the man's face and said, "Looks like you don't know everything about this situation and if you all had remained in contact with me instead of blocking me you would have known sooner!"

When he was finished, Davis left the office and slammed the door behind him. Walking down the hall Davis heard the door reopen as his siblings chased after him. When they caught up and were in private Jacob asked, "What do you all think?"

"Well, they're determined that's for sure, but their arguing isn't going to settle anything until we're dead." said Alex.

"We can't trust them," said Davis bluntly. "Look what happened, they left and only when they got attacked, then they cared. On top of which each one of them have their own agenda. But it's never a bad idea to stay near people like them with good intel, and if either side is looking for the presidential football then we have got a problem."

"Guys I have been with these people for months, they seem like they really want to get things to the way they were before. I'm not going to lie they can be difficult and snotty but it's not like they want it for themselves." said Jacob again.

"Jacob if they really want to end this, they would have told you all the truth, even if everyone had got mad, to stop this war and work with the Venvoss to conclude this situation. But instead, they chose to lie to you all and drag you offshore before the attack and left us at their mercy," Alex stated firmly.

"I know that everyone was pissed when we found out why they did it and more when they abandoned their people. But right now, we have to deal with this situation and deal with them later!" said Jacob sternly.

Davis looked out the window from one of the terminals and saw hundreds of soldiers from every branch marching and moving equipment around as he began to think of what they needed to do. Leaving with either side wasn't an option, one was already trigger happy and who knows what the other was going to do with it when they got it. But before they decided on anything they needed to check up on the others and see what they were currently doing. Davis asked Alex where the teams were as one of the politicians came up to ask Davis about something in private. Before Davis was escorted back Alex told them they were set up in hangars five and six and to come find them when he was done. Davis hated the idea of talking to them alone especially since his arm was acting up more now, he didn't want to get caught so soon after coming so far, whatever they wanted he prayed they made it quick.

Davis was dragged back into the office with the politicians as he sat down, he said, "Okay, what the hell do you want now? To send me on another wild goose chase like you did the first three months?"

"Davis, relax I know you're angry, but please calm down, would you like something to eat or drink before we talk?" said Tenor. "No, what I want is answers so stop beating around the bush and come out with it. I know you want something your body language tells me everything. You're twiddling your fingers, tapping your desk, and barely making eye contact. All the signs are telling me you're nervous, impatient, and afraid because you need something from me otherwise you wouldn't have asked me to come back alone!"

"We just want to talk."

"Please even an eyeless man can see you want something."

Mrs. Tenor ground slightly and told Davis, "No wonder they picked you, you have good perception." She sat down at her desk and explained, "Look, whatever you need to do with the Hope Diamond will help you do it, but when you're done with it to destroy it."

"Why? Why should I do anything else for you people. All you have done is made me and my people run around in a hostile environment for months while you went into hiding."

"We don't want the information to tear us apart any further than what it has. Davis, we don't want to have the rest of the world come back and everyone be at war with each other because of a past mistake. We're afraid if that information remains intact and someone besides you discovers it, they're going to find a way to show the world."

"Oh, I get it now you want me to not only clean up the mess, but you also want me to make it go away and throw it into the void so it can be lost to time!"

Mrs. Tenor smiled and said, "If you are successful then we will be able to reset all of America, and the world."

Davis was confused and asked, "What do you mean by a reset?"

Tenor looked Davis in his eyes and said, "The governments of the world, or what's left of them, agree that if this comes to an end then every country will start off fresh. No debt, and everyone will chip in to help rebuild our homes and lives. It's a win-win for humanity and the other races affected by this unfortunate war."

Though Tenor explained the situation, Davis wasn't convinced, there was no way it was going to be that easy or simple for any government to accept. Davis got up from his seat and told them unless they were going to be honest with him then there was nothing left to say as he made his way to the door and left.

Davis walked away from the office again, but the stress he was feeling along with his anger made him feel nauseated, or that's what he thought. He began to feel his arm throb with pain once again, but this time it was different from the other time. The pain felt sharp like he had been stabbed by a knife, he figured it was the stress that made his muscles tense up, which in turn aggravated whatever was inside his arm. Davis slowed down his walk as he tried to find his way out to the landing strip. His arm became numb like it had fallen asleep, he noticed his vision starting to go blurry, and he was becoming disoriented. Davis shook his head and slapped his cheek trying to refocus his sight and ignore the numbness of his arm, but it was in vain. His arm slowly woke up to a pain that felt like fire in his arm. Davis stopped and nearly collapsed on the nearby wall, he held the wall with whatever strength he could muster and said to himself "Damnit! Please, body, hold on a little longer, we're almost there!" Davis began to hold the wall as he made his way to the outside door. Desperately hoping that with a miracle they wouldn't notice his poor health.

Outside he could see the operations up close and personal as he made his way to hangars five and six, it seemed that these men and women were doing everything they could to prepare for battle, yet he could see that they were nervous. That's how it always started, the calm before the storm, or in their case the war. Davis found himself near the hangars as he stopped dead in his tracks, he could not find the strength to move forward without feeling like he was going to barf. He took a moment to try and get himself comfortable enough to speak and chat without looking sick when someone had grabbed his left arm and dragged him off behind some cars. Davis hissed at the pain from his arm but did everything to keep his composer as a soldier pinned him against the car. The man explained that he worked for the A.K.R. and that he needed to talk to him quickly before he got caught. Davis was willing to listen as he told the man to let go of his arm and explain himself to him without the aggression. The man did as he asked and explained that his name was Jackson, and he was trying to get information about the Seeker's and what they were up to. He further explained that it was this side who was trying to get the football to stop the aliens and that they had hid massive amounts of critical data about why they were here. He also admitted that both sides were guilty of desertion, but they were the ones trying to actually find a peaceful solution.

Davis shook his head as he knew that this was a possibility, both sides blaming the other to try and solve a problem they both created but in their own image. The soldier explained, "Once the football is on our side we need you to get the Diamond without looking into it until we can decide it is safe or not. I'm not going to lie, we know every little bit of why the Hope Diamond is so important, but we want to be sure that it is okay to use. That whatever it was, whether it is a chase of information, or a weapon, too valuable to lose or destroy."

Davis looked deeply into Jackson's eyes and couldn't tell if he was honest or not but told him, "I will speak to my team and get a plan together, but I don't make any promises." The soldier looked at Davis, knowing he wasn't going to persuade him and nodded his head with contentment. He stepped away from Davis to give him the space to walk away, as Davis went around the car. When he was out of sight Davis could hear Jackson's feet hit the ground as run off it. Once he couldn't hear them anymore Davis headed toward the hangars, even though he was a little in shock at the man's information, it was still good to get an understanding of what both sides wanted. Davis had to speak with his sibling and team to find the best course of action before things got worse or if it was too late. Davis came up to the open doored hangars his thoughts came to a halt. The hangars with his teams were bursting with activity. Everyone seemed to be like the soldiers in the airport, it looked like they were preparing for the worst as men and women alike were grabbing and loading guns, checking supplies, and making sure their vehicles were okay for travel. Even the guards that watch the front entrance seemed to be nervous and watching the entire world around them, as if they were expecting something to show up. Davis always saw this type of activity back in their own base, but everyone there was more at ease because they were used to the area, out here in unfamiliar territory even Davis could tell they were scared of the unexpected.

As he entered inside the fifth hangar, he began to search for his sister Alex and her team to get things underway. As he asked around, he still did his best to put on a smile and show confidence even though he still felt horrible. His body still wasn't doing any better and he could feel himself slipping away little by little. He stopped looking and sat down on a foldable chair and tied to rest his body, but it didn't last long as he heard someone from behind say, "There he is!"

Davis turned his head slowly with pain and saw his sister coming up to see him. Davis panicked inside, knowing his sister was going to notice that he looked terrible and would demand to see his wound. Davis turned his head back quickly as she came up to him and asked, "I'm glad to see they didn't do, well anything to physically harm you as I can see. But I'm pretty sure they gave you some info that's disturbing; seeing how disturbed you are and how terrible you look? What do they give you?"

Davis felt relief and in the back of his mind he said to himself, "Thank you God for making my sis so thick she wouldn't notice!" As he sat up to face his sister he put on his serious face and told her, "Ya, they did, and I got some more from another source of information. Where's everyone, they need to hear this too?"

"They're in the hangar next store, they're preparing to get everything ready for the mission and making sure there are plenty of provisions around."

"Let's go then, too much stuff to do, every little time to do it."

As my sister turned away to leave, Davis struggled to stand up and had to use the chair for support. When he made it to his feet, he could feel the dizziness come back as he saw Akio in the distance and called him, "Hey are you two coming or not?"

"Keep your walnut size brain in that head of yours were coming!" yelled Alex.

Davis shook his head to regain his composure and made his way to the entrance with his sister. Once outside they were greeted by John, Jackie, Adalard, and Jacob who were glad to see Davis. Adalard couldn't help himself and before anyone could say a word, he hugged Davis tightly saying, "When you stayed behind, I thought I wasn't got to see you again!" Though Davis did like that Adalard was worried, he really wished he hadn't hugged him. As Adalard squeezed his body it almost left like an anaconda was constricting itself around his body and putting so much pressure on his body, it left like he was going to be crushed. Adalard stopped hugging tightly as he could feel Davis shaking and asked, "What's wrong? You okay?"

"Ya, just a little too tight for my liking," said Davis still shaking with pain.

"Oh! I'm sorry!"

"It's okay, look I'm glad to see everyone, but there is something we need to discuss, in private."

As he said that Akio quickly showed Davis into the sixth hangar and led him to the back office with the others. As they entered, she told the guards not to let anyone in unless it was a life-or-death situation. She closed the door behind her and showed them a simple table with chairs with a single light illuminating the room and said, "It's not fancy but, hell, it works."

"So, what do they want?" asked John questioningly as everyone sat down.

"Look I'm not going to sugar coat this so let me explain everything." Immediately Davis told them what they wanted and how everyone was during their private meeting along with the soldier from a few moments ago. This made everyone more nervous than it did before they got there, but his younger brother was furious.

"Bro, I know these people, they are tricksters, they don't care what happens to anyone!"

"Bubba, in my meeting it seemed that your leaders don't care either, if they did, they would have solved it a long time ago."

But before Jacob could say anything Davis cut him off saying, "There are two other things we need to worry about."

"What?" asked Alex.

"One, the hope diamond itself, it seems both sides aren't too keen on keeping it around when or if I use it. One wants the information to be erased from history due to the fact that four governments went behind the world's back and did something to piss off eight other races and the other just doesn't trust them."

"We can work around that, but what is the second problem?" asked Jackie.

"We have a mole." said Davis frankly.

Everyone in the room looked confused and asked what he was talking about.

"Someone has been deliberately giving information about our operations and our mission to save earth but hasn't been giving these people everything. The way they reacted when I have told them that billions were still alive, showed me that they had no idea what was really out there. Meaning however the mole is has their own agenda and is clever enough to evade us."

"Okay, so what do we do?" asked Akio.

"The answer is obvious." said Jackie.

"No, that's why I'm asking?"

"We have to figure out how to get the Seekers and the A.K.R. to stop fighting each other and help us, along with finding the mole, getting the Hope Diamond, and saving our world before they Venvoss get tired of waiting!"

"So how do we do it?" asked Adalard.

"We need to get the mole!" said Akio.

"We need to get the A.R.K. to back down." yelled Jacob.

"No, need to get the Seekers to back down." yelled John.

Everyone began to argue once again about what to do next. Eventually they stopped listing to each other and began calling each other names, being disrespectful to each other's ideas and opinions, and and began to make threatening gestures. Davis rubbed his temples as the stress made his body become stiff and though this arguing was nuisance to him it was a good distraction from the pain in his arm. "Will you all shut the hell up, please!" yelled Davis.

Everyone stopped arguing and looked to Davis as he stood up. Everyone thought he was going to yell more, but they saw him with a calm face say, "We can't be at each other's throats when it comes to this. I'm so sick of all the arguing and fighting over deciding what to do. This almost feels like a presidential debate every day now where everyone losses their collected shit over the tiniest differences in opinion. We need a solution, and we are going to find one, but with no yelling and threatening gestures."

Everyone looked at each other and those who were still mad, that Davis could see they were a little embarrassed by their behavior. Jacob spoke up and said, "Okay, let's look at this situation. We can't let either side get the football or the Diamond, we must stop them from fighting each other, and above all worry about the Venvoss and mole. I don't see any way this is going to go smoothly."

"When does anything?" asked Akio.

As the teams sat in silence trying to figure out a plan Davis was hit with another case of nausea as he could feel the pain from his arm getting worse. He put his hand on his face to make it look like he was thinking of something, but he was trying to stop himself from vomiting. Davis desperately tried to keep down the bile and as he kept his hand to his face it began to become tighter, trying to keep his mouth closed. Davis was unable to hold it for any longer and said quickly, "Excuse me I need to go to the restroom."

Nobody seemed to acknowledge his statement as he plotted out of the room with a sudden burst of energy. Though he didn't know where the energy came from, he was glad it came when it did at that moment. As he ran out of the hangar, past all the guards and people he had known for the last few months, he began to become afraid, not of them finding out about his injury or illness but of dying. Outside, he quickly looked around for a place with no people and without thinking rushed behind the hangar. Away from the teams he began to vomit on the ground as he desperately tried to keep himself up with his strength. In those moments, he was more afraid to die even if it was to save others. In his mind he always accepted death as a part of his life, it was supposed to be natural, but his wasn't. After all the bile was expelled from his body, he laid against the hangar wall to recover, but found it difficult as his arm continued to rise in pain. With whatever strength and courage Davis had he gently pulled off his glove and saw that the once silver veins had turned violet, and his skin had turned red like it was fighting off an infection.

"Davis is everything-" Akio said as she came up from behind, but her thought came to a halt when she saw his hand. Akio gasped loudly and ran to the front of Davis, "Davis what the hell happened to your arm?" But he couldn't respond, he didn't know who she would take it if she found out that he was hiding something like this from everyone. But Akio it didn't take long to figure it out all she had to do was see where it originated from.

"Davis why didn't you say anything before? Why did you come along knowing you were going to get this bad? You could be dying right now!"

Davis managed to lift his head up to face Akio and told her, "I'm the only one who can use Icin's sphere as far as we know. I have no idea what's happening to me or even if its treatable. If I had stayed behind and something happened to me before you could get it back, then we never would have gotten the spheres last clue and end this. I did what I had to in order to save everyone, even though I'm scared shitless right now of dying."

"Davis, do you have any idea how much you risked! If the A.K.R. or Seekers ever found out about this, they could use it as an excuse to attack the Venvoss' strong hold or honestly God knows what! In all the time I have known you this has got to be the most idiotic thing you have ever done!"

Davis took a moment and replayed her words again, "If anyone found out about this," did that mean Akio wasn't going to tell anyone? "Wait, you're not going to say anything?"

With a heavy sigh she said, "No I won't, but you will have to eventually."

"Wow, Akio, I'm surprised I never thought you would help me with this?"

"I know what it's like to keep a secret, so don't worry. But I want you to listen carefully, stay hidden until I can find some pain killers and something to bring down your fever and try to get some rest." said Akio checking Davis temperature with her hand.

"Fine, but you better hurry, I can't be hidden for too long."

Akio understood and ran off back around the corner to find anything could help Davis as he lied against the wall. The cold metal felt heavenly on his back as it was sturdy and cool from the summer night. As he waited, he noticed the horizon begin to change color from its black and blues to its multiple color aura. Davis was agitated by the sun rise as he wanted a few more moments of the cool night to wash over him before the blazing day came. The sun crawled over the horizon with black spots beginning to come into view.

Davis was thinking that his eyes were playing tricks on him from whatever was in his system, but as it drew closer, he could see it was moving in great numbers. At first, he thought it was a flock of birds but when he adjusted his eyes in the light, he could what they really were. Davis's face was filled with terror as he found new energy rising him. He jumped off the ground in pain and quickly made his way back inside the hangar. Even with all the pain in his arm and the sickness still in his system he didn't seem to notice as he made his way inside the hangar and yelled out, "The Venvoss are coming!"

"What?" said one of the many people there.

"Hundred if not thousands of those serpents are coming in fast from the east!"

Everyone stopped what they were doing and looked out the open door of the hangar and saw as them. Hundreds of serpents beginning to eclipse the sun partly and flying with great speed.

Akio came up to Davis with some medicine and said yelled out, "EVERY-ONE, GET READY FOR BATTLE!"

As people began to scramble to find weapons Jacob ran out of the hangar and yelled into his radio, "MAYDAY, MAYDAY, WE HAVE MULTIPLE BOGIS COMING IN FROM THE EAST, GET LIVE ROUNDS!" Once he finished, he began to run back to the port as Davis slipped on his glove and sat down. Whatever adrenaline he got from the fear was dissipating quickly as he was trying to catch his breath with his people preparing for battle. Akio pushed her way through the crowd and came up to find Davis sitting down shaking.

"Davis how the hell did you get back inside?"

"Adrenaline from seeing the serpents, quick give me the medicine before what energy I have left fades away."

Akio helped him take the medicine as Alex approached, "Davis come on we have to get to out there!"

Davis wanted to help but he found it difficult to stand up or even lift his arms, whatever he had left was gone and Alex was right in front of him. He thought his secret was going to come out when Akio told her, "I don't think he can! He had some homemade jerky I made, and I think it gave him food poising!"

"HOW DO YOU GET..." said Alex as she growled with anger. "It doesn't matter, Akio get him out, we will deal with it after words. Davis stays here and out of trouble." said Alex as she was turning away from him.

Davis felt terrible that Akio had lied to cover for him and for being left behind so he thought of something, "Sis wait, I might not be able to fight, but I can still protect you."

"What do you-" said Alex as she turned to face him only to see his sphere wrap around her. Alex was shocked by her brother's actions at first, her face told Davis that she was betrayed but when she stood still for just a moment the dust turned to into armor around her body.

Alex and Akio were amazed as they asked, "How did-"

"When we faced off against Vomanin he reviled that the Venvoss armor is the same as the material as the dust, you are as of this moment you can't be harmed, or at the least chopped in half. Now go kick their asses!" Alex was astounded that her brother was able to do something like this, but there was no time to celebrate. Alex rushed out with her people to hold off against the armies of the Venvoss as Davis was left inside the hangar. Akio asked Jackie, "Jackie help me with Davis!"

"What happened?!"

"We don't have time, just help!"

Jackie quickly helped flit Davis out of the chair and laid him on an air mattress and was covered with a medical tarp to keep him warm. As he lied there Akio quickly grabbed some painkillers and gave them to Davis saying, "Quick swallow these!"

Davis put them in his mouth and found it hard to swallow without water. His mouth and throat felt dry with the painkillers in his mouth. It was almost like all the moister from his body was evaporating from the inside.

Davis took on big gulp without any liquid and got the pills into his body, though his throat felt like hell after it. To Davis it almost left like someone strangled him and he was his last breath of air. Davis looked to Akio as she grabbed an AK-47 and headed outside to join the others with Jackie. Once they two were out of sight all was quiet as he laid in his bed waiting for the first shots to be heard. He could only imagine what was going on outside for he couldn't see the battlefield or the hangars opening. In his mind he remembered all the times they faced off with the Venvoss before, the fear, anger, and sense of hopelessness in the air as the Venvoss drew in closer each time. Even now as he lied in the bed, he could feel it again as the hordes drew closer. His sister along with everyone else was going to be fighting for their lives again, but this time he wasn't going to be much help in any way. All he could do was wait and hope his sister could hold off the hordes as he stared at the ceiling of the hangar.

Yet every passing minute felt like an hour as he listened to the sounds in the wind. Then after a time the sound of a beast roar broke the silence, the earth began to rumple afterwards, telling Davis that there were hundreds outside, charging towards everyone. But even with the rumple of the Earth Davis could hear his sister call out and rally their people, "Everyone don't let your fear halt you. We have beaten these things before and will do it again." Everyone cheered and yelled with joy knowing with the strength combined like before, they could win again and again. No matter how many times they got knocked down.

"Everyone, take these bastards down!" Alex said as their people began to fire at their enemy.

Davis closed his eyes and wished them well, but then something happened to him. When he reopened his eyes, he was on the battlefield and standing right next to his sister, "Sis what's going on." He said weakly.

Alex didn't respond to his question and as he tried to place his hand on her shoulder his, it went through her. It startled Davis as he quickly removed his hand, "What's going on?!"

Davis thought he might have been dreaming what was going on outside and just decided to sit back and let his imagination unfurl since he couldn't do anything, and at the very least get an idea of what happened.

She wielded two katanas in this battle and in a single sweep of her swords, she sent a massive wave of energy and heat toward the beasts on the ground as her people shot the serpents in the air.

As they fell to the ground, the Venvoss came out of it with its swords on it sides and charged at Alex with great speed with its remaining beast behind it.

Alex stood her ground waiting for them to get closer as she charged her swords, when out of nowhere multiple rocket launchers from the airport came and bombarded the horde that was coming after them and Alex's team. The force of energy and sound wave was so intense, the beast near the explosion died instantly. The Venvoss was thrown from the explosion and staggered for a few moments before it got up and shook off its shock. Alex was finished charging as she released not a wave of energy, but instead turned her blade into thousands of white-hot small spheres and thrust them towards the Venvoss. It saw her attack and quickly created a shield to protect itself from the onslaught of belts. As they ricocheted off the shield, Alex ran towards her enemy with her sword on her side with the determination to end this fight quickly. As she got closer her blade reformed and she stopped swirled around, as she did, she lifted her leg to show the hell of her foot. The Venvoss lowered its shield to soon and saw Alex's foot coming in quickly, but it was too late to put its shield back up. Alex's foot contacted its helmet she, with one decisive motion, energized her shoe and sent the Venvoss hurdling down the runway.

The Venvoss smacked the ground repeatedly as it tumbled on the pavement with Alex quickly following behind. As she got close, the Venvoss managed to get its stance back and the two began to clash swords. Both desperately trying to land a hit and dodge out of the way. The two clashed their swords together until they were face to face and then forced themselves way. As the bullets fly toward the enemy knocking some down others got to them. They managed to save their own but when it came to the Seekers, they were losing so many men and women to the alien force.

Davis was impressed by his sister's abilities and was relieved to know they were winning or at least that's what he had imagined. However, as he watched he started to feel something was off, but he didn't know what it was. Then without thinking he closed his eyes and when he reopened them, he found himself back in the hangar and was still able to hear battle outside growing louder as he laid there on the mattress. He wished he were out there alongside his sister, not laying on his possible death bed. Looking up at the ceiling he could see the flash from the gun shots as the battle went on, but out of the corner of his eye he saw something move. Davis couldn't tell what it was and tilted his head towards where he saw it, even though moving his head was painful. When he saw nothing, he brushed it off, thinking he had just imagined it, after all he couldn't really see too well with his vision being blurry. He moved his head back into a comfy position but as he lied there, he saw something move again. He used his eyes to look in every direction he could but saw nothing.

As he lied there, he tried to figure out what was going on and he started to remember everything about the Venvoss' tactics. Then he remembered something from the first day, when the world went to hell, he felt like he was being watched by something from the roof of another building, but he didn't see anything at least not fully. Davis eyes became wide as he said out loud painfully, "Oh crap!"

Then hanging over him a Venvoss removed its camouflage to reveal itself to him. Before Davis could react, it placed a mask over his mouth from its own dust, silencing him as he lied there. He tried to move his body, but it had gone numb, and wasn't responding to him. Davis was helpless as the Venvoss moved around to his left side and spoke in its own tongue as it pulled a knife that was color orange. It picked up Davis's hand, waited for a moment and uttered a single word to him a word he understood, "Sorry." Then it plunged the blade into his hand, in the exact spot as the last one. Davis's screams were muted as his blood dripped from his hand to the ground, but it was no longer red, it was indigo. The blade was removed from his hand and materialized a part of it into a vail.

It slowly gathered his blood as the battle continued, only ever to look away to see if anyone had turned around. Once it was done it removed Davis's mask and left Davis alone with his hand still bleeding out on the ground. Eventually, like before, it closed and his arm started to feel better and whatever paralyzed him eventually wore off. Things for him just kept getting weirder as he wondered why it would do this and what was it after? The battle ended outside when the Venvoss that attacked Davis sounded the retreat. The beast and serpents followed their masters as everyone was mentally exhausted and many had been taken by the serpents. They thought this was a victory, it was anything but. Davis got out of his bed and made his was outside as his team began to come back in.

Alex was surprised to see the Venvoss swift retreat and wondered why they had come in the first place as Davis approached saying, "Alex we have a problem."

Alex ran quickly to see her brother out of bed and asked, "Davis are you feeling better already?"

Akio came from the side wondering why Davis was out of bed and then saw the blood from his hand. "Davis?" she said in a panicked tone, "What happened to your hand?"

"This battle was a diversion, whatever they want I think is inside me and it seems they have stop it, at least for now." said Davis bluntly.

Akio was surprised to hear him say it aloud in front of his sister and said, "Davis your sister?"

"I already know what happened to his hand," Alex replied to Akio.

Akio was shocked to hear that she had already known about the wound but asked if she had known how bad it had gotten. Alex had no idea what she was talking about and that's when Davis told her what was going on for the last few weeks. After he was done explaining himself Alex looked at him with such disappointment. She thought that after what happened with the people back home, he would have been more truthful, especially to her. He had always come to her in need of advice and wanting to confine secrets, but she never dreamed that he would do it to her. Alex demanded to have his armor removed from her in a furious voice as Davis wanted to give her a hug and apologize, but he was no longer concerned about that. Alex's eyes were filled with rage as she told Davis that what he did was irresponsible and childish as Davis pulled off her armor. Akio immediately stepped in between the two and told them both to chill out.

"No, Akio I will not chill out! I will not have my brother constantly keep getting hurt because of me!"

"What?" said Akio and Davis almost in unison.

"Wait, you still think that this is your fault." said Davis as he should his hand to her.

"Yes, you idiot, it was my fault you got hurt and it my fault you were sick. If I had just kept my guard up for a few more seconds you wouldn't have been stabbed." Alex said on the verge of tears.

"Alex, I don't blame you for any of this, this wasn't your fault. I chose to take the hit to save you, if I hadn't you would have had to deal with this bull crap, or worse die." said Davis upsettingly.

"Then that's the price I should have paid, not you. I'm your older sister I have always looked out for you and protected you. But in that one moment I failed, and you got hurt and almost died a little while ago. How do you think I would have felt to see you die right there? How do you think anyone would have felt?" Alex said with tears in her eyes.

"Alex, I hid this because I didn't want you to worry or feel regret for what happened, none of what happened to me is your fault. You weren't the one who lied to everyone and put our entire species in danger. Not to mention the fact that none of us knew what was happening to me anyways, there was nothing you could do, there was nothing anyone could do, not even me, and I was the one who got hurt. You can't save anyone if you don't know what's wrong, I made this choice because it was the only logical one."

Alex wiped her tears away and said, "I know it's just, the two of us suffered for our entire lives, I just wanted one moment that you and I didn't have to."

"We are all struggling now sis, and when that moment comes it will be when all of us are reunited and he begin to rebuild our lives."

For some time, the two relaxed and eventually hugged each other and started to head back to the hangar. Akio looked at them wondering what biological creatures these two were. Nobody in their right mind would get that angry and fight, only to change their minds in mere moments. Jacob came from behind Akio and explained, "Weird, right? Those two are plain nuts and that it had been like this for years, but they overcame issues by leaning on each other, even if the issues were themselves."

Even though Akio could understand, she still had a hard time accepting it, she couldn't accept that people were like that. "I just don't understand, how can they still love another after all the betrayal in their lives, all the pain, all the lies?"

"Because they have hope, it's the one thing that keeps them going. Not everyone gets such a luxury to enjoy everything we were given, some get incredibly unlucky with a terrible life while others get to live the high life, but in the end it's not the role you play that matters, it's how you play it. I have seen people from rock bottom reach the top and the people at the top fall, but in the end it's not about the destination that matters."

"It's about the journey getting there." said Akio remembering something from her past.

"Just like it is all about saving our world." said Jacob as he smiled at them.

But Akio could see his smile wasn't what it was all cracked up to be and asked, "Are you jealous or your brother and sister's kinship?"

Jacob looked at Akio with sincerity and said, "More than they even know, I was spoiled when I was young and those two were always the last thing on our mother's mind. She never had to worry about Alex since she got good grades, but when it came to Davis, he was always overlooked. So, Alex's opinion to him is the highest he has ever looked up to, because she was the only one who saw him, at least that's what I think he believes."

As the two headed back to the hangar, Akio could understand how complicated their family was. Out of the five children, two were the last priority and three were the top. Maire was being spoiled because their father was too strict on her, never really giving her leaser, and Jacob and Amelia were the youngest so they needed all the help they could get. Akio finally understood why Davis couldn't remember most of his childhood or why Alex never wanted to talk about hers. But she also remembered Davis telling her that his mother tried so hard to help, but in the end she couldn't.

Akio remained silent as she walked into the hangar with Jacob, noticing Davis and Alex talking to the others about what happened outside with them and the plan they were going to execute tomorrow. Akio and Jacob rejoined the others and discussed what happened. Davis and Alex did tell the others about the Venvoss attacking him and his wound. Their team was scared and started to ask questions, "Why did they attack just to get to you?" said one of their members.

Everyone was about to return to the office to discuss the plan when a group of the Seekers came out of nowhere and demanded that everyone come with them to speak with the politicians for an emergency meeting. This news surprised everyone, they thought that the siblings may have terrified the politicians with their fighting. So, Alex, Davis, and Jacob started to head with the soldiers to the politicians' office while the others would come up with a plan. It wasn't long before they were back in the office, sitting down back at the table, but this time the politics were quiet and seemed nervous. They first started off by thanking them for their help with the Venvoss and their pets, but it was clear they were somewhat terrified about Alex and Davis being in the same room together.

"Look we may have some issues, but know now we are all good to go," said Alex reassuringly.

"That's not why we called you here." said Mrs. Tenor.

"Oh, then why did you call us back here?" asked Jacob.

Mrs. Tenor took a deep breath in and said, "Because we sent a team to the natural history museum, where the Hope Diamond was, and it.... gone."

"Gone, what do mean it's gone?" yelled Davis in a panic.

"It's still in the museum, it's just we can't get to it." said Mrs. Tenor.

"Okay, you're not making any sense right know, why do politicians have to be so cryptic?" said Alex annoyed.

"Let me explain," said Mrs. Tenor, "When we have an invading force from other countries try to take over ours, we take some of the most valuable treasure our country has and lock them in vaults below the museums. This way we can preserve our culture and history even if America falls."

"Okay, how is that a problem?" asked Jacob.

"Because right before the attack, they moved a few things down in the storage facility along with the Hope Diamond. Which the storage facility also happens to be a vault and has four different floors. But the problem is that the person who hid the Diamond was taken by the Venvoss at the beginning. So, in short, we have no idea where it is down there and to top it off, we can't get into the vault."

"What do you mean you can't get in? The power is still on and with our current technology we could easily bypass any door." said Jacob.

"The vault door has its own electrical circuit, so when in situations like this happen, it automatically shuts down and won't power back on for a set period of time. In our case we would have to wait another seventy-five years before we could get in there again." said Mrs. Tenor

"Not a problem me and my sister can just use our spheres to break in." said Davis confidently.

"Actually, you can't, the entire vault has the same material as your spheres surrounding it."

The three looked at her in horror as they said trembling in unison, "Oh, shit!"

CHAPTER 13

The insidious Vault.

The three sat in shock at the news and wanted to know everything they knew about the vault without sounding enraged. The politicians explained that after the event in 1946 they had taken more than what they were given and used the same dust to build the vault. But something wasn't adding up to Davis, the museum and the vault were made decades before, and asked how they made it. They clarified that just like their spheres they can dematerialize and rematerializes into whatever they want, so they took the material and had it surround the exterior of the vault in a thin layer and the vault door.

"You better be playing a joke right now because if you're not I will make you wish you were!" said Alex, infuriated.

The politicians looked at her in fear hoping she wasn't going to let her sphere turn into a weapon as Jacob asked, "Alex calm down, please." Alex sat back down as Jacob continued to talk but kept her eyes on the politicians. "First off, how do you know that is surrounded by this material, two, how did you know that it was stolen, and three, how do you know if it's down there?" Mrs. Tenor pulled out a laptop and showed them a video of them using a laser on the door, but it didn't work. Then she explained that when they tried from other walls it was the same result, even on the vault door, it seemed it was air-tight. Then she pulled out files about the vault's creation during the building process decades ago and found out they made the hole for the vault a few centimeters too big which was easy enough to fill up with the dust. She put those files away and showed them a black and white video of some scientist using the dust during the cold war to make shapes and six dumpster-sized containers that must have had tens of thousands of pounds of dust inside. Mrs. Tenor explained that in the original event with the Venvoss, the records show no indication that they had this much at their disposal and had no idea how they managed to slip that much out from under their noses. She finally came to the last question and told them that her husband was in charge of moving the Hope Diamond to safety.

"Safety? It seems more like a tomb than a vault." said Davis bluntly.

"Look we just found out about this a month ago and we have tried everything to get inside, but we can't. That's why we want to see if you two can find a way in. You both know about this material more than we do, than possibly anyone!" said Mrs. Tenor.

"Barely," stated Alex, firm. "We are still discovering new things about these, if anything we possibly only know as much as those scientists did back then."

Mrs. Tenor rubbed her eyes and said, "You two have more experience than they did. You both made swords that can unleash energy and disintegrate people, a pair of boots that make you fly and can change them so fast that its impressive. I am quite sure you are leagues ahead of their research."

"Well even if we are, we still don't understand what it is or what it's made out of and to top it off we don't even know if this thing limited." explained Davis.

"That's why we need you look at the blueprints to see if there is away in, there has to be a way inside." said Mrs. Tenor.

"It could take us weeks to find a way inside and after what just happened, we don't have much time. Some of the Venvoss have shown that they are getting impatient. The only way we would be able to pull it off is if we had more help." explained Davis.

"You already have all the help you can get, you have an entire army at your disposal." said Mrs. Tenor a little offended.

"Really, then why haven't you found a way in yet?" yelled Davis.

Mrs. Tenor was about to yell him out, but she realized he had a point. Even with their armies and multiple eyes they still could find a way in. Davis told them, "If we're going to succeed then they were going to need more help, not just from you, but from the A.K.R."

The politicians looked at Davis with scorn and told, "Ya, that not going to happen!"

Alex interjected, "Well we don't have much of a choice, we need every available set of eyes then could get, and it would make it easier if they had more scientists around." The politicians were indignant about this plan, they didn't want to side with their political enemy. "Look, whatever problems you both have with each other or whatever their own agendas are, will be on hold until they figure out how to get the Hope Diamond. After all everyone on Earth was counting on us!"

The Seekers hated the fact they were being forced into a corner, but then Jacob had an idea. He explained, "I have a great idea, with the A.K.R. right on their doorstep they could watch them like a hawk and make their pursuit for the football more difficult and give us an advantage to find it first!"

The politicians sat for a moment and asked, "Would you three leave so we could discuss it in private?" The siblings got up and left the room as the politicians started to whisper amongst themselves, debating whether it was a good plan. Davis smiled at his brother as he knew what he was up to.

"If this works then we own you big time," said Davis quietly.

"What, why?" asked Jacob.

"Because if this works, then the two side will watch themselves, our group can go and find the football before either one of them. They'll be so busy trying to keep an eye on each other they won't have time to go look, and since our team isn't on either side, we won't be watched that closely." explained Alex.

Jacob didn't even think of that, he was just trying to get people to work together, but his siblings were right, this would be the perfect opportunity to find the football and the Diamond. Jacob nodded his head in agreement as they were called back into the office. They entered and stood there waiting for their answer, with an irritated groan they agreed to the terms, but it would be Davis who would ask for their corporation. He agreed, but Mrs. Tenor would have to occupy him there, he explained that they needed to see that they were serious. Mrs. Tenor hated the idea of going to the A.K.R.

headquarters and negotiating with them, but she saw that she didn't have a choice.

Everyone left the office area as Davis and Mrs. Tenor were escorted by some soldiers to a truck, it was supposed to be sent out on a recon mission, but instead it would be taking them into the lion's den. The drive wasn't long as the A.K. R. setup shop in the harbor with the navy ships still under their command. Davis asked the team to stop the truck at least a mile before they got there, he was worried if they went in with a truck full of soldiers and guns it would end badly. However, the soldiers didn't listen to him and continued till they reached the main gate where the main ship was.

It wasn't long before men and women from the A.K.R. sounded the alarm and began to point guns at the tuck. Some of the Seekers got out and began to ready themselves for a shootout as Mrs. Tenor began to have a light panic attack. The soldiers told Davis and Mrs. Tenor to stay in the truck while they tried to get the A.K.R. soldiers to back down. Davis told them to stand down, that they were trying to make peace not more war. But none of them listened as they took cover around the area. Both sides were yelling and screaming at each other to drop their weapons and surrender, but they were doing everything but that. Eventually Davis got sick of the yelling, grabbed Mrs. Tenor, and exited the truck.

Some of the soldiers tried to stop him, but Davis used his sphere and created a tread to tie them up and pinned them to the tuck as Davis approached the gate with Mrs. Tenor under his arm. When they were far enough, Davis let go of the Seekers as the soldiers at the gate saw who was approaching them and asked, "What do you want and why are you here with her?" Davis let go of Tenor and gestured to her to ask, but she was being difficult. She took a few moments to compose herself as she approached the gate a little closer and asked, "I need to speak with Mr. Henry about a temporary truce."

The people at the gate looked suspicious as they asked her, "Tell your people to lower their weapons." Davis thought this was a good start, but it was immediately destroyed when she refused.

Then things got heated as the A.K.R. soldiers repeatedly told her to give the order which made the Seekers begin to walk up behind Davis and them demanding that they lower their firearms first. The situation was out of control as both sides had their fingers on the triggers, while Tenor was yelling at them that she would not be bullied by some trigger-happy punks. Davis got irritated and quickly turned more of his sphere into string, grabbing all the guns, and yanking them way from everyone, keeping them twenty feet in the air so on one could get to them.

"There, now nobody is a threat," said Davis enraged. "Now, please get your boss. We really need to talk with him about a problem that we need help with."

The A.K.R. soldiers looked at each other and sent two to fetch their boss as Davis lowered the weapons back down towards the ground. After half an hour the Seekers, Tenor, and Davis became impatient. Then Tenor saw some coming their way and made herself presentable as Davis joined her side. But out of curiosity he asked her who this guy was. She explains that he was in Miami when the invasion started and joined up with the Marines a few weeks later, soon he rose to power, and formed the A.K.R. when they split. Davis thought to himself that was a fast transition and asked her what his name was. She told him his name was Henry Duskman and that he was a bit of a jerk.

When Davis heard the name, he asked her, "Is his middle name Kenny by chance?"

"Yes…wait how did you know that?" Tenor said shocked by his question, "Do you know him?"

Davis rubbed the back of his neck as he sighed heavily, "Yes I do, and he's got some explaining to do himself." As he said that the gate flew open with their leader approaching with his two soldiers as he came face to face with Mrs. Tenor and Davis. He looked at Mrs. Tenor with discontented, but when he sifted his gaze over to Davis he brightened up with a smile.

"So, you have finally come to me." Henry said smiling.

"Yes, I have, only to find out that you have been with these people this whole time, where you could communicate with me! I was trying to communicate with you for months!" yelled Davis.

"Davis how do you know this man?" asked Tenor.

Davis got in between them both and said "Mrs. Tenor, this is Henry Kenny Duskman, my biological father."

"What?" She screamed.

"I'm afraid it's true and because of his Marine experience and his position as a major general in his time, makes his knowledge of warfare highly valuable. That's how he managed to take power and people from you all." said Davis.

"Look, Bubba, I..." before he could explain himself, he grabbed his father's mouth and told him to shut up and listen. Henry stopped speaking as Davis's hand moved away and explained what was going on and why they needed their help. After twenty minutes of explaining, Davis and Tenor waited for Henry to respond, but he was taking his time to soak up all this information. For him this was crazy, but at the same time he knew that most things were these days, and came to his conclusions. He agreed, but on the condition that he attend the briefing when it came to getting into the vault. Davis thought it was fair, but made a condition of his own, Mrs. Tenor would accompany him in the briefing. Henry hated this idea, but knew he wasn't going to get any were with them, so he agreed but added another condition, to spend time with his kids. Davis was so close to immediately refusing the deal when his father made the condition but held his words back as Mrs. Tenor agreed to the term.

Henry told them he would be there in a few hours to set up a small shop for his people and in exchange they could do the same. This news made Tenor smile gently as she shook his hand and began to head back to the truck. Davis looked at his father one more time, knowing that his siblings were not going to be happy when he told them. Henry waved at Davis one last time before he left, but Davis was trying to avoid his gaze. When the Seekers were down the road a bit Tenor asked Davis why he didn't say anything about Mr. Henry. Davis looked at Tenor and told her if he knew that his father was the A.K.R. leader then he never would have gone to their front gate. She could see that Davis didn't like his father, but she thought of this as a serious advantage. With his kids on their side, she could get him to stand down and make one massive army again.

However, before she could ask anything Davis told her whatever she was thinking about to drop it. She opened her mouth to speak, but Davis gave her his sister's death glare, instantly shutting her up. The rest of the way was quiet and uneventful as they drove down the road. Back at the airport, Davis got out of the truck and stormed off towards his teams as Tenor followed behind asking Davis to calm down. But it was clear that he wasn't listening, all this time his father could have been talking to him and he chose not to, he had every right to be mad. His father, the guy who spent months with the military, with a working internet connection, didn't think to respond to any of his emails made him furious.

When he entered the hangar, his team greeted him and asked about the negotiation and if he was okay. Davis wasted no time and told his siblings, "You're not going to believe the hell is in charge of the A.K.R."

"Who?" asked Jacob.

"Henry Kenny Duskman."

"DAD?" said Jacob and Alex in unison.

"Believe me I was just a shocked as you two are." said Davis.

"But the last time we saw him wasn't he in jail?" asked Jacob.

"Ya, and now we're going to be saving the world together, what incredible irony!" said Alex annoyed as she rubbed the sides of her head.

It wasn't long before the A.K.R. came rolling in with their trucks and began to set up their outpost. His father's men and women seemed to be prepared and well equipped for the tasks at hand, yet even if they were Davis didn't care about it, though a thought did cross his mind. Jacob could see him thinking as he stared at the A.K.R. set up and asked what was on his mind. Davis told him, "It's strange how our father managed to gain power so quickly and that he wants the football." Jacob agreed that it was indeed strange Henry had never been power hungry before. But after what happened before, they were afraid that he never wanted to go back to that life, even if it meant losing himself.

It was nearly noon when the A.K.R.'s camp was made and as promised the siblings, Henry, and Tenor made their way into the operations tent to be briefed about the situation and what was needed from everyone. A.K.R. soldiers guard their encampment intently as they made their way inside. These people seemed to be more on edge with the Seekers than the aliens, which was what Davis and Alex wanted. As they made their way to the center of the encampment, some soldiers escorted them inside their largest tent. Inside they saw a table filled with diagrams and schematics of the natural history with a few white erase boards around the tent with information about the dust and aliens. On either side of the table were three soldiers from each side standing near the far wall of the tent, it seemed that they were meant to be there for security and safety.

Everyone sat down as some other soldiers came in with Henry, giving him a file and then sat down next to him as if they had the right to be there. This made Tenor distraught; she believed that only she and her guards would be allowed in this area, but she believed that Henry had brought in more back up. Tenor demanded, "I insist that your soldiers leave immediately, that this wasn't not we Seekers they signed up for." However, Henry refused and explained, "These people stay with me because you to have an army outside the tent, and it makes me feel better having the best by my side." Then they begin to argue, blaming each other, and saying this was a waste of time and that if they didn't want to listen to reason then they could just leave.

The two argued for twenty minutes before Alex used her sphere to muzzle their mouths shut. She demanded, "Will you two shut the hell up and stop acting like children and just grow up? The more time you both argue is more time we could be using to save our world, remember?" As Alex removed the dust from their mouths the two reluctantly kept their arguments out of their conversation as they discussed what they needed to do.

Jacob took a picture of the Hope Diamond and place it on the white board in front of them and began to explain, "Okay, this is our target as we all know, but the questions we have are why do we need it, what its purpose, and where it was along with the problems that will come with it!" He continued to explain, "We all know the situation with the vault and the Venvoss becoming inpatient. We all know that we might not have much time left, that is why we need to be quick but smart as we go over the plan."

"So let's go over what we do know about the vault, its impenetrable and has four floors of stuff we have to explore to find the Diamond, and on top of which has a timer that won't open for the next seventy-five years." said Tenor.

"Which is why we need to find a loophole somewhere, a weak spot, something." said Henry.

"Which is where Alex and I come in, once we find this weak spot or loophole, we use it to get into the vault and destroy the vault doors mechanism in order to gain access."

"Then we finally search for the Diamond and when found we give it to Davis, get the last clue, and end this nightmare."

"The plan is straight forward we just don't know how to execute it."

"Don't worry, Pops, I got you covered." said Alex as she stood up. "Okay A.K.R. and Seekers, take two groups from both sides and do some recon on the museum, look for anything that could get us inside. I'm talking about false walls, air vents, anything that we can exploit. Meanwhile, find someone or hopefully some people that have a construction background to have a look at the schematics to find anything out of the ordinary like a back way in. Davis and I will practice making something that will get inside and destroy the vault door's mechanism, we will need something that can help us see what we're doing."

"Wow, way to take charge honey." said Henry happily.

"So, everyone agrees with this so far?"

Everyone at the table and the guards agreed that was the best course of action. "Okay let's get this show on the road. Remember, be fast and smart, the faster we end this the more we can begin to fix our home and our lives."

Everyone immediately went to work as the guards were sent out to find someone with a background in construction and do their recon. Jacob went with some soldiers on both sides to the museum for recon while Tenor headed back to the other politicians to discuss the plan. Alex and Davis headed back to the hangar as their father followed behind. The three stayed quiet as they marched on, the only thing they could hear was the men and women around them marching with people shouting out in the distance. Then Henry asked, "So I know it's possibly the end of the world, but either one of you dating someone?" The two looked back at their father wondering where that question came from.

The two said in unison "No."

Henry looked a little disappointed and asked, "Why not?"

"WE ARE IN THE MIDDLE OF A WAR," screamed Davis. "We don't have time to find someone if there is no one to find!"

Henry was stunned at Davis's words and rephrased the question, "I mean did you date before?"

"Okay why is this so important to you right know?" Alex stated bluntly.

"I just wanted to check up on you two. Is that a crime?" asked Henry.

"No but screwing your children out of thousands should be. Oh, wait, it is!" Davis replied angerly.

Henry sighed and tried to explain himself to the two, but neither one wanted to listen and continued to the hangar. Until Henry yelled out, "HEY, don't you to walk away from me when I'm trying to talk to you!"

"Well, we don't want to talk to you so deal with it." said Davis without looking at Henry.

At that point Henry decided to head back to his tent as Davis and Alex entered the hangar. The two called for a quick meeting with everyone and asked if anyone had a construction background, lucky two people immediately put their hands up and exclaimed that they were. Alex told them to head to the A.K.R. camp and start looking over some schematics for the museum, that they were going to need their experience to do this mission. The two immediately took off running towards the A.K.R. camp as Davis and Alex explained what happened at the meeting and what the plan was, but also what they were going to do on the side lines. A group of seven people would look for the football while everyone else helped around the airport. They would switch every four hours to avoid suspicion, but if they find it to re-hide it somewhere, only they would know just until the mission was over.

The plans were in motion as Davis and Alex started trying out a few ideas with the sphere. Yet everything they came up with wasn't good enough. Everything they thought of was either too complicated for them to do or wasn't good enough to cut the vault's mechanism. Until they had a sure-fire way to get in, they were stuck. However, it did make them question how much they could make with their spheres. Back at the meeting Alex said they barely understood them and that wasn't a lie, but she didn't think that they were any different from the scientists' conclusion either.

When they practiced, they only stuck to the basics of what they knew, but they never actually tried to make something different. For them, the simplest things to make were things that they knew how to make. But in the last few weeks they have made a string-like wire, antigravity boots, controlled energy waves, armor, a form of saranwrap, and thousands of small spheres. Even after months of having these things, they still didn't know what their extent was, but in the last week and a half they began pushing the limits of these spheres. Davis started goofing around with his, making stars, triangles, and eventually a whip. It was strange to him, after all this time he thought he had least understood how it worked, but he knew that him and his sister had only just grazed the surface of knowledge they had floating in front of them.

But in the back of Davis's mind, he couldn't help feeling disappointed in himself for being so cruel to his father for just trying to interact with his family. He began to regret the things he had said to his mother on the first day of the invasion. He felt terrible, the last thing he said to her was, "Look at you just sitting in silence again, how pathetic, you clearly are more comfortable being a failure than being a good mother, and you know what is worse, I don't feel sorry for you anymore." In his heart he knew his mother was trying to bring the good out of Don, but the pain that came with it became unbearable.

She may have not been a good mother, but she was still his, and the way he had treated her was the way she had been treated her whole life, as a nobody, that she couldn't do better than what she could and that she had to accept it. Davis told Alex, "If we ever make it back home, we need to find our mother and talk to her, to make amends, and to help raise her confidence, even if she didn't do it for us then maybe they could do it for her."

"You know something Davis?" asked Alex.

"What?" he asked.

"We both heard the saying that you never know how much something means to you until you lose it. We knew what it meant, but we never truly knew what it felt like till now." said Alex.

"Ya, so I'm guessing that the two of us should go talk to our father, right?" said Davis in a bit of a regretful tone.

Alex nodded her head and the two got up from their seats and made their way back to the A.K.R. camp knowing if they couldn't make amends now, they may never. They asked around to find their father's tent, but it seemed that their father didn't want to talk to them, as the soldier told them to leave their campground. Before the soldiers could do anything, Alex told them, "The deal is, we have access to this area and the briefing tent, so either you move, or I will use my sphere and make you both dance like a pole dancer."

Davis looked at her for a minute and asked her, "Is that the worst you can do?"

Alex faced her brother and said, "Well its either that or have them strip tease the other men."

Davis's face turned red as a tomato and commented, "Damn it, Alex! Just use your sphere to tie them up for a few moments."

"Fine!" Alex said annoyed as she tied up the two soldiers and moved them away.

As the soldiers were moved away, Henery approached them saying, "You both will not make my soldiers strip tease performances here, do it in your own tents."

"Where's the fun in that?" said Davis bluntly.

Henry sighed and asked, “Look just don’t harass my soldiers while they are on patrol. If you two have come to talk, make it quick.”

The two said nothing as Henry escorted his kids to his tent and asked, “Either one of you want something to drink or eat?” Neither one said anything as they sat down at his desk as he went around it. When Henry sat down, he told them, “Kids, I understand why your two are so angry with me. What happened before this invasion was inexcusable and I have no right to ask for forgiveness.”

“Ya we might still be angry with you, but at the end of the day we have all done stupid things.” said Alex.

“But the reason why we hated you so much is that you got on to use so much about overspending and wasting opportunities, that when you did it, made us feel betrayed. That you went against your own wisdom.”

Henry sighed and said, “Kids, I can’t tell you how much I have screwed up in the last few years, but I can tell right now no loving parent ever wants to put their children in harm’s way. But you both were right, I did put you in harm’s way, you gave me your trust and I used it against you for my own selfish reasons. No matter what my reasons were I had no right to trick you into putting your lives on hold just so I can get something.”

The two just stared at their father as he smiled back at them feeling better and told them, “I might not be a good father but for what it’s worth even with all my stupidity I’m still proud of the lot of you for having the courage, wisdom, and humility that I never had.” The two looked at him and told him, “We just did the opposite of what your crazy ass did.”

“And yet somehow the two of you still turned out crazy,” said Henry.

“It must be in our genes,” said Alex sarcastically.

Henry started looking through his pockets as he said, “Well, I know I had some crazy in my pockets early today, but it seems I’m out right now would you take a check.”

The two shook their heads as they smiled hard, trying to keep the composer and not laugh at his dad joke. Though their time together was brief it unfortunately came to an end as one of the soldiers came into the tent and told everyone, “Everyone, the recon team is back you need to head to the briefing tent, Tenor and Jacob are already waiting.”

“And the craziness continues, let’s just hope it ends soon, I don’t think I can take much more of this.” said Davis as he raised himself out of his chair.

As they made their way to the tent, Davis noticed that the team that came back wasn't as big as when they left. "What happened?" asked Davis.

"It's better if your brother tells you." said the soldier as she opened the tent to reveal Tenor looking over Jacob with medical officers. Jacob looked terrible, he looked like he had gotten into a brawl with a rhino. "Oh my god!" said Davis as he quickly approached his brother.

Everyone gathered around Jacob as Henry asked, "Bubba, what the hell happened to you?"

Jacob sat up and explained with his face swollen and blacked. "We went to the museum, looking for the weaknesses you asked us to find. When we were nearly finished another team we had never seen before came out of nowhere. I don't know who they are, but we never stood a chance. They had killed about six of our team and started beating the life out of the others, including myself. We managed to get away, but not without sacrifice."

Henry couldn't stand to see his youngest son like this as he said, "Do you know what they wanted?"

"No, they were speaking in another langue they said, 'Wathi tchi no jma ni nra-' or something like that."

Davis looked shocked as he heard his brother and said, "Did he say precisely 'Watashi tachi no jama ni nara nai you ni suru.'"

"Yes, exactly," said Jacob surprised. "Wait how do you know..."

"Back in college I took a foreign language class, guess which one I chose, Japanese. They were saying, 'Stay out of our way.'"

"But why have they come here of all places." asked Tenor panicking.

"It could be possible they're after the Diamond as well, but for what reason I can't say."

Tenor explained, "I think I know the Hope Diamond was basically a winning lottery ticket, it was worth millions and if they know the secret behind it, on the black market it would be worth billions. If this rouge group knows about it whereabouts in the vault and get it first, then we can kiss our chance goodbye."

"True, but don't forget they cant get in the vault just like us, which means we have time to think of another plan." said Alex.

"Actually, I think we and they have found a way inside." said Jacob in pain.

Everyone's bodies went cold as Henry as, "Did they get the information out of you." Jacob shook his head, "No I got away before they could break me, but they did steal my camera, so it was a matter of time before they found the way in."

Tenor grabbed Jacob's arm and demanded, "Tell us where it is before the rouge team discovers it so we can get the in!"

Davis grabbed her and threw her to the side saying, "Back off Tenor he's in pain and jumping on him isn't going to help. Besides which we need a new plan, we can't just go inside and get it then stroll out."

Tenor was now frustrated and told them all, "We have a time race on our hands people. Fighting the Venvoss is one thing but now we have to deal with the Japs! If this rouge team gets the Diamond first, the fate of earth could be in tremendous danger."

"I think making a deal and screwing over another race put us in tremendous danger first don't you think?"

Tenor looked at Davis with rage as the medic told Jacob, "Okay Jacob, you have three cracked ribs and a fractured wrist, luckily, you won't need surgery, but you won't be in the field for a while."

Jacob tried to stand up, but the medic and Henry stopped him before he could even get his stance. Jacob told them, "Guys please, help me to the table." With the help of Alex and Davis's spheres they helped him over painlessly as he explained what he discovered.

"As you all know the vault is covered with that alien's dust. When we were looking around the vault door, I realized something." said Jacob a little excited.

"What did you find?" asked Henry.

"I didn't realize it before but when I looked at the door there were flashing lights around it. According to your schematics there are cable pipes that run throughout the museum for the lights, including the ones in the vault."

"Yes, but the vault has its own power circuit breaker. It doesn't need to be connected to the rest of the museum." explained Tenor.

"I'm not talking about the power source, I'm talking about the cable pipes themselves. The ones for the museum run through the vault and don't have the alien's dust on them." said Jacob excitedly.

Alex realized what he was saying and intervened, "We can cut the pipe open and have our spheres go through it, then when there on the other side we can cut the vaults mechanism down."

"We can get in and get the Diamond before the rouge team even figures out what we're doing. Jacob, I could kiss you, you genie!" Tenor exclaimed.

Davis looked at his brother with joy, but then he realized something to and said, "It's a good plan, but one problem. How in the hell are we supposed to see in the vault?"

Everyone's smiles faded quickly as they started rattling their brains to figure out what they were going to do. This plan was great, but without any visual aid to help them, they were screwed. Then a sudden flash of realization hits Henry as he said, "A snake camera!"

"Snake camera?" asked Tenor.

Davis and Alex took a moment to process what he was talking about, then they understood what he meant but Tenor wasn't following as she said, "Snake camera? What that?"

Jacob explained to Tenor, "A snake camera is used by plumbers to look for pipe damage or blockage. If we used one in a cable pipe, then we could slither it down while the dust followed behind. When it was inside, they could use the dust to make the adjustments they needed to see the door and begging breaking it down."

"That's exactly what we need, where do we find one?" said Tenor, overjoyed.

"Hold it Tenor, even if we get the snake camera we still have the rouge team standing around the museum. We can't just stroll in!"

"Ture but that's what distractions are for." said Alex confidently.

"What?" said everyone.

Alex explained her plan in detail, "First we have some soldiers make some noise close by the museum to lure them away. When the rouge team follows them, we get inside and go to work. Davis, Tenor, and a few soldiers would wait by the door until me and my team open it. Once you're in, start looking for the Diamond. Tenor, since it was your husband that was responsible for hiding it, we're counting on your insight from him might help find it. When the Diamond is found give it to Davis and let him do whatever he needs to do to get the final clue. Then leave the Diamond and get the hell out of dodge before the rouge team finds you all. With that then hopefully we can finally end the conflict between the Venvoss and humanity."

"God, I am so damn proud of you sweetheart!" said Henry.

"I have to admit you do tend to take charge when you're under pressure don't you?" said Tenor.

"So, when do we start?" asked Davis.

Alex smiled and said, "Now, cotton candy."

With their new plan in place, they began to prep for the battle and mission ahead. Tenor and Henry had some of their scavengers go looking for a snake camera while everyone else started to load weapons, fuel tanks in cars and trucks, and make sure they had ammunition and medical help. Davis and Alex took their brother to the hangar and placed him into a bed as everyone began prepping again. However, Jacob didn't want to stay laid up, he desperately wanted to go and help more. The two siblings reassured him they were good and that he had done enough, now it was their turn to handle this situation. Jacob laid in his bed in a bit of pain as Davis asked Jackie and Adalard, "Guys please keep an eye on him while we're gone, he tends to be reckless when he's in bed."

Jackie agreed and told Davis, "Sure Davis, I will tie him down if I have to," which made Davis think of something that made him chuckle.

"Don't you dare think dirty thoughts, Davis" said Jackie sternly.

"Ten years too late Jackie," said Davis chuckling.

Adalard chuckled back at Davis response while Jackie said, "That's my que to leave now, you rainbow reject."

Davis, Jacob, Alex, and Adalard started to laugh out by her harsh words as she walked away smiling. Everyone stopped laughing after a few minutes as Tenor arrived with Henry. The two looked at everyone as they wiped the tears from their eyes wondering what was so funny, they were about to enter a war zone with their own people. Davis explained that Jackie was just relieving the tension everyone was feeling and said something funny to help them out. However, Tenor didn't look amused, she seemed irritable, this wasn't the time for jokes in her mind, and demanded that they grow up and act like adults. She stormed off while Henry looked at his kids and told them to be on their guard not just with the rouge team, but with her as well. Davis and Alex didn't need him to say anything about her.

They were already skeptical about her when they saw her at first, but she changed way too dramatically within the last hour. Something was clearly eating at her and she was now starting to show it. Granted, they admitted it wasn't the best time for jokes for some people, but in this situation, it made them relaxed and focused. That was how they succeeded all this time, by thinking positive and trying to make themselves smile, for if everyone saw them happy even when things were bleak, then maybe they had nothing to fear. Everyone said their goodbyes one final time before they headed out, but before Davis could leave the hangar, Adalard asked him to talk with him in private before he left.

The two went behind the hangar and as he could see his sister Alex follow behind. She always did love watching romance between people bloom, but for Davis this wasn't going to be a pleasant conversation. Adalard put his back against the wall as he desperately tried to say something, but his words found it difficult to make their way out, and Davis was getting impatient. Alex waited behind the corner and listened closely as Jackie made her way up behind her to listen in. But this conversation was so quiet that even a mute person use sign language to say, "Will you just say it?" Davis looked at his imaginary watch and told Adalard that he had to leave. Adalard freaked out and tried to speak but the words still couldn't find any escape from his throat. Eventually Davis told him, "We should only be friends."

"What?" said Adalard confused.

"We should just be friends. Look I know that for the past few months you have been trying to hit on me and that…" Davis took a moment and screamed out "ALEX AND JACKIE NEED SOMTHING BETTER TO DO WITH THERE TIME!" Alex and Jackie immediately scrambled away, but then they tripped over something that crashed on the ground, making massive noise, proving that they were indeed easily dropping. After they fled, Davis turned his attention towards Adalard and continued speaking his mind, "I know we have gotten close in the past few months, but I think of you as my best friend, not a boyfriend. Now, I'm not going to lie, sometimes I may give off the wrong signals without realizing it, and it causes problems. Know that you are special to me, just not in that way. I hope you are not too crushed but this information."

After he was done, Adalard looked completely confused and asked, "Wait, you don't like me in that way? But Alex said and I quote, 'He has been wanting you for months now, you should totally get that before some other guy does.'"

"I'm so sorry for my sister, she has a good heart, it's just she is not that good with romance." said Davis.

"Well, she did just embarrass the hell out of me. But I'm not going to lie either. I grew curious about same sex relationships, I don't understand it completely, but I can respect it. I honestly wanted to try with you, but now I see that it was all a deception." explained Adalard.

Davis put his hand on his shoulder and told him, "Being curious is not a problem, but people need to make sure it is their choice to do these types of things and not be peer pressured or tricked into doing it. Otherwise, they might have a lingering regret that hangs over them forever."

Adalard laughed it off and said to Davis, "Your sister and Jackie are real pieces of work. I'm surprised they wasted this much time, they could have used that to help each other figure out their own feelings."

"No kidding," said Davis smiling, but then he stopped as he asked him one last question before he left. "Was Jackie the one who started it and then just recruited Alex when she came along?"

"You just won the daily double and got one thousand pints." said Adalard as he was walking back to the front of the hangar with Davis following behind.

"Don't you mean points?" asked Davis.

"Screw points I want to drink again once this is over. Can I half of your pints?" said Adalard.

Davis smiled at his joke as he got into his car full of soldiers and told him that once this all over, he would take him out for a drink, but he was not going to let him drink that much. It would be incredibly awful and hilarious if he survived till the end of a galactic war and died from alcohol poisoning. Adalard was going to hold him to that as the truck started up and rolled out. Davis closed the door as he said goodbye again, the men and women inside asked if that was his boyfriend. Davis smiled and told them that he was the closest friend he had in this world, but they weren't together. Some of the soldiers looked at Davis and asked if he wanted to meet someone.

Davis screamed out loud in anger, "GOD DAMMIT ALEX! IT HASN'T BEEN MORE THAN TWO MINUTES AND YOU'RE ALREADY TRYING TO SET UP ANOTHER TRAP!"

CHAPTER 14

The truth and the fall.

After the fiasco with his sister, father, the politicians, and everything else that had happened, everything was now set for the vault's heist. The men and women that were to go were already gathering and loading into their trucks as the sun rose over the sea. But soon, the bright sunny day began to turn grey with looming clouds over all of D.C. In the distance, the clap of thunder could be heard echoing out, calling to all that were still around that a storm was coming. Yet all who were not taken knew that the storm they were in already was far worse than what earth could through at them.

The drive to the museum of natural history was quiet as gun fire could be heard in the distance. The plan was going smoothly so far and the soldiers seemed nervous. In the air, smoke and ash could be smelled with the fresh smell of iron. Blood had been spilled and everyone prayed that it wasn't their comrades. Normally humans couldn't smell blood, but due to the Venvoss's war people had to rely on more of their other senses rather than just sight and sound. The soldiers were quiet, some had their heads down while others were muttering to themselves. Davis could hear some of their words, they were praying to God, for safety and protection, they were afraid that they were going to die.

The soldier that sat next to him started to shake, his leg bumping into his, as the man bowed his head and began to mutter something to himself. Davis placed his hand on his back and said, "You, okay?"

The man stopped and looked at him and said nervously, "Sorry, I'm not bothering you, am I?"

"No, I'm just worried for you, are you sure you can handle going into this battle?"

"I've seen my fair share of death. I had served three tours in Afghanistan, and after seeing my brothers and sisters die right in front of me, I thought I'd be used to it." said the soldier, shaking still.

Davis rubbed his back and said, "Death is not an enemy, but it's the way you die that can be. I saw someone fall to their death on the very first day when all this happened. But it wasn't death that scared me it was the way she had to greet it."

The soldier stopped shaking and looked at Davis confused and said, "It almost sounds if you aren't afraid of dying?"

"Of course I'm scared of dying, but death is a part of life as light is to the dark, you can't have one without the other and you can't separate them, the only thing you can do is to make peace knowing that one day you will be on the other side and walk with death to whatever comes next."

"Okay that sounded a little gothic!"

"Ya, I went through a weird goth phase in high school, but what I have said still is true. It's not death, but dying that scares people, it's the fear that they will never be able to come back to this world, that drives them to be afraid of what comes next. But if we succeed today, then no one will have to worry about it for a long time, at least that's what I believe, because that's all we have right now, hope."

The soldier smiled at him as Davis could no longer feel him shaking with fear. "You amaze me, I don't know you and in the single minute you have talked to me, you have shown compassion, wisdom, and strength in ways, that even adults my age can't achieve."

"We all can achieve it but only if we stop tearing each other down to get it."

Davis removed his hand from the soldiers back as the driver yelled out, "We're here!"

The truck came to a stop as Davis looked to the soldiers saying, "Alright everyone let's do this quickly and quietly as possible."

One by one the soldiers made their way out of the truck with Davis being the last one out as Alex's truck parked behind them. Davis looked at the museum wondering how something like this, a place that hold the discoveries of the world would also be the crypt of a dark secret.

Alex walked up and stood next to him, Davis knew he couldn't hold back his expression of being distraught from this place, and she asked, "You always wanted to see this place, right?"

"Yeah, I just never in my imagination thought I was going to break into it."

"I know this isn't important to the mission, but I hoped one day I could bring our nieces and nephews here. To show them how much humanity had accomplished and to inspire them to never give up."

"But now it's nothing but an empty building with possibly no artifacts left."

Alex placed her hand on her brother and told him, "I wish to it hadn't turned out this way."

"It's not the fact it turned out this way, sis, it's the fact that we're stuck in it, and the grand babies, Irina, Jerry, Darren, Cassy, and Lilith, they're the ones who will have the most difficult road ahead." said Davis on the verge of tears. "Our ancestors left us this as a sign that we are all united no matter how divided we are. But it was nothing more than a literal coverup for what they were really hiding. This entire place was literally built on a lie, and now the generations that are to come will be paying for it. By the time this will all be resolved, all of us will be gone."

Alex turned her bother to face her and slapped him across the face and yelled out, "Don't you ever talk like that again!" Davis raised his hand to check as Alex continued to yell, "Yes, what happened decades ago was terrible and yes, what's happening now is unacceptable, but you can't worry about what you can't fix, you need to focus on what you can. For God sakes, Davis, I have seen you give wholesome advice to people twice and even three times your age. You have always inspired people to do their best and have always given confidence to others even when you didn't have it. I'm not going to lie, the road ahead will be hard, but if we do what we are doing know that the other generations including the grand babies won't have to worry so much. So, put the blues away and get out your rainbow back out, because if you don't, I will make you become one!"

Davis wiped his eyes and said jokingly, "I am technically already a rainbow according to everyone at the mall and to every soldier you tried to have hook up with me in the truck."

"Did any agree?" Alex said excitingly.

"Nope sorry, this rainbow can't be followed so easily, after all no one can find me pot of gold!" said Davis in a terrible Irish accent.

"See that's the attitude I want to see from you, understand." said Alex while embracing Davis tightly.

The soldiers saw Davis and Alex hug each other as Tenor was helped out of her truck and looked disgusted. She shoved the soldiers out of the way and approached the siblings saying to them, "Stop hugging you two, you can hug all you want we get save humanity, so get to work." Alex stopped hugging her brother and turned her head slightly to reveal her left eye menacingly at Tenor. Tenor stopped in her tracks and looked horrified she had stood up to psychotic politicians and murderers, but Alex's eye alone was more fearful than God. Alex turned all the way around and told her, "NEVER interfere with me being a loving sister again!"

Tenor backed away slowly as she told her soldiers, "Everyone hear that, be respectful," in a stuttering voice. Alex rolled her eyes at Tenor and said, "Alright everyone this is where we split, my team led the way, Davis get your team get into position." Alex's team separated from the rest and lead the way to the pipe with the snake in tow. Alex looked at her brother and gave him a look that told him to be prepared for anything. Davis gave his sister a nod as Tenor came up to him and said, "Shall we?"

"No, I thought we should just stand here for nine hours and adore the sunset over the ruins of D.C.!" said Davis sarcastically as he headed up the steps with the soldiers following close behind.

Climbing up the steps of the museum they found the doors to the main entrance ripped off with trash flying inside by the wind. Davis went in and as he took his first step inside the museum, he found it to be in almost perfect condition. Everyone could see all the inspiring knowledge of the world begins to flow through them as they took their steps inside. It seemed that this place had hardly been touched, with little to no damage, from their perspective, inside that building it was like the world had never fallen that somehow in some way the time stopped in this one place. Davis looked around seeing all the things humanity accomplished still standing in their glory, but the feeling he had before when he wanted to see this place was gone. "I thought this place would have been at least broken down or rare things stolen, but I wasn't expecting it to be almost clean."

"Men, start searching the area, make sure we are safe." said Tenor, barking.

The soldiers obeyed her orders and began to sweep the areas around the entrance, as Alex and her team went to their position, but all unaware of Davis wandering around on his own. He stood before a skeleton of Mosasaurs on display, admiring its ancient figure that was left behind for the world to find, and for one moment Davis remembered what it was like to be a child, always curious about the world around him. As he looked down at the plaque of information, he was brought back to reality as he saw a bloody handprint on the bottom corner. He saw the blood drip down to the ground and it showed him a small trial that led around the display. As he made his way around one of the displays, he saw blood all over the floor and bullet holes on the nearby walls. He followed the blood trail around the corner to find one of the soldiers from the recon group, but it was only his head. Davis couldn't unsee the horror in front of him but did his best to keep calm. Tenor grabbed Davis's shoulder and said, "What's-", she turned her head to see the soldier's head on the ground, she gasped with fear. Tenor couldn't look away for more than a few seconds and she immediately vomited on the ground. Davis rubbed her back trying to aid her, but she quickly forced him away saying, "I don't need your help!"

"Not use to seeing death like this?" asked Davis. "Well get used to it because this is what war really is. People like you clearly don't have an actual grasp on it until its staring at you right in the face."

"I understand this happens! I just never-"

"Thought you were ever going to see it. This is the fate of many men, women, and children because of your greed. What's worse is that so many must fix the mess that people like you left behind." Davis stepped away from her and entered the next room, but this place was far worse than what he had just seen. The room was bathed in blood and body parts, that scattered the floors, and seemed to be desecrated. One of the soldiers came up behind Davis and saw what had happened to their recon team. He dragged Davis away from the room, closed the gate around it, and radioed to everyone, "No one is entering here, it's not good, we'll have to find another way around."

Though Davis was in shock he got a grip on himself and pulled out the blueprints, looking for another way to the vault. A few went on ahead to make sure the coast was clear as Davis told Tenor, "Whatever happened in there wasn't a fight, it was a slaughter." Tenor tried to peek into the other room but Davis immediately turned her away and told her, "You couldn't even handle the head, if you saw what was in there would have second thoughts about coming here."

Tenor could see the fear in his eyes and decided to take his word for it. The soldiers singled the coast was clear as Alex radioed in, "Davis.... We're in position, are you?"

"Not yet." said Davis on his radio. "We have to take a detour, why don't you open the pipe so you can get to work."

"Oh, she already doing it," said one of her soldiers on the radio.

"Good job, sis!"

"Well, I do love a good pole."

Davis groaned and said, "Alex I love your jokes but now is not the time. We just saw the recon team and it's not pretty. We need to hurry and get what we need and get before we are discovered."

"Okay, sorry about that, Bubba, just trying to lighten the mood."

"And I love you for that but know one thing. I'm the only one here that plays with the pole."

Alex started to laugh into the radio as Davis found a new path to the vault. He called over his team and everyone started to head to the vault. It did take a few more minutes, but eventually they found themselves standing in front of the large door. Davis radioed his sister telling her they were ready for them. It wasn't long before the radio crackled again with Alex's voice, "We're in guys, we see the door, and the mechanism. I'm going to start and I'm not going to lie it's going to get loud so get ready to-" Then Alex went silent, but only for a moment, "LOOK OUT!"

The radio went silent as echoes of gun shots filled the halls. Davis and Tenor looked down the hall with shock as the door started to hum and turn red. Whatever was happening upstairs didn't stop Alex from getting the door unlocked.

Tenor yelled out, "Crap, the rouge team must have figured us out! Soldiers get up there and help Alex, give her the time to get this damn thing open!"

Some soldiers ran down the hall as Davis tried to flow behind but was immediately stopped by Tenor and another soldier, "What are you doing!"

"That's my sister out there, what do you think I'm going to do?"

"We need you here, your sister can handle herself, but if you die then we won't be able to fix anything!"

Davis looked at Tenor with rage, but knew she was right. Even if she was using him, he was using her, and if he botched up his own plan then there might not be a second chance to stop this war. Davis relaxed and nodded at Tenor, hoping his sister was okay and could hold on long enough for him to get what he needed and get to her before it was too late. Men and women on her team were screaming in pain, the echoes reached Davis even from where he was.

"Come on Alex you got this," Davis said under his breath.

As he waited the door was beginning to cool and the radio crackled with Alex's voice, "Its open, go, go, go!"

Davis told the other soldiers to assist Alex as he opened the vault door and pushed Tenor inside, saying that they needed to buy them time till they found the Diamond. They ran down the hall as Davis closed the door behind them.

Davis turned to face Tenor once the door was completely shut and told Tenor, "Okay we got you here so now it's your turn look around quickly!" Tenor looked around the vault shelves on the first floor as she was desperately trying to think like her husband. She asked herself, "Where the hell could he have hidden it?"

"Tenor, hurry up!"

"I'm trying!"

"Think about what makes him special! What's his favorite food, animal, anything that might give it away?"

She calmed herself down and began to think about her husband, she took a moment and remembered her husband as she looked around. "Davis, I think I'm looking for something hidden that also blends in!"

"What? Wait, are you telling me he might have camouflaged the damn thing!"

"It's possible! I remember he loved chameleons for their camouflage abilities."

"Why the hell can't things be easy!" said Davis infuriated. Davis looked around on the floor they were on and spoke. "You check over there I'm going to check some shelves on the east side!"

"No, stay and guard the door, that rouge team could be here any second."

"Which is why you need help! We have four floors to check, and this place is huge remember!"

Before Tenor could say another word Davis ran to the east side walls and shelves and franticly started to look for something that the Diamond could fit in and hide. Searching on each shelf, Davis became more frustrated as he looked, wondering how anyone found anything in this vault. Everything he saw was in either crates, boxes, or glass displays. When he found nothing, he went to the second floor and checked, to find nothing. "Oh my god this is taking too long! There has to be a system to find something down!" he said as he leaned on a shelf. When he looked at the crate in front of him, he could see the words 1950 fashion and the shelf lined with the letter F. Davis face turned red from embarrassment as he realized the displays were organized by the first letter of the topic. "God damn it!" said Davis as he headed back to the staircase where he came down. When he checked to see what its alphabetic letters were it read E-G for the second floor and the stairs below read H-O. "Good I'm only one floor up," he said to himself.

As he descended the stairs to the fourth floor, he found himself in the H section and began to search for the Diamond. When he walked down the row of shelves, he saw they had turned into cupboards. He opened one to find jewelry cases stacked inside and labeled by their size. Davis closed the cupboard and moved down to the larger side to see if it was there. He opened the small door to see multiple larger shelves with cases and looked carefully. Near the bottom right he found the largest jewelry case and took it out. A tag fell from the side of the case and hung as Davis looked at the name on the tag. Davis looked closely at the tag and even with its old and worn paper it still red as the Hope Diamond.

"Oh, thank Christ" Davis said relieved on as he hugged the case to his chest.

Davis wasted enough time and flung the case open, but his joyous smile vanished as he saw the case was empty. "Its… not here." Davis said, heartbroken. Davis put the case back and closed the door as he thought to himself,

"Why the hell did she bring me down here?" In the corner of Davis eye in the shadow of a corner there was something sticking out near the end of the cupboard. Davis got closer and saw that there was a larger brief case in the corner, and it looked brand new. He quietly pulled out the brief case and opened it, but it wasn't the thing he was expecting to find.

Davis quickly closed it as he heard Tenor's voice echo out, "Davis have you found it yet?"

Davis took the briefcase with him as he ran up the stairs yelling out, "Not yet check the next floor I'm still looking on this floor!"

Davis ran up the stairs to the top floor and looked over the side to seen Tenor looking over crates and boxes looking for what he had found.

Davis used his sphere to open the door and as it creaked open Tenor looked up to see Davis staring back down at her, "Davis what are you-"

"You politicians are all the same, you claim you want what's best for our world, but in reality, you only look out for yourself!"

"Davis this isn't the time to bicker, we have to find-"

"THIS!" Yelled Davis as he lifted the briefcase.

Even from the height he could see she was horrified by what he had in his hands. "Davis, please give that to me."

"LIKE HELL I WILL!!!"

"Just let me explain!"

"Oh, I can do that for you. You were trying to do what was best for your country and wanted to serve it in the most noble way. Even if it meant covering up or destroying anything that got in your way! Am I right?"

Tenor got frustrated and said, "You don't understand!"

"Oh yes, I do, I didn't realize how expendable our race was to people like you! The Venvoss attacked us out of desperation, but you-" Davis said with rage. "You were going to commit genocide, just to try and keep this damn secret and your damn role as a leader!"

"The world would fall apart if the people knew!"

"Look at the world now! Its already in ruins even before the Venvoss ever showed up! Our ancestors left us in this mess and instead of the generations after trying to fix it, you became part of the problem!" Tenor was about to speak until Davis cut her off as he continued. "The only real threat to this world, hell to our universe, is people like you!"

Davis turned around and took the briefcase with him as Tenor began to rush through the crates and shelved areas to get back up the stairs as she screamed, “Davis you can’t take that, it’s our key to our survival!”

“It’s the key to our extinction!”

Davis exited the vault ignoring the rest of her pleas as he slammed the door behind him. He quickly ran down the hall and with his radio tried to call his sister, what he had really found, but there was no answer. Davis ran around the museum searching for his sister hoping she was okay as he continued to radio, but there was still no response. He stopped for a moment to catch his breath, but then he realized how quiet it was. There was no gun fire, no screams, or footsteps, it was like nothing had happened when they had entered the vault. Davis deiced to go to the room with went to the room with the pipe to the vault. As he approached Davis took his sphere and had it swallow the briefcase to keep it safe and secure. He drew closer, he could hear people breathing heavily and as he turned the corner, saw Japanese soldiers holding everyone hostage. Tenor came screaming down the hall saying, “DAVIS GIVE ME THAT DAMN BREIFECASE!”

As she ran towards Davis one of the Japanese soldiers went around Davis, tackled Tenor, and pinned her to the wall. She struggled with all her might, but it wasn’t good enough, the man managed to sedate her and was dragged in and laid on the floor.

The Japanese soldiers pointed their guns at him and immediately soldiers screamed in Japanese. Davis tiered to understand them, but they were taking all at once that he couldn’t understand what they were saying. But a familiar voice clued him in, “He said for you to freeze and not move.”

Davis went white he knew exactly who it was, “Akio?!” said Davis.

Akio came around into his view as she said, “Don’t look so angry Davis, you wanted to find the football, and now you have it.”

In that moment Davis began to look back on everything they went through and pieced it all together. “It all makes sense.” said Davis realizing the horrible truth. “Your resilient attitude and dedication were exactly what I needed when we first met, there was no way our meeting was a coincidence. You knew you could hide in plain sight without me questioning you because you knew I was desperate to keep the peace and you collaborated with other departments to gain as much information as you could. But I don’t understand why.”

"You wanted to protect your people, so I did what you needed me to do." said Akio, facing away from him.

"You played on every side, you became the mole and pitted us against one another so we would not be able to trust each other. That way we would betray each other, and the football would land right in your hands." elaborated Davis.

"Davis, even you cannot understand the severity of his situation," said Akio. "Do you really think after all this everything will go back to normal, or everyone would have a clean slate? Even after this is over everyone is going to try and get new territory and statues any way they can, even if it means life is lost. Japan thought it was possible and our fears came to light when we intercepted a transition from what was left of your government, so we acted, we're not after the football to cause pain and suffering, but to stop it from coming."

"Oh, I'm sorry, but deliberately cutting the heads and limbs off of soldiers and arranging them into a horror flick scene is not really trustworthy." said Davis.

"That was all fake Davis, just some movie-magic we came up with to scare you guys into freaking you out, the real soldiers are hidden, and all the gun shots were deliberate misses to add to the believability that you were under attack." explained Akio.

"Okay let's say I believe you, my questions for you are, even if its cliché, is why did you deliberately withhold the information we needed and placing not only humanity in danger, but eight other races?" yelled Davis.

Akio turned to face him and said, "Because we were trying to preserve Earth's future and its multiple cultures. Even though this museum has multiple exhibits, it doesn't have everything. Civilizations were lost and we have no record of them ever existing. If your government got its way, they would have destroyed everything they saw as a threat to themselves. We can't let that happen again!"

"Why didn't you just tell us what you were planning from the start, we could have rallied everyone together to stop anyone who threatened our home when this was over!" yelled Davis.

"Davis you're not thinking this through, even if we do get out of this, how many people will believe us! You know as well as I there are people who would rather accept a lie over the truth because it makes them feel safe. We both know that if anyone told the truth, they would never be heard or worse, killed.

You're a good man, Davis, but even you can't make the truth come to light that easily, and I can't stand by and watch you die for it." Akio said with a gentle smile, but then it turned into a frown. "Just please hand over the football so we can be done with it."

"You're not getting any closer to this until you tell me this, we both know the Diamond isn't here, Tenor already revealed that to me. But I have sneaking suspicion that you know where it is!"

Akio sighed and then looked him straight in the eyes and said, "Its back in Wichita, back home."

"What the hell did you just say?" Davis said, shocked.

"Right before the attack I was stationed here to oversee a mission of a traitor to Japan. I was here in this building watching him when the Venvoss attacked. After hiding myself in the ventilation duct, I managed to find my way to the Hope Diamond exhibit, where I saw Icin doing something with the Diamond. I don't know how, but he managed to turn off the alarm but when he was done, he put it back and left. Back then for some reason I had a feeling that it was extremely important, so I got out of the vent and stole the Diamond. Then I got new orders before the world went quiet. I was assigned to get the football and our informants told me it was here right under our feet, but then we ran into the vault problem. We thought we were screwed, but fortunately we heard about you and your sphere, so I went looking for you. But when I got there, I couldn't figure out a way to get you out here."

"But the opportunity came when I told you how that Diamond was important. You couldn't pass the opportunity to use us."

"Yes, and it's back in my safe." Akio turned away from Davis. With her back turned she said, "At first it was my job to destroy the football, but knowing it's in your hands, I know you will keep it safe. I can't ask for your forgiveness, but please understand I did this with no joy."

Davis, Alex, and everyone on their team was infuriated, this whole time everything they did was a complete waste of effort and energy. They could have ended this a week ago, but no, everyone just had to have the football, constantly delay their efforts, and endanger billions of innocent lives. Davis told her to give him what she was using to communicate long distance to call Amelia and make sure the Diamond was there. She gingerly pulled out a satellite phone and handed it to him, he snatched it from her hand and proceeded to call Amelia. He had to call her three times before she picked up wondering who it was. Davis announced himself to her and asked her to check Akio's safe for anything out of the ordinary. He waited on the phone impatiently as Amelia made her way to the peacekeeper department.

Amelia's voice came through the phone as she asked for the combination. Akio said out loud "45,2,31."

It only took her a moment to open the door and peek inside. Amelia gasped as she saw what was in the safe. "Let me guess, the Hope Diamond!"

Amelia immediately replied, "Yes?! Wait why does Akio have it and what do I need to do with it?"

"I'll explain when I get back but for now put it in my safe. I'm going to be on the first flight out of here, I will see you tomorrow, and the first thing I will do is see what the damn clue is so we can end this!" He looked at Akio and Tenor with disgust and told her, "I'm also going to bring a souvenir home!" Amelia was relieved that everything was going to be settled tomorrow. As she was about to say goodbye there was a muffled sound in the background.

"Amelia? What was that?" asked Davis.

She wasn't sure, she closed the safe door, and made her way out of the department as another muffled sound was made, but this time it sounded louder. Amelia's voice started to shake as the noise got louder every few minutes. Then a massive explosion could be heard on the phone as Amelia screamed. Davis panicked and asked, "Amelia are you okay, what's going on?" The crackle of the cell service started to cut in and out as he listened, it was all silent now as he said asked, "Amelia, please say something, for God sakes say something!" Alex rose to her feet as she heard Davis speaking on the phone as she said, "Put it on speaker!" Davis quickly changed the setting and had everyone listen in as he asked again on the verge of tears "AMELIA PLEASE!" Then they all heard it, the roar of the beasts and serpents, as they heard the sound of glass and walls being broken down. Gun shots began to come through the phone along with men and women screaming in a massive panic. Everyone's blood ran cold as Davis kept calling out for Amelia over and over as the massacre continued. Eventually he could hear someone breathing rapidly through the phone and eventually heard her voice. He felt relief but it's was only for a moment as picked it up saying.

"DAIVS, ALEX, THE VENVOSS ARE HERE! THEY'RE KILLING PEO-" screamed Amelia before the line went dead.

"Amelia? KITTEN?" screamed Davis in a panicked voice.

Everyone in the room heard what she had said on the phone, the Venvoss were there, they were attacking. Davis looked to Akio and Alex and said, "We're out of time."

The Japanese soldiers lowered their weapons as the Americas rose off the ground, in shock, it was over, and they all realized they had failed. Akio could not bring the words out of her mouth, she tried to say how sorry she was but that wasn't good enough for Davis. Davis made a gauntlet and quickly punched Akio in the jaw, a loud crack was heard by every when he made impact. Akio flew towards the wall, smacking into it, cracking the dry wall. As she fell to the floor, Davis charged towards her as he made his sword. He was moments away from killing her when the Japanese soldiers stood in his way. But his rage blinded him, all he could think about was killing Akio. The Japanese soldiers pointed their guns at him, but he wasn't showing them any fear. As he drew closer, he used his sphere to create threads that wrapped around their guns and sliced them into pieces. When they saw their guns were destroyed, they took out their daggers and tried to assault him, but only in vain. Davis grabbed one of their knives and said, "Next time don't bring a butter knife to a sword fight!"

With one quick motion he cut the man's hand clean off and kicked him to the side. The man rolled around in pain as he looked at his severed hand on the ground and the blood that came with it. The others charged towards Davis to avenge their comrade, but they fell victim to Davis's rage. As they charged at him, Davis took his sword and dogged out of the way. He took his blade and ran it straight through one of their remaining Jap's legs. One came from behind and tried to stab him in the back as the other attacked from his side. Davis stepped out of the way as he removed his blade and slashed it across the side attacker's chest, ripping through the bullet proof vest and ammunition he had and creating a huge gash in his torso. As the last Jap saw this, he stopped in his tracks as he was too afraid to get any closer to Davis.

"Jesus, I didn't think Davis was that dangerous." said one of the soldiers.

Davis turned his back towards the Jap and stood in front of Akio's motionless body. He took his sword down with all his rand and without hesitating, put his blade was stopped by another, it was Alex's blade. Davis demanded, "Stand down, Alex, Akio and Tenor deserve to die after what they have done!"

Alex struggling to keep her blade in check forced Davis away from Akio and said, "We don't have time to deal with her or Tenor right now, if the Venvoss are attacking the mall, not only are our loved ones in danger, but with Diamond is as well, if we don't get back there right now we can't finish this!"

Davis took his sword and slashed down at his sister who blocked it and yelled, "Did you seriously ignore the call! It's too late! We have failed because of Akio and Tenor, they wasted all our time and even if we do get back there, we have no chance to stop their attack and find the Diamond."

Alex shoved her sword to the side and told him, "There is still a chance to fix this, we're so close."

"Well maybe I have had enough." said Davis as he smacked his sword against his sister's again. "I am sick and tired of the next generations always having to pay the price for mistakes they had nothing to do with! I am sick of constantly having to pick up the pieces of failures that came before us and fixing their mistake! And above all I'm done with all the lying and deceiving just so they can live it up why the future is thrown away!"

"What those idiots did was unforgivable, but right now killing them isn't going to end this! All it will do is make you a killer! I have had enough, too, but the only reason I kept going was because you!" said Alex as she forced him away again.

Davis lowered his sword and let her speak her mind, "Davis there were days that I thought of ending my life because I couldn't handle this either. But I never did because you always found the light when I needed it. If you lose hope and fall into that darkness, then we have failed."

"But she-"

"You're not the only one who is suffering! She is my sister, too, and I'm scared to death of what's happened to her and all our friends. So please let this go so we can save them."

Davis looked at Akio as she looked at him, "Every moment of your life, good and bad, is a gift from Alex. Get out of my sight!" She looked to the floor with shame as he turned walked out of the building as men and women from their side followed him from a safe distance.

Once they were gone, Davis stormed out of the museum, swinging his sword to the ground to clean off the blood. He dematerialized it afterword's when he approached the entrance. He could hear someone's footsteps approach rapidly but then stop as someone said, "Don't, let him go, he needs time to cool."

Davis could only guess that it was his sister trying to comfort him, but he didn't want to be around anyone right now.

The winds began to store more as the weather began to change from bad to worse, the clap of thunder came more frequently, but no rain had dropped yet. The leaves flew with the wind as he descended the stairs. But with each step he felt like he was dying a little, his anger changed into sorrow. Davis didn't want to deal with this right now, he couldn't, he refused to, but knowing his sister, Amelia, was possibly dead, along with his so many others, made his every being break down. His last step on the stairs made him wish this was nothing but a bad dream and that any moment he would wake to the sound of his alarm clock telling him to wake up. But he knew this was the reality he had to face and even though he knew this was already a nightmare he couldn't escape, he wished he had the chance.

His feet touched the sidewalk as he looked to the trucks they came in and he didn't want to go back with them, at least not now. He began to walk back to the airport with the briefcase in hand, but even in his broken state he saw something blue not too far away. He approached it and found a motorcycle in good condition lying on the sidewalk. He picked it up off the ground and managed to get it to turn on and drove it back. Along the way in the empty streets, Davis couldn't help but imagine the lives that were destroyed, the memories of their time on earth that would be forgotten, the joy that would never come to pass. His eyes began to fill with tears knowing this was the end of his life, everyone's life, on earth.

He managed to get back in one piece and everyone asked him how it went and where everyone was, but he couldn't bring himself to tell them. Davis went into the back office as he stole a bottle of tequila and a soda from one of the people and locked himself inside with the light off and said to himself, "What the hell am I to do?" as he sat down in a chair, opened the soda and started drinking it. In the darkness that surrounded him he closed his eyes and found himself back the museum with everyone loading up and heading back. "What the-" said Davis confused. "God dammit, it's the end of the world and I fall asleep again!"

He wiped away his tears and watched as the trucks pulled away, then he found himself next to his sister in the front seat driving. Along their way back,

Tenor started to wake up and felt sick as the truck swerved back and forth. She climbed over everyone and vomited out the back. When she was done, she demanded, "Davis you will hand over the football this instant or so help me I'll make you public enemy number one!" But she didn't see him, only the soldiers who looked at her with cold eyes. Tenor panicked as she realized she wasn't alone with Davis anymore, and her secret was out.

"Everyone…. how did we?" asked Tenor, unnervingly.

"We left about twenty minutes ago, after one of our people betrayed us and left us." said Alex as everyone sat quietly.

Tenor looked sad for them but then a look of Terror came upon her face, "WAIT, DID THEY?" she screamed with fear.

"No, they didn't get the football," said Alex. The news made Tenor relax a bit, but it soon faded as Alex said, "and you're not getting it either. You lied to us, made us waste our time, and now because of you and Akio, our home is gone, our little sister is possibly dead because of you two, and to top it off the VENVOSS ARE PISSED!" Tenor looked at Alex in anger and was about to say something when one of the soldiers grabbed her arm and threw her on the ground of the truck and told her to shut the hell up, that she had done enough talking. Tenor looked around at everyone to see the hatred once again in their eyes, but she could also see the pain in their hearts. She looked at the back of Alex's head and knew that she was telling the truth, they just lost their home, because of her. Tenor sat on the floor in silence as the truck continued its ride towards the airport. The sun was begging to set as the truck pulled in, many soldiers stopped what they were doing and looked at the truck as soldiers began to step out one by one, pushing and shoving Tenor as they climbed out. Alex got out of the truck last and waited for Tenor to get out, but she didn't, she couldn't after what she had done. Henry came running up to her and hugged his daughter with tears in his eyes. He explained that when Davis arrived without them, he assumed the worst. Alex looked stunned, Davis hadn't told anyone yet about Akio, Tenor, the football or what they heard on the phone. Alex pushed her father off and asked where Davis was. Henry pointed to the hangar and told her that once he got there he locked himself in the office and hadn't come out just yet, plus he took a bottle of tequila inside with him. Alex told her father to stay put and deal with Tenor while she would talk to him. Her father asked why and what happened to her.

Alex looked at Henry and said bluntly, "It's not what we did to her it's what she did to everyone. We found out the truth about what was down there, and you were right not to trust her."

Henry didn't understand what she meant but he could tell his daughter needed to speak with her brother, after all she knew him better than he did. Henry let her pass and asked the soldiers what had happened, she wasn't more than fifty yards away when she heard her father scream, "What!" It echoed out all the way to the hangars. People looked outward towards the airport as Alex came up, they asked what had happened, but she didn't respond. Jackie rushed up to her and asked what had happened out there and why did Davis look so crushed. Alex tried to move past her, but Jackie put her hands on her soldiers and asked her again, the same question. Alex looked up at Jackie with tears being to swell up and asked her to stand aside, she needed to talk to her brother.

Jackie had never seen her this way and stepped aside. When Alex approached the door, she used her sphere to unlock it and then entered the pitch-black room. The light shine on him and for that one second Davis reopened his eyes to see his sister standing right in front of him. Davis was surprised but at that point he didn't care how he imagined it, he just wanted to be left alone. But even without her words Davis could feel the same pain of loss and confusion as she did. She wanted to face him in the light, she needed to see how bad his state of mind was. Instead of turning on the lights she energized her sphere and made her own soft light to see in the dark.

She moved her sphere above his head and sat down next to him as she asked, "Can I have your tequila?" Davis didn't respond but he gave her a look saying he didn't care what she did. Alex opened the bottle and began to drink it straight, even though she never liked tequila, she was willing to drink anything at that point.

As she down the tequila, she began to feel the burn of the alcohol warm her throat and make her feel better for a short while. The two sat in silence for a few minutes before Alex started to cry out her tears. Davis wrapped his arm around her and placed his head on her shoulder to comfort her, but he to caved into his emotions. Alex through her sobbing said, "Akio is right, even if we do stop this war another will begin. Everyone who tried so hard to fight for Earth, the things we did so we could stop the war and bring back the peace, was in vain. Earth will never find the peace and history will always repeat itself."

Davis hugged his sister tighter as she spoke knowing the truth was hard to swallow, but she was right. They both knew they were so close, but they were half a country away and now the Venvoss were killing people, and it was only a matter of time before they brought the fight to them. As they sat in the darkness, they could feel the weight and burden of being a leader overwhelming the two of them. They sat in the dim light the door opened, and the silhouette of a man stood in the door. He closed it behind him and as he approached them his face came into the light; it was their father. He saw how much pain they were in and sat down in front of them and said, "I'm not surprised by you drinking alcohol, Alex, but after what happened I thought for sure you would Davis."

"I don't drink when I'm depressed."

"Which tells me you haven't lost hope yet, if you did then you would be drinking that tequila, too." said Henry with a smile. "Alex, Davis, you two need to get up, there are people out there who still need you."

"No, they don't need us they want us." said Davis.

"We two are the most powerful humans right now, an asset to any army that could replace thousands of soldiers at the expense of our souls," said Alex.

"Listen I can't even begin to know how you two feel right now, but there are people out there wondering what has happened, you two need to face this evil and strike it down." said Henry.

"Then why can't you do it? If you can do it don't ask us for something that you can do," said Alex while taking a swig.

Henry looked at her sphere and smiled as the light cascaded down on his face as he said, "Because, I'm not you." The two siblings looked at their father confused as he continued to talk "You two have accomplished more than anything anyone on this planet ever could. You two bring out the best in people and refuse to let them fall. You two have the strength that me and your mother could never give. You can do the impossible and lead during a galactic war while our leaders ran, and in turn you gave others the same chance to do the same."

"Anyone could do what we did," said Davis.

"Then why didn't they?"

Alex and Davis had never heard their father give such a pep talk before. In the past the ways he wanted to give them confidence only so that way when they succeeded that he could make his way into their spotlight, but now it seemed to them he was stepping out of the way. Everyone still needed them to lead after this because others didn't want to, and they were going to need all the guidance they could get. Alex put the bottle down and stood up. Davis however stayed down and still drank his soda. To him it didn't matter what his father had said to him.

Yet despite his father's manipulated nature he was right, but Davis told him, "You know many of your generation complained that our generation was to blame for everything wrong in the world, but look at yourself, you are willing to throw your children headfirst into a fire because you don't want to do the hard things. The fact that we can, only proves that people like you can't survive without someone to take the fall, and personally I feel sorry for you."

Henry looked way from Davis and said, "So am I."

With that Davis stood up and helped Alex to the door as Henry stayed in the room. Before they left Davis turned on the light and told his father that he needed to stay in the light. The two closed the door behind them and saw that people were gathered around the office door waiting for them to come out. Davis sat down, Alex and asked Jackie for some water, as he began to give them the news. He tried to make a joke to break the tension, but it wasn't that good. People looked a little irritated as they waited for him to tell them what had happened. Davis took a deep breath in and told everyone that he appreciated all of them coming out to D.C. for this mission, but he had some news about the Diamond, the football, and what happened back home. He went into great detail of what happened in the last few hours, how Akio and Tenor had betrayed everyone to get the football, the Diamond being back home, and the worst news of all that their home might not be there anymore.

Everyone was in shock and disbelief, they weren't just angry they were blood thirsty as much as he was. People began to scream and shout about going to the airport and killing Tenor as many others wanted to use the football on the real enemies of Earth. However, Davis put his hand up and told them, "Chill everyone please!" But no one was listing to him then from behind a gun shot was fired.

Everyone turned to find Henry holding a gun in the air as he said, "All of you keep it together and listen to my son for a moment!"

"Thanks, pops."

"Look we are all angry and hurt, but right now the most important thing is ending this quickly."

"My sister is right, we can't undo the damage done but we can heal from it and believe me it's a hell of a lot easier said than done! But we aren't done yet! We know the Diamond's location and still might have a chance to end this. I'm not going to lie if the Venvoss had truly gone mad with rage then heading home was a suicide mission!" Davis looked to the ground for a moment and told them, "But if I…. if we give up then the future, we give our world will be more horrible than we could ever imagen."

Davis wiped the tears from his eyes and looked at them with a smile and continued, "I'm going back and ending this and if anyone wants to join me then they are welcomed." Everyone got quiet from what he had said, no one made a sound or even tried to talk him out of it. In those moments everyone had no idea what to do or what to say as they just stood there. Davis could see the hesitation in their eyes as they stared at him with fear of the unknown.

That is until Jackie pushed her way through the crowd. Jackie approached Davis and said with a smile, "We have all been to hell and back," then she put her hand on his shoulder and said, "and I'm up for it again!"

"You two have led us for months, even went behind our backs, but you never did it for power, you did it for us. Whether in life or in death I will follow you." said Adalard.

"What the hell, I haven't been an angel, so if I am going to hell anyways, I might as well go out on my terms." said John.

Soon others began to speak their minds, but not many. Others didn't want to go back after everything and decided to quit this mission and Davis didn't try to sway them. They had every right to stay after such a devastating blow of information. However, with no hesitation Henry told him that they had his armies at their disposal and after the exposure of Tenor's treason then maybe he had hers. Alex and Davis hadn't even thought about that, with Tenor out of power they might be able to persuade a part of her army even with the other politicians in the way and with a part of their father's army, they would be able to keep them all least at bay long enough to get the Diamond.

The two felt the strength of the friends come back into their hearts and Alex said, "Okay enough mush let's get to work!" Although the two were afraid for their people and the soldiers, they knew that they would go with them to face death if it meant that there was a chance that their loved ones could see another dawn rise on earth.

As the sun disappeared before the horizon the red hues on the as dark clouds began to cover the sky, making it look of blood before the night came. The people on every side started to talk for this might be their decisive moments on earth, to say goodbye to the people they fought with, the siblings that were made by the bonds of friendship, and to close their stories not with their deaths, but by their final words. The leaders from every army gathered in the briefing tent once more to discuss the plan that they were going to need. Everyone argued about strategies and unforeseen attacks when Tenor entered the tent. All grew silent as she stood there, asking Davis to step outside for a moment. Everyone was against this, but Davis went with her and told them to continue with the planning.

The two left the tent as Tenor said, "I know you have no right to trust me but there is more information I have for you."

"Oh, really?" asked Davis questioningly.

"Look you were right we all have our own agenda, but there is something that I know that the others don't." explained Tenor.

"Then by all means, indulge me." said Davis sarcastically.

Tenor seemed nervous at first but then poured it all out, "You know about the cure that was made for the other eight races, and when our mole told us what you told her, I did some digging. But as you know all the information from that time was gone, it's like it never happened. However, there was one thing I did find, the cure's formula. I gave it to one of our head scientists and they said that the formula wasn't complete. They did say that it would still be able to cure the diseases hypothetically, but not without severe side effects."

Davis sighed with irritation and said, "Well they're still alive and pissed, so I bet it's safe to say that there was an unforeseen side effect. Also, I want to add this shit is exactly why we won't trust you."

"Okay I admit it we suck! When we found out about the cure's incompletion, we were so afraid of what side effects there were and the chance of them repelling. But they didn't show up for more than seventy years after our past leaders gave them the cure, so we assumed everything turned out fine. That is, until we had reports of strange figures barely invisible, when we heard that, we panicked and left." said Tenor irritated.

"Tenor, our ancestors didn't mean to cause this type of pain to us, but they certainly did with the other races. They knew that the cure was incomplete and even if it could cure them, they still gave something that might cause more harm than good. I can understand that even with the Venvoss help and tech there was no way they were going to be able to make an actual cure in the time span that our ancestors had been given. But if they had just told them that the cure was only a prototype and that they would work out the kinks during their time away, then things would have turned out a whole lot different. However, all of you knew that there was a chance that they would return with vengeance and what did you do? You ran when your entire world needed its leaders, and what's worse you were willing to go to kill billions and even your own family!" said Davis.

Before Tenor could even get a word in, they heard a thump. Everyone stopped what they were doing and listened again. Another thump rang out into the night as they felt the ground shake. Davis asked the soldiers to call the watch tower to see if anything was coming their direction as another thump rang out and the ground shook harder. The soldiers got on the radio as Davis turned to face Tenor again, but she was gone. "Typical," Davis thought as the soldier's radio crackled with static. Then another thump came and then a split second later so did another. The ground shook more violently with as each thump grew louder, until it stopped. Everyone waited and listened for anything, any sound that could be heard, was now silent. The solider came up and told Davis that there was nothing coming from any direction inland.

"Use the observation tower, look around, and check out the river and sea," said Davis as soldiers began to gather their guns.

The soldier radioed the tower and asked to look around the river and sea to check if anything was coming. The soldiers wasted no time and used their night-vision goggles, franticly searching in all directions. The soldiers looking north, east, and west cleared them, but the soldier south turned pale as he saw something large swimming towards them.

"Sir?" said the soldier as he gave him the goggles. His commander took them and looked through for a single moment and said under his breath, "Oh shit!"

From the edge of the runway that connected to the sea, the waves began to come on to the pavement as whatever it was caused giant swells. As he continued to look, he noticed it wasn't alone. The man dropped the goggles and radioed all the soldiers below, "Everyone look south, somethings coming and its huge!" Everyone turned their heads south and waited for what was coming. Everything was quiet and calm as they all waited, wondering what was out there. Then from the sky they heard the call of thousands of serpents coming from the sea. Then from the sea itself, six monstrous heads burst out and roared, echoing throughout the moonless and starless night. They managed to climb out of the sea and began to make their way to the airport. They stood thirty stories tall, and their appearance was horrific, they had only one eye and it was on a spiked chin, massive jaws, a giant fin on their necks and tails, and were bipedal. Compared to Earths tyrannosaurus rex it to would have run in fear from this beast.

Everyone had begun to panic as the six creatures made their way to them slowly as the serpents began to fly faster to them. Everyone stood paralyzed for a moment before Tenor yelled out, "WHAT ARE YOU ALL DOING? FIGHT!"

Soldiers began to grab guns and ammunition as Davis went to find Alex, Jacob, and their father. The creatures continued to roar as Davis ordered the quick evacuation of children, injured, and elderly while he looked for his siblings. Helicopters began to fly overhead, some stayed hovering over the crowds, as others headed straight towards the creatures, and opened fire on them. The serpents with their vast numbers overwhelmed them fast, they began to spin out of control, and plummet to the ground. Davis desperately searched the crowds of people, pushing and shoving everyone to see if he could spot his sister, the panic of the people was overwhelming as people began push others to the ground. It was like the first day of this war all over again.

In the distance, Davis could see Alex deferring kids and elderly people away from the camps and into the airport to protect them. He pushed his way through and was glad to see her before a helicopter began to fall towards her. Davis quickly used his sphere and made threads, rose them over the crowds, and at wrapped them around her as the last of the elderly went inside. The door shut and Davis quickly yanked her away as the chopper nearly fell on top of her. As she was moved, the safety chopper didn't stop when it hit the ground, but skitted on the ground towards some trucks.

It only took a moment for the chopper to detonate as it hit the truck. The explosion caused the truck to jump out and barrel-roll in the air as one of the blades from the chopper flew out from the explosion and flew right into another choppers cock pit, killing the pilot instantly casing another chopper to crash. The truck came down landed on top of another truck carrying passengers, everyone could hear the screams of people who survived the burning to death. Soon other choppers began to fall even more quickly from the sky and bursting into flames as they came to the cold ground. Everyone saw the serpents were systematically attacking the choppers with great movements. As the choppers came close to the ground, some people inside tried to jump down, but the serpents grabbed them and instead of taking them the rose high into the air and let them plummet to their deaths, others grabbed them and took them to the titans and dropped them into its mouth. Davis and Alex got up and couldn't believe the chaos, they knew the Venvoss were impatient, but this wasn't a hostage situation anymore, this was extinction. People tried to flee anyway they could think of but with the lay of the land they would be to wide open.

Soldiers were desperately loading trucks up with people and previsions as they shot the serpents out of the sky, even when they began to sky bomb towards them. As they held off the serpents, they managed to fill up the trucks with civilians. Some parents said goodbye to their kids and began to join the fight as their kids drove off screaming for them in tears. Alex and Davis began to help load the people onto the trucks and get them inside as more serpents came down faster and faster, like a rain shower. The soldiers kept up with them as the shells of their bullets began to littler the ground. As they loaded up another truck with kids and injured people, some serpents came in low near the ground. As they approached rapidly towards the truck the soldiers turned their attention to the ground. The serpents that came to them had some strange attachment on their heads it looked demonic in appearance, but this didn't phase the soldiers as they began to fire at them. But their numbers were too great as they came closer and closer. Davis and Alex and other soldiers finished getting people inside the airport. As the last few people went inside, Davis ordered some soldiers, "Stay inside and find somewhere to hide, we'll take care of this." The soldiers didn't argue with him and ran inside as the siblings slammed the door shut. They looked towards the trucks and soldiers still fighting on the field as the chaos ensued around them.

From a distance they saw the last person got into the last truck as the soldiers that surrounded the trucks ceased fire. The soldiers emptied their guns and tried to reload, but when they looked for their other clips they stopped in fear, they had run out. As the soldiers looked to the serpents, they saw them all coming once. One solider threw her gun to the floor and took out her grenade from her belt and yelled out, "No matter the cost, don't give them an inch!" She pulled the pin out from her grenade and rushed towards the serpent with her brothers and sisters following behind her, with their own grenades ready. The siblings knew what they intended to do and began to run towards them, only to be attacked by other serpents. The siblings formed their weapons and began to defend one another as the serpents. Desperately trying to get through the mayhem they could see the soldiers and serpents charge towards each other and when they were close enough the truck drove away as the serpents began to rip the soldiers apart.

Whatever was on their heads was made of metal and had sharp teeth in their jaw. Blood splattered into the air as the soldiers screamed in pain, but in their last moments let go of their grenades. Then a flash of light and fire came from the ground, and a loud explosion followed. Ripping the serpents apart and sending the limb bodies all over the battlefield.

The two looked at each other and looked into their eyes, knowing that they need to end this now. The two had seen watching the Venvoss for a while and with their own experience managed to form some belts and jumped into the air, far above the ground and hovered.

"Davis, do you think you can take those creatures without me?"

"With that thread trick, definitely. But what are you going to do?"

Alex formed her small spheres around herself and had them begin to spin around each other in a certain number, "Today's forecast, thunderstorms."

The siblings waited as the serpents charged towards them roaring with rage. Davis changed his sword into treads and rushed towards their enemies as Alex stayed behind and concentrated on her spheres as she flew high into the sky and hid in the clouds. Davis flew towards the serpents screaming, "GET THE HELL OF MY PLANET YOU SNAKE REJECTS!" He flew right through the horde of serpents, dodging their bites as he wrapped some thread around the ones he passed. In the heart of the horde, he began to spin his body like a dancer as the serpents began to circle him. The serpents didn't understand what he was doing but without hesitation they all flew towards him in all directions like multiple missiles. Davis smirked as she stopped dancing, and with one tug of his string caught all their serpents in the sky.

Then closing his eyes, he dropped out of the sky with the string wrapped around his hand. As he landed on the ground, the concrete cracked by the force of energy he created from the fall, and with one motion he yanked all the threads down towards him. The serpents were instantly sliced into thousands of pieces and their blood rained down on top of him. As he rested for a moment, more serpents came from the sea and the sky began to rumble with thunder and spark with lightning, illuminating everything in sight. The giants stopped and looked into the sky as the lightning became more frequent and lasted longer. Davis looked into the sky as the lighting began to connect in a circle.

Above the clouds, in the full moon's light, Alex was having the spheres circle one another. As they circled around each other faster the air in the center became hot and electric until they formed white-hot halos. In the halo's center was a ball of energy with tendrils of electricity escaping, as the energy continued to build. Back on the ground, the dark clouds became so bright that it almost looked like the dawn had begun to rise. Davis's hair began to rise into the air and felt it become more electric. Davis pulled out his radio and yelled into it, "EVERYONE TAKE COVER!"

As the last of the energy was stored Alex looked below and said under his breather, "Let's get electrified!"

All the energy burst down below with a loud crack, ranging throughout the sky, like a giant spider web. Bolts of lightning struck the ground and the aliens and everyone took cover in the buildings and areas outside. It lasted a for some time as it illuminated the world around them. Davis looked around him to see the serpents were scorched as the titans shocked, but as he looked above, he saw the beauty of the lightning and power it created. When it stopped, thousands of serpent's flaming bodies fell from the sky, crashing on the ground and bursting into dust as the titans struggled to keep on their legs.

After the waves of serpents, Davis and Alex regrouped with some soldiers and some of their own. "ALEX! That was to close!" said one of the soldiers.

"Sorry, but even I can't predict where the lightning will strike!"

"Yell at each other later we still have massive titans there stunned for now, so anyone have a plan?"

"We don't have shit! All of our air support is gone and we're running low on ammo!"

"There has to be something we can do!" yelled Davis.

"There is, stay safe everyone I be back!" said Alex as she went flying towards the titans.

"ALEX GET YOUR ASS BACK HERE!" screamed Davis.

"What do we do?"

"Don't know, but I'm telling you what you're going to do, get inside, and stay there!"

"We're not going to-"

"Don't argue with me just do it!" said Davis as he caught off the soldier.

One of the soldiers gave Davis a radio and told them they were on channel three and to contact them when they were done. Davis thanked them and flew after Alex.

When Davis caught up with Alex, he asked, "What's the plan?"

"Wing it!" said Alex.

Davis never heard his sister say 'wing it' before, she always had a trick or two up her sleeve, but this was a first. The titans roared at them as they flew past them with their weapons drawn. The creatures were huge, they were slow. Davis deliberately plummeted down towards them with his small spheres charging with energy followed behind. Alex took her stings and used them to keep the titans immobilized as Davis got closer to the titans. Before Davis could throw the small spheres towards the titans, a Venvoss stopped him in his tracks. It dragged him to the ground as Alex tried to finish off the titans with her string, but their skin was just too thick for it. It made Alex wince as she realized that she couldn't beat them alone, but she did think of something else. She raised them up and hurled them around a few times like a lasso and flung them back far into the ocean.

As Alex was dealing with the titans, the Venvoss rushed to the ground with Davis struggling to get free. Davis quickly used one of his small spheres like a bullet and fired at the Venvoss' face. The Venvoss was stunned for a second and loosened his grip, giving Davis the opportunity to escape. Once he was free, he had the other small spheres assault the Venvoss. However, this Venvoss was quicker and made a shield that absorbed the blows from the spheres and the energy they had created. Its shield grew red as the energy from the spheres transferred and returned to Davis. When his assault ended, Davis took his sword and rushed towards the Venvoss, but the Venvoss was ready for him. It dematerialized its shield and swung its own sword in an arch. Davis managed to dodge its swing but not without loss. The tip of the blade had managed to cut horizontally across his face. His blood flew into the air and Davis noticed it looked like a metallic sliver and once he regained his posture, he turned to face the Venvoss, who was already charging towards him with his back turned.

But as the Venvoss saw the tip of his blade covered in sliver blood, it stopped right in front of Davis and grabbed his neck, looking very deeply into his laceration. It could see the silver blood dripping out little by little, and even though Davis couldn't see its face, the amount of pressure it put on his neck was intensifying; it was furious. Davis didn't understand why it was so angry, but he was more focused on not being choked to death. He tried to use his sword to get away, but because of its four arms it just held his two arms in place. Davis's vision became blurrier as it became hard to breathe, and he could feel his sword begin to disintegrate and his hand begin to loosen.

Then Alex appeared out of nowhere and tried to stab at the Venvoss, its armor deflected the blow as it tried to grab Alex. Davis felt its grip loosen and he took a chance. He quickly made a belt around the Venvoss which had the ability to amplify gravity. The Venvoss fell to earth ten times faster and, without realizing it, let go of Davis by mistake. As the Venvoss created a crater in the earth, Alex helped Davis to the ground as he was coughing and hacking. Once on the ground, Davis and Alex saw the Venvoss was able to stand up normal, it seemed that it had decreased its own gravity in order to counterbalance the belts. It ran towards the siblings with full force as Alex was trying to help Davis catch his breath. Alex quicky covered Davis's body with her own to shield him from the sword.

However, when the sword hit her back only the ring of metal could be heard. Davis demineralized everything to make her armor again as they descended to the ground, but he made it camouflaged, and Alex was so worried for her brother that she didn't even realize. Davis looked her in the eye and said, "Even the playing field, sis."

Alex smiled, reviling her armor, and formed two katanas as she stood up, she faced the Venvoss saying, "You don't mind a dance do you, Vomanin?" It didn't take a genius to see that it was the same Venvoss from a week ago that attacked their home back in Kansas, but it was surprising to see him already back on his feet and able to prepare for an assault in a short amount of time.

The two began to clash swords and the sparks began to fly as they made contact. Davis got onto his feet and made his way around the Venvoss as they fought, when there was an opening, Davis would use his sphere again, but until then he had to stay out of the way. The swords began to turn red as the air became hot and electrified like the first time they fought. Alex was beginning to make two waves of energy as the Venvoss began to charge it's own blades with it's own power. Alex's blades became white-hot as the Venvoss' become an orange colored. The two waves of energy were released for the blades leaving molten rock in their wake. As the wave collided the energy fused together and became unstable, creating a massive explosion of both thermal and gamma radiation. Alex and the Venvoss fought back from the force as Davis watched the energy come towards him and thought to himself, "Well I did always want to out with an explosion, I just thought I would be the one to cause it."

Davis closed his eyes and waited for death to take him but out of the corner of his ear he heard that strange chirping sound again. He reopened his eyes as giant wings quickly surrounded him, wrapping him up like a cocoon as the wave of everything hit him. The wave blasted Davis and this strange creature back once they were inside its wings, but the radiation still managed to seep in, and Davis began to feel sick. When they landed half a mile away the creature unwrapped its wings around Davis as he began to lose his vision and succumb to the radiation. The creature called out to someone as Davis managed to squint its eyes and see what this creature really was.

Its entire body were shades of bule and small with an hour glass shape, eight tentacles coming out of the bottom, three green eyes on a mushroom like head with two swirls on its side, and four eight-foot wings. Davis wondered why this creature kept looking out for him as it kept calling for something just as he passed out.

CHAPTER 15

Into the unknown end.

Back in the darkness of his mind, Davis found himself next to his sister in the battlefield or what was left of it. She was frantically searching for Davis or at least his body. She leaped over the melted cement and was relieved as she found him, unconscious and alive, but the mysterious creature had vanished.

Okay, this is getting weird?" Davis said to himself. "I know my imagination is… well imaginative but there is no way I can constantly make these scenarios. I wonder… No, it can't be!"

Davis could see Alex trying to wake him up, she didn't know how he survived but was determined to keep him alive. She demineralized her swords and made another anti-gravity belt for her brother to make him weightless. She grabbed him and flew off towards the other end of the airstrip where soldiers were still evacuating. She begged for someone to help her brother, but everyone was in such chaos that she didn't get an immediate response. She waited for almost an hour before someone came to her and asked what had happened.

Alex brought him into their hangar and told them "When that Venvoss and I clashed, we both released a massive amount of gamma radiation. I thought mine would overpower his and cancel it out. But instead, I think it absorbed it, it became unstable and well, you saw what happened! I thought he was dead, but I found him just near the outskirts of the molten pavement!" The medic quickly got a radiation detector and checked his levels, they showed them that he was in the 50 rem/500 mSv section. Though his life wasn't in danger, his blood cells would be damaged due to the exposure. Alex was relieved that it wasn't too serious but still was worried for him. One particular man appeared behind her and asked if she would like some help. When she turned, she saw her brother Jacob and her father Henry helping him over. Alex hugged the two of them and was grateful that they were okay, but even they couldn't hold back their fear when they saw Davis lying on the ground.

"What happened?" asked Jacob.

"Vomanin, the Venvoss that attacked our home back in Kansas, he was responsible for all of this." Alex said bluntly.

"Where is he?" asked Henry.

"I don't know, I was looking for him, but wherever he has gone I'm sure he won't show his face to us or the Venvoss anytime soon." said Alex.

Henry looked to his son Davis and saw the cut across his face and noticed the silver liquid coming out of it. "What the hell is that?" Henry said out of fear as he moved past his daughter to his son. Henry used his index finger to pick up a little blood off his cheek as Jacob moved past Alex and saw what his father was talking about. Alex told them, "I think it's his blood."

"WHAT?" screamed Henry.

"Wait, why is it silver?!" asked Jacob.

"There is something I need to tell you both." said Alex worried. The soldiers looked over Davis while he was unconscious, and Alex explained everything to her brother and father. About the attack months ago, the mysterious Venvoss, and the side effects of whatever Davis had. Even from his position Davis could see the horror in his father and brother's eyes as his sister told them about how he got like that.

"Alex is it permanent?" asked Jacob scarred.

"I don't know, the Venvoss did this I think only they can undo it."

"NO!" yelled Henry.

"No?" asked Alex.

"I....I can't let you guys go out there, not again." Henry said grabbing his daughter's arms.

"Dad we are already in a war zone, and Davis doesn't have a choice, he needs the Diamond, and I won't let him go off alone. Besides why are you now suddenly acting like this? A few hours ago, you were all for us doing the right thing and protecting the innocent. What changed?"

I didn't know you both were in the smack damn middle of this situation! I...I didn't know you both were in this much danger!"

"Dad, you have known the whole time and the world is in danger! It didn't matter if it was me or Davis or anyone, someone was going to be in this position, whether we liked it or not!"

"I don't care! You two will not leave this place, I forbid it!"

"BOTH OF YOU SHUT IT!" screamed Jacob. The two stopped arguing and looked at Jacob, "Look this situation you two are in is messed up and I don't want to lose you two, and honestly I wished it was someone else, but you have to go, and dad you have no right to stop them." said Jacob almost looking like he was on the verge of tears.

Henry lowered his head down to face the ground and said, "When this all started, I knew it was going to be rough, but nothing like this. I just got kids back not just from the war but from my own selfishness, and I don't want to lose you again! I might have already lost Maria and the grandkids, I can't lose another child."

"But could you ever look at us in the face again, knowing you gave up generations of children." Said Alex.

Henry took a deep breath in as he raised his head, he exhaled, and said, "Please come back safely."

Alex smiled at her father and brother and held them both tightly as she hugged them with delight, but at the same time Davis could see in her face a certain sadness showing itself through her smile.

"Okay, I'm glad that this is settled but there still a problem.... how do we get back home? The cars and trucks are being used, and dozens of helicopters are down." said Alex attempting to end the conversation to move forward.

"Got you covered on that, sis!" said Jacob as he took her outside and showed her a private jet being prepped for takeoff. She wondered how he managed to pull that off as Jacob explained, "When the attack started Tenor ran, she left a lot of her stuff behind including the keys to the jet, though I do not know how she managed to get them?" Alex didn't care how or why Tenor had keys to a jet, but she was glad Tenor wasn't smart enough to take them when she ran.

"How long before takeoff?"

"An hour, two tops, I suggest you say your farewells to your friends and gather some supplies before you leave."

As she waited for the jet to get ready, she took her time gathering supplies and checked up on Davis now and again to see if he was still okay. However shortly after some of the politicians came to the hangar and visited Alex and Davis. They wished them luck, but Alex saw past their ill-gotten sympathy. She knew what they wanted from her and Davis, their precious football. But before she could say anything to them Henry stormed over to them and said, "Get away from my daughter, you vultures!"

"We want the football, after last night's debacle, it's clear that it should be used to eradicate the Venvoss." said one of the male politicians.

"You are not getting the football, and neither am I. It is going with my kids to make sure that hopefully nobody will make a rash or idiotic decision!"

The politicians were about to argue as they saw many soldiers with their guns pointed at them. One of the soldiers demanded, "Go back to your little offices, quickly and quietly, we will come get you when everyone else is safe."

Out of fear for their lives some agreed to their demands, while others put up a fight, but in the end, they were all dragged back to the airport.

When the politicians were out of sight, Alex thanked the soldiers for their help as she began to finish up her supplies. The soldiers told her that after all they had done in the last few days for them, protecting them was the least they could do. As Alex smiled at them for their kindness some soldiers began to gather her supplies and escort them to the jet as other soldiers wished Alex and her brother luck on their journey. Knowing that so many people were rooting for her, and her brother made her feel at peace and gave her the confidence and hope that they might just actually manage to pull this off. But as the jet was being loaded, Alex wondered where her people were and thought that they might have been evacuated during the attack as the last of their stuff was loaded.

She sat down next to her father and brothers as they waited for time to dwindle way, hoping that her friends were okay, but then a familiar voice caught her ear saying, "Hey! You're just going to leave without saying goodbye to your friends?"

Alex looked towards the doors of the hangar and was surprised to her John, Jackie, and Adalard with many of their people still there. Alex was overjoyed to see so many still standing but asked, "I'm glad to see you all, but why didn't you leave?"

"Because you and your brother never did." said John.

"Even when things got really difficult." said Adalard.

"Hell, someone of us didn't even deserve your help, but you still gave it. Our past may have messed up and made us look like we were weak, but with people like you two in the world, make us see a future worth fighting for." said Jackie with a huge grin on her face. Then she turned her attention towards Henry and said, "You have some damn good kids, you should be really proud of them."

"I am," said Henry nervously.

"Okay, thank you all, but please save the speeches for after we save our world!" said Alex trying not to tear up which made her team laugh lightly. "Thank you for your encouragement, but I don't want to celebrate yet until this is over. I want to celebrate when all of us have been made whole, when our world is safe and rebuilt. I'm not going to lie, the future ahead is going to be difficult for all generations, past, present, and future. So, for now, in this moment, instead of celebrating, lets reminisce before we leave."

Everyone could see Alex wasn't going to be happy until this was over and indulged her as they reminisced about the funniest things that had happened to them in this war, just to pass the time. They all laughed about the good times they had during their time in the mall, but the more they talked, the more upset they became, realizing that when everything was finished, that they would all go their separate ways. When time was almost up everyone became silent, their adventure was starting to reach its conclusion and the worst part was that the others weren't going to be there in the end. Alex asked, "Does anyone what to come back with us?" But nobody said a word, it was clear that they were done with all the fighting, at least for now, and Alex couldn't bring herself to force them into going. Everyone started to feel depressed as they realized that this was possibly the last time they would get to see each other.

"Oh, for God sakes you idiots, stop being so depressed!" Jacob said irritated. "I know is a cliché, but your adventures are far from over." Jacob said more calmly as he sat down next to his sister. "I'm not going to lie this has been a hell of a nightmare, but even though you might never see each other again doesn't mean what you didn't matter. It's because of all of you that we are going to end this, and earth will still stand. Even if all of you aren't going, you helped them reach the end. You didn't allow your differences to divide you and because of that you were able to do something many would have shied away from. When this is over, I'm sure all of Earth will be rejoicing in what you all have done, and if not then we all will make them see that you all didn't give up that easily, that you all didn't fall."

Alex and her team felt a little better by Jacob's words but knew this was a goodbye when the pilot for the jet started to approach. Alex stood up as some men carried Davis's unconscious body to the jet. Alex started to walk slowly towards the jet with the briefcase containing the football, knowing once she went on, there was no turning back. She was already at the stairs of the jet, and she took a deep breath in and told herself that they could do this, just once more. The door closed behind her as the soldiers sat her down and told her to make sure she was secure. Alex buckled her belt and looked to the seat with her brother on it. She wished that he were awake to at least say goodbye, but they didn't have the time to wait any further.

Alex looked out the jet window at her friends, brother, and father as they waved gently goodbye. In ten minutes, they would be airborne and on their way, back to a possible desolated home with the only way of stopping this nightmare, she only prayed that the diamond was still there along with the rest of her family. The jet began to drive down the runway and slowly started to accelerate as the engines on the other side of the jet began to roar. It took only a few moments for the jet to lifted of the ground as they became airborne. It made its way into the sky it circled around the airport to get into the correct positions for travel.

From above Alex could see the damage that she and the Vomanin had caused, this made her turn her head towards her brother and say to him, "How could you have survived such a devastating explosion and how did he get so far without the dust?"

Davis looked at his own body as it lied in its chair from the ally he stood in and accepted the truth. "I don't know why or how, but I now know that somehow, I have been astray projecting my mind this whole time. Or some sort of trippy side effect of what happened to me."

Davis looked out the window and saw the plane no longer circling but was now flying away from the airport. The airport was disappearing from his gaze as the jet began to fly away from D.C. and began its journey back to the west, with the last bit of hope of their people that they would succeed. Davis looked back at his sister seeing her look outside the jet looking below to D.C. to the new ruins of the once capital of America. Many of the buildings were gone along with its people and the only survivors that would be found would endure the horrors of an unforeseen future. As she looked out, Davis placed his hand on her shoulder and felt her emotions run into himself. He could feel her anger, fear, and sorrow all at once, he felt this before when he first saw the devastation of the first attack, wondering how much life was lost, the struggles of the ancestors trying to build a new future their beliefs, and the dreams that never came into the light. All because their leaders had let them down. Alex turned away from the window as she couldn't look at the destruction any longer. She had seen the ruins of her home back in Kansas, but she never had a chance to grieve for everything she had lost.

In that moment she prayed for something and said under her breath, "Dear lord, please allow the future to know our mistakes, so that way they don't suffer the same fate as we have to."

When she was done with her prayer, she sat back in her chair as the seat belt sign turned off, allowing people to roam about the cabin. Some soldiers began to talk about strategies and plans as others kept an eye on Davis as he slept. Even in his astral form he could see his sister pondering over his survival from the blast. It was a mystery to her and everyone on the jet, but no one dared asked anything about it to her, in a way Davis could see that they knew she didn't even know.

After some time in the jet, a soldier asked Alex to join them in the back of the plane to discuss the plan for when they landed, but her mind was somewhere else. It wasn't till the soldier tapped her shoulder when she looked at them. She was startled but she collected herself, "I'm sorry what? I wasn't paying attention?"

"It's okay I was just wondering if you would like to join us for making a plan." said the soldier.

Alex looked over to her brother and said, "Okay, but please can someone who isn't going to be a part of the planning, keep an eye on him."

The soldier looked over her shoulder and told her, "I'll keep an eye on him, if he wakes up while you're gone I'll come and get you." Alex left the room and made her way into the back of the plane where there was a bedroom with men and women waiting for Alex with Davis's astral form following behind.

"Thank you for joining us miss Ring, we need some input on what we could be facing." said one of the soldiers.

"Well as you all saw from the attack at the airport, the Venvoss are pissed and only a few hours prior to the attack they struck Wichita first. My little sister, Amelia, answered a phone call from us when we were at the museum, during which the Venvoss's creatures attacked. In the background we could hear…. Destruction. I cannot begin to tell you what I heard, it was happening all too fast that the noise was almost gargled. So, if the building and people are okay then we need to assume that the Venvoss are nearby waiting for an attack. If they're gone then we need to check for survivors and for Akio's safe, which should hopefully still be in her department on the bottom floor."

"Okay, so what are best points of entry?" asked one of the soldiers.

"Well… let's see!" said Alex as she began to discuss the lay out.

The teams planning lasted for hours as the jet flew back to Kansas. Yet throughout planning Alex's mind was always somewhere else and Davis knew what she kept asking herself "How did he survive?"

As Davis watched on his vision even in the astral plan became blurry and faded in and out of darkness, like he was tired and worn out. He became curious and left the room to return to his body and saw himself sweating as the soldier tried to wake him up but as she shook him the darkness consumed him. Then he found himself in a familiar sight, the same dream as before the one of him with his skin becoming black his blood bursting through while it began to fall off. Only to fall to the ground to have the pain stop and find himself in a barren wasteland. At this point he finally realized that he was dreaming about the plague that ravaged the other worlds, the horror, fear, and pain that he could only imagine in his mind. Yet as he dreamt something changed while he lied on the ground. The pain began to fade, and his crimson blood turned silver and he fell. As he fell into the pool of blood, it to turned silver and the sand absorbed it. Soon grass began to grow with wildflowers, and the once endless desert turned into a lush green field with rivers and a few forests.

The sun rays beat down on his head as he left new life beginning to breathe in him. It was like whatever happened to this place had long since passed. In his mind he believed that this was what the other races wanted, what they needed, a chance to begin again, just like humanity. In the distance he saw someone sit up from the grass, like they were looking into the skies above. He approached the being and they looked towards him. He stopped in his tracks as he saw this person stand up. They turned towards him and revealed that they were elderly and frail, but still full of life and had beautiful eyes. Davis's heart almost stopped as he saw her eye, he almost began to tear up as he saw, his sister Amelia's eyes. Yet it wasn't Amelia, it was his youngest niece Diamond smiling at him. In the distance a woman called out, "Mom, come on the grand babies want you to tell them a story."

"I'm coming sweetie, it takes forever to get round with this old body." Diamond replied.

As she headed towards her daughter she passed through Davis, like he was a ghost. Davis turned after she passed through him to see her with her own grandchildren coming up to her in the field, giving her an eminence of love. Then he saw an elderly man and woman with a cane with a few other adults helping her play with the children. Davis got closer and saw that it was his sister, Maire and her husband, Daniel, with their children Jerry, Lilith, Cassy, Darren, and Irena all grown up with their own kids.

Davis felt overwhelming joy as he saw this dream, this was what he wanted, his family to continue with all the love and joy they could get. When he tried to get closer, he smacked into something that stopped him in this track. Davis rubbed his face and shook it off, he approached again but this time put his hand on it as it. It was some sort of wall that stopped him from getting closer. As he looked beyond this translucent wall the image of his family disappeared and the desert came back. Davis was startled and quickly removed his hand, but then everything good had come back. Davis didn't understand as he watched from the distance, he was trying to figure out what it meant. Then without warning the day turned to dusk and a voice from behind him spoke.

"I'm sorry but this is the only way now, you can't go back, you can only go forward, so please make your peace," said an unfamiliar voice.

Davis was so startled by the voice he forced himself to wake up. His eyes shot open, and the soldier jumped back in fear, screaming. Alex bulldozed out of the back room and came to the soldier asking what happened. Davis butt in and told his sister he had startled her by accident. When Alex heard her brothers voice, she turned to face him and immediately hugged him with delight. She pulled away from him and started asking so many questions: how he survived, if he was okay or if he was sick, and about his blood being silver. The soldier pulled Alex away and told her to take minutes for him to fully wake up first. Alex realized she jumped the gun a little and went back to the bedroom as the soldier began to do a standard check up on him. During her checkup she asked the same questions as Alex did. He did admit he felt a little woozy and a little nauseous, and that he didn't know why his blood turned sliver, but he didn't tell her about the alien.

She looked at Davis and told him that he was one lucky S.O.B. That no one on earth could have survived a massive amount of radiation dose, not even him. Davis grew curious and asked how much there was when the explosion happened.

"Let's just say there was so much that you would have been vaporized into dust, or that's what would have happened, but something strange occurred on that field."

"What do you mean?"

"Well, something diluted that radiation levels in less than a few seconds that regular time could never do. It went from 100-rem to 50-rem in less than a few seconds. If say the football had been used, it would take five thousand years for the radiation level to be depleted naturally overtime to reach that same range, and its cause for concern."

"How is it cause for concern?" asked Alex.

"Because 50-rem, is enough to damage white blood cells." she said as Davis flinched. "Don't worry I have medicine that will curve it so your body can heal properly."

Davis relaxed for a moment but then remembered the strange creature that saved him and realized what it had done. "Holy shit so that's what that thing did, but why?"

"Thing? What are you talking about?" asked the soldier questioningly.

Davis explained the events of what happened to him on the field of battle along with the strange creature that saved him. The soldier asked Davis to draw the creature from memory as she became curious about it when he explained it. She handed him a paper and pencil; he sat up from his chair and did his best to draw out every detail about the creature. Though his skills as an artist were more on the cartoony side, he showed his drawing to her. She looked at it for a while but had no idea what to think.

"This is the thing that saved you?" She asked. "I mean I still believe you, but I have never seen an alien like this during the war." She then called Alex back into the room to get a better understanding of what she had seen. Alex came in quickly and the soldier showed her the picture of the strange creature and explained to her what Davis had seen and wondered if she had seen it too on the battlefield.

Alex looked at Davis and said, "I didn't see this out there because I was fighting."

"I think this was what saved me from the explosion and I believe that this was the second time this creature saved me."

"Second time?" questioned Alex.

"On the first day, when all the world went to hell, I think it saved my life from the car wreck."

"You didn't tell me that!" screamed Alex.

"I didn't want to upset you and I don't know why it saved me, but the one thing is that thing, whatever it is, has been following me ever since that day."

"Maybe it's taken a liking towards you otherwise you might have been dead sooner." said the soldier.

"No.... it's like.... It's keeping me alive for something else."

"Like what?" asked Alex.

"I don't know. But the reason I woke up was I was startled by a voice I didn't recognize. But one of the things it said was 'You can't go back, you can only go forward, so make your peace.'"

"It was just a dream." said the soldier.

"What if it wasn't? Out of all the things we have seen and heard, I wouldn't be surprised if there was something out there with telepathic abilities talking to me."

"Well, whatever is going on, we'll find out when we end this, but first your medicine and more rest." said the soldier forcingly dropping the conversation.

When they were finished talking, the soldier gave Davis a potassium iodate pill for the radiation and some water to help wash it down. Alex sat behind Davis and explained that he had been out cold for hours and that they were heading back home to Kansas to get the last clue.

"How did our father take the news?"

"He wasn't happy, and it took our brother to convince him for us to leave. He was still angry when we left, but he understood we had to go."

Davis was disappointed he didn't say his goodbyes to his friends or family, but he was glad his sister was still around with her armor. That's when he realized his sister was still wearing the armor, he made for her and took it off of her, "Sorry about that, it must have been horrible wearing that for so long."

"I didn't mind, but I am grateful to have it off." said Alex as she stood up and stretched her body.

"Well, I'm glad you're okay, but what's the plan for the base back home?"

Alex put her hand in front of his face with one finger in front of him symbolizing to be silent for a moment. She went into the back of the jet and brought everyone out into the seating room. When everyone was settled, they all went over the plan one more time as a precaution and to lay out their strategy for Davis. The plan to Davis was straight forward and to the point with extra caution, but his mind was somewhere else. He still listened to the plan but that strange voice he heard kept ringing in his head as he asked himself, "Was it real or just a dream?"

Their plan didn't take long to explain to Davis for he already knew what was going to happen when they landed as the pilot called out to everyone on the intercom saying, "Everyone, we are about to reach our final approach into Wichita, or what's left of it, please fasten your seat belts, and have all chairs in the upright position."

Everyone did as they were told and as the plane turned on its side, everyone on Davis's side of the plane saw the city of Wichita annihilated with only one tower hardly standing. Davis wasn't surprised that this happened, but the feelings of fear and uncertainty for the survivors in the mall wouldn't go away.

Approaching the airport, they saw it too was in ruins and the destroyed planes were scattered all over the runway near it. The pilots had no choice but to land and hope they didn't hit any debris on the runway. The wheels were deployed and kissed the ground as the wind roared around it, slowing the jet down. The pilots managed to land but had to make some quick maneuvers with the jet to avoid taking damage. The pilot called out on the intercom, "Everyone hold tight!"

The jet swerved around debris, desperately dodging the wreckage as they tried to find an opening to stop. Everyone in the back was gripping the arms of their seats as they held on for dear life. After what seemed like a roller coaster ride the jet came to a stop. The pilot came out and asked, "Everyone all right?"

"We're okay." said one of the soldiers.

"That was sort of fun, it was like we were on a rollercoaster."

"NO, IT WAS NOT," screamed Davis. "Rollercoasters are designed to swerve, twist, and all that other shit. A jet is not supposed to!"

"Davis calm down, it's over and we're okay," said the pilot as he opened the jet of and let down the stairs.

Davis stayed seated as the soldiers exited the jet and began to survey the area. Alex came up to him and said, "Shake it off, you're okay."

Davis collected himself as his sister went outside with the others. He stood tall and made his way outside the jet. Outside, Davis stepped down onto the ground as the soldiers began to fan out and look for a vehicle. The soldiers were being extremely cautious about their surroundings as they were looking for transpiration, it was like they were expecting an attack. Some soldiers managed to find a truck that was damaged but still working enough to get them around. When the truck came up to the jet Davis began to examine the wreckage of the planes. Looking closely, he saw that the planes had been, cut, bent, and smashed by something. Continuing to look around he saw the slash marks on the ground and the mangled metal of some planes.

"Sis?" Davis asked, "Please tell me you are seeing what I'm seeing."

Alex approached him and looked at the wreckage, but she didn't know what he was referring to and asked, "What am I looking for?"

"The damage of these planes, was caused by the spheres dust material."

"So? Why is that unusual. I mean the Venvoss were destroying everything in sight."

"Ture, but on the first day I saw javelins thrown on the pillars of the highway that detonated and collapsed it. So why would they crush, slash, and bend metal planes?"

Alex understood what he was saying, it made no sense why they did this. Then out of the corners of the siblings' ears they heard one of the male soldiers scream out in fear. The siblings rushed over to find the man getting off the ground as others investigated some other debris. The soldiers saw the siblings and told them, "It's a severed arm."

"Human?" asked Alex.

The soldier shook his head as Davis looked inside the debris. The arm was burned and crisped, but still showed signs of reptilian scales as it revealed it only had three fingers. "This is a Venvoss' arm." Davis explained.

Alex looked around the airfield and put all the evidence together as she said, "This wasn't a random attack, this was a battle field between the Venvoss."

"I believe you're right Alex, if the Venvoss fought each other then there is anarchy in their ranks."

"But, regardless of knowing why this place was destroyed we still have to go." said a soldier as he turned around and headed towards the truck.

"Alright people listen up half of us will go with Davis and Alex, the rest of you refuel, if you can and try to figure out a way to clear some of the debris from the airway. Keep up your guard everyone we're in hostile territory now and whatever you do don't engage the enemy alone."

The soldiers all yelled out, "Sir, yes sir."

The team split up and as Davis and Alex jumped into the truck and told them what route to take to get to the mall as the other soldiers stayed behind and began to look around. As they drove through the destroyed neighborhoods, the siblings began to fear the worst and wondered if everyone was still alive. Davis took out Icin's sphere and looked at it, hoping that the last clue was really the last, but also wondered what the final clue was. He looked to his sister and explained what Tenor had told him about the incomplete cure and the possible side effects that might have caused them to act out so violently, even though he wasn't sure about it himself. Alex wasn't surprised that Tenor was hiding even more crucial information about this, she was possibly going to ask to be acquitted for her aid in this mess, at least that's what she thought. Some soldiers started to discuss what they were going to do when the war was over, like have a long vacation or be reunited with their families, go to bars and meet up with their friends again. Davis turned to face them and told them not to raise their spirits and hopes just yet, they still had to figure out the last clue, and figure out what to do next.

Then suddenly the truck came to a screeching halt as the drivers in the distance saw another car approaching them, fast. The soldiers jumped out of the back and pointed their guns at the car as it slowed to a halt. It was a hundred feet away as two people stepped out slowly with their hands in the air cautiously. From the distance they asked who the team was, why they were there, and if they could help. The soldiers looked at the two suspiciously and told them to keep their distance. As they talked, Davis and Alex began to recognize the voices of the other two, they popped their heads around the truck to see who they were. The siblings smiled with delight as they saw two of their friends stills standing.

"Mathew, Emily!" yelled the siblings as they jumped out of the truck.

"Davis, Alex, you're alive!" yelled Emily back.

"Everyone lower your weapons these two are friends." demanded Alex to their team.

Mathew and Emily were relieved to see them again as they lowered their hands down. Emily looked like she was going to cry when she saw Davis still standing, after all the last time she saw him was when his strange aliment had spread across his body. Though she was relieved that he was alive she came up to Davis and slapped him across the face and began yelling at him, "Davis, you are the most moronic man I have ever met! How dare you put your life and mine in danger!"

"Okay I'm not going to lie I had that coming. But I couldn't let you stop me from doing what was right, and honestly it was worth it, though I do wish I didn't have to drug you to do it."

Emily slapped him again and said, "Don't you ever drug me again!" Then when she was done, she hugged him, "I am still angry with you, but I am also relieved to see both of you still alive."

Davis hugged her back and told her, "I am so sorry for doing that to you, but this reunion will have to be cut short. We needed to get back home immediately."

"I'm guessing you know how to end this?" intervened Mathew.

"Not yet, which is why we need to get back home."

"What I thought you needed the hope diamond that's in D.C.?"

Davis and Alex both looked at them surprised. "Amelia didn't tell you, did she?" asked Alex.

"Tell us what?" asked Matthew.

"The Diamond is in Akio's safe."

"Are you kidding me?! Why would she even have it?!" Emily yelled.

"Look, we will explain everything on the way home, just get us there." said Davis concerningly.

Davis and Alex went with Emily and Mathew in their car as they told the soldiers to follow close behind. Everyone piled into the car and truck, speeding off towards the mall with great haste. Along the way Davis and Alex explained everything that had happened out in D.C., the attack, Akio's betrayal, their leaders knowing why this was happening, and it made them sick.

"How could she do this? She knew how desperate we were to fix this and she just…." said Emily on the verge of tears.

"I'm not happy about what she has done either, but there is one thing I can agree on with her." Said Davis.

"Seriously, you can agree with her on something?" yelled Mathew.

"Yes, Matthew when this is over and the Venvoss are gone, we need to make sure that when we rebuild and dismantle the nukes." said Davis.

"Why, those are our defense?"

"No, it's a weapon that can be turned on us." said Alex. Mathew wondered where she was going with this as she continued to explain. "When this is over and we survivors tell our stories, there will be no government on this planet that won't try and coverup what happened or try to gain new territory."

Mathew looked in the review mirror and said worried, "I…. I think you could be right. I just pray it never comes to that."

"I think it will," said Davis worried. "A politician named Tenor said that once this was over the world would have a reset. Thinking back on it, I believe they would have used the football regardless of any deals they made."

Everyone in the car became silent as their conversation ended. Now knowing what they know, they became scared of the future. Emily asked, "I know this isn't the time, but Davis when we get back, mind if I have a look at your arm and take a sample of your blood? I need to see what that Venvoss did to you."

"I don't see an issue with it, but before we do anything we need to know what happened to the mall when we left."

Emily and Mathew seemed worried for a second and took a moment to collect their words, then Mathew told them. "It was fine in the beginning, though Amelia was struggling with her duties to the people, but with our help she managed to get it together, but it didn't last long. You all were only gone for two days, and people were gloomier than normal with their loved ones half a country away. Amelia did her best to cheer them up but nothing she did seemed to work. I don't think she had any idea how you two could constantly bring smiles to peoples face day in and out with all of the responsibilities. The other night, eventually everyone went to bed, and we were wakened up by some loud thumping noise. It kept getting louder and louder, like bombs going off in the city drawing closer. When it stopped, we thought it was over, but we were far from being right."

"It was absolute pandemonium. The Ssrpents broke in through the ceiling and swarmed the second level of the mall. The beasts broke down the barricades and entrances to get inside. At first, we thought they were going to take us, but then...." "Dear God," said Emily unable to hold back her tears.

"They began to rip people apart. It didn't matter what age or gender they were, they killed anyone in their path. By the time we managed to get the guns and fight off the first wave but we lost so many people, then when we started to push back, the Venvoss showed up and all bets were off. Many of us were forced to retreat into the storage facility below and waited for the end. Those of us that got underground could feel the facility shake as the carnage above. It lasted for hours then for some reason they just stopped, they seemed to give up and they left." said Mathew recounting for Emily.

"We waited for hours even after they left, we were so afraid that we wouldn't even near the surface. When we had finally gathered the courage to leave the storage and got to the surface, our home was destroyed with... body parts everywhere."

"How many did we lose?" Alex asked hesitantly.

"We lost eighty-seven people, 36 men, 34 women and 17 children, there are only 39 of us now."

Alex and Davis were horrified by the news and asked, "Who survived?!" as pray that their sisters name was on the list of survivors.

Emily looked at the two and reassured, "Your sister is alive and so is your niece, but your brother-in-law; he didn't make it. But he didn't die in vain, he gave his life not just to save his own child, but many other children as well. If it hadn't been for him some many more children would have died."

The siblings were indeed glad that their sister was alive and so was their niece but knowing their brother-in-law's fate made them feel sick and depressed.

They made their way to the only intact highway, they saw the view of their home and there was nothing left standing. Not one building was left erect in its formal glory, this once proud city was just gone. Wichita may have not be their favorite city, but it was still their home, and they could feel the sorrow of losing it as they remembered their childhoods, when they played in the parks, went to the festivals, saw the fireworks on the fourth of July, and the family reunions. As they passed the ruined city they wondered if this last step would be enough to end this and bring peace back. Turning off the highway and losing the view of the destroyed city they turned their attention towards the mall. Passing through the surface streets of the neighborhoods near the mall, everyone could see that they suffered the same fate. But as they drove onward to the mall Davis realized that even if they did succeed, it would take decades to get everything in order, and survive. Without their means of survival, humanity will find itself at death's doors. Davis knew that the future generations would have to be stronger and that they would suffer, but he never knew just how much until he saw the ruins of houses.

After they passed the neighborhoods, they finally saw it, the east mall, or what was left of it. The car came to a stop and Davis immediately jumped out and took it all in. The building had taken massive damage. Much of the roof and walls were gone, chunks of bricks still stuck together by concrete were scattered all over the ground, and not too far laid the bodies that were covered with sheets. Nearby, Davis could see only a few people on guard, protecting the few survivors that were left. The others exited the car as the truck came to a halt, and everyone got out as some of the guards came out to see who was there. When they saw that it was Davis and Alex, they seemed relived, but also confused, wondering where everyone else was. People began to swarm the two asking questions about what happened out there? Did he find out what he needed? Where's everyone else? The soldiers had to pull some people who were getting a little too rough as Davis and Alex answered their questions.

"Everyone please, remain calm!" said Alex. "I know you all have questions, but please, let us give you your answers without us yelling over you all!"

Everyone didn't hear her as they continuously kept probing her for questions. They kept asking the same questions repeatedly, until one of the soldiers yelled out, "SHUT THE HELL UP." and fired a few shots into the air.

Everyone went quiet and backed away as Davis said to them, "That was uncalled for, but effective." He cleared his throat and explained to them the situation of what was going on and that their families were safe. The people were relieved that their family and friends were still alive, but angry about everything else. After everyone had their questions answered they asked what they needed to do now.

"You need to get as far from this place as possible." said Alex.

"Alex is right, this place isn't safe anymore, we need to find what's salvageable and go."

"Where? There is no place left to go!" yelled out one of the survivors.

"South," said Davis, "You all need to head south as far as you can. Into the countryside, find dense forests, and if you can, start to rebuild."

Some were about to argue when Mathew stepped in and said, "You heard him! Let's get going."

"What about the dead?" asked another survivor.

Davis struggled with the words but was forced to say them "Leave them, we need to keep the living going. Even if we leave behind the dead like… this."

Everyone began to scream and shout at Davis for his harsh words towards the people who had died. Alex intervened and said, "You don't have time to bury or cremate them. We don't know if or when the Venvoss will lose their patience again. I know this is hard, but you don't have a choice. So please say your goodbyes and go, otherwise you might meet the same fate."

Many survivors were angry but couldn't argue with her and reflectingly began to scatter, looking for supplies. Others went over to the bodies and sat next to them, saying their last goodbyes. The soldiers began to help everyone clear debris and look for supplies as Alex went looking for their sister and Davis went into the crumbling ruins of their base to find the Diamond. As he entered the darkness he used his sphere to light the way with its radiant glow but made sure it shined in one direction. Making his way through the rubble he found himself climbing up to the second floor and found himself near his department. Peering inside, he began to remember the days when he just did research, the days when they first setup shop, the fights, the fun, and above all the joy of helping people. He walked away from his department and found the catwalk mostly still intact. As he continued heading forward, he saw the sunlight from the torn roof ahead, glistening down into the food court. Akio's department wasn't far from this place, but he couldn't help but smile as he remembered the kids playing in this court and with him and some of the other adults joining in. Giving them moments to forget the state of the world was in made him feel happy, but the moment passed as he knew that many of their last moments were them being killed.

Davis pressed on from the food court and tried to avoid any more eye contact with other places, but even though he didn't look at them, he still remembered all the good and bad times this place had. Davis placed his feelings aside and kept moving forward. Eventually the memories faded, and Akio's department stood in front of him as one of the least damaged areas. He entered Akio's department and wondered if anyone else in Akio's area knew about the diamond, as he slowly walked into the darkness. The light from his sphere guided his path as he looked around the department. Even though he didn't what to reminisce about the place, his memories came nonetheless. The hard times when he and Akio were at each other's throats came back, but also the fun they had when scavenging for supplies and helping people. Though Akio's actions were unacceptable, he couldn't truly hate her for what she did. For he knew if the roles were reversed, he would have done the same to ensure Earth's survival.

Perring into the darkness Davis saw Akio's desk and put it in light, he stood in front of it and felt regret for hurting her. Looking over the desk he saw the safe behind her desk and made his way around. The sphere cast its light on the dial and Davis entered her combination in. He heard the click of the door unlocking and opened the safe, laying right in front of him was the Hope Diamond. Davis took it from the safe and held it in his hand while he grabbed Icin's sphere from his pocket, waiting for the clue to come forth to him, but nothing happened. He placed it down on the table in frustration as he stared into it. "I don't get it, in the past, I discovered the clues from data I gathered, I did the same for this, so why isn't it showing me anything?" said Davis frustrated.

"Okay Davis relax, think, what do you know so far." said Davis to himself as he sat down at Akio's table. "Nearly a century ago Canada, Russia, China, and America made a deal with eight other races to help cure them from a new strain of the bubonic plague, the cure worked to an extent, but something went wrong, and it made the other races so angry they sought out revenge. They kidnapped more than seventy-five percent of humanity and holds them hostage until they have the cure."

Davis went over the information again and again in his head, but he couldn't figure it out. He put his head on the table and screamed in anger, he wasn't getting an answer and said out loud, "What the hell do you want? The cure we gave you worked! So, what is the problem?" As he calmed down, he started to remember other details his mind he heard as he heard Icin and Tenors word's replay, "There was one thing I did find, the cure's formula. I gave it to one of our head scientists and they said that the formula wasn't complete. They did say that it would still be able to cure the diseases hypothetically, but not without severe side effects."

"What's happened to my race along with the others isn't something that can kill us like before. Granted it is still an issue that can lead to the end of multiple races, but not for a few hundred years."

As the words faded from his mind he realized the truth, the reason why they came back. Davis looked into Icin's sphere and said, "Our ancestors took their future away." The sphere glowed a bright blue as the blue ring began to break apart and form the light in the dark flame. The lustrous blue color of the diamond faded until it was pure white, and the blue light had completely formed in the black flame. The three lights in Icin's sphere went out and as the flame disappeared and the only thing that remained was a form of radiant light made of the three colors.

Davis looked deep inside the sphere and began to see images of the Venvoss home world, Tenatros, lying in ruins because of the bubonic plague. Then the memory changed as he saw the city being rebuilt and the Venvoss started to burst with celebration when the disease came to an end. They were overjoyed and filled with new life, but as the years began to pass, their cities began topass, their cities began to become empty and almost lifeless, with every few Venvoss around. Davis was shown the other worlds in the same condition. He saw the races work tirelessly to figure out what caused this new problem. The memory sped through time, the years passing in the blink of an eye, until it stopped at a particular event, the day they discovered what caused the problem. Icin had brought the last vial of the cure that earth gave to them decades ago and had his researchers study it. Davis could see on his face, he was worried about his people, but also saw the fear of being right. It took the three researchers a few hours, but they concluded that the cure that was given was indeed the culprit.

Icin looked devastated and he ordered his adviser to, "Call the Zenitharus that had been given the cure, we need to tell them."

The memory changed and Davis found himself standing next to Icin with seven other beings in a meeting about this issue and what Davis noticed was that they all were covered in shadows except their armor. It had the same star and ring symbol on their clothes and armor. Davis thought it was the symbol for the Venvoss, but now he realized that it was the symbol for these "Zenitharus."

"Thank you all for coming on such short notice," said Icin.

"Well after we heard the news about the 'cure' I am sure everyone here wasn't going to turn a blind eye!" yelled one of the other beings.

"Of course, we're not going to turn a blind eye! Look at what humanity has done!" screamed another. "In the last forty Ziphoners, all of our populations have dropped to nearly half!"

"You can't just blame humanity for what happened, we put them on a time crunch, what did you think would happen?" yelled another.

"They could have warned us! But instead, they gave us false hope and took everything from us." yelled another being.

"Humanity should be wiped from existence for their treason!" yelled out another being.

The arguing went on for hours, until one being showed itself. The other aliens became silent and bowed their heads respectfully as the being approached the center. It asked them to raise their head and explain what had happened and why some of its Zenitharus were in disarray. During their conversation Davis realized something he hadn't before, their title 'Zenitharus' was only a few letters different from Zenith which on Earth meant highest point, though it was unusual that their words were close he believed it might have meant something else in their tongue. He let go of that wonder in his mind and refocused on the memory that was playing right in front of him. The strange beings stopped their bickering and said, "I understand your struggles, so now you must go back to Earth and claim your cure and heal your worlds by whatever means you deem necessary. But know this the cure that was made for your species will need a particular piece of a puzzle on that is rare to find and can only be found in humans."

"What do you mean Deregain?" asked Icin.

"You need to find one that has a natural immunity the sterilization, one who is born with the genetic sequence that can fight against it and come out victorious, it would be in their genes and maybe no longer active. From there you will take the cure that was given to you and infuse it into that human, it will be painful at first and there is a chance that human may come close to its end, but if you place the element xancron into its body it will save them while it changes their genetic code to, in a sense, change their code and restore that ability; thus a new cure will be born that will correct the side effect. Then and only then can you have the cure to save your worlds."

"You know the chances of finding a human with that immunity is like finding a samtren fruit, correct?" said one of the beings.

"Which is why you must take all of humanity at once, capture billions, test them, and see which one has the genetic code you need."

"Alright so now we know what to do, I shall lead this invasion against humanity." said Icin. "It was my race that started it, it's my race to finish it."

Deregain agreed with Icin and told him that he could do what he needed to get the job done. But he stressed about the severity of humanity's betrayal and that there was no excuse for it. Icin told Deregain that the fault lied with humanity's leadership, not their people. If they were going to get what they needed, then they were going to have to seek out some who would go great distances both physically and metaphorically to discover the truth. Icin did agree on the invasion, but he was clear that humanity wasn't going to be executed, not at least until they got what they wanted, and if a human did happen to help them then they would negotiate the punishment. Deregain agreed once again and told him to be careful and to be witty, he may not know what evil, but they might have cooked up something in the time that they were gone, if the cure could be made then the blood would turn.

The memory faded and Davis was back in in his living hell of a reality. He raised his left hand and looked at it and said, "Well, shit. I guess I am literally the savior of humanity."

Davis got up from the safe and walked away with both the Diamond and sphere in his hands. After seeing the memory, he believed maybe he could convince them to spare humanity. If they could find Icin and speak with him then they could work something out. It was going to be a long shot, but after everything that happened between them all, he believed that they could have a chance to set things right with each other.

The other side of the mall that still stood was enough to block the rain and winds of summer, but it wouldn't do if the Venvoss started to attack again. The people there were beginning to pack up and move out of their ruined fortress. Emily and Mathew told Davis they were going to move south and see if they could find some other place to live until things were settled. Davis understood and wished them luck, but then he saw Amelia and his niece, Diamond, in the back of the car with Alex talking to her.

"She's going with you, isn't she?" asked Davis.

Emily and Mathew said nothing, they knew Davis already knew the answer. He asked them to keep an eye out on them and to keep an out for Maria and her family, too. He didn't know if they were alright but if they were going to need all the family they could get. Emily and Mathew agreed to Davis's terms as they asked if he got what he needed from the sphere. Davis looked to them and told them that he did, it's just he wasn't expecting how steep the price was. The two looked at him suspiciously and asked one last question.

"You're not coming back, are you?"

Davis looked them straight in the eyes and told them "I'm not sure, there's a chance I might, but…."

"You don't want to get our hopes up," said Emily.

Davis smiled and nodded at her as Mathew asked, "What about Alex?"

"You know her, she will go to hell and back ten times if that's what it takes to end this, but I just hope we can end this peacefully and in far better shape than what our ancestors did." said Davis as he saw Amelia wave to him to come to her. Davis approached her slowly as Alex went to Emily and Mathew to wish them luck on their journey. When he approached the car, he could see his niece sound asleep in the car seat as Amelia tucked her blanket around her. Davis was glad to see them off, but it still was heartbreaking. Amelia told Davis that her and Alex talked about the possibility of them finding a nice place to grow up in the countryside, to get away from the cities, and have a nice peaceful life. Davis smiled knowing that her idea was a cliché, but he had a hunch why she was really going.

After discovering what some of their government had done there was going to be a target on everyone he loves back. Even if they were dismissed from their seats of power there was no way they wouldn't seek revenge for revealing the truth. It was better if they went into hiding for a few years, at least till the people of power were gone. They might try and pin the blame on others but after everything that had happened and with millions of people to tell the tale along with the hundreds that knew the truth, it was going to be hard to keep this quiet for long, at least that's what Davis hoped.

Unfortunately, Davis got around to the painful news. He looked his sister in the eye and told her what he saw in the sphere, he promised her that he would do everything he could to make sure humanity was spared from being enslaved or annihilated, though in the back of his mind he wasn't sure how. Amelia wasn't really that surprised of the news, she told her brother she expected something like that. To her it didn't matter whether she was going to die by an alien hand or their own race. All that mattered to her was keeping her daughter safe for as long as she could, she was all Diamond had left right now. Davis looked at his niece and smiled as she lied there sleeping like nothing had happened. Then he remembered the dream seeing her as a full-grown woman. He didn't know whoever was talking to him was showing him a future or it was something he just made up, but it gave him peace. Davis hugged his sister and told her that he would try and make it home if he could.

Amelia hugged him back and told him, "You better, because if you die, I will find your ghost and keep you prisoner just to be with our family."

They stopped hugging and Davis closed the door as the driver said they were ready to head out. Alex said her final goodbyes to Emily and Mathew as they made their way to the car. Once everyone was inside Alex rejoined her brother and they stared at their sister through the window as the car began to drive off. As they saw their little sister drive off with the remaining people of their once home, the soldiers came up and asked if they had gotten what they came for. Davis didn't even look at them as he said he knew what they needed to do now, and that they needed to talk to Icin at his facility in Great Basin Desert.

The soldiers knew it was back to the plane as they began to get in their cars, but they noticed that Alex and Davis hadn't followed. The two quietly spoke to themselves about the sphere, the Zenitharus of other worlds, and what needed to be done. Davis took the sphere out and looked into and told her that if they had just come to them in the beginning instead of making them run around, then things would have been simpler. Davis formed a glove out of his sphere and crushed the sphere into shards. When he did a column of light shot up into the sky and a massive flare could be seen hanging over the ruins of the mall. He didn't know what this meant but he believed it was important. Then two siblings were about to enter the cars when a voice could be heard from the flare.

"You both have done well to make it this far but know that there is still one final test. I know that in the sphere's memory you saw me tell them to punish you all for what you had done. However, due to recent circumstances and unacceptable acts of the Venvoss Vomanin, we have decided to make a deal with you two and you both alone. I already know that you're heading to your desert, I might not be there myself, but know I am always watching. So be on your best behavior, your people are depending on you, for their lives," said Deregain. The light faded and Icin's sphere reformed and flew off towards the west with an aurora trail to follow.

"Go into the light!" Alex said quickly.

Davis looked at her and said, "You can't help yourself can you!" as they got into the car.

"God, forbid I do!" she said while laughing.

Davis looked at his sister with a smile as they drove off to the airport again. When they arrived, they could see the soldiers left behind refueling and checking for any damages when they landed. The soldiers explained the situation and the pilots told them they would be up in an hour, two tops and that the closest airport near there was in Salt Lake City, they would have to find a car from there. Everyone reentered the jet and waited again for the time to run out. Inside of the plane the soldiers found a bottle of Prosecco and started to pass it around to everyone to take a sip. When it got to Davis Alex told them that he wasn't a drinker.

Davis shrugged and said, "Not even when I'm depressed would I drink, but instead of letting me drink how about I give a toast."

The soldiers didn't say anything and allowed him to speak as the one with the bottle gave it to Davis. He raised the bottle in the air and said, "To the future and the hopes that things will not be the same but better." The soldiers cheered at the toast and continued to drink as the jet left the runway.

Once they were in the air and everyone was free to roam the cabin Alex sat next to her brother and said, "I hope you know what you're doing."

"I already know what to do sis we just need to get there."

The siblings sat in their chairs and looked out the window seeing the aura and for an instant they were glad they got to see something so beautiful before the end. "You know the Venvoss maybe a little bit extreme when it comes to this, but you must admit. Their technology is indeed extraordinary."

CHAPTER 16

The final decision.

The flight from Wichita to Salt Lake City was not a long one, but it sure felt like it. Everyone was becoming nervous when they got closer to the Great Basin Desert. They didn't know what they'd find out there besides the Venvoss stronghold. Though everyone knew the risks of dealing with the Venvoss, and with a new alien in the way, they weren't sure what to expect. One race of aliens was a problem, now they had to deal with one constantly watching their every movement. It was a bit creepy, and to Alex and Davis, mysterious. This Deregain had been watching them the entire time, but the question was, why? They may have been brave enough to seek out the truth and overcome adversity, but it still didn't make sense why he was watching them. Anyone could have done what they did, they weren't chosen to pick up the mantle, they did it because they were, the only ones that would, do it for the right reasons.

They had to face so many problems with the Venvoss and their own people. They have had to unite the many and save what was left of humanity, take life to preserve it, hurt the guilty to spare the innocent, and bring out the traitors into the light to face justice. They had done so much in the past six months, but there were people that had done what they did far longer than they had and weren't under surveillance by an alien. It made them wonder what was so important about them, what was their role to Deregain? Whatever it was it made them shake in fear, wondering what he was planning to do, and the roles they played in whatever plan he had cooked up.

The captain announced on the speakers that they would be landing soon and that the siblings needed to prepare for their departure. The soldiers looked to the two and wondered if they really were up for the task ahead, if they really didn't need any help. The two didn't have to prepare too much, they already had everything on their person, but still looked through their items one last time. Alex pulled out her phone, wallet, and a small blue gemmed necklace. The neckless was precious to her because it was once their great grandmother Willow's. Alex and Maire were really close to their great grandmother, but Davis had no real memory of her besides him telling her that he didn't eat pink meat when she made him a ham sandwich.

When she died, Alex and Maire had been given most of her jewelry and Alex's favorite was the blue topaz necklace she wore all the time. She never saw Willow without it on, but when she died and was laid to rest, it was left behind for Alex to find, in a way it was her final way of being remembered. Maire and a few gems here and there, but her favorite was the emerald ring Willow wore along with the topaz. It was dark green and was in the shape of a leaf. Willow never told Maire how it made the emerald into a shape like that, but it was so impressive she didn't care, so things were and still out to Maire, one of a kind.

In Davis's pockets he found his wallet, Icin's sphere, and something he didn't realize he had, it was his mother's engagement ring. He wondered how it even got into his pocket, then remembering back to before they left for D.C., he was in such a hurry he just grabbed the important things in his safe, and his mother's ring must have slipped into his mind, so he grabbed it. As he held his mother's ring between his fingers, he wondered how she was. Was she safe, alive, or captured, these thoughts made his stomach turn. She might not have been a great mother, but she was still a damn good one. It had only been recently that she started to neglect her duties as a mother, but when he was younger, she did everything she could do to help him. She protected him, encouraged him, and tried so hard to give him a good life, but all he ever focused on was the pain, for that was what he was taught by the world around him.

He knew it was human nature to remember the good and forget the bad. Yet in Davis's case he remembered everything, the good to help him remember there was still good in the world and the bad to help him learn from the mistakes of others and his own. He also knew Alex did the same thing, but her wisdom grew stronger than her brothers, she took each lesson to heart, and made sure she followed it through. The two looked at their items a little longer as they could see the memories of their past flood into their minds, bringing them joy and sorrow, things they feared they might never get to feel again.

Suddenly they felt the jet land its wings and were brought back into the present. They pocketed their items and saw they were already on the ground; they didn't even hear the captain say they were landing. The soldiers saw them in a bit of a panic putting their belongings away and worried for them both. The jet came to a slow crawl as the roar of wind once again hit the wings. The jet continued to slide on the ground for a few more hundred feet before finally coming to a stop.

Everyone got out and saw in the distance, Salt Lake City or rather the Salt Lake ruins, but unlike them this place didn't have fires or any sign of life, it seemed that this place had been abandoned like Mt. Hope. Some soldiers went back the way they had landed to see what they hit as Davis and Alex looked at the city. Just like the civilians in Wichita, they didn't stand a chance against the hordes of alien pets, and Vomanin. Somehow, they were going to have to find a car in all that mess.

"This nightmare just gets worse!" yelled Davis.

"I think we established that already, hell, I'm pretty sure in another universe there is another version of you writing about this and is so annoyed with the word 'nightmare' he is going to delibly break the fourth wall for a slice of comedy." said Alex.

Davis looked back to his sister thinking she was crazy, but then he took a moment and said, "You know might be right… God have mercy on that poor shmuck."

Alex laughed at the fact he actually agreed with her as the soldiers came up to them asking what the plan was. Alex stopped laughing and looked at them and told them the plan hadn't changed, they were going to the Basin Desert while they went home. The siblings wanted them to leave for their own safety, but it was clear they were going to refuse them. The two told them that it was their job to protect the many, not the few, and that they were going to be needed to pick up the pieces when everyone was free. But the soldiers insisted that they stay, they wanted to help end this hell, but the siblings couldn't allow them to follow. Then for some strange reason everyone began to smell something sweet in the air. It made the soldiers feel relaxed and calm and in just a few seconds the soldiers fell to the ground, while Davis and Alex remained awake.

The siblings looked around the airfield and saw a light mist roll in. It blanketed everything and one that was in its path. The sweet smell was coming from the mist itself as Davis and Alex smelled it all around them now. The vision was slightly obscured by the mist, but they could hear something coming their way. The sound of metal struck down on the pavement, along with low growls. The siblings saw in the distance silhouettes of something coming their way as the sounds drew closer to them. The image became clear as the mist began to part way from them and their group. Venvosses stood tall when the mist disappeared, a small pack of Hornfangs and one small little fuzzy creature on his shoulder the same one that they encountered near Mt. Hope. The two siblings recognized that it was Icin and walked right up to him, moving away from the sleeping group.

"Welcome two siblings to the end of your journey you have done the eight races and your own, well. I knew I could trust the common folk rather than your leaders, my faith was placed in the right hands." Even though he gave an enthusiastic congratulation, he could see the two siblings were not happy. "I know that you both have many questions and you both want answers."

"Ya putting two people through a dangerous adventure that nearly got them killed over a dozen times comes with questions." said Alex offended by Icin's response.

They were sick of being kept in the dark on this matter, and they wanted the truth. Icin took his helmet off and revealed his face to them as he began to speak. They had seen the skin and body of a Venvoss, but not the face. Icin's head was squared with four eyes, no nose, and a simple mouth. The two were a little shocked to see Icin's facial features, they were close to that of a human, and it threw them off. However, unlike Vomanin's skin color, Icin's was jet black and looked glossy, almost like a gemstone.

Icin explained he was sorry for the rouge Venvoss and what they had done, they managed to find them and would be punished severely. He knew that Vomanin was angry, many of them were, but he didn't think that they would deliberately kill. In the Venvoss culture, it was forbidden to kill other races unless they struck first and even though what happened was tragic it didn't warrant such violence, but he believed it did. Icin looked them in the eyes and told them that he was sorry, but they still needed to discuss humanity's actions. He further explained that he didn't send them off, he just happened to find Davis on the second day and took a shot in the dark, hoping that he would be able to help the other races. But he feared that Davis wouldn't have believed him, so he set in motion a series of events that were already in place and unfolded by his discoveries of the sphere he had given him. Leading straight to the undeniable truth and forcing the humans that knew to come out of hiding.

Davis had believed this to be a scenario a few months ago, but there was always another way to find or tell someone the truth. It would be difficult to accept at first, but the more people went over the facts and information they were given, the more it would come to light. Alex could understand Icin's idea for seeking truth, but all of humanity wasn't only to blame for what happened. She agreed that the people that helped them should have warned them of the possible side effects, but they came to Earth during a time where they were still trying to make sense of medicine and only gave them six months to create a cure for something that they had extraordinarily little information about. Even with the Venvoss technology the chances of making a totally successful cure weren't going to happen, even in the century they lived in curing diseases was still a problem. Also, the Venvoss, by Earth standards, had almost eighty years to notice something wasn't right, and just like humans they too didn't fully understand how they did things, and because of their rush and ignorance, they too had made a mistake. Besides which he could have spoken to them again and gotten an actual response.

Icin explained that they had tried to speak with their leaders, and they were arguing so much about whether they should help, they began to stall the Venvoss, that was the actual reason they began their invasion. They had to go against their own culture because they couldn't wait, seven other races were in danger because of them. They may have rushed to find a cure for a version of the bubonic plague for themselves and the other seven, and even if humanity back then weren't preparing for the hardships of working with another race, medical advancements, or the technology, they still could have warned them of the consequences.

All this pain that was caused, because of them both, and seven different worlds suffered from past problems. Though no one knew how the disease got off Earth, they could have handled controlling this better. Icin told Alex she was wise and honest, but it still didn't change the fact that they still had a problem, and they couldn't just look away either. That's when Alex told him to only punish the ones who were responsible for what happened instead of punishing the generations that came after them. Icin told Alex it wasn't just up to him alone he had to speak to the other races before deciding, though he did like her idea. This way humanity still could live and prove themselves to be better than the last generation of their kind and still make peace among the stars. Icin accepted her idea and told her that the other Zenitharus would be difficult to pursue, but they would be able to pull it off. But they still had to make a cure for their sterility and if the two would follow him back to his stronghold, then they could get started.

"You don't have to wait for it, it's already done. At least I hope it is." said Davis as he stared at Icin.

"What are you-" said Icin before he stopped his own sentence. Then Icin noticed the cut on Davis's face along with the dire silver blood and asked, "What happened to you?"

Davis explained that he had stabbed him twice, showing him his arm and all the damage that had occurred from it. Icin's eyes widened, and he grabbed Davis by the arms demanding to know if there were any side effects.

"Side effects?" asked Alex.

Icin didn't spare the details as he bluntly said, "Your kin's blood has changed, we had prepared what you would call a synthetic strand of DNA, that in theory would be able to awaken the gene we needed to make a cure. It seems whoever did this went behind our backs, made one, and forced it upon your kin. In short, your brother is the cure we need."

Davis wasn't too surprised by this information like his sister was. It made sense the moment he saw the last memory, when Deregain said that their blood would change, he knew what it meant. However, he was angry that the Venvoss that stabbed him forced the cure on him like that, it was no different than the people who gave them a faulty cure.

"HOW DARE YOUR FOURCE THIS ON TO HIM." Screamed Alex. "WHICH VENVOSS's ASS DO I NEED TO KICK."

When Icin heard her say a Venvoss did this to him he immediately scooped them up and told his guard to remain put and escort their soldiers home once they were awake, then morphed his wings and flew off towards the great basin desert.

Icin may have had four arms but even he was finding it difficult to carry them both, even with his armor. The two made their belts and forced themselves away from him. At first Icin was terrified when they forced themselves away, but when he saw them flying alongside him without wings, he was astonished. The two wondered why he was so surprised by what they did, he had the sphere armor longer than they did, so he and his people should have been able to uncover more secrets about the orb than they could in the few months they had them. But they didn't ask, they just followed him to the desert quietly, they knew they would get many answers in time, but they needed to be a little more patient.

It didn't take long to see something in the distance simmer in the morning sun, even with the mountains coming into view. The closer they got the more they could see the top of the stronghold, high above the mountain peak. When they flew above, they could see the roof of the stronghold go on for miles, the space photo they had seen months ago was almost accurate, the only thing that they missed were hundreds of triangle tessellation spheres surrounding them in a spiral spin. Inside they saw multiple Venvoss at work and speaking to one another while looking at some humans hovering in midair. It seemed that they were looking over the bodies and healing them with the strange mucus that the two siblings wear given. They were trying to save humans from the original attack six months ago, but due to how many they had it became a long stacking process. It was no wonder why they hadn't found someone with the gene they needed. They had to scan humans one by one to fix the damage they inflicted while healing them. Looking for any signs that there was a chance at finding a cure.

Icin dove down and landed on a platform on the roof in between the triangle tessellation, the two siblings followed his lead. When they had landed, the platform began to descend into the stronghold. It was a slow ride down and the two became impatient, they just wanted this to end, but then the walls began to open, and they saw why this place was so big. Inside the stronghold there were hundreds of massive towers interconnected like an underground cave system. Icin saw that the two were impressed and explained to them that this stronghold was made from thousands of ships that could interconnect with one another. However, there was a drawback, they could not keep their camouflage on when they began to merge with one another, otherwise the system would malfunction. Icin further explained to them that these strongholds were used specifically for emergencies, just in case their planet ever died some day or if there was a huge catastrophic event.

That made Davis realize that this massive ship was like the ark in America. Davis enlightened Icin about how humans in their country had something similar, but nothing like this. The ark could only fit a few hundred thousand, maybe, but this place could easily fit a few hundred million people, give or take. Icin looked at him and told him he was smart, explaining that this stronghold could hold over one billion of any species or race. However, they had to cut that in half to bring their Hexwings, Fanghorns, Feneve, and the Scotros. Alex and Davis were confused on the last two and asked him if the Scotros were the same giants they faced at the airport and if the Ferncrats were the little thing on his shoulder. Icin nodded his head and told them that the Scotros were an endangered species back on Aqunaua, they were only used for extreme circumstances, but not like that. Icin did greatly appreciate Alex staying her hand from killing them, he had sent a few scouts to retrieve them and take them back to Aqunaua. The Feneve were from his home world, but there were not used for war but only for companionship or as humans called it "pet."

The three were tolerable with each other's company the siblings brought up a difficult conversation about Vomanin. They asked Icin why he attacked again and why he tried to kill Davis. Icin sighed heavily and explained that he couldn't take the waiting anymore, he was fed up with it and after being beaten by two humans he felt depressed. He gathered some other Venvoss who felt the same way and began a rampage around their world, trying to wipe out all of humanity, that is until he ran into them. It had only been a week and they could do far more than what they were cable of, and it scared him. He tried to do a massive assault, but he failed. Alex was shocked when he heard the word failed, she immediately pointed out that he killed dozens if not thousands of humans for crimes they had nothing to do with. Icin told her that Vomanin would be stripped of his title and any Venvoss that aided him in this would be sent with him to Volowskan. A planet that had only two massive sources of water, endless deserts or forests, and small islands on the water, with a tower called Beleanon watching over the planet. They didn't have to worry about escapees because they never strayed too far from the water and the towers would alert the entry or departure of ships and bring them down quickly.

However, Icin wasn't sure why Vomanin tried to kill Davis other than the fact he is human. But he did have a theory that made him believe that Vomanin must have figured out that David had the cure inside of his body and couldn't accept it. So, he tried to kill Davis and end the chance of an actual cure to be made endangering all nine worlds. If his theory was correct, then Vomanin had more punishment heading his way than he first thought.

The two were glad that there was going to be justice for the humans that left but looking around they felt this place wasn't appropriate. Alex asked him about the human facilities they had, if they were humane. Icin didn't understand what she meant but assumed that she meant if they were tolerable and showed them the insides of the towers. The platform moved through the wall as it parted and they could see thousands of humans laying on the walls face up, it almost looked like they were part of the ship. He explained that this tower was for the elderly of humanity past the age of forty, the younger generations were placed in the center to keep them safe from harm. The children were the first to be treated and scanned, the elderly was the second and so on. They kept them placed vertical to help keep their blood flowing properly and get proper readings on their genetics. They only took them up top for more advanced research. As for him trying to kill Davis he had a hunch but wanted his own personal healers to be sure first.

"What hunch?" asked Davis.

"Well to see if your body would be able to sustain even though you're still a child."

"Child?! I am a fully grown adult." said Davis irritated.

"By human standards and cultures, yes, but amongst the stars you would be considered a child still. In fact, you're considered not to be an elderly being until your over forty and ancient after you're seventy, at least that's how we see you all."

"Seriously?"

"Davis please relax he's just trying to enlighten you about the cultures of the Milky Way." "Yes, and that's fine in their culture, but we as humans don't want to be corban dated while we are still alive." said Davis.

Alex stood there and giggled and said, "There's nothing wrong with hearing someone else's perspective."

"I understand that, but I don't what to be called a fossil when I'm old. Do you remember the last time Maire called someone a fossil?" said Davis.

"Yes, I do she called me a fossil and I smacked her ass so hard I left a red handprint; our aunt Matilda could not stop laughing, she didn't know whether punish me or congratulate me." said Alex.

Icin looked at the two and asked, "Is this a normal conversation for you two?"

"Yes," the two said in unison and a little annoyed.

The platform came to a stop at one tower and Icin got off, the two followed suit and were met with two smaller clothed Venvoss. Davis recognized them from the second memory and greeted them with respect. Shenral and Yanton greeted them both and asked them to follow them to the examination chamber. Alex was skeptical at first, but Icin told her that they were perfectly safe, if anyone tried anything then he would put an end to it. Davis allowed Shenral and Yanton to guide him into the chamber as Alex and Icin talked for the moment. The two Venvoss asked him to remove his shirt so they could see why he was brought to them.

Davis removed his shirt and when their saw his body they eyes filled with fear. The origin of his injury had spread across his torso and down his left leg. His veins were still sliver in color, but they looked darker than before, and his hand looked like it had been consumed by the cure. It was turning purple and black, his scar had turned crimson red, and the areas surrounding it were orange like fire. The two Venvoss were completely in shock of how this turned out as Icin and Alex entered the chamber. Alex hadn't seen the extent of the cure spread and when she saw it, she almost collapsed. Icin managed to keep her steady as he asked the two to do a biometric scan on Davis to see which Venvoss might have left behind their palavien or by human standards ancient nano when they attacked him.

"Ancient nano? Wait you mean nano bots, is that what our spheres are made out of?" said Alex surprised.

"Yes, they are, these were made by the Hannar race long before the time of, well any of any race. They can generate plasma and radiation, morph into things for survival, and even clothing. Granted we still are discovering knew things every day about the ancient nano, but it still takes time. We tried asking Deregain about it, but when we did, he just stayed silent." Explained Icin.

Alex was overjoyed hearing more about their tech as the two Venvoss had Davis stand still for a moment and used his belt to keep him in place and turn his gravity off to float weightless as they examined his body with screens. Icin further explained that the palavien that they had were left behind for anyone to find, but he didn't think that they would be able to use them. Normally palavien was only given to one master at a time and in order to use them requires a special means to use them, like a special bound. The palavien was also synced to their owners mental and emotional personality allowing them to sift them into anything they needed. However, when the owner dies it remains in its current structure like statue or gravestone, if it's being loaned out it disintegrates. While Icin continued to explain its usages Davis was hovering in the air and the two Venvoss took a sample of his blood. However, his mind wandered to a specific question about Deregain.

"In the last memory you all bowed your heads to Deregain, he was the highest Zenitharus, correct?" Asked Davis.

"Yes, and he also happens to be the last of the Hannar, that's why he never discusses his people, he is the sole survivor." answered Icin.

"I know this is jumping a little off topic, but what is a Zenith anyways, and why couldn't Davis see his figure?" asked Alex.

"Zenitharus, by your world standards, are considered demigods. We are powerful beings entrusted with the energy of the universe itself. Our goal is to protect and preserve life, for as long as we can. We Zeniths rarely age and can regenerate faster than any of our people without the slineslan, the mucus that heals you. Each one of the orders is what makes up parts of life, there are currently fifteen, and each represents a specific category. Support, which is time, dimension, dawn, dusk, rejuvenation, change, deconstruction, and reconstruction. Voice, who is thought, self, choice, determination, inspiration, belief, and balance. These are the current things the universe needs to keep everything in check and each Zenitharus represents one of them. As for Deregain's appearance, he is what humans call a shapeshifter, in the memory he deliberately hid himself in the dark, for reasons even is still don't know." Explained Icin.

"Strange but other than that I'm guessing that you're the Zenith of belief, right?" asked Alex.

"Every perceptive, I am, I'm duty is to spread belief and keep hope alive, though in the last few decades I have been failing." Answered Icin.

"It's hard-to-find light in the pools of darkness even when it shines, but that doesn't mean it's not there, sometimes you have to adjust your perspective a little to find it or ignite it." said Alex.

Icin was shocked to hear a human offer such wisdom, especially since she was still considered a child. He looked at Alex and said, "I have only seen you three times and you have shown me that you are far wiser than the average human. Most would dismiss such notions, yet you run straight towards it."

"Knowledge is born by the mistakes and success by the past, if we fail to learn from it, we are always doomed to repeat it. Many of our people refuse to because they believe they think what they're doing is right, but in truth, they become blind by fear and rage. Not all of them do, just most of them, and it causes pain, heartache, and death. There will always be those who spread the good and there will be those who bring destruction. That is why many keep hoping that they will find the real light that has been right in front of them all along." Said Davis as the two Venvoss checked his arm for any signs of infection.

Icin removed his helmet once again and chuckled to himself, "It's not every millennium you meet creatures filled with this type of belief, it's comforting to know that there are some humans that can find it still, even without my aid."

"Well, we try, but getting back on topic how did Deregain's people die out and how do you even become a Zenitharus." said Alex.

"We have tried to speak with Deregain about that, but we had no luck and Zeniths aren't made they're born. Every once in a while, the universe begins to lack certain things and makes us to keep it in check. Think of us as an extra safety precaution. We give specific abilities or powers that best suit our needs to help keep our races and others going, mine for instance is Benston, I have the power to bestow upon someone specific knowledge from one being to another, mostly its healing, since my species has some of the most cultivated herbs in the stary flower." answered Icin.

"Stary flower?" asked Davis.

"I believe you called it the 'Milky Way.'"

So that's why you have so many Venvoss in those spheres, they're healing centers, and the hemisphere must help them keep patients asleep, by blocking out the sun and bringing it back to make sure they stay warm." said Alex.

"Yes, but it's also a kind of hypnotism trick with lights, so they stay oblivious to what's happening. I brought you both here for privacy, this place is my own personal healing center." Said Icin.

"One more thing, I understand that you used some specific knowledge to unlock your sphere but why was the Hope Diamond a physical clue?" Asked Davis.

"Honestly, I thought the first clues were so stubborn, so I changed it up a bit. For your own understanding I didn't know it was called the Hope Diamond. I just saw a shiny rock in a display and thought 'great hiding place' and placed the memory inside." Said Icin.

"That's funny, but how did you put a memory inside a rock?" asked Alex.

"All I did was use the palavien to project the combined memory into Davis's head. I did it for all the clues, but there can be side effects, I'm sure you have already experienced that." Said Icin.

Davis nodded and everyone seemed to be comfortable with each other now, but just like everything else that happened so far it didn't last. Shenral's monitor began to beep loudly and glow blue, she quickly began looking through her notes on Davis's structure, there was no sign of the ancient nano but trace amounts of the Slineslan in his wound, whoever did this was clever. They left the nanos inside his hand to check progress and when it was time to complete, they then took them out to cover their tracks. Though the news was disappointing, Shenral had to ask if he had come in contact with radiation.

Alex intervened and explained that Vomanin and her clashed with high amounts of gamma radiation, but it had somehow disappeared, and Davis miraculously survived. Davis explained to them that he saw something cover him with its wings and shield him from the force and radiation, but he had no idea what it was. Yanton looked skeptical and asked if the creature's wings were massive and if it was blue with green eyes. Davis only nodded as Shenral pulled up a picture of the creature. It was an old sculpture hieroglyph of eight different creatures reminiscent of the one he saw. They all circled the symbol that Deregain wore and the blue one was on the bottom. Shenral asked if this was what he had seen that day. Davis nodded again and she looked like she was about to scream.

"YOU SAW AN AZURITE!" yelled Yanton.

"Azurite? What is an Azurite? I mean on earth we have a stone called azurite, but we have never heard of an alien called that?" said Alex.

"You might have, the stone might be a symbol of the Azurite's, they basically are the very foundation of life itself. When they find a dead planet they terraform it then give it an extremely specific element to reestablish life, it wouldn't be the same as before, but something new. In your culture you possibly use this stone as a representation of the alien." Explained Icin.

"A phoenix, the Azurites are phoenixes of the universe!" Exclaimed Alex with excitement.

"I don't know what that is, but if it's a creature of rebirth, then yes. But the thing is the Azurite disappeared eons ago." Answered Icin.

"Wait, why would a creature of rebirth shield me from a massive radiation explosion?" asked Davis.

"It makes sense, you hold the key to rebirthing eight different races, they would defend you with their lives if that meant you could bring back what was lost. But there is a complication, the Azurite was not able to absorb all the radiation, in fact the amount it did absorb was a miracle. But unfortunately, your blood has taken damage, as well as the cure." Said Shenral.

Everyone went quiet as Icin with a shaking voice said, "Wait, are you telling me, that the cure is useless?"

"No, we can distill the healthy blood from the damaged, but we would need more than half of it, and forty percent of his blood is damaged, so in other words…" said Yanton regretfully.

"In other words, you would have to take the healthy blood, but leave the damaged, I would have to die in order to give you your cure." said Davis unfazed.

Once again everyone went silent as the information washed over them. They were so close to what they needed, but now they were beyond its reach, they were back they started. Until Davis told them to do it, to drain his blood and make their worlds whole again. Alex immediately tried to forbid it, she wanted to fix this too, but she didn't want to lose her brother in the process. Davis told her this wasn't up for discussion, though it wasn't his fault this all happened, he would end it, and that was his choice. Yanton and Shenral argued that it wasn't his to keep anyways, that it was theirs by right, even if it was forced upon him. Icin looked at Shenral and Yanton and told them that the cure was supposed to be a choice, but due to this mysterious Venvoss forcing the cure on him it was his by right to either give it or keep it of his own accord.

Yanton and Shenral couldn't believe what they just heard, he would give it up willingly, they argued that one life wasn't worth the lives of billions, and he already gave his consent, so it was theirs. Icin looked at them and told them he understood what Davis just did but it was still his choice, and it wasn't theirs even if they took it, even after he was gone it would still be his.

Alex, infuriated, told them she refused to let her brother to pay the price of others, that wasn't his job, and even if he did what was to stop the people from doing it again. There was a chance that what he did wouldn't matter to them. Icin agreed, but it was his choice and he made it of his own will, and if she stood in his way then she was denying his right even if he was forced into it. Alex didn't care, she didn't want to lose her brother when they had gotten this far. Acknowledging her determination to save her brother, everyone in the room showed empathy, but they were done waiting and needed his blood. Alex drew her katana out and pointed at Icin's head saying that this time he didn't have his protection to save him now. Either they found another solution, or she would tear them apart.

Shenral smacked the sword out from Alex's hand and grabbed her arms telling her that they had to and that she was sorry, but this was their only chance, and they weren't going to lose it. The two began to duke and soon the air was filled with red and violet blood. The two were covered with bruises and blood coming out of their mouths. Shenral was about the throw another punch but was stopped by Yanton who grabbed her, interrupting.

"Will you both just stop it, fighting now isn't going to change anything. Even if you to beat each other senselessly we still have this problem." Yanton said annoyed.

"So, what would you have us do, let him go and the cure along with him?" yelled Shenral.

"No, I'm just saying there must be a way to get the cure without causing Davis's death." Said Yanton.

Then in the back of her mind Alex realized the obvious and smacked her head while saying, "I'm and idiot, there is another way, though I really don't like it."

She explained that they had the same genetic blood type so they could use his blood to get the cure and hers to replace the blood that was lost, this way everyone one won, well, almost everyone. Yanton and Shenral thought for a moment and did some quick calculations. After the two collaborated with each other they saw there was a good chance it would work, but there was a catch, they would take her blood and give it to him after they got their cure, but he wouldn't be able to return to earth until his bodies were restored to human standards. They would take him back to their home world Tenatros and keep them in a suspended animation until his body was restored and as a precaution. If everything went according to plan, then they would be back in a year or two, by Earth's standards.

The two siblings looked at each other seeing the fear in each other's eyes, for Davis to leave Earth made them both nervous. Alex put her sword away and groaned, she didn't want to do this because of her promise she made to her father, but if this were the only way to stop this and save her brother, she would take it. She looked to Icin and agreed but on the conditions that they bring him home safety, to punish the guilty and to leave the rest alone, and what she meant by guilty, she meant the people who willingly tried to stop this from ending because they wanted to keep it secret and commit genocide, but also to leave behind his sphere, they wanted everyone to know everything when they were gone. Whether they accepted it as fact or fiction was up to them from that point until they returned, even if the other Zenitharus disagreed. Icin was hesitant at first but eventually agreed to her terms and thanked them both for what they were doing and that when he awoke the next time, he would hear about them like they were legends.

Alex looked Icin dead in the eyes and said, "Are you calling me old? If you are, I will leave a perfect impression of my hand on your ass!"

Davis smiled and chuckled at his sister and thought to himself, "You're right, God forbid if you ever take anything seriously."

Yanton turned Davis's gravity back on and asked them to follow them both to the next chamber as Icin called his Venvoss to release the humans from where they were taken, but to avoid the destroyed cities until they were up to the task of rebuilding. They understood his order but had to go into detail about how they were going to accomplish this task as the siblings began to follow Shenral and Yanton. Their spheres flew to Icin, and he explained that he would be taking them back, since they had no longer any use for them.

The siblings were disappointed that they lost their spheres, but what they got out of it was worth it. Davis asked for one favor, he took out his trinkets and asked Icin to hold on to them, that way when he woke up, he wouldn't feel lonely out among the stars and could reminisces about his life back on Earth. Icin smiled softly at Davis and took his stuff and allowed the spheres to engulf them. The siblings watched as his stuff disappeared into the thick silver metallic dust. Icin told them he would be back in a bit to see him off to sleep after they got cleaned. With the two Venvoss leading the way they all entered the chamber. The two Venvoss explained that the relaxation chamber basically was an illusion chamber, it made the place they longed for most in their dreams. The chamber had eight large, elongated cubes standing on a single point, slowly rotating, and filled with a gelled chemical they called davtrins, it helped them to relax and numb their bodies, so it wasn't unpleasant.

The two Venvoss explained that Davis would be placed in one shortly after they both were clean and sanitized. Their reason why they wanted them both clean was to make sure nothing else messed with their cure and at the same time send Alex back better than ever as a sign of good faith to the other humans. Shenral regretfully took Alex to the other side of the chamber and Yanton took Davis. Each one entered another chamber with floating spheres of water above a pool and they were asked to strip and enter the pool and it would do the rest. The two didn't understand, but they did as they were told, but they didn't remove their undergarments, they made certain of that.

When they entered the pools, it was already warm and it began to swarm around them, it was almost alive, they couldn't see it but they the water was being manipulated by the ancient nanos, one molecule at a time. As they began to sink deeper into the water, their bodies were cleaned quickly and rigorously as the spheres of water began to go in and out of the pools, removing the dirty water and replacing it with new fresh water. Davis felt the water being a little rough on his skin but was sure it was cleaning of any radiation that had been left behind.

After a nice cleansing bath, the siblings got out and found the two Venvoss with some new clothes, that were more for Venvoss than humans. It was a simple elongated loin cloth and some waist low ponchos that were readjusted for them. As Davis approached his sister in the main chamber, he realized her skin looked lighter than usual and asked, "Why does your skin look lighter than normal?"

"It's because of the Hexwings blood it was all washed off in the bath." Alex said as she brushed out her hair.

Everyone was regrouped in the main chamber as Icin came in attendance with a few Hornfangs and Hexwings, he wanted to wish Davis a restful sleep and that he was going to leave some of his personal companions in the sanctum for him. He was grateful for what they were doing, they didn't have to do this, they shouldn't have had to do this, but if any one human was going to save their races, he was glad it was them. The two shook his hand and said their goodbyes to him. Then they turned towards each other to say their own goodbyes.

"I guess this is it, isn't it?" asked Davis.

"Ya, it is."

"Sis, before I fall asleep, I just want you to know you have always been my favorite sister."

Alex laughed and said sarcastically, "The feeling isn't mutual."

"I'm going to miss you, and everyone else." said Davis as he hugged his sister.

Alex hugged him back tightly and said, "Don't worry so much you'll be back in a few years. So, no tears or regrets okay."

Davis let go of his sister and shook his head in agreement and began to enter the cube. The gel was warm and moved around his body like the water only this one felt like it was massaging his body. Alex stood by Yanton who began to take the blood she needed as Shenral placed a palavien mask on Davis face as it formed around his head and neck, she explained that the mask would recycle his breath over and over until he woke. She also let him know that even though his body would be in this gel it will stop him from aging, or starving, but not growing, so when they woke up, he might have longer hair and fingernails.

Davis got the message but before he fell asleep, he asked for one more thing, he looked to Icin and asked, "If things were to go south with Earth again, don't let them fall."

Icin agreed and told him that he would do his best, but with luck they wouldn't have to worry about it. When he woke, he would see his home again and begin to build a glorious future for not just their people, but for the other races as well. Davis smiled as his eyes began to drift into the darkness and with his final strength, he said, "Please watch over them and don't lose faith in them, I still haven't."

"I will try, Davis, but understand it will be a difficult road for everyone." said Icin.

"True but that's why I'm placing my trust in you, I know that some of my people have failed, but I want to give you my trust, because they didn't. The future can be great or more fearful than ever but know that the journey of rebuilding our worlds begins when my eyes shut. So please, I am not demanding you, but asking you as an equal to have faith in them, even if it seems hopeless, and never let them fall." Said Davis as his eyes finally closed and he drifted to sleep.

As Davis was asleep, he Astro projected himself near his sister again and saw everything unfold. Icin said nothing but he nodded his head to him one last time as Yanton and Shenral got him set up and began to drain the blood from him as Alex was escorted out of the base by other Venvoss. It was painstaking to separate, but eventually they managed to get what they needed, and eventually tested it. The results were better than they expected, even without being damaged, but they still feared the worst just in case. As promised, Icin kept his word and let the captive humans go. But then just as he begun, Davis fell back into the darkness of his dreams and everything after that became uncertain to him.

EPILOGUE

It took a few weeks to return everyone and capture the guilty, but eventually they left with their prisoners. They also left behind Icin's sphere for others to find and learn from their mistake, but to always find the faith in each other and among the stars.

Humanity was brought back to their home and though many lives were lost, they began to rebuild with the guidance of the survivors that prevailed. It was unpleasant to hear what had happened and as expected everyone thought they were just nuts, but many eventually came around to the truth. The Venvoss began to disperce their ships from the stronghold and began the journey home themselves. Things for humanity would be difficult from time to time, so Icin would keep an eye on them, but if humanity were in trouble, he would do his best to aid them, although he was sure the other Zenitharus were going to be furious if he did. As for the many survivors they had a long way to go in rebuilding their civilization and heading into a future that was unknown. But prayed that no one would ever have to pay that price again and would do their best to avoid doing things like this again, though they knew the odds were against them.

As for Alex and her family, they waited for Davis to return home, but unfortunately, he never made it back. Icin told them in person what happened on his way to Tenatros. Their fleet was attacked by an unknown force. Whoever attacked boarded their ship and took the sleeping chamber Davis was in and disappearing into the darkness between the stars. The Venvoss looked everywhere, in all directions for any sign that they had gone that way, but they never found them. The cure for the sterility was a success, but that didn't stop them from looking for them. Even the other races began searching for them, but over time the searches became less frequent, and they eventually stopped searching, all except Icin and Deregain.

After that Alex found herself, along with many of her family members, investigate the stars and pray their family would be whole one day. But as the years passed no living being in any world knew of his final fate, but some still hope he is out there, waiting to be woken up again, or that he was enjoying a new life away from Earth. Soon their story became legend to some, but to others a nightmare, and humanity began to recede back into the darkness again. Many tried to defend the siblings and what they did while others began to despise and fear them. Once again, the lust for greed and power started, but now there was a new story to tell, not about the end, but how they became icons of hope or fear for their people, just like others did before. They became another story about being human.

But just like all truths his story scattered into the void of uncertainty and eventually was forgotten.

364 Years Later. . .

That was until the day he came back.